I0822818

The Case of the Weeping Hamm

A Freddy Falcon Mystery

By
R.B. Willis

Hardcover: 979-8-218-12863-0
Paperback: 978-0-578-34382-2

Edited by Kirsten Kennedy
Cover art by Scott Beasley

For Jim.

I love you more as each day passes.

Chapter One

An Unexpected Visitor

In the basement of a pizza restaurant lives Otto Von Snaut. It isn't a damp, dark, dingy basement. It is well kept and quite cozy. There is a small kitchen in the corner. The kitchen has a gas stove, a microwave, a mini-fridge, and a utility sink. A small bar separates the kitchen from the rest of the basement. A couple of wingback chairs sit in one corner. There is a small table with a lamp sitting between them.

A small office had been built along the far wall opposite the kitchen. There is a workbench along the wall. Two computers sit on the workbench. On the left is a desktop tower with three displays. On the right rests a laptop with two displays. Otto uses the laptop for everyday work, leisure, research, etc. The desktop, on the other hand, has a dual purpose. It is set up as a media server. A VPN is constantly connected and running. He found an anonymous VPN service that allows him to pay using gift cards purchased over the counter at any retailer. He pays cash for the gift cards. This allows him to stay anonymous and untraceable on the dark web. An extra benefit to this is the ability to illegally download movies, TV shows, music, and video games to his media server.

A pool table is along the back wall. This is strange because he has no interest in billiards. He uses it more as a torture device. A young woman is lying in the center of the table. Ropes tied around her wrists and ankles. Her arms stretched above her head. Each of her arms and legs are extended toward the four corners of the pool table. The ropes are connected to a device with a mechanical lever. It works in a way that is similar to torturing someone on the rack during medieval times.

Otto Von Snaut is a stocky, balding man who loves his cigars. He has been using this basement as his headquarters for the past fifteen years. It is attached to his favorite pizza restaurant, *Hold the An-*

chovies. Otto and the owner have entered into an agreement that benefits both of them. Otto will not release proof of tax evasion and is thereby allowed free reign of the basement with no questions asked. Mario, the owner, has not paid taxes for the past twenty-five years. Otto discovered this interesting fact and uses it to his advantage.

He is sitting in a chair next to the pool table. His hand resting on the lever for his make-shift rack. A cigar in his mouth. He has a slight grin on his face.

"Tell me what I want to know."

"Or what?"

Otto leans in close to the woman's face. She turns her head in disgust from his stinking breath.

"Or...you will undergo pain unlike any you have experienced before."

He pulls the lever slightly. This causes the ropes to tighten. Her arms and legs feel like they are being pulled out of their sockets. She lets out a small scream. Otto releases the tension, and the ropes relax.

"One more time Ms. Atworth..."

Noise could be heard above. A customer entered the pizza shop. Otto quickly places his hand over the woman's mouth. He grabs his gun from a nearby table and points it at her head. "Not one word, or I WILL kill you."

***

A red Mustang flies down the road. The driver is a tall, thin redhead. This is a classic 1965 Mustang convertible. It doesn't have any modern conveniences. Only two upgrades had been made to the classic car. The radio had been upgraded to add an aux port, and a police siren had been added. The aux port is so he could use his phone, hands-free, in his car. The siren rarely got any use. The car originally belonged to his grandad. It had been handed down to him after his grandad passed away. He made sure this Mustang is kept in pristine condition. It is his way of staying connected to the man that raised him.

He never knew his dad. His dad had been sent to prison before he was born. His mom raised him for the first ten years of his life. She passed away from cancer when he was young. His grandparents gained custody of him and raised him as their son.

That's why these drives were always so important to him. The memories of his rides with his grandad always came flooding back. There used to be a small country store where they would stop for lunch, *Marcell's* if he remembered correctly. The place had caught fire and burned down years ago. The owner never rebuilt.

The car races down the highway. No other vehicles are in sight. He knows he will have to slow down the moment he reaches town. The man takes full advantage of the isolated highway, passing through the wilderness. This is a drive he makes any time he needs to get away and think. The rush makes him feel alive and free. He does his best thinking on these drives. Despite the high rate of speed, he is cautious in case he does encounter another vehicle or a pedestrian. It hadn't happened in the past ten years, but his opinion is, " better safe than sorry." He sees an intersection ahead. The town is not far. It is time to slow down.

***

The town of Terra Loch was founded over 200 years ago. There was a rush on the area by would-be treasure hunters hoping to find their fame and fortune. The legendary treasure of an ancient people is rumored to be buried somewhere in the area. After a while, people began to settle and make a new life. The stories of the legendary treasure were forgotten, by most.

Terra Loch surrounds Lake Terra, the largest lake in the county. These days, it is mainly a tourist trap. People come through here hoping to find some sort of treasure. They mostly just buy souvenirs and trinkets to show off to their friends and family back home.

All the downtown streets are arranged in a grid. Streets going east to west are named after former presidents. Streets going north to south are named after states. They all end at Congress Avenue. Congress Avenue runs around the lake, and all streets in town are connected to it. It is apparent the town planner loved puns, due to the naming of Maine Street. Maine Street is the main street that runs down the middle of downtown. Maine is the only road in town that goes over the lake. Figaro Bridge is a drawbridge that connects North Maine Street to South Maine Street. Though Maine is the only street that goes over the lake, all other streets have the words north and south or east and west, depending on what side of the lake they are on.

The red Mustang enters the town from the south. It takes a left on West Jefferson and a right on South Illinois. It is half-past noon, and the driver is looking for a place to eat. He passes restaurant after restaurant. He isn't craving burgers or tacos. He finally pulls into a spot directly in front of *Hold the Anchovies*. That's what he is craving. He leaves the car and steps inside.

***

The restaurant is small. There are a few tables across the right wall. The left wall has one large table that can seat a group. There is a hall on the left behind the table. A restroom sign points to the door on the left side of the hall. There is a door at the end of the hall with an "Employees Only" sign. The counter is toward the back of the small restaurant. A chubby man, who looks to be in his sixties, stands behind the counter. He reads the man's name tag as he approached the counter. It reads "Mario."

Mario smiles wide, "Welcome to *Hold the Anchovies*! How may I help you today, sir?"

He smiles back. “Hello, Mario. Let’s see…” He looks up at the menu board behind the counter.

He peruses the menu board: Pizza, Calzones, Pasta, Soups, Salad, Drinks, Deserts. He can’t decide if he wants a calzone or a pizza. After a moment, he finally decides on pepperoni pizza and a small salad.

“I’ll take a medium pepperoni pizza, a small Caesar’s salad, and a....”

He reads the beverages a second time. It isn’t there.

“No coffee?”

“S...sir?”

“You don’t offer coffee, I take it.”

The chubby man shakes his head. “No, sir. Just what you see there.”

He looks at the beverages again. “I’ll take a large, iced tea then.”

“Excellent choices, sir.” Mario rang up the order. “That will be $14.83.”

His detective badge is revealed when he opens his wallet. Mario flinches when he sees the badge.

“Is everything okay?” he asks as he hands the man his debit card.

Mario takes the card and cashes him out. The man looks nervous. He could tell the man is trying hard to play it straight.

“Sir?”

He sounds nervous when he speaks.

The redhead smiles, “You flinched when you saw the badge.”

“Sir?” Mario tries to play it off.

“Look, I’m a detective. I’m good at reading people.”

Mario hands the card back and starts making the pizza.

“Oh,” he let out a nervous laugh. “Police officers do come in occasionally when they are off duty. I’ve just never seen a real badge before.”

"It's okay. So how long have you owned this place?"

He is casually looking at all the decor around the restaurant. There isn't anything unusual about the decor. It looks like your typical Italian-American restaurant.

"Thirty years," Mario says while making the pizza.

"Ah. Did you inherit it or purchase it outright?"

"It was a speakeasy at one time. This area was a storefront. Downstairs is where the bar was. After prohibition was abolished, the downstairs was gutted for storage, and the storefront was converted to a bar."

"A speakeasy? Interesting."

The chubby man nods and continues. "The bar never did well. I purchased the place thirty years ago. I'm not much of a drinker. My passion is cooking. So, I converted it into the place you see today."

"If these walls could talk, I bet they would have interesting stories," he says.

***

Sweat pours down Ms. Atworth's face. Otto sees her shaking as she eyes the barrel of the gun.

"Will you stay quiet if I put the gun away?"

She nods.

Otto puts the gun down on a nearby table and takes his hand from her mouth. He leans back in his chair. The woman relaxes slightly. They listen in on the conversation above. The moment he hears the stranger's voice, Otto sits up straight.

"Could it be?" Otto stands up and walks toward the bottom of the stairs. He wants to hear the conversation better. He wants to be sure.

"Sir…"

He waves his hand toward her.

"Sir…"

Otto glares at her. He places his index finger over his closed lips.

"Sir!"

Otto runs over to her. "Shut your mouth!"

She mouths, "I have to pee."

"Hold it!"

Otto runs back over to the bottom of the stairs. He trips over his own feet and takes a tumble.

***

A loud crash could be heard from below.

"What is that?"

"What is what?"

"It sounded like someone fell. It came from your employee's entrance."

He walks toward the back hall. Mario starts shaking.

"S...s...sir… N...n… D…"

"Okay, what's back there?"

"N...n...no!"

He opens the door. It leads to stairs. A light can be seen at the bottom of the stairs. He starts down the stairs.

Mario screams, "Otto!!"

***

"Shit…"

Otto quickly picks himself up, runs over to the billiard table, and gags the woman with a bandana. He covers the billiard table with a sheet. He bolts to his workbench, tripping over his feet and almost missing the chair. Otto quickly launches a spreadsheet application. Footsteps grow closer. He hears the footsteps hit the basement floor.

"Otto Von Snaut..."

Otto looks up to see a tall, thin redhead glaring at him. He gives the man a grin as if to say, "there's nothing to see here."

"Hey, Freddy…" Standing and walking over to the man, Otto continues. "I thought that was you up there! How are ya, old friend?"

Otto spreads his arms to hug Freddy. Freddy backs off. "What are you up to now?"

"What do you mean?"

"Otto, we've known each other since we were kids. For as long as I have known you, you have always been hatching some scheme. I know you are hiding something."

Freddy starts walking around the basement. He keeps one eye on Otto. He is looking for the slightest reaction. He gets it as soon as he nears the billiards table. A small movement of Otto's bottom lip. It causes his cigar to bounce ever so slightly. He uncovers the billiard table.

"What the hell…"

"I...I…"

Freddy looks at Otto, "Please don't say, 'I can explain.' Otto, stop right there! Don't go any further!"

Otto turned and darts for the stairs. He stops in mid-stride, as if he were a dog obeying his master's command.

Freddy removed the gag from the young woman and unties her arms and legs. He helps her onto her feet.

"Otto, what's going on?"

"It's not what it looks like." Otto has a grin on his face as he walks toward Freddy. He heads toward the small table behind Freddy.

"Oh really? That's good because it looks like you had this poor woman tied up to a make-shift rack, trying to get information out of her. It also looks like you are trying to sneak toward this table behind me. Perhaps trying to get to this gun?" Freddy grabs the gun from the table. Otto stops in his tracks.

"Freddy…" Otto smiles.

"C'mon Otto, it's my day off." Freddy gives an exasperated gesture with his head. He exhales, "All I wanted to do is grab some lunch on my way home. Of all the evil lairs in all of the restaurants in town, I had to stumble into yours. Otto, man… I gotta take you in…"

"Well, you still can grab your lunch and head home. Just pretend this never happened." Otto smiles.

"No, I can't. Otto, you are clearly kidnapping and torturing this poor woman for some nefarious purpose!"

"No, I'm not. It's nothing like that."

"Yes, it is," Ms. Atworth speaks up for the first time.

Otto glares at her. He looks back at Freddy. "No, it's not."

"Yes, it is." She excitedly demands.

"Freddy, in all of the years you have known me, have I ever lied to you?"

Freddy laughed, "All the time."

"See, he's lying. Save me, sir." She grabbed Freddy's arm in a pleading gesture.

Freddy looks at the woman and back at Otto. He keeps eyeing both of them. Otto notices what he is doing. He is reading them both. This would be it. Freddy would see the truth. He would see…

"She's lying," Freddy exclaims. He shakes his arm, and she releases her grip.

Otto smiles.

"What's really going on here?"

"You remember Harry?"

Freddy nods. "You're brother?"

"Adopted brother," Otto interrupts.

"Your brother," Freddy states. "How could I forget Harry?"

Ms. Atworth creeps toward the stairs. Otto reaches out and grabs her by the shirt collar.

"As I was saying, this...woman…" He thrust the woman toward Freddy. "...was in on that murder. I am just trying to find out the details." He smiles. "Just tryin' to solve a case, Freddy. Same as you."

“Not like me,” Freddy says. Freddy shakes his head and throws up his hands. “Otto, I was there. I saw the entire thing go down… You know what...I don’t care. I just want to grab lunch and go home. You do what you want. You two settle this.”

Freddy walks toward the stairs to go back up. The woman looks frightened.

“Hey, Freddy…”

“Yeah, Otto?” He doesn’t turn around.

“Can I have…”

“You can pick it up at the station.”

Freddy heads up the stairs. Otto turns to look at the frightened woman. He grins.

“Now, where were we…?”

***

Mario catches Freddy coming back into the restaurant.

“M...M...Mr…”

“Look. I don’t even care. Whatever you and Otto have worked out is between y’all. Just give me my food so I can go home.”

Mario hands Freddy the bag with his food, along with his tea. Freddy heads out the door and heads home.

Chapter Two

Murder on an Oriental Rug

"The test came back," the doctor says.

The office is small. There is a small window behind the doctor. Across the desk sits a couple holding hands. The short, chubby man is no taller than five feet. His husband is about average height and relatively thin. They both appear to be in their forties.

"And…?" The chubby man looks nervous. He wraps his hand tightly around his husband's. He could feel the other man shaking as much as he is.

"It came back positive."

The thinner man sighs. "Well, that's a relief."

The doctor has a puzzled look on his face.

The chubby man leans over to his husband. "Positive is not good. He means I have cancer."

The thin man looks at his husband and then at the doctor. He looks back at his husband…

"I have to pee."

***

"Cut!"

The director is of average build and stature. He isn't thin, but he isn't fat either. He is fit and muscular as if he worked out daily. He throws his headset off. "What the hell, Richard?"

The chubby man snickers.

The director glares at him.

He clams up.

"I have to pee, Marcus."

"Hold it, Richard! This is the 14th take! It's the final scene in the doctor's office! We only have this location for two days! It's late, and we are all tired!"

"I have to go to the bathroom."

"There is no bathroom!"

"But, Marcus…"

"Shut up, Hampton!" Marcus puts his hand up in front of the chubby man's face.

The chubby man glares at him. It is evident, that comment angered him.

Marcus either doesn't notice or just ignores the glare from Hampton.

"One more time from the top. Nobody goes to the bathroom. Nobody eats. Nobody does a damn thing until we get this scene! Now, everybody into position!"

The cast reset their positions. The doctor picks up the phone receiver. The two men leave the office and close the door.

"Quiet on the set!" Marcus places his headphones back on his head. "Now, one last time! Action!"

***

The car pulls into the long driveway. It is a single-story house out in the country. The house sits back off the road in a sizable two-acre lot. A privacy fence surrounds the backyard. The backyard has a wooden deck with a pool and a hot tub.

The garage door opens, and the car pulls in. Hampton gets out of the passenger's seat before the engine is switched off, slamming the car door. He grabs his bag and the gift basket from the back and storms inside without a word to the driver.

Hampton walks into the mudroom from the garage. From the mudroom, he enters the kitchen. The kitchen is open, with a large counter and bar facing the living room. The counter contains the sink and dishwasher. The stove is on the left side of the kitchen. The refrigerator is to the right. Cabinets run around the outer walls of the kitchen. There is a small breakfast nook on the right side of the kitchen, on the opposite side of the bar.

Behind the kitchen is a large dining room. There is an opening to the right side of the kitchen that leads to a sitting area. From the sitting area one passes into the master bedroom. The wall opposite the sitting room, opposite the bedroom, leads to the front door. Hampton lies the gift basket on the counter and walks briskly to the master bedroom.

The master bedroom is enormous. There is a walk-in closet off to one side. There is a master bath that contains a walk-in shower, a separate tub, and two sinks. The bathroom has another door that leads to the toilet.

The bedroom has a separate door that leads out to a lanai. A patio table and chairs and two rocker recliners sit on the lanai. The wooden deck leads from the lanai and wraps around the pool and hot tub. The entire area is screened. There is a separate sliding glass door on the left that leads directly into the living room. Opposite the sliding glass doors and to the right side of the lanai, a screen door leads out into the yard. Another entry on the other end of the house opens to a second bathroom.

Hampton throws his bag on the bed and steps out onto the lanai. He sits down in one of the rocker recliners and just stares out at the pool. He knows he needs to calm down.

Hampton can hear the glass door from the living room slide open and footsteps walk onto the lanai. The man remains focused on the pool as the footsteps close in on him. He can hear someone sit down in the rocker next to him. The chubby man never takes his eyes off of the pool.

"It is a nice gift basket. Chocolates this time. Your favorite."

Hampton just sits there in silence.

"C'mon Hampton. You know how tired I am. You know how stressful this is. We were in a time crunch. We needed to get that..."

Hampton glares at the man. "Shut up, Hampton! Really? Shut up?"

Marcus sighs. "I know. I shouldn't have..."

"No, you shouldn't have. We've never told the other to shut up. Never..."

"I know. For that, I am so, so sorry."

Hampton shakes his head. "I know Richard can't act. He just doesn't have it. I get it. I was just as frustrated with him as you were. Do you think I wanted to do that scene again? The guy smells as if he had been eating out of the garbage. I hated every second we were on set together. We still ended up shooting that scene ten more times before we got it. I understand how stressed you are. This is your first big break directing a major studio film. I have always been there for you, and I always will be."

Marcus reaches his hand out to rub Hampton's arm. Hampton quickly moves his arm away.

Hampton shakes his head. "No. I'm still mad. Just give me time, please. This isn't the first time. You have treated me like trash during this entire project. Marcus, please leave me alone right now."

"Hampton..." Marcus pleads.

"Leave me alone," Hampton says, matter-of-factly.

Marcus nods. He stands up and turns to walk back inside. "I love you."

Hampton is silent. He doesn't even turn to look at his husband.

Marcus leaves through the sliding glass door into the living room. Hampton hears the TV turn on. He reclines back and closes his eyes. The sound of the TV slowly fades away into silence. Before long, he is asleep.

***

Hampton wakes in the recliner around three o'clock in the morning. He knows this because he had glanced at the clock hanging on the lanai wall. He notices the TV is still on. This is not like Marcus. Marcus is strict about his bedtime. Hampton enters the living room and sees the sight immediately. Marcus is coughing up blood while holding his side.

Marcus lies there on their antique oriental rug. The rug takes up the majority of the living room floor. Marcus stops coughing. No sound could be heard from the man. He laid there, unmoving. The rug starts changing to a reddish color as it soaks up blood. Hampton runs over to his husband and kneels beside him, grabbing Marcus's left hand and holding it tight.

Hampton keeps moving his lips as if he were trying to speak. No words would come out. He feels Marcus's hand loosen its grip. Marcus's left arm flops to the floor. Hampton falls to the floor in tears. He wraps his arms tight around his husband's lifeless body. A shower of tears flood down his face.

It felt like a knife had been plunged through his chest, directly into his heart. The pain felt deep. As if it had pierced his soul. All he wanted to do is hold Marcus and never let him go.

He had no idea how long he had been lying there. Time just slipped away. It felt like an eternity. A phone began to ring. Hampton just laid there, holding his husband. The phone continued to ring.

***

The house is busy. Three cops are there. Hampton is sitting in one of the chairs in the living room. He is staring at the blood-stained rug where Marcus had laid. One of the cops is looking in the two guest bedrooms to the left side of the living room. A bathroom is between them. Another cop is in the back of the house. A small hallway leads from the back of the living room to another bedroom and bath. This back bathroom contains a door that leads out onto the pool deck.

The third cop is tending to Hampton. The man stands around six feet. He is thin and has bright red hair. He had just brought Hampton a glass of water. Hampton takes the glass from the officer. The officer sits in the chair beside him. Hampton stares at the officer as he takes a sip of water. Except…

"I don't look like a cop," he says with a smile.

Hampton just sits there.

"I'm not going to ask if you are okay. I know you aren't. Nobody would be. Just sit there, okay. Take as long as you need to."

Hampton nods.

"Freddy…"

The man looks up at the officer emerging from the back bedroom.

"What is it? Did you find something?"

"Perhaps…"

The officer walked into the living room holding his nose with one hand. He had a shoe in the other. Both men recoil as the officer approaches. The stench is unbearable.

"What the hell…"

"It doesn't fit the victim. It doesn't fit the chubby guy either, I'd wager."

Hampton glared at him.

"Mr. Hamm," the redhead starts, "has been through enough. His husband died in his arms. Please have a little sympathy Shawn."

The other officer nods. He gestures at the smelly shoe. "What do you want me to do with this?"

"Over there with the rest of the evidence." He looks back at Hampton. "Now, Mr. Hamm…"

"Hampton."

"What?"

"My first name."

He smiles. "You're joking."

Hampton sighs, "I've heard every joke you can come up with."

"I'm sure you have. Well, Hampton Hamm, how about you and I talk in my office while these guys finish up here? There's no sense in you staying here and letting those horrible events play out in your head."

Hampton nods. He sets the glass down on the end table beside him. The officer helps him up and leads him out the front door. He directs Hampton to a 1960's red Mustang.

"This isn't a police car."

The man smiles. "And I'm not a police officer. I'm a detective. Freddy Falcon, the world's greatest detective."

Hampton glares at him in disbelief.

"Okay, the city's greatest. I'll be right back. I'm going to let them know we are leaving."

Hampton nods.

***

"Hey guys, I'm taking Mr. Hamm back to the station to talk. You guys finish up here," he says as he enters the living room.

They nod.

"What about this?" Shawn points to the glass Hampton had been drinking from.

"Lift the prints. See if they match anything."

"Sir?"

"He was the only one here at the time of death. Find out if his prints are on any of the other evidence."

"Sir, he lives here," Shawn says.

"I know that." Freddy sighs. "I'm trying to clear him, not convict him. The spouse is always looked at first. There is no evidence of a break-in. The doors were locked. Nothing was tampered with. No sign of a struggle. Find out what happened. Lift every print in the house. And guys, find the murder weapon."

With that, Freddy heads back to his car. He pulls out of the drive and embarks for the station.

Chapter Three

When Hampton Met Marcus

It begins to rain on the drive back to the station. By the time Freddy pulls into his parking space, the light rain had turned into a thunderstorm.

"Give me a minute," says Freddy. He reaches toward the back seat and reveals an umbrella. "Stay there a second. I'll come around with the umbrella."

Hampton nods. He watches as Freddy opens the driver's side door, extends the umbrella, steps out, and walks around the car. There is something about this guy Hampton could not figure out. He had watched enough television and films to know that he should be the prime suspect. He had been there when Marcus...Marcus… He shakes his head. It is impossible for him to even think the words. Whatever the reason, this guy is acting too friendly to someone who should be the prime suspect.

Freddy opens the door and helps Hampton out of the car. This is the first time he had a good look at where they were. The rain had been beating down on the windshield so hard that he could not tell where they were until now.

The station is on the corner of North Delaware and East Garfield. There is a donut shop and a coffee shop across the street. He and Marcus had been over here a few times. The station is located in the northeastern most part of the city. This area was once farmland. There used to be a farmhouse sitting on the very spot the police station now stands. There is an ice cream parlor just a few blocks from here on East Garfield, right before it intersects North Missouri. Hampton remembers that this particular station is known as 'The Farmhouse' due to its specific location.

Freddy puts his arm around Hampton's waist. He knows it is only to keep them both under the umbrella. It feels nice, though. It reminds him of Marcus. The feel of another man's arm around him. The warm body so close. He starts to tear up as he thinks of Marcus standing close to him instead of this cop.

"It's okay. Let it out. There is no wrong way to grieve." He realizes the detective must have noticed his tears.

"It's not that. It's just…"

Freddy smiles, "Let me guess. You miss him. Something about this particular situation either struck an emotional chord or brought back a particular memory. Like I said, it's okay."

Hampton is puzzled. True, this guy is a detective, but how is he that perceptive? It's as if he had been in this situation before. "I miss his touch."

"Let's get out of the rain. We'll get you something to drink and let you dry off. There's no pressure to talk."

Hampton nods. They walk inside.

***

Freddy leads him through the front door into a small reception area. The detective waves at a large, burly man sitting behind a glass window. There is a rectangular slot at the bottom. Just large enough to transfer items through.

Freddy closes the umbrella and shakes the water off of it through the open door. He closes the door and starts to set the umbrella against the wall.

"Not in my office," the large man says. His voice has a deep bass sound to it.

"Good morning to you too, Norman," he says with a smile.

"You know my rules."

Freddy sighs and nods.

"New suspect?"

Freddy shakes his head. "He watched his husband die. I thought I'd bring him in while Shawn and Eddy finish up at the crime…" The man glances over at Hampton, whose head is still hanging low. "...at his home." He motions to Hampton as he states the last sentence.

Norman frowns. He looks at Hampton. "I'm sorry to hear that, um…"

"Mr. Hamm," Freddy says.

Norman nods, "Mr. Hamm… Well, you are absolutely with the right man."

"Okay," Freddy says to Hampton.

Norman hands Freddy a tray. Freddy holds it out to Hampton. He has a confused look on his face. What is he supposed to do with this?

Freddy smiles. "Norman's rule. Nobody is allowed in with anything. No phones. No wallet. No keys."

"No umbrella," Norman interrupts. Freddy glares at the man. Norman's face remains stoic.

He turns his attention back to Hampton. "Empty all of your pockets and place everything on this tray."

"All I have on me is this." He holds up his left hand to show his wedding ring.

"You're good," Norman says. "You can leave it on."

Freddy empty's his pockets. Hampton watches as the man starts placing items on the tray. Wallet, phone, car keys, and his gun from its holster on his right hip. Freddy hands Norman the tray and his umbrella through the open slot in the glass. Norman presses a button under the counter. A door sits along the right wall. A red light next to the door changed to green. Hampton could hear the click of the lock releasing. Freddy leads Hampton inside.

***

"It's bigger on the inside."

Freddy smiles at the astonished look on the man's face.

"That's what everybody says."

Hampton takes in the sight of the large room. The interior of the station has a wide-open floor plan. Cubicles line the entire area. The cubicles are arranged in sections. Teams, perhaps? Along the outside walls are offices and interrogation rooms. There is a spiral staircase that leads to a second floor. He allows his eyes to climb the staircase. The stairs lead to a catwalk that encompasses all sides of the room. He can see an enormous office at the far end of the second floor. A thin, short black man is sitting behind a computer, hard at work. Hampton assumes that this man is the captain.

Freddy leads Hampton down the center of the room, saying 'hello' to folks as he passes. They turn to the right at the end of the second row of cubicles. A few more turns and Hampton sees the destination. Freddy is taking him to a small glassed-in office along the right wall. Freddy opens the door and lead him inside. The man closes the door behind them.

***

It is a decent-sized office. One wall contains a small coffee bar. He notices a drip pot, espresso machine, and one of those single-cup machines that use those coffee pods. He also sees a French press and a machine that makes cold brew. There are shelves above, that house all varieties of powder creamers. He notices varieties of different sweeteners as well. Underneath the bar is a mini-fridge and glass door cabinets. The cabinets contain all flavors and varieties of coffee and espresso. He can see hundreds of coffee pods as well. He assumes the fridge has milk and liquid creamers. On the left side of the counter, to the immediate right of the fridge, sits a double basin sink. It is a deep, stainless-steel sink. The faucet could detach and double as a spray nozzle. The man loves his coffee, he thinks. Freddy's desk is against the opposite wall. It is situated so that Freddy could look out the glass, with his back to the wall. The desk is organized. Every folder is labeleled. He has desk organizers and trays of neatly stacked papers. All labeled and in a particular order. It appears the detective is a little obsessive-compulsive. Strange though. There is no computer on the desk. He assumed that every officer would have access to a computer, at their fingertips, in this day and age. He shrugs it off. Some people don't work well with technology. Perhaps this detective is one of those people.

Freddy pulls back a rolling chair and offered it to him. "Would you like something to drink?"

"I'm not a coffee drinker."

"Neither am I."

Hampton looks at the coffee bar and back at Freddy. "But…" He points to the coffee bar.

Freddy laughs, "I'm joking with you. Would you care for some hot tea?"

Hampton shakes his head, "I'd like something cold to drink."

Freddy heads to the mini fridge. He opens it, and Hampton can see the variety of cold drinks inside.

"I have iced tea, juice, milk, soda, water."

"I'll take a soda."

Freddy hands him a bottle of soda and heads over to the coffee bar. He turns on the single-cup machine.

"So," Freddy starts, "How long have you been married?"

Hampton watches as Freddy does not use a pod. Instead, he grabs a mesh filter and fills it with Cuban coffee.

"Ten years this month. We've known each other for twenty-six."

"You guys must have been young when you met."

He watches Freddy place the small mesh filter in the hole for the pods and close the lid.

Freddy smiles, "I don't have any pods of Cuban coffee."

Hampton nods, "We met in high school. Our theatre teacher wrote her own plays. Every year ended with a murder mystery dinner theatre production. This is always a who-done-it with audience participation. The audience would get to guess who the murderer is. Every night the killer rotated to a different character. She did her best to include everyone."

"Murder mystery? That sounds like a lot of fun."

He nods. "It is. I looked forward to it every year."

"So, were you both in the show?"

Hampton shakes his head, "Marcus was never an actor. Ms. Bruno never wanted to exclude anyone. This was never a competition for her. We were high school students having fun. It did not matter how wretched of an actor you were. She wanted everyone to have a part."

Freddy grabs his cup of hot, black coffee and walks back to his desk. He rolls his chair to the opposite side of the desk beside Hampton.

"You drink it black?"

Freddy nods as he takes a sip of coffee.

"What's with all of those creamers and sweeteners if you don't use them?"

"For anyone else who might come into my office. And for the other officers. They are all welcome to coffee at any time." He motions for the man to continue. "I'm listening."

Freddy sits back in his chair. He sips his coffee as Hampton spoke.

"Marcus is happier behind the scenes. His mom and sister showed up to the last showing of our senior year. Ms. Bruno was determined to get him on stage for them. She wrote a part specifically for him and made him the murderer that night."

A smile starts to form on his face as he speaks of Marcus. He felt all of the tension lift. Joy starts to fill his heart and mind.

"Marcus and his sister were raised by his mom. His dad left them when he was eight. She struggled to raise those two kids by herself. She did the best she could with what she had. Anyway, he was horrible that night. That was the worst acting I have, to this day, seen from anyone. No emotion in the delivery. No life. He acted like a robot reading ingredients for a recipe."

Freddy smiles.

"It was glorious, though. His mother lit up watching him. He stole the show in her eyes. Anyway, when it came time to guess the killer, everyone got it wrong. They all guessed either me or someone else. Nobody guessed Marcus."

"Not even his mother?"

Hampton shakes his head. "Nope. Because Marcus was written in at the last minute, it was a minor role. Nobody had time to get to know the character. His delivery did't help with that either. Ms. Bruno felt so bad. He told her not to worry about it. He said he loved the opportunity, and it was enough just watching his mom's face light up.

"After the show, I slipped in the dressing room. I hit my head on the floor. Marcus immediately ran over to me. He felt as if it were his fault for not being backstage and taking care of things. He felt so bad about it. He invited me out to dinner with his family to make up for things."

"And the rest is history…" Freddy smiles.

Hampton shakes his head. "Not exactly… He is not my type. We weren't even friends. I was a stuck-up and prissy rich snob. At the moment he asks me out, his mom walks backstage. I laughed in his face. I told him I would never be caught dead eating with poor trash like him.

I was such a fool. I embarrassed him to death. I told him that I am going to be a famous ac-tor…" He embellished the word to sound a little stuck up. "...and he is going to become a famous fry cook."

Hampton hangs his head with guilt. Freddy puts his hand on Hampton's shoulder. Hampton looks up. Freddy smiles.

"How did you guys fall in love?"

The man takes another sip of coffee.

"Well, it would be a while. A lot of missteps and struggles before we get there. We crossed paths again in college." Hampton leans back as he starts to tell the story. "I was studying theatre, and he wanted to direct. At the time, I had no clue he was there. Marcus Peterson had long left my memory. I was studying in my dorm room when there was a knock at the door."

***

"It's open."

Hampton looked up from his work as the door opens. In walks the most handsome and well-dressed man he had ever seen. It isn't until the man spoke that Hampton knows who he is.

"My roommate has a girl over. I was walking down the hall and saw your door. I thought I'd stop and say hello."

"Marcus Peterson?"

Marcus smiles and nods. "I'm not exactly the poor kid in rags you knew in high school."

"Well, don't just stand at the door. Come in and sit down."

Marcus closed the door and steps inside. Hampton brushed off a spot on his bed. He motioned for Marcus to sit there, and he sits next to the man.

"How long has it been?"

"Since you saw me last?"

Hampton nods.

Marcus shrugs. "I dunno. Maybe five years. Since high school."

"Has it been that long? Time flies. Tell me about yourself."

"There's not much to tell. Mom married after we graduated. He is an executive for a large software company. We moved into a nice home. We have all new clothes. I started working out and taking care of myself. That's how I ended up here. I'm studying film. I want to be a director. What about you?"

Hampton's life had changed too, but not for the better. His dad lost everything in the stock market. He is in college solely on financial aid. His folks lost their home, and they were living in a trailer park. That had been a bust to his ego. He applied for any grant or scholarship that would get him out of, as he sees it, that slum. He is going to be an ac-tor. He is determined not to allow anything or anyone to stand in his way of achieving that goal. In his mind, he is too good to be poor and would never be poor. He lied to Marcus.

"Oh my, life has been a whirlwind. My folks purchased a new house after high school. We moved to an exclusive community. They heavily encouraged me to pursue acting."

"Wait, isn't your dad in the stock market?"

Hampton swallowed hard. "Yeah, he is."

"He did't loose everything when the market crashed?"

He shakes his head to continue the lie.

"Oh, I thought no one came out of that unscathed. My understanding is thousands of families lost everything; their homes, cars, possessions. How did you guys come out okay?"

"Dad got a tip that it was all about to crash. He sold before that happened."

"So, your dad is in prison now for insider trading?"

"What?"

"Isn't that illegal?"

"Insider trading is illegal. That's not what dad did."

"I thought..."

Hampton roles his eyes and sighs. "Insider trading is when an employee, officer, or board member of a corporation buys or sells stock of that corporation, artificially influencing the market and not allowing someone outside of the corporation to purchase any of the stock. Dad got a tip and acted on it to save his family."

"I see." Marcus smiles at Hampton. "You've always wanted to be an actor. I'm glad to see you here. It's been hard getting to know

folks. I'm too smart for the jocks. I'm too muscular for everyone else. It's good to see a familiar face."

"Would you care for something to drink?"

Marcus scooted closer to Hampton. They were right next to each other now. "I have an idea. Why don't I take you out for dinner?" Marcus had his arm around Hampton now. "I don't know about you, but I am sick of cafeteria food and ramen."

Hampton smiles. He allowed his head to rest on Marcus's shoulder.

"I'd love that."

***

Hampton has tears in his eyes now. Freddy grabs some tissue and hands them to him.

"You don't have to continue."

"No," Hampton shakes his head. "I'm almost done… I have to verbalize this..." Hampton wipes the tears away with his arm and blows his nose into the tissue before continuing.

"He took me to an elegant restaurant that evening. It is one of those places where the meal is always onc hundred dollars a plate. We ate and talked. I had no idea he had been watching me for months. He had been trying to get up the nerve to talk to me. He knew I was lying to him. He knew my dad had lost everything. He just let me talk. Marcus had had a crush on me since high school. I had been too stupid to notice."

***

"How is your steak?" Marcus asks.

Hampton shoved a piece of steak in his mouth as he looked up. "It's amazing." Hampton wiped his mouth and takes a sip of wine.

All of the circular tables were covered in white cloth. The cloth napkins wrapped tightly around the silverware and were bound with a wooden ring around them. Everyone is dressed in their best elegant clothing. The lights were dim. The servers were doing their best to wait on everyone. This is the first time he had eaten at a place like this since before the market crashed. This is never the type of place Marcus cared for, though.

"You never cared for places like this. You always recoiled every time I would talk about my life when we were in high school. I would go on and on about every restaurant we ate at the night before. You would roll your eyes. Why the change?"

Marcus laughed and shakes his head. "I never eat at these places. I'm a fast-food nut. This is for you."

"Me? Well, thank you." He smiles at the thought of this handsome, muscular man thinking only of him. It is a selfless gesture that he appreciated.

Marcus put down his wine glass. "Look, Hampton, you haven't changed. You are still the same self-absorbed prima donna I knew in high school. Truth is, I like you. For some ungodly reason, I've always been attracted to you. I see something in you that is more than what you present."

"I know that." Hampton waved his hand as he says it. "Please, every gay boy and straight girl in high school wanted a piece of this."

"Cut the shit, Hampton." Hampton is in the middle of taking a bite when Marcus says that. The tone came with such ferocity that Hampton nearly dropped his fork. "Look! I know you're bullshitting me."

"What do you mean?"

Oh crap, he thinks. He doesn't know how Marcus knows, but he is sure the man knows. He smiles and attempted to look innocent to continue the lie.

"C'mon Hampton, I can read you like a book. You're lying. I know your dad lost everything when the market crashed."

"No, he... My folks are vacationing in Europe right now...."

"Cut the crap! No, they aren't. Your dad stocks shelves at the local supermarket. Your mom is a housekeeper in a hotel. They lost everything. Your ego would not allow you to stay. You left to pursue your own interests. You haven't talked to them in years."

"How did you know that?"

"My step-uncle owns the hotel."

Hampton wanted to crawl under the table. How could this man lead him on like this? Is this all a setup? Is he leading him on as some type of cruel joke? He is infuriated at the thought.

"You're a jerk."

"Why?"

"Is this your idea of a cruel joke?"

Marcus put down his fork and leans back. He folded his hands and rested them on his chest. He continued to speak in a calm, even tone.

"Of course not. Quite the opposite. I know you are capable of more than this box you put yourself in. It's my goal to wake your ass up. The fairy tale is over. Welcome to real life. Now, talk. Let's have a real conversation. No more of this bullshit."

Hampton opens his mouth to speak. Marcus put up his index finger.

"Talk about the truth. Your life. Your goals. Your real passions. I want to get to know you. The real you."

Hampton laughed. "Look, we haven't even spoken since the night you embarrassed me by asking me out."

"Embarrassed you?"

"That was in high school, Marcus. Get over it. Anyway, the only reason I accepted is that you are hot now. But you are still the same loser you were in high school. I am going to be a great actor...", he embellished the word again, "..., and you can still become a famous fry cook. You're nothing. A loser. Scum. Not even worth wash-

ing my feet. I'm like a great elephant, and you are the mouse beneath my feet."

"Elephants are afraid of mice. They are spooked by them." He continued his calm tone.

Hampton continued as if he doesn't hear the comment. "I will run circles around you. I will crush you. You are a loser and will always be a loser. I am destined for greatness, and you are destined to scrub floors."

With that, Hampton holds his head high and walks out. He would be happy for the rest of his life if he never sees this man again.

***

Hampton is crying hard now. Freddy just sits there for a moment.

"I have so many regrets. So much I missed out on. I treated him like crap for so long. He kept loving me."

Hampton wipes his tears away with his arm again. Freddy hands him another tissue. He uses it to blow his nose.

"Well, you obviously fell in love. When did you meet again?"

"It was some years later. I auditioned for a movie. It was my first big break. Marcus was the director." Hampton starts laughing. "He gave me the role of a fry cook."

Freddy laughs.

"I hated him for that. He used that to get to know me. We dated for a while and fell in love. I almost lost him, though. I cheated on him with his best friend. It broke his heart. He had worked hard for a year to win me over, and I did that to him. It takes another year before he gave me another chance. After twelve years of knowing each other, we finally moved in together. We lived together for four years. We eventually married in Canada."

"In Canada?"

Hampton nods. "We married in 2010. Gay marriage wasn't legalized in the US at that time."

"I see. That's a nice story. It's real. Honest."

"I was an idiot. I squandered twelve years."

"But you had fourteen."

Hampton smiles.

"Hey," Freddy says, "are you hungry? I'm hungry."

Hampton nods. Freddy looks at the clock. It is one o'clock in the afternoon.

"Let's grab some lunch."

Chapter Four

Two Guys, a Crook, and a Burger Joint

Otto Von Snaut had been eating nothing but pizza and pasta for months now. It is an unfortunate consequence of living in the basement of an Italian restaurant. He had decided to go out for burgers. It is something different and something he had been craving for a while.

Otto walks down North Maine Street, perusing the shops. He rarely came to this part of town. The restaurant is south of the lake, on South Illinois. Otto typically just stayed around the south side of the lake.

The streets were bustling with people. Everyone scurried off to whatever destination they had planned. Families heading one way. Kids running into and out of the local arcade. Men and women heading to and fro. The only businesses that were not packed were the bars. It is one forty-two in the afternoon, after all.

As he walks down Maine, he passed by an antique store, ice cream shop, coffee shop, and a few restaurants. He passed by a pub which is next door to… Perfect, he thinks. Otto steps inside *Burger Palace*.

***

"You don't care for the fries?"

Hampton sits there staring down at his plate. He had barely touched his fries. It isn't that at all. The fries and the burger were delicious. He had barely had an appetite after watching Marcus… He can't bring himself to think the rest of it. The events of the previous night kept playing in his head like a movie on repeat. He remembered the sounds, the smells, every single moment. He still felt that pain. It is a stabbing feeling that went down deep into his soul. Every time he felt it, it made him feel sick to his stomach. He wishes for the pain to end. He wishes he could rewind time. He wishes the last thing he had said to Marcus had been, “I love you” instead of...

“Leave me alone…” he mumbles.

Freddy nods, thinking Hampton is talking to him.

“I’m going to get a refill. Would you care for one?”

Hampton just sits there, silent.

“Okay.”

Freddy stands up, grabs his and Hampton’s empty cups, and casually strides toward the fountain drinks. Hampton sits there, drowning in his misery.

***

Otto walks through the burger place, carefully watching everyone. He feels for his wallet the moment he enters. All he feels is his car keys. All his other pockets are empty. Had he driven across town without it? What would he do now? Perhaps find a sap he could use or rob.

There he is…, Otto thinks. He notices a lone loser sitting at a table. His head is down, and he had barely eaten anything. There is a second place setting with an empty plate. It appears that someone had been sitting there moments ago. A bad break-up, perhaps? This poor sap had been left in the lurch to wallow in his pity. He is the perfect target.

Otto sits down in the empty chair across from the sap. The chubby man never looked up. How long could he sit there before the loser noticed him? Otto sits back and folds his arms. He sits there in silence, determined not to speak until the short, chubby man sees him.

“What the hell are you doing in my chair?”

Otto jumps at the sound of Freddy’s voice. He is so focused on this chubby loser that he never notices the tall redhead approach from behind.

He turns around and smiles at Freddy. “Freddy, small world, ain’t it?”

“Get out of my chair.”

“Hey, sorry about that, Freddy. I didn’t realize you were here with this guy. Working a case?”

“Up! Now!”

“Okay, okay… No need to shout.”

Otto stands up and holds his hand out, motioning for Freddy to sit. Freddy sits down and glares at Otto.

“Leave,” says Freddy.

“Is that how you talk to an old friend?”

“We aren’t friends.”

“We used to be.”

“Yes, before I became a detective, and you became a petty crook. Now, what do you want, Otto?”

“I thought that tubby, here….”

“Mr. Hamm…”

Otto looks confuses for a moment. He then realizes that is the loser's name.

“...Mr. Hamm, here, would lend me some money so that I could grab a bite to eat.”

Freddy just stared at him.

‘See, I left my wallet at home….”

“So, you drove across town without a license?”

“Well, yeah. I left my wallet at home.”

“Are you seriously admitting to a cop that you have been driving illegally?”

Otto quickly realizes Freddy could arrest him for this.

“I mean, my money. I have no cash and left my debit card at home. See, I was purchasing something online and left my card….”

“You talk too much, and I don’t care.”

Freddy pulls out his wallet and throws a few dollars at Otto. “There. Go buy some food, and leave Mr. Hamm and me alone.”

"Hey, thanks, Freddy. I'll pay you…"

"No, you won't."

"Yeah, I won't."

Otto turns to leave. Freddy grabs his arm.

"And Otto, don't give me a reason to take you in."

He jerks his arm from Freddy's grip. He smiles as he turned to walk away.

"Hey, Freddy, it's me."

"I know."

That guy is a pain in my ass, Otto thinks as he walks off.

***

That guy is a pain in my ass, Freddy thinks.

"I'm sorry about that," he says as he turns his attention to Hampton.

"So, you guys were friends?"

He jumps at the sound of Hampton's voice. The man had been silent for so long, it startled him a little.

"I'm sorry. I didn't mean to startle you."

Freddy shakes his head. "It's fine. Yeah. Otto and I go back a long way."

"Tell me about yourself. How did you guys meet?"

He smiles. He notices Hampton lighting up a little. Perhaps Otto barging in is a much-needed distraction. It appears to have taken Hampton's mind off of the events of the last twenty-four hours.

"We were friends in high school. I was much different then. So was Otto, actually."

"Weren't we all…" Hampton smiles.

Freddy grins. "You know that all too well, too."

Hampton nods and starts to frown. Freddy can tell memories are coming back.

"So, yeah, we knew each other in high school. We used to hang out together and cause a little bit of mischief. Otto came from a stable and loving home. I was raised by my grandparents. Mom died from cancer when I was young. Dad had been in prison my entire life. My grandparents did the best they could, but they had already raised their kids. I know they loved me, and I still love them. It just isn't a stable home. Otto's family was my bastion of stability."

Hampton reaches for his burger. Freddy pulls his plate away from him. At that moment, a server approaches with a fresh plate. Freddy motions toward Hampton. The server sits the plate down in front of Hampton.

"The plate is hot, sir."

Hampton grabs the plate to pull it close.

"Ouch!" He jerks his hands away.

The server looks puzzled. "Why did you touch it? I said it's hot."

Freddy hands the server Hampton's old plate.

"Thank you," says the server. She looks back at Hampton. "Let it cool down before you touch it."

"Thank you for bringing the fresh plate," Freddy smiles.

The server takes the plate and smiles.

"My pleasure."

The server turns and walks off.

Freddy smiles at Hampton. "I thought you could use a fresh plate."

Hampton looks at his burger. He removes the top bun and smiles.

"Exactly the way I like it."

Freddy nods. "I have an attention to detail. It makes me good at my job."

Hampton takes a bite of the burger. "Oh my, this burger is amazing."

Freddy laughs.

"So," Hampton speaks between bites, "go on." He motions for Freddy to continue. "His family was a bastion of stability for you."

"Just that. We were like brothers. In fact, I got along better with his adopted brother, Harry."

"Adopted?"

"Yeah. His mother almost died, giving birth to Otto. His folks were told they could not have any more kids. It could kill her. So, they wanted to give Otto a brother. They chose to adopt."

"Are you and his brother still close?"

Freddy shakes his head.

"Harry got involved with some bad folks."

"Like Otto…"

"No," Freddy says, shaking his head. "Otto is a petty crook with illusions of grandeur. He likes to think he is an evil genius or my arch-nemesis… I dunno... Perhaps he believes he is James Moriarty to my Sherlock Holmes. I don't know, and I don't care. In my mind, he's more like Lou Costello to my Bud Abbott."

Hampton almost chokes on a fry with laughter. "So," he coughs as he says it. He takes a sip of soda and coughs again.

"Sorry about that. I didn't mean to make you choke."

Hampton waves his hand as he drinks more soda. "It's okay. That just struck me funny. I expected you to call him Gracie Allen."

Freddy burst out in laughter.

"So," Hampton continues, "what happened to Harry?"

Freddy frowns. "He was…"

He stops himself. He doesn't like to lie, but he thinks this necessary. The last thing he wants is to dredge up what Hampton just went through.

"...put in prison a few years ago. No parole."

Hampton nods. "That's sad. It shows that it never matters where someone comes from. We are all responsible for the choices we make in life."

Freddy smiles. "You astonish me at how perceptive you are, Mr. Hamm."

Hampton smiles. "Call me Hampton."

Freddy shakes his head. "Mr. Hamm, I'm sorry." He knows what is happening. Hampton's emotions are taking over. He needs that connection. He still longs for it. And here Freddy is, showing him the attention he craves. He is mistaking it for an attraction. "Mr. Hamm, I am working a case."

Hampton starts to speak and quickly closes his mouth. He lowers his head.

Freddy frowns. "I know what you are going through is impossibly hard. Trust me when I say, I know what that pain feels like. You remember when Norman made the comment that you are with the right guy?"

Hampton nods.

"I have been exactly where you are now. I watched the love of my life die. I want to get to the bottom of this case for you."

"So, you don't think I…"

Freddy shakes his head. "I know you didn't. I have that feeling about you. You couldn't have done this. You don't have it in you. It's my job to prove it. Look, Mr. Hamm, perhaps we can be friends when all of this is over. Right now, I must stay professional. You are part of a murder investigation. I am the lead detective. Do you understand?"

Hampton nods.

Freddy sits back. "Also, I want you to understand something else. Life will get tough for you during this investigation. My heart breaks for you."

At that moment, Otto walks by as he heads for the door. A takeout bag in one hand. Otto pats Hampton on the back and says in passing, "You'll be okay. Prison ain't so bad."

Freddy rolls his eyes, "How would you know? You've always weaseled your way out of it."

"I hear things."

Freddy looks at Otto in disgust. “Otto, leave.”

“I’m going. I’m going,” Otto says as he walks out the door.

Freddy sighs, “I’m sorry about that idiot.”

Hampton laughs. “It’s fine. I think I needed that.”

“Good. Now, I don’t envy what you are about to go through. You will have to deal with being a suspect in the murder of your husband while grieving for him. You will be asked to talk about the events of last night. This will get hard. Do you understand?”

Hampton nods. “As long as you believe I didn’t do it.”

Freddy smiles. “Let me work my magic. It’s time for the investigation to begin.”

Chapter Five

An Interview With Richard

Freddy's phone rings. He is in the middle of frothing his milk for his cappuccino. The espresso is almost ready.

As he uses the rest of the steam to froth the milk, "Shit," he says.

He finishes frothing the milk and set the container down. He runs over to his desk and picks up the receiver.

"Hello."

"Hey, Freddy." It is Norman.

"Hey, Norman. Is he here?"

"Yup. You ready for him?"

"Hold him there. I'll be out in a minute."

"You got it."

Freddy hangs up the phone and heads back over to the coffee bar.

This will give me time to finish my cappuccino, he thinks.

The espresso is finished. He turns off the machine. He takes the carafe and pours the espresso into a large cup. He then takes the container of frothed milk and pours it over the espresso. He uses a spoon to hold back the froth. After the milk is poured, he scoops up the foam with the spoon and places it on top of the espresso. He should have been a barista. He always makes interesting designs with the froth. Today is no different. It is a smiley face.

He dumps out the espresso grounds and cleans up after himself. He takes his cup over to his desk and sits down. He skims through a folder labeled "Richard Olstroski" while sipping his cappuccino. He asked for as much of a history on everyone related to this latest film project Marcus Peterson was directing as he can dig up. There is something about Mr. Olstroski that doesn't sit right with him. He can't quite put his finger on it, though. That's why he had asked Mr. Olstroski to come in to talk. He needs a good read on this guy.

He closes the folder. "Well, let's not keep Mr. Olstroski waiting."

***

Norman sits behind his desk, watching Richard Olstroski. This is one odd individual. He doesn't have to be a detective to tell this guy is nervous. The man could not sit still. He is pacing the waiting room, looking at the walls. He is straightening the pictures on the walls, which weren't crooked. If they were, then it is only by a minuscule amount. He is counting the lights on the ceiling.

I could tell him how many there are, Norman thinks. I helped install them.

There is a smell about the man. Norman wishes Freddy would hurry. He knows that if this guy stayed in his waiting room much longer, he would never get this stench out.

At that moment, the waiting room door opens, and Freddy steps through. He sees the cappuccino and rolls his eyes.

"I had to babysit this guy while you were making coffee?"

Freddy smiles at him. "Priorities, Norman. Is that him?"

Norman nods.

"Why is he whispering to himself?"

Norman shrugs.

"What is that smell?"

"Your problem now," he says matter of factly.

Freddy sighs and walks over to Richard.

"Mr. Olstroski," Freddy says, holding his hand out to the man. "I'm Freddy Falcon, the lead detective on the case. I'm glad you could come in."

Richard shakes Freddy's hand. "Of course. I don't know what I can offer, though. I don't know Marcus that well. I told the officer that I had been brought onto the project late...."

"Mr. Olstroski," Freddy interrupts him. "Let's talk in my office."

"Freddy," Norman says. He holds out a tray for Freddy.

Freddy smiles. "Before that, Mr. Olstroski, would you mind placing all of your possessions on this tray? You will get them back when you leave."

"But..."

"My rules," says Norman.

Richard starts to object again but stops himself when he sees the burly man behind the counter stand up. Norman stood six and a half feet tall and was built like a brick shithouse. He had been a linebacker in college and still looked the part.

Richard empties his pockets: Keys, wallet, phone, gum, change.

"Just your pockets. This isn't airport security," Norman says. The man had started to take off his shoes.

"Oh," Richard says. He put his shoes back on.

The red light on the door turns green. Freddy leads the man through.

Norman shakes his head. He sits back down and sighs with relief.

"I'm getting too old for this shit."

***

Freddy and Richard walk through the station. They were not heading toward Freddy's office, though. As they walk through the rows of cubicles, people would show visual signs of their disgust of the foul smell emanating from Richard. These folks deal with unkempt people constantly. The smell protruding from Richard is too much for them.

"So," Freddy says with a smile, "did you win Survivor?"

Richard has a confused look on his face. "What?"

"From that smell, I just assumed you had been stuck out on an island for thirty-nine days."

"What smell?"

"You're joking, right?"

Richard smells his armpits and then lifts his shirt to his nose. "What smell?"

Freddy shakes his head as they approach the far back wall of the station. A female with short, curly hair and glasses is standing near a door reading *Showers*.

"Hey, Freddy," She says.

"Hey, Meg."

She clears her throat. "Sergeant."

Freddy had forgotten. Meg had been recently promoted to Sergeant.

"Sergeant Strickland. I'm sorry. I'm still not used to the new role yet."

She recoils as she smells the stench coming from Richard.

"Uh…" It takes her a minute to compose herself. "You just bring this guy in?"

Freddy shakes his head. "He's part of the Peterson case. He's an actor who played opposite Mr. Hamm. I brought him in to discuss the case. I don't want that foul stench in my office. I think a shower would do him some good."

"Understood, Detective."

"What are you doing back here now that you're in 'management'?" He smiles.

She sighs. "I had to go out on a case. I'm about to get cleaned up, myself. I'll walk him back there."

"You sure?"

"Yeah. Why not? Besides, it will give the famous detective some time to make himself some coffee," she says with a smile.

"Ah, you know me too well."

Freddy turns to Richard. "The sergeant will show you to a shower stall and where to grab clean clothes. When you are done, my office is over there. The small, glassed-in one."

Richard is still sniffing himself with a confused look on his face. He looks to where Freddy is pointing and nods.

"Thanks."

"No problem, Freddy." She turns to Richard. "C'mon, let's get you cleaned up."

Meg leads Richard into the showering area.

Freddy heads toward his office. "Time for more coffee," he says as he gulps down the last few drops of his cappuccino.

***

He sits down with his second cup of coffee. He had been reviewing Richard's file while waiting on the man. At that moment, there is a knock at his office door.

"Come," he says.

The door opens, and Meg pops her head in. "Freddy," she says.

He looked up in surprise. "Meg?"

She looks annoyed.

"Sorry. Sergeant."

"No. I'm not annoyed at you."

"What is it?"

She holds the door open, and Richard is standing there.

"I got lost," he says.

"Somehow, he ended up in the captain's office. Captain Youngblood was not impressed."

"I'm sure he wasn't. Alright, come on in and have a seat."

Richard walks into Freddy's office. Meg closes the door behind him. Freddy stands and walks over to the other side of the desk. He pulls out a chair for Richard to sit. Richard takes the chair. Freddy sits back down behind his desk.

He watched Richard for a few minutes before speaking. He leans back in his chair, folds his hands together, lays them against his chest, and looks up at the ceiling. He is trying to think of the correct way to start the conversation. He needs to know everything about this man.

Well, he thinks, let's start from the beginning.

He is still leaning back in his chair as he speaks. He turns his eyes toward Richard.

"How was the drive over?"

This caught the man off guard. "What?"

He smiles. Perhaps the man had expected him to start in on the case. Asking him questions about his location the night of the murder or some such. He suspected this man's only knowledge of an investigation came from TV and film.

"How was your drive? How was the traffic?"

"Oh," Richard starts, "it was quite nice. Traffic is a little hectic in spots, but nothing too bad."

"That's good. Is this your first time in this part of town?"

Richard nods.

"It's not a bad area. We have a coffee shop and donut shop across the street. I know, cop stereotype." Freddy smiles. "Honestly, I don't care for donuts. I'm an ice cream man, myself. There's a great little ice cream parlor a few blocks from here. They have an amazing caramel-mocha sundae. The 'Sundae Mudslide' they call it. That's my favorite." He could taste the flavors of the sundae as he talked.

"I'm not big on ice cream."

"What is your favorite dessert?"

He shrugs. "I guess I don't have one."

"Oh, c'mon now. Everybody has some type of favorite dessert. It may not be sweets, but there has to be something."

"Well," he says, "I like apple pie."

"There ya go. How long have you lived here?"

"I don't live here."

"Oh?"

"I'm just in town while the movie is being shot."

"Where are you from?"

"California. L.A."

"Swimming pools. Movie stars," he says with a smile. The theme from *The Beverly Hillbillies* starts playing in his head.

"What?" Richard had a confused look.

"Nothing. Just making a joke." He shakes the thought off and swerves back on topic. "Are you married? Do you have kids?"

"No kids. Neither of us are good with kids. They get in the way."

Freddy doesn't have kids either, but he was always good with kids. He had heard those statements before. "Kids get in the way" or "Kids are too much trouble." He always saw the joy in the innocence of a child. Perhaps it's because of where he came from. He isn't sure. He had seen so many so-called parents do a lot of horrible things to their children. Perhaps it's good that this man knows he and his wife are not cut out for children.

"Detective?"

He just realizes Richard is in the room. He had gotten lost in his thoughts again. He decides to continue.

"So, you're married then?"

Richard nods. "For twenty-three years."

"Is she here with you?"

"No. Maggie doesn't travel much. It's not her 'thing.'"

"Are you staying here in town?"

Richard nods. "With Marcus and Hampton. They let me use.."

He bolts up as soon as he hears this. He cuts Richard off mid-sentence. "You're staying where?" He starts looking through his notes and folders on the case. It isn't listed anywhere that Richard Olstroski is staying with the victim and his husband.

"With Marcus and Hampton. They are letting me use their back bedroom and bathroom during the shoot. I was brought on at the last minute. They felt bad about it, so they offered me a free place to stay. Is that a problem?"

"Yes, it's a problem. You've just become a suspect."

"What? But I wasn't even there that night," Richard protests.

"It doesn't matter. You just made yourself a suspect."

"But…"

Freddy holds up his hand. Richard closed his mouth. "Mr. Olstroski," he starts, "you are not under arrest. You are just a suspect now. You can't leave town."

"But I have a new project starting tomorrow. I flew in just for this. I fly out tonight."

"Not anymore, you don't."

"Listen, Mr." Richard stands and places his hands on Freddy's desk. "I came in as a courtesy to Hampton. I felt bad that he had to deal with that jackass husband of his. You can do whatever investigations you want, but I will be back on a plane heading for LAX later tonight." With that, he turns and starts for the door.

"You walk out that door, and you will be spending the night in a cell instead of a hotel."

Richard freezes. He had just opened the door.

"Sit down, Mr. Olstroski."

Richard closes the door and heads back to the chair. He sits down.

"Good," Freddy says. "So, why didn't you mention you were staying with the Peterson-Hamm's when you were interviewed?"

"They never asked."

"You didn't think to mention it?"

He shakes his head. “I didn’t think it was relevant.”

“You didn’t think…” Freddy takes a breath, trying to calm himself. “So, Mr. Peterson is found dead by his husband in their living room. You were staying with them, and you don’t think it important to mention that?”

“I wasn’t there that night.”

It is rare for Freddy to get this heated in an interview. He made an effort to stay calm while allowing the interviewee to squirm a little. He could feel his blood pressure rising. His entire body is pounding from his pulse. He is close to coming across the desk and tackling the man. He takes a breath and allows himself to calm down.

He picks up the phone and dials. A gruff voice answers.

“Yeah?”

“Oscar, come to my office.”

“What?”

“Now, Oscar.” He hangs up the phone.

A few minutes later, Oscar enters. He is a short, thin man with dark black hair.

“Yeah, Falcon?” he says in a gruff voice. “What the hell?” He is taken aback by the stench emanating from Richard.

“This is Mr. Olstroski. Please ensure that he has a comfortable place to stay nearby. He is not to leave this part of town. I want an officer always stationed with him and eyes on him at all times. Understood?”

“We’ll make a detour by the showers first.”

“He’s already had one.”

Oscar starts to comment. Freddy interrupts before the man could say a word.

“Just do it, Oscar.”

Oscar sighs. “Come with me,” he says to Richard.

Richard starts to protest. Oscar reaches for his handcuffs. Richard freezes.

"Come with me," Oscar says again. "You will either walk out with cuffs or without them. The choice is yours. I could care less either way."

Richard nods. He follows Oscar out. Oscar closes the door behind him.

Freddy sits back in his chair and thinks for a few minutes.

"Why had this not been mentioned? Why hadn't Mr. Hamm said anything? Why wouldn't he? He's the prime suspect. This changes things for him. This would help him, a lot."

He dials another extension. "Shawn, could you come in a minute?"

A few minutes later, Shawn strolls in.

"What's up, Freddy?"

"Well," he says, holding up a bag with the smelly shoe in it. "I think we know who this belongs to. Did Mr. Hamm say anything to you about a guest staying with them?"

Shawn shakes his head.

"Could you check with the other officers that were there?"

"It was just me and Eddy. We were nearby at the time the call came in."

"Did Eddy talk to him?"

"No. Eddy was helping the paramedics with the body. I was comforting the husband until you arrived."

He nods. "Thank you, Shawn."

Shawn nods and leaves.

He sits back in thought.

Chapter Six

He Only Sleeps When He's Crying

Freddy moved into his grandparents' house after his granny passed away. He could not bear to sell the house he grew up in. It is a simple house that sits on a fifty-five-acre farm. His grandad, whom he called "Papa," never raised animals. He was, primarily, a peanut farmer.

He turns off of North Van Buren and drives down the dirt drive. Both sides once contained rows and rows of peanuts. He remembers his summers in these peanut fields. He remembers how much he hated spending his days pulling the weeds from these fields while his friends were out having fun. He looks back on these memories fondly now. A smile forms on his face as he remembers how he would always complain, every time his Papa would tell him to help in the fields. His Papa always responded with, "Boy, you are allergic to work. Now come on."

The drive goes around the house. The old cow pasture still stands on the side of the house. His Papa never had cows. He allowed a friend to use this pasture for his cows to graze. The old grain bin still stands there in pristine condition. As a child, he always wanted to climb to the top of the grain bin and play inside. His Papa, wisely, forbade it. As an adult, he understands the grain would have sucked him down like quicksand.

Behind the house, there are more fields where peanuts and corn once grew. His Papa used the first few rows of one of the fields as a garden. He would grow peas, beans, and tomatoes in the garden. That is something else he loathed when he was younger. He remembers sitting on the living room couch with a five-gallon bucket full of peas at his feet. He had a pan in his lap to place the shelled peas in and a bag by his side for the empty husks. His evenings were spent watching TV and shelling peas.

He pulls into the carport behind the house. He gets out of the car and heads for the house. He passes the old, above-ground well that had long since been modernized to have running water in the house. All of the water they used; washing dishes, showering, washing clothes, and drinking came from this well. The same well had rodents, frogs, and snakes living, pooping, and peeing in it. He finds it funny that people today are grossed out by the thought of drinking pond water. Hell, he used to drink water from this very well, growing up. He swam in ponds and rivers as well. As far as he sees things, he turned out fine.

***

He enters the house and flips on the living room light. Back behind him and to the left is the master bedroom. He never moved into this room. This would always belong to his grandparents. To the left is a small bathroom. A door leading to the kitchen is along the wall directly opposite the front door. He makes his way into the kitchen. There is a small breakfast bar on the left wall and an opening to the right of the bar that leads to the dining room. Along the wall behind him, there are cabinets and an electric stove. More cabinets and countertops are along the right wall. A sink is in the center of the right countertop. The marks of a knife are still in the Formica, to the right of the sink.

That was the worst spanking he had ever received. He doesn't remember the details anymore. He remembers he had gotten so mad at his grandparents that he stabbed the knife into the countertop, leaving the marks. His granny approached him about it, and he threatened to hit her. His Papa stepped in and said, "Boy, if you hit my wife, you will never forget it." He remembers threatening to report child abuse. His Papa said, "I'll show you child abuse," and gave him the worst spanking he would ever receive.

He left those marks in the Formica to remind him of the lesson learned that day. He doesn't need them to remember the events. They would forever be etched in his memory. The marks were there as a constant reminder of a lesson he learned all too well. From that day forward, Freddy never threatened to hit his grandparents. In fact, violence would always be a last resort for him.

The far wall contains more countertops and cabinets, as well as a refrigerator. To the left of the fridge is a small entryway. He walks through the entryway. On the right is his bathroom. On the left side is his bedroom. So many childhood memories were contained in this room. His old stereo still sits on the chest of drawers along the left wall. The CD player barely works anymore, but the radio still picks up all of the local stations. The dual cassette players that he used to make mixtapes had long since stoped working. This is a relic of a simpler time. His bed is against the left wall. The right side has a small desk. A window is along the back wall. He used to sit on the edge of that bed doing his homework while recorded episodes of *Ren and Stimpy*, *Animaniacs*, *Quantum Leap*, and *Star Trek: The Next Generation* played in the background. He didn't watch them all at once, of course. He would grab a VHS tape, pop it in the VCR, and let it play while doing his homework. He didn't care what it was. There had to be background noise while he worked.

Perhaps that's why he did his best research in coffee shops or restaurants these days. He finds the chaos and commotion soothing somehow. It allows him to get a rhythm going and get into his groove. He sets his notebook on the desk and returns to the living room.

A couch sits along the left wall of the living room. There is a window behind it. Sitting catty-cornered between the sofa and front wall is a recliner. A television is against the right wall, to the left of the bathroom. A coffee table sits in front of the couch. He grabs the television remote from the end table by his recliner. He powers on the TV, drops the remote on the table, and returns to the kitchen.

He had never been much of a cook. His granny had attempted to teach him a few times. No matter how close he followed the recipe, it never came out quite right. His granny always said the secret ingredient is love. He never could figure out what love had to do with it.

His inability to cook never stopped him from trying. Every once in a while, he would attempt it. Tonight, is not one of those nights, though. He grabs a TV dinner out of the freezer. "Mac and Cheese with Broccoli" is written on the package. He warms it up based on the directions and returns to the living room. He sits down in his recliner and realizes he forgot silverware.

"Shit."

He sets the dinner on the end table and grabs a fork from the kitchen. He sits back down and starts eating. It isn't as good as the homemade his granny would make, but it would have to do. He sits back and looks at the TV.

"What the hell is this crap?"

***

"Thirty years ago, they were part of a phenomenon. Comics, toys, video games, cartoon series, and a theatrical motion picture. Every kid knows their names and their origin. Now, for the first time, watch them live on stage!" Says the disembodied voice.

The scene changed to something he recognized but looked slightly off. It is the climactic battle against Shredder at the end of the first Teenage Mutant Ninja Turtles movie. Splinter had just knocked Shredder over the ledge of the building. Shredder is holding on for his life. Suddenly, Splinter burst into song.

Death
It comes to us all
Yes, death
It comes to us all

The Turtles echoed the last word.

All, all, all

Splinter continued.

Death
It comes to us all
Oroku Saki

But for you

The Turtles echoed.

But for you
But for you
But for you

All five of them sang the following lines.

It will be
It will be
It will be

Leonardo steps up and sings.

Yes, Oroku Saki
Death will come to you
And it will be

Splinter sings solo.

Without honor

Splinter lets go, and Shredder falls to his death.

The disembodied voice returns to say, "Teenage Mutant Ninja Turtles the Movie the Musical." Each word of the title appears as he says it. The title card resembles the movie poster from the original film. "Get your tickets now."

***

Freddy sighs.

"Oh, brother."

He powers off the TV and finishes eating. He places the empty tray on the end table and reclines back. Folding his hands and laying them on his chest, he gets lost in thought.

"I can't put my finger on it, but there is something I am missing. The husband is too obvious, but I can't completely rule him out. This Richard guy, though. There is something odd about him. It just bothers me. There was no struggle. It had to be someone Mr. Peterson was expecting or knew. But who? The doors were all locked. Nothing had been tampered with. No sign of a struggle. No footprints. No blood trails. Just Mr. Hamm and Mr. Peterson.

"What if the suspect showered? Would Mr. Hamm have heard it? No, he was asleep outside. But nothing was tampered with in the bathrooms. Shawn and Eddy checked them. Besides, there would have been a blood trail. Or would there? Was Mr. Peterson the intended target? Or was he just happenstance? Why was Mr. Hamm spared? What stopped this person from attacking him?

"Mr. Hamm was asleep outside on the lanai. Asleep looking out at the pool. The pool enclosure!"

He sits up and reaches for his phone on the end table.

"Damn!"

It isn't there. He starts looking around the house. No phone.

"Damn, damn!"

He checks his desk where he had set his notebook. Nothing.

"Where is it?"

He suddenly remembers where he left it. He never took it out of the car.

"Ah, shit."

He heads for the car to grab his phone.

***

Hampton has his arms wrapped around Marcus's pillow. It still has his smell on it. He had spent the last few hours?...minutes?...he can't remember...crying into the pillow. However long, it seemed like an eternity. All he could think about is how much he missed Marcus. He sits up and starts looking around, expecting Marcus to walk through the bedroom door. Tears are streaming down his face. He is half expecting Marcus to laugh and tell him it is all a practical joke. He would be furious with the man for putting him through this. He knows exactly what he would say. He knows the anger that would follow. But it would all be okay because Marcus would still be there. After all the anger subsided, he would wrap his arms around his husband and express how much he loves the man. He wishes Marcus would do that. He hopes he would. He prays this is all some horrible joke.

He looks down at the floor. No clothes. No dirty socks. This used to annoy him a lot. Marcus always left his clothes on the floor. He would go behind him, cleaning up his mess and placing his clothes in the clothes basket. What he would give to see just one sock on the floor right now. One piece of trash lying next to the garbage can. One empty soda bottle sitting on the dresser because Marcus knows he will throw it away. That would mean Marcus is still here. He would still be with his husband. Still breathing. Still alive.

But he isn't. There are no socks on the floor. No trash surrounding the trash can. No empty bottles of any kind lying around. Just a clean bedroom. No signs of Marcus being around at all. More proof that he is gone.

is still there, though. It sticks with him as if it were a f his essence. So is that sick feeling in the pit of his stomach. He wants it all to end. How much longer could he endure? Would this nightmare ever end? Would it get easier? When would it all be over?

He was going through the stages of grief. He knows them well. He had taken a few psychology courses in college. "Dogs and bears don't agree" is how his psych instructor taught the class. It worked well. He had never forgotten it. "Dogs" is for denial. "And" is for anger. "Bears" is for bargaining. "Don't" is for depression. "Agree" is for acceptance. It's funny, though. He is not experiencing them in order. He jumps back and forth through the first four stages constantly. He wonders when acceptance would finally come.

At that moment, his phone rings. He wipes the tears from his eyes with his arm and composes himself before he answers.

"Hello?" he says with a shaky voice.

"Hey, Mr. Hamm," says Freddy from the other end. "Is it too late for me to stop by? I have a few questions to ask you."

He hesitates a moment before replying. "S, sure. I'm up," he says with a cracking voice. He hopes the detective can't hear it.

"Alright. I'm on my way over. Goodbye."

"Goodbye."

He jumps up and runs to his closet. He throws on a shirt and a pair of shorts. He runs into the living room and straightens up. Why would Detective Falcon want to come over this late? he thinks. What questions? He shakes the thoughts from his head as he cleans the living room and washes up his dishes.

***

Freddy had been there for half an hour. He sits in the left theatre chair and Hampton in the right. They both were drinking a glass of wine. He rarely drank wine. It surprised him when he said "yes" to Hampton's offer. It seemed the natural thing to do at the time.

The television is on, but he isn't paying attention. He is giving Hampton all the time he needs. He wants Hampton to have the first word.. He can see that Hampton wants to talk but keeps hesitating. Freddy finally speaks up, hoping this would initiate the conversation and get the other man to open up. He's glad Hampton feels comfortable enough to talk about his personal life with him. He needs this man to talk about the case. He needs him to talk about the details of that night and everything that led up to the murder. But, of course, he doesn't.

"How are you holding up?"

Hampton looks over at him. "I'm scared."

He nods. "That's normal. Understandable. You're alone. You're confused. Your anchor is gone."

Hampton nods. "The pain, too. It won't stop. I think of that night. The smells. The sounds. The images. It's all fresh in my head. I remember every second. It's like a record on repeat...No... More like...Have you ridden (if you want to call it riding) one of those 4-D attractions at a theme park? You know the ones. They incorporate smells and even special effects into the audience."

He nods and takes a sip of wine.

"Well, it's like that on constant repeat. At times, I am still in that moment. Holding my dying husband in my arms.

"I screamed out at him yesterday. I spent hours yelling at him for abandoning me. I was screaming at the top of my lungs. I stood right there…"

He points at the base of the blood-stained oriental rug.

"That's where I was when I watched him… When I watched him…"

Tears start rolling down his cheeks.

"It's okay. Take your time."

"I only sleep when I'm crying. I cried myself to sleep last night. My arms wrapped around his pillow. It still has his smell, you know. It happened at three AM. I remember looking at the clock. That time will forever be burned into my mind. That's the witching hour, you know. How odd is that? I feel so lonely. He is so young. He is forty-two years old. Forty-two.

"Losing him isn't what scares me. It's that I don't feel him. I don't feel his presence. People talk about how they can feel the presence of a loved one after they pass. They say they see signs from the beyond to let them know their loved one is okay. Butterflies. Birds. The loved one's favorite quote or song suddenly plays. I feel nothing but pain, guilt, anguish. There's no presence. No spirit. No signs. Nothing. Just emptiness.

"A piece of me is just...gone. I have a hole in my soul now. I can physically feel it. It's as if a part of me was cut out the moment he died. Just...gone. People say, 'as long as they are in your heart or memory, they aren't really gone.' That scares me more than anything. It's meant to bring comfort, but it frightens me. Right now, I can still remember what he sounds like, what he looks like. I can remember his smell and his touch. I remember what it's like to feel him or to be in his presence. What happens when that fades? What happens when I can no longer remember what he sounds like? What he looks like? What he smells like? Will he be gone forever?

"We were so happy. Things were finally going right. We purchased this house three years ago. This film was his big break. I had been in a few movies and TV shows prior. Marcus had mainly directed commercials, music videos, and a few Indy projects. We were about to wrap on this one. His star is rising high. The thought of it fills me with so much joy. I am proud of what he has accomplished. He worked so hard for it. It is his time to shine. Sure, there were a few bumps in the road. The original actor hired to play my husband turned it down once he found out he would be playing a gay man. What an idiot. Anyway, we were lucky to get Richard. He's a bit of an oddball, but he's not a bad guy. Richard was excited to take the role. He had no issues playing a man in a homosexual marriage. He never batted an eye. He's a nice guy but a horrible actor. I didn't think we would ever finish all of those takes in the doctor's office. We only had that location for one more day. We finally got all of the shots, though. Richard is hard to work with and can be a bit annoying, but he's not a bad guy. That smell, though. Have you spoken with him yet?"

Hampton turns to look at Freddy. It is the first time he had taken his eyes from the bloodstain on the rug.

Freddy nods. "You aren't kidding about that smell. I made him shower before entering my office, and he still had a stench on him. I had a car that got a stench like that once. It happened after a valet brought it around."

Hampton laughs. "The valet? How did you get the smell out?"

"I sold the car."

Hampton smiles.

He could see Hampton lighten up a bit. Just a bit longer, and he might be in the right mindset to discuss that night.

"So," Freddy starts, "where are you from, originally?"

"A small town in central Florida. I moved back home after college."

"Back home?"

Hampton nods.

"With your folks?"

Hampton shakes his head. "I still hadn't learned anything. The situation still embarrassed me. They would have welcomed me with open arms if I had let them. I moved into an upscale apartment in Orlando. It wasn't until Marcus and I finally got together that I reached out to them. That man was good for me in a lot of ways."

Freddy takes a sip of wine.

Hampton continues, "It was hard getting a job. I worked in the theme parks for a while. Most people wait tables. That is not for me.

Hampton Hamm did not serve. He is served." Hampton rolls his eyes. "I'll be right back," he says.

Hampton gets up and heads for the bathroom off to the left of the living room. Freddy sits there looking around the room. He is trying to piece it all together. How could Mr. Peterson not notice? Was someone already in the house? There is no sign of a break-in. Possibly the sliding door? No. Mr. Hamm would have noticed. Or would he?

He hears the toilet flush and then the sound of running water. A few minutes later, Hampton exits the bathroom. He sits back down and takes a sip of wine.

"So, where is I? Ah, yes…I've had a few types of jobs from self-storage facilities to call centers while trying to get work. What about you?"

"Me?" Freddy smiles. "Here, I thought I was the one interviewing."

Hampton laughs and smiles at Freddy.

He did find the man attractive. Perhaps something would happen afterward. Perhaps not. He knows he has to keep it professional for now. Plus, he knows what Hampton is going through. He isn't even sure if Hampton's feelings for him were real or just the emotional need for attachment. He has no real feelings for the man outside of a friendship, though.

"I've lived here my entire life. In fact, I still live on my grandparents' farm and still sleep in my childhood bedroom."

"Oh? Do you take care of your grandparents?"

He shakes his head. "No. I live alone." The conversation is going too well. He decided against telling the man they had passed on.

"I bet you have a lot of stories from childhood too."

"I do. How about I tell you about them at dinner sometime?"

Hampton lit up at that. "That would be great!"

Freddy put up a hand. "As friends. After this is all over. Remember, Mr. Hamm, I am still on a case."

Hampton nods. "I understand."

"Okay, I want to ask you a few questions about that night. Is that okay with you?"

Hampton nods.

"I already know what happened on the set. What happened after you arrived home? Where was Richard Olstroski that night?"

"Richard?" He looks puzzled. "Why Richard?"

"Because he was staying here. He was sleeping in that room back there, was he not?" Freddy motioned to the opening that leads to the back bedroom and bathroom.

"He was. As far as I know, he never came home. He wasn't here when Marcus and I arrived."

"How do you know? Was the door locked?"

Hampton shakes his head. "He doesn't have a key. We leave the screen door unlocked."

"Screen door? What screen door?"

Hampton pointed to the lanai outside. "The one that leads into the pool enclosure from the yard."

"Show me."

The men stand. Hampton leads Freddy out the sliding glass door. He turns on the lanai light as they exit. Hampton leads him across the lanai. They pass the rocker recliners and the patio table. They approach a screen door to the pool enclosure.

"We leave this door unlocked for him." Hampton reaches for the handle. Freddy grabs his arm to stop him.

"Don't touch it. This is very important, Mr. Hamm. Did you or your husband touch this door after you returned home?"

Hampton shakes his head. "No. I came out here from the bedroom that night. Marcus entered from the living room. We leave that door, and the glass doors, unlocked for Richard. I haven't been out here since that night. Richard left for the shoot that morning. No one has touched it since."

"He never touched it when he packed and left?"

"No. We all went out the front door when we left that morning."

"And, after the events of that night, we have controlled who and how people enter and exit."

Hampton nods.

"So, this door has not been touched at all since that night?"

Hampton shakes his head. "No, it hasn't."

"So, this door is still unlocked?"

"Yes, it should be."

He grabs his phone and places a call to Shawn.

"Hey, Shawn."

"Do you have any idea what time it is, Freddy?"

"This can't wait. Did you or Eddy touch the screen door on the pool enclosure?"

"What? What screen door? No. We concentrated on the house. That's where the murder took place."

"So, you didn't lift prints from anywhere on the lanai or pool deck?"

"No. We concentrated on the scene of the crime."

"So, after I asked you to lift every print, you didn't go outside?"

"You said to lift every print in the house. We didn't go outside at all. Why?"

Freddy sighs. "Okay," he says, ignoring the last question. "I want you and Eddy to meet me at the crime scene at eight in the morning."

"But," the man starts to protest.

"And bring a fingerprint kit. Have a good night."

"But…"

Freddy ends the call and turns to Hampton. He has a huge grin on his face. Hampton looks confused.

"Wait a minute. You think…" He points to the screen door.

"Yes."

"And you think…" He turns to point to the sliding glass door.

"Yes."

"But I was…" He points to the rocker recliner he had been sleeping in that night.

"Yes."

"And you think this person…." He movs his hand in a motion that drew an invisible line from the screen door to the sliding glass door.

"Yes."

He shakes his head. "No, no, no. I would have heard this person walking by."

"Would you?"

He starts to nod. He stops mid-nod. A look of confusion on his face.

"Are you a heavy sleeper, Mr. Hamm?"

He pauses and then nods. "Marcus always says I could sleep through a tornado."

"We never thought to ask you that. It didn't occur to us that the suspect would have walked right past you into the house. Here's what I think happened.

"The suspect had been waiting for you to arrive home. This person knows several things. They know Mr. Olstroski had been staying with you. They know you had been leaving this door unlocked for him. They know that Mr. Olstroski would not be returning that night.

"This person sneaked in after your argument. They bided their time until you had fallen asleep. This individual headed directly into the house. Your husband would not have thought this odd. This would not have alarmed him at all. He would have thought it was you. That's why there was no struggle."

"He thought it was me? Oh my God! That means, he thought..."

Freddy pauses. He sees the look of horror on Hampton's face.

"No," Freddy says. "He didn't think you…"

"You don't know that!" Hampton exclaims. "The only person that knows that is Marcus! Oh my God! I never told him I love him! My last words to him were 'Leave me alone'! His last thought was that I murdered him!" Tears were streaming down his face.

"Damnit," Freddy says. He knows he screwed up. He can get on a tangent and forget who he is speaking with. Why did he have to verbalize every theory he had? He had to make this right. He put his arm around Hampton and walks him back inside. He sits Hampton down in the right theatre chair and sits down beside him.

Hampton is crying heavily now.

"Look at me," Freddy says.

Hampton keeps crying. He is looking directly at the blood-stained oriental run on the floor.

"Mr. Hamm," he is firm now. "Look at me."

Hampton turns his head toward Freddy. Tears are still streaming down his face.

"You've had arguments before, correct?"

Hampton nods.

"And some a lot worse than this, correct?"

Hampton nods.

"He knew that you loved him. That you still love him."

Hampton nods. He is calming back down now.

"He knew that wasn't you after the attack started. As much as you love him, he would never think that. He knows you can't, just like, you know he can't."

Hampton wiped the tears with his arm. He nods.

"I still don't know what happened. I am still trying to figure this out. This is just one hypothesis. This may not be what happened. It makes sense based on the evidence and the facts that we know so far. The only person that knows exactly what happened is still out there."

Hampton sits there without speaking.

"I'm so sorry, Mr. Hamm. I get so involved in a case. I run with any thoughts that pop in my head. I should not have expressed this to you. For that, I am sorry."

Hampton stopped crying. He is starting to relax. His cheeks still damp from the tears, he sits back in his chair. Freddy does the same.

"How long did it take you to get that smell out?"

Hampton chuckles, "It's still there. Perhaps I should cut off that end of the house and sell it."

They both laugh. Freddy looks at his empty glass.

"May I have some more wine?"

"Of course. I could use a refresher too."

Hampton grabs both glasses as he heads for the kitchen. He returns a few minutes later with two full glasses of wine. Hampton hands Freddy one of the glasses as he sits back down.

"Thank you, sir."

"You're welcome."

The two men sit there, drinking their wine, in silence. The television is still on in the background. Freddy looked at the television for the first time. There is a weird horror show that he did not recognize.

A woman in a white dress is on her knees. She lets out a blood-curdling scream. Her mouth opens wide. A black, scaly right arm shot out of her mouth. The clawed hand hit the ground. Outshot a black, scaly left arm, clawed hand hitting the ground. A grotesque alien creature, to who the arms belonged, crawled out of the woman's mouth and stood, facing her. It towered over her as she cowered in fear. The creature shoved its right claw through the woman's open mouth, out the back of her head. Blood poured out of her mouth and dripped down the white dress. He, or it, removed its claw. The lifeless body fell to the ground.

"What the hell?"

"I don't know," Hampton says, looking at the television for the first time. "I'm not into horror."

"Neither am I."

Hampton grabs the remote beside him and turns off the television. The two men sit there drinking their wine. When he finished, Freddy gets up and sets his glass on the counter.

"Are you leaving?"

"Yeah. It's getting late. I need to get some sleep before heading back over in the morning."

"Why not just stay the night?"

"Mr. Hamm, we've been over this."

"In one of the guest bedrooms."

Freddy smiles. He shakes his head. "Thank you for the offer, but I can't. I will be back over here at seven-thirty in the morning."

"Let me show you out."

Hampton leads Freddy to the front door. Freddy opens the door and heads out. He spoke to Hampton one last time as he is walking away.

"Thank you, Mr. Hamm. This evening has been extremely enlightening. I have enjoyed my evening with you, and I think we have a break in the case."

Chapter Seven

Dial M, For Maggie

Oscar pulls into the drive of the old motel early the following day. The sun has not come up yet. He and Phil Wilcox were taking turns sitting with the suspect. It is his turn to sit with the man.

It is a single-story old-style motel. The only one in town that is not modernized. All of the rooms, or cabins, were in a straight line. The office is attached at the end. It reminds him of something out of a Hitchcock film. There is a house sitting back behind the motel. The owner isn't a bad guy. Oscar knows him well. That's partially why he chose this place.

Falcon asked to keep the suspect close by, but Oscar has decided against that. He trusts Frank, the owner. They go back a long way. They were close friends at one time. That was a long time ago, before the incident with Frank's brother. What choice did he have at the time?. Oscar had to take the man in. Frank never did understand that. Oscar tried explaining it to the man. He never could get the man to understand. Things would never be the same after that. They were at least cordial, and this is the safest place to hold a suspect.

The motel is south of the lake and relatively secluded. There is a pizza place just a few blocks away. It isn't bad food. He had eaten there a few times when he was off duty and in his street clothes. The owner, Mario, always came across as a bit of the nervous type. He was a nice guy, though.

He pulls into an empty spot right in front of room twelve. This is where they are keeping the suspect. It is next to the last room. The next room over is room fourteen. Frank is superstitious and would never allow a room thirteen on his property. He grabs the bag sitting in the passenger's seat before exiting the car and approaches the door. He knocks and exclaims, "It's me."

The door opens. A muscular man is standing there. He looks like the stereotypical officer that you would see on TV, with a chiseled chin and a shaved head. "It's about time, Oscar."

Phil steps aside to allow Oscar in. Oscar closes the door behind him.

"I brought you breakfast," Oscar says as he hands the bag to Phil.

"Thanks." He opens the bag and takes out a biscuit, hash browns, a straw, and a container of orange juice.

Both men sit in the two empty chairs. Richard is lying on the bed watching them.

"How is he?"

"How am I?"

Oscar turned his gaze to Richard.

"I am locked up in a motel with two cops. I start work on a new film in a few hours on the other side of the country. I haven't spoken with my wife. My agent has no idea what's going on. You took my phone. I'm not allowed to leave. And, apparently, I'm a suspect in a murder investigation. How the hell do you think I am?"

"We never said you can't call your wife," Oscar replied.

"How the hell am I supposed to do that? You took my damn phone!"

Oscar points to the phone lying on a table next to the bed. "You pick up the receiver, listen for a dial tone, dial the number, wait for her to answer, and talk."

Phil had just taken a bite when Oscar said this. He almost choked with laughter. He starts coughing.

"I don't know the number."

"You don't know your wife's phone number?"

Richard shakes his head. "Who the hell remembers phone numbers these days?"

"I know my wife's number," says Oscar. He looks at Phil. "What about you, Phil? Do you know your wife's phone number?"

Phil nods. He is taking a sip of orange juice to wash down the food. Still coughing.

"Well, good for you. I can't. I just call her from the contact list on my phone."

"Alright." Oscar sits back. "Phil, hand me the man's phone."

Phil reaches in his shirt pocket and pulls out Richard's phone. He hands it to Oscar.

"It's powered off to save battery," Phil says.

Oscar powers on the phone and waits for it to boot up.

Oscar looked at Richard. "Does this thing have a fingerprint scanner, or does it use face detection to unlock?"

"Both," Richard says. "But I have to enter the PIN code to unlock it after a restart."

Oscar understands that he can not force the man to give him the PIN code as much as he wants to. Damn new privacy laws protect it. PIN codes and passwords ware considered "in a person's head," and you cannot force them to hand over that information. It is treated as thoughts. If it isn't written down, you can't force it. He hates that. It made his job a lot harder. He walks over to Richard and hands him the phone. Richard enters the PIN code and hands the phone back to Oscar.

"What's her name?"

"Margaret. She's listed as Maggie."

"818-555-2847."

Richard dials the number.

"Hey, sweetie," he says. "I know, and I am sorry. I'm still here in Terra Loch. No, we finished shooting. Well, I'm not sure. I know I have a new project in a few hours. But Maggie, listen! There's been a complication. The director was murdered. Filming has stopped."

Oscar is watching Richard intently. The man sighs in frustration. He rolls his eyes a few times. It is clear who is in charge in that marriage. Oscar is fortunate his marriage is an equal partnership.

"No, I can't! Maggie, I'm under arrest!"

There is a long silence before Richard continues.

"No, I didn't do it! Just listen to me for once!"

Richard takes a breath.

"Marcus and Hampton allowed me to stay with them during the shoot… The director and his husband… Yes, they're gay. No, I didn't sleep with them. What the hell, Maggie! Just listen. We had a long shoot the night of the murder. After we wrapped, I went out with a few members of the cast for some drinks. I never returned that night. I was too drunk, so I slept it off in my car. Marcus ws murdered… Jesus, Maggie, he's the damn director. Hampton and I are the two primary suspects… His husband, Maggie. No, Hampton didn't do it. No, I wasn't there to witness it. I know the husband is always the primary suspect. You watch too much True Crime. Just listen, please… They are not going to allow me to leave until this is over. But… But… But… Alright, I'll call him. Goodbye."

Richard hangs up the phone and lies back in bed. Silence fills the room. Oscar finally breaks the silence.

"That went well," he says sarcastically.

"Can you find me the number for Cecil Knight?"

Phil had just finished eating. He throws his trash away and stands up. He taps Oscar on the shoulder. "I'm out of here. Have fun with this guy." Phil leaves, closing the door behind him. A few moments later, Oscar hears a car pull off.

Oscar focuses back on Richard. "Cecil Knight, you say?"

Richard nods.

"818-555-2217."

Richard dials the number.

"Mr. Knight, please. He's not? Okay, send me to his messaging service."

Another pause.

"Thomas? Thomas, Richard Olstroski here. I want to leave a message for Mr. Knight. Can you have Cecil call me as soon as possible? No, I'm not. I'm still in Terra Loch. Have him call me at..." He looks over at the top of the phone, where the number is posted. "...229-555-7947. Thank you." He hangs up the phone.

"Is that it?"

"Yes."

"You sure?"

The man leans his head against the headboard and lets out a sigh. "Yes."

"I could get you room service. I could order you a pizza. You need me to shine your shoes too?"

"Stop with the sarcasm. That's it."

Oscar powers off the phone and places it in his shirt pocket. "Just relax, Mr. Olstroski. Let Falcon work his magic and figure this thing out. We'll find this guy, and you will be out of here in no time."

Just then, they hear a loud noise outside. Oscar jumps up and looks out the window. He sees a car speeding down the highway.

"Shit," he says. He turns and points at Richard. "Stay."

Richard smiles, "Where am I going?"

Oscar races out the door, gets in his car, and drives after the motorist.

***

Otto is a bit tipsy as he speeds down the highway. He had been on a wild goose chase all day. Damn Freddy. If he hadn't barged in. Shit! He never had the chance to interrogate her more. She gave him a nice punch in the gut and kick in the balls before she took off.

At that moment, he notices flashing lights behind him.

"Shit…"

He pulls the car over. The cop rolls to a stop behind him. He quickly puts a few breath mints in his mouth to mask the smell of the alcohol. After a few minutes, a short, dark-haired cop gets out of the cruiser and heads toward him. He sits back and waits.

The cop approaches the window. He doesn't have to lean over much.

"Do you have any idea how fast you were going?" the cop asks in a gruff voice. This takes Otto by surprise. He doesn't expect that voice to come from this tiny man.

"Look, officer, I know I was speeding. Just give me the ticket."

"Have you been drinking?"

"No," he lies.

The cop stands there, looking in the car. He looks in the back seat, then he looks back at Otto.

"Alright," he says.

The cop writes out a ticket and hands it to Otto.

"Don't make me come after you again."

He nods. The cop gets back in his car. He waits for the cop to drive past, turn around, and head back the opposite way. Otto drives off after the cop is out of sight. He decides to get the car back up to speed and race down the highway as he heads home.

***

Oscar pulls back into the motel parking lot. He steps up to the door of room twelve and notices the door is unlocked. Did he leave it unlocked? He can't remember. He had rushed out in a hurry. He opens the door and steps inside.

"Okay, Mr. Olstroski. I'm...shit!"

He looks over at the empty bed. Panic overtakes him. He can feel his heart start to race. Had he just made the biggest rookie blunder? He looked around the room. It is empty. He checks the bathroom and closet. Nothing. This guy is gone.

He runs outside and to the front office. Frank looks up as he barges in.

"Oscar?"

"Not now, Frank. Room twelve. Did you see the man leave?"

Frank nods. "He borrowed my phone to call for a ride a little bit ago. Why? I figured you released 'im. Wasn't he supposed to leave?"

"No, he wasn't."

"I just figured…"

Oscar shakes his head and turns to leave.

"I'll let ye know if I see or hear 'im," Frank says.

Oscar heads for his car.

"Shit!"

He makes a call on the radio. "Put out an APB for a Richard Olstroski. He's five-nine, 180 pounds. Black hair. And...You will notice the smell. He's probably headed for the airport. He would be flying to California, possibly LAX."

He picks up his phone to call Freddy.

"Freddy's going to be pissed."

***

"Dammit! You had one job, Oscar! One job!" Freddy is yelling into his phone. He is standing in his bedroom with just a shirt and underwear on. He is supposed to be over at Hampton's in a half hour. The man had slept through his alarm. Perhaps he should have taken Hampton up on his offer.

"Why did you leave him alone?

"I was chasing after a speeding car."

"What speeding car? Why? Where is Phil?"

"He left already. There was no need for him to stay. The guy was calling his wife and agent…."

"Okay. Just find him."

"I've already put out an APB."

"Good."

"I'll ensure we have two men on him at all times when we bring him back."

"No. I want him behind bars. That way, we know he won't try to flee. He blew his chance. Dammit, Oscar!"

He takes a deep breath and exhales slowly. "Well, I have to get over to Mr. Hamm's place shortly. There have been new developments."

"Alright. Bye."

Freddy ends the call and throws his phone on his bed. He finishes getting dressed, snatches his phone off of the bed and places it in his pants pocket. He grabs his wallet and keys while rushing out the door.

He calls Hampton while getting in his car.

"Mr. Hamm?"

"Detective? Are you on your way?"

"No. I'm running late. I overslept. When the officers arrive, show them the door that I want prints taken from. Don't touch that door. I'll be there shortly."

"Okay," Hampton replies. "Bye."

Freddy ends the call and drives off.

***

Hampton is busy cleaning the house. It is a quarter till eight. He spoke with Freddy twenty minutes ago. The officers should be there shortly. The house isn't messy. It is immaculate. He just needs to keep himself busy. It keeps his mind off of Marcus and the pain.

The television is on in the living room. He has old episodes of *Cube*, his first professional sitcom, playing in the background. The show is set in a call center, revolving around a group of co-workers and less about the call center itself. He played the lead, Jason Andrews. Jason was the straight man that all the craziness revolved around. The show took its inspiration from *The Office* (U.K. version) and *Seinfeld*. Its humor was uncomfortable at times, and the anti-heroes weren't always likable. He remembered how it felt filming the final episode. He wasn't as sad as his other colleagues. He was moving on to the spin-off, *Storage Locker*. The last episode of *Cube* ended with Jason losing his job due to a layoff. *Storage Locker* was set in a self-storage facility. Hampton's character, Jason, is the manager of the facility.

Neither of these was too far from his real life. He had worked in call centers and storage facilities between jobs. These jobs were always fond memories for him. He loved the character of Jason Andrews. He would love to return to that role one day.

The doorbell rings. Hampton looks at the clock. Five minutes to eight. "It must be the officers." He quickly finishes washing off the refrigerator. He drys his hands and heads for the front door.

"Hello, Mr. Hamm."

"Hello...Officer Braxton? Is that right?"

Shawn nods. "And this is Officer Hickly." Shawn motions to the man behind him. "May we come in?"

"Yes. Of course."

He moves aside to allow the men entry, and closes the door behind him. He notices Officer Hickly is carrying what he assumed is a fingerprint kit and a laptop computer.

"Freddy… I mean, Detective Falcon asked me to show you the door."

The two men glance at him with puzzled looks. He smiles as he realized how that sounded.

"I mean, show you the door he wants the fingerprints taken from."

The men nod.

He leads the way through the kitchen and living room, onto the lanai.

"That's the door," he says as he points to the screen door that Richard uses.

"And no one has touched this door since the night of the murder?" Officer Braxton asks.

He shakes his head.

"Alright," the officer says, "let us work. Go and relax, Mr. Hamm."

He nods and heads back inside. He continues cleaning until Freddy arrives.

***

It is a quarter past eight when Freddy finally arrives at Hampton's house. He pulls in the drive and parks next to Shawn's car. He heads for the front door.

Hampton answers with a smile. "Good morning, Fre...I mean, Detective."

"Good morning, Mr. Hamm. I'm sorry I'm late. I slept through my alarm. Perhaps I should have taken you up on your offer." Freddy smiles as he says that.

Hampton moves aside to allow Freddy in.

"How was the drive?"

"It was fine. Thanks for asking."

They talk as they walk through the house toward the lanai.

"We have a small complication."

Hampton freezes. "What?"

"Richard Olstroski."

"What about him?"

Freddy explains to Hampton they had Richard detained and how he escaped. They continue walking outside.

Hampton shakes his head. "Richard didn't do this. I know it."

"He ran, Mr. Hamm. That doesn't look good."

"Richard may be a lot of things, but he's not a killer. I would believe that I could do this before I would believe it is him."

"So would I."

The men had just approached Shawn and Eddy. They had completed lifting the prints from the door.

"What did you find?"

"The only prints on this door belong to Mr. Hamm."

"What!" Hampton is excited. "But… No… It can't be… I…"

Freddy looks at Hampton. "You didn't touch this door, did you? Even by accident?"

"No." Hampton shakes his head in a panic. "I didn't… I...I...I can't…"

Hampton collapses on the concrete. He rolls into a ball, crying.

"He didn't do this, Shawn."

"You said it yourself, Freddy, on the day after the murder."

Freddy helps Hampton to his feet. Hampton glares at him in horror. "You told him that you think I did this?"

"I said he didn't do it. I said that I'm trying not to convict him."

"You said the spouse is always looked at first. The doors were locked. There were no signs of a struggle. He was the only one here at the time. There is no evidence of anyone else being here that night." Shawn shakes his head. "I'm sorry, Freddy. Everything points to Mr. Hamm. I'm the officer that answered the original call. I have to take him in."

Hampton looks scared. He is about to burst into tears.

"You guys head on out. Let me talk to him. I am the lead on this. I will bring him in."

Shawn opens his mouth to protest.

Freddy shakes his head.

Shawn nods. The two men gather up everything and leave. Freddy walks Hampton back inside.

"I'm sorry, Mr. Hamm. They are right."

"You think I did this? You think I murdered my husband? I poured out my soul to you. I trusted you. I thought you were working with me. I thought you were helping me."

"I am," Freddy says firmly.

"No, you aren't. I'm a suspect in a case. That's it. That's all I am to you. Just a number. You don't care about me. You care about solving this case. Is any of that even true? Have you ever felt the pain of losing a spouse? Do you even know what I am going through, or is this all a ruse?"

"Listen to me. I want to make this very clear. I know you did not murder your husband. I can't explain how I know. I just know. Call it a feeling. Everything I have told you about myself is true. This case is personal for me because I know that loss. I know that pain.

"You remember me telling you about Harry? Otto's adopted brother?"

Hampton nods.

"He isn't in prison. He's dead. Harry and I were together. It killed me when he died. So, yes, I know how you feel.

"You are not just a number to me. I will do everything, including giving my life, if necessary, to prove that fact. We will bring this criminal to justice. As much as I don't want to, I have to take you in."

"But, I...I didn't..."

"I know that. It's not about that. I must be able to prove it, and I can't. Not yet. It's about the law. The law doesn't care about feelings or intuition. The law cares about facts. All the current evidence is pointing to you." Freddy starts to tear up for the first time since he took this case. "Please, Hampton... Please don't make me cuff you."

Hampton nods. He glances at the TV. Freddy looks too. He recognizes the show. The TV is showing the final scene from *Cube*. Hampton's character, he can't remember the name, is walking out carrying a white box full of his belongings. He stops at the desk of another character and places a purple stapler on the desk. Hampton's character walks off. The other character did a double-take as he picked up the stapler. It fades to black, and the credits roll.

Freddy chuckles. "I remember that. That is a good role for you. That is a payoff to a season-long gag. He spent the entire season looking for that stapler, and you had it the entire time."

"You know that is based on a true event."

Freddy shakes his head. "Really? I thought it was more of a reference to *Office Space*."

Hampton shakes his head. "That was my addition to the script. I had a co-worker exactly like Tim Hadley. He did have a purple stapler he lost. I have no idea what happened to it, though. He searched everywhere for that thing. As far as I know, he never found it. I thought this is more of a satisfying ending."

Hampton powered off the TV. The two men walk through the house, turning off all the lights and ensuring nothing is left on. They walk out the front door, locking it behind them.

Chapter Eight

Meet Jacob Wexler

Freddy hated having to place Hampton behind bars. He knew deep down that the man did not kill his husband. It doesn't matter what he thinks or believes. The law needs facts. The facts were that Hampton is the only person who could be placed at the crime scene when the murder occurred. No other evidence was found. None that would indicate an intruder. Even the screen door on the pool enclosure had no prints beside Hampton's. Nothing added up.

Neither man spoke on the drive back to the station. He felt the hurt and frustration emanating from the man in the passenger's seat. His heart is breaking as he rolls each of the man's fingers, one at the time, over the ink and then rolls them onto the card. Neither man speaks as he walks Hampton to his cell. The cell door closing sounds like a sonic boom compared to the uneasy silence. He leaves the station and drives.

It is a beautiful day for a drive. He always did his best thinking behind the wheel. His evidence folder is sitting in the passenger's seat beside him. He is out looking for a quiet place to park and go over the evidence.

As he drives down the open road, he hears his stomach growling. He needs to find a place to eat. He doesn't feel hungry, but his stomach says otherwise. There is a restaurant up ahead. It reminds him of *Marcell's*. It even has a blue and white striped awning like *Marcell's*.

"Thanks, Papa," he says to no one in particular. He never was too religious. He has faith in God and does believe in an afterlife, but organized religion was never for him. There is no logic in it. No hard facts. Yet, as odd as it feels, he honestly does believe his grandparents are watching over him. "I need to stop by and visit you both some time."

He finds it hard to locate a parking spot. The parking lot is a mix of gravel, dirt, and grass. There are gravel parking spots near the building. Off to the right side lay marked spots in the dirt. There is a grassy field behind the building for additional parking. That is where he finally finds a spot. He grabs his evidence folder, locks the car, and heads inside.

"Welcome to The Golden Pancake!"

He is greeted by a cheerful woman dressed in a blue and white outfit.

"Table for one?" she asks.

He nods. "Yes. Thank you."

"This way, sir."

She leads him through the small country restaurant. They pass by tables full of families, couples, and other patrons as they enjoy their lunch. They arrive at a small table, for two, near the back of the restaurant. He sits down with his back to the wall, and she sets a menu in front of him. From this vantage point, Freddy has a view of the entire restaurant.

"Samuel will be with you in a moment," she says and walks off.

He opens his evidence folder and starts reviewing everything. He could kick himself for solely focusing on Richard Olstroski and Hampton Hamm. The situation with Hampton is causing him to lose focus. He wants to help the man through his grief, but not at the cost of solving the case. Hampton was right about one thing. His main goal is to solve this case. Hampton isn't a number. He had been frank with the man. But he had to step back. He has to focus on this case.

"All of these people who were on the set that day, and I have yet to speak with them?"

He shakes his head as he flips through the folder. He is reading the testimony of a Jacob Wexler when he hears someone approach.

"Sir, my name is Samuel. Would you care for something to drink?"

He looks up at the scrawny kid. He can't be more than eighteen. Samuel has short, black hair. He stands about six feet in hight.

"I'm sorry. I haven't even looked at the menu yet."

"I can come back," Samuel says, turning to walk away.

"No." He shakes his head. "Give me a second."

He turns to the beverages and smiles as he sees it. "I'll take a coffee, black."

"Sir?"

"No sweetener. No cream."

"It's lunchtime, sir."

He nods. "Yeah. Wait, do y'all not serve coffee after breakfast?"

"I'm not sure. I've never had someone order coffee during the middle of the day."

Freddy smiles. "I'll take a black coffee."

"Yes, sir. I'll be back with it and to take your order."

He peruses the menu and finds what he is craving. A few moments later, Samuel returns. The kid places a cup of hot coffee in front of him and a large stainless steel coffee pot down beside him.

"Just black," Samuel says.

Freddy smiles. He takes a sip. "Perfect. Thank you."

Samuel takes out a small pad. "What can I get you, sir?"

"I just want a chicken sandwich and a side of fries."

Samuel looks puzzled.

He assumes the kid had never taken a lunch order with coffee to drink before.

Samuel writes the order down.

"Would you care to add cheese?"

"Sure," Freddy says. "And lettuce."

"It comes with lettuce. Would you like the mayo on it too?"

Freddy shakes his head. "Mayonnaise is the devil," he says with a smile.

He can tell the kid isn't sure how to react. "Yes, sir. So, that's a chicken sandwich with lettuce and cheese. No mayo. With a side of fries."

Freddy nods.

"It will be out shortly." Samuel walks off to put the order in.

He looks back down at his folder.

Where was I, he thinks. Ah, yes. Jacob Wexler.

Jacob played Dr. Gavin Tengel. He was on set that day playing opposite Hampton and Richard. This guy would be good to talk to. He writes Jacob's name, number, and address down.

He keeps flipping through the files of everyone who was on set that day. Adam Greenbriar, Miguel Alvarez, Stacie Hampton, Lucy Singleton, and Aaron Chatsworth. Everyone's stories seem to match. There is nothing out of the ordinary. The shoot went long due to complications with Richard. A few of them went out for drinks afterward. Nothing special that night. Nothing out of the ordinary.

At that moment, Samuel returned.

"Be careful. It's hot," he says.

"I will. Thanks."

"Would you care for anything else?"

Freddy shakes his head, then stops. "Actually, yeah. Would you mind refilling this?"

He hands Samuel the empty coffee pot.

"No problem, sir." The kid takes the coffee pot and walks off.

He starts nibbling on his fries while looking through the folder.

"What's this?" He pulls aside what looks like an insurance policy. He looks it over carefully. "Ah, shit."

He reads through it again to be sure. This is precisely what he doesn't want. Before he found this, all they had was evidence showing that Hampton was the only one at the scene of the crime. This changes things, for the worse. This gives him motive. This is a five million dollar insurance policy for Marcus Peterson. Hampton is the sole beneficiary. If anything happens to Marcus, then Hampton is to be paid five million dollars.

There is also evidence showing that Hampton's career isn't as rosy as the man made it sound. It looks like Hampton's career had been on the downswing since *Cube*. Even *Storage Locker* was a mediocre success.

Marcus, on the other hand, sees a massive upswing in his career. *Collision Course*, a comedy about a race car driver, turned fast-food mogul after a car crash, was his breakout film. After that, he directed films such as *Danger Zone*, *The Pawn*, and now *Blackrock Hill*. This was the film he was working on when he was murdered. This was his first big break with Hollywood.

Marcus had cast Hampton in the lead as a way to help boost his career again. He played a man coming to grips with his mortality through his battle with cancer. It was the first serious drama that Marcus had worked on.

"What's this? Interesting…"

That's when he noticed an interesting correlation between this film and *Collision Course*. Jacob Wexler played the lead in that film. It appears his career took a nosedive after that. The article doesn't go into details, but there had been a rift between Wexler and the deceased after that movie.

"Now I really have to talk to him."

He had been too involved in his work to notice Samuel. He had brought the full coffee pot back and sat it on the table. His arm bumps up against the scorching pot. He jerks it away on instinct. That's when he notices it is there. He pours another cup of coffee as he reads. This is looking worse and worse for Hampton.

"I've got to talk to him too."

"Sir?"

He jumps at the sound. The kid's voice startles him. He didn't realize the kid is still there.

"I was thinking out loud," he says with a smile.

"Would you care for anything else, sir?"

He shakes his head. "No, thank you."

Samuel lays the check on the table. "You can pay at the counter when you are ready. There is no rush," he says as he walks off.

He finishes his meal and gulps down the last of the coffee. He looks at the total on the check. He reaches into his wallet and pulls out a few one-dollar bills, and places them under his plate for the tip. Freddy grabs the check and heads for the front. He notices a jar of mints sitting on the front counter as he is paying for his meal.

The cashier noticed him eyeing the mints. "They're complementary," she says.

Freddy takes one. She cashes him out, and he leaves.

He throws the evidence folder in the passenger's seat as he gets in the car. He sits there for a moment in thought. He shakes his head and activates his phone's voice assistant.

"Call Captain…," he pauses for a moment.

"Did you mean 'Call Captain Youngblood'?" it asks.

This needs to be discussed in person. This is not the type of thing you discuss over the phone.

"No. Call Shawn Braxton."

"Calling Shawn Braxton."

A few moments later, Shawn answers.

"Hey, Freddy."

"Shawn, you guys busy?"

"Nope. Nothing's going on at the moment. You need something?"

"We need to find Richard Olstroski. I'm following up on a few other leads on the case. Would you guys mind following his trail?"

He hears Shawn and Eddy chatting. After a moment, "Sure."

"Good. Thanks. Start by speaking with the owner of that hotel. Mr. Olstroski used a ride-share app on this guy's phone. Find out where that driver took him. Find him. Catch him."

"We're on it."

"Get the address from Oscar. Also, find out the name of that motorist he stoped that night. Perhaps that guy saw something."

"Alright. Anything else?"

"Just keep me updated...by text. Don't call. I'll be interviewing a few folks. I want this case solved."

"Alright. Bye."

He ends the call and flips through his evidence folder. He stops on Jacob Wexler.

"There it is."

He enters the address for Jacob Wexler into his navigation app.

"Alright, Mr. Wexler. Let's see what you know."

***

"Jacob Wexler?"

"Yes. May I help you?"

"Detective Falcon. May I come in?" Freddy shows the man his badge.

"S, sure. Come on in, Detective."

"Thank you."

The Wexler house sits on a half-acre lot on the west side of the lake. The housc sits off of the road a little. It is a modest two-story home. According to the file, the Wexlers purchased the house five years ago.

Jacob Wexler leads Freddy inside. A staircase sits at the end of the foyer. The right side of the foyer leads to the kitchen and dining area. Jacob leads Freddy left, into the living room.

Freddy takes a seat on the couch, and Jacob Wexler sits in a wingback chair close to the sofa. The couch is placed against the left wall, underneath a large bay window. A fireplace is in the center of the back wall. There are two wingback chairs on either side of the fire-place.

"This is a nice place you have here," he says as he looked around the living room.

"Thank you, Detective. We like it."

"Have you and your wife lived here long?"

"Five years."

"Do you have any kids?"

Jacob nods. "Just one. Matthew. He's five. Do you and your wife have any children?"

"No," Freddy says. "I'm single, and I do not have any kids."

"Ah. Any girlfriends?"

"Boyfriends, and no."

"Oh, I see," Jacob says. "I'm sorry. I didn't mean to… You just don't seem like the type."

Not that type? What the hell does that mean? He will never understand that close-minded stereotype attitude. Not every gay man is flamboyant, not that there's anything wrong with that. And what does it matter anyway? I'm here to solve a case. As much as he wants to say something to the man, he thinks better of it.

"I hope you don't mind if I get down to business?" is the response he decides on.

"Of course. I'm curious to find out how I can help you."

"Mr. Wexler, I am investigating the Marcus Peterson murder."

Freddy pauses to gauge a reaction. The man did flinch just the slightest.

"Oh?" Jacob replies. "I thought you arrested the murderer? I read his husband was arrested for it."

"Mr. Hamm is a suspect. That is normal. We always look at the spouse. No one has been officially charged."

"Well, I barely knew Mr. Peterson. How can I help?"

"You barely knew him?" Freddy asks.

Jacob nods. "That's right."

"You didn't work with him on a film called *Collision Course*?"

"Detective, that was years ago. That was a rough shoot. We had a lot of drama on that set."

"Oh? What type of drama?"

"There was so much, Detective. I don't remember now. It's been more than ten years."

"Everything could matter. You brought up the drama. Obviously, it still bothers you. Think, Mr. Wexler. Did anything happen back then that could be relevant to this case?"

The man sits back and thinks for a moment. "Well," he starts.

At that moment, a five-year-old runs into the room, arms outstretched, pretending as if he is flying. Jacob grabs the kid up when he "flies" near him.

"And this little guy is Matthew," he says. "Hey buddy, say hello to the detective."

Freddy smiles at the boy. Matthew looks at him and quickly turns his head away.

"He can be shy."

"And that's perfectly fine, Matthew. I was too when I was your age."

Matthew looks at his dad. "Can I have something to drink?"

Jacob smiles. "Go ask your mom. I'm talking to the detective."

"She's asleep."

"Alright," he says. "Would you care for anything, Detective?"

Freddy shakes his head. "Thank you, but no. I had lunch a little while ago."

Jacob nods. Matthew runs to the kitchen. Jacob follows.

Freddy stands up and walks around the living room. He looks at the pictures on the wall. This guy looks like an ordinary family man. Pictures of him and his wife. Pictures of Matthew. He sees Matthew's kindergarten graduation picture. Photos of the Wexler family out on a boat. There is nothing out of the ordinary with this guy. He appears to be a typical American family man.

A few minutes later, Jacob returns. Freddy is looking at pictures from a cruise. The Wexler couple looked a lot younger then.

"That is our honeymoon," Jacob says.

"You both look so happy."

"We were in love. I adored her. Detective, there is nothing out of the ordinary here. I met my wife eleven years ago. We fell in love and were very happy."

"I see," Freddy says.

Both men sit back down.

"Where was I?" Jacob asks.

"You were remembering something that happened on the set of *Collision Course*," Freddy says.

He nods. "That's right. Well, there was a lot of drama on that set. Marcus and Hampton…" He shakes his head. "Those two. I'm surprised they ever married."

"What do you mean?"

"Are you familiar with that film?"

"I've read the synopsis. Something about a race car driver opening a fast-food restaurant."

"Yeah. So, Hampton is cast as a comic relief fry cook. He hated that role for some reason. I dunno...Maybe he thinks he should have had a larger role. Anyway, those two had vicious arguments on set. Now, don't get me wrong. Hampton was a bit of a prima donna back then. Marcus knew exactly how to push that man's buttons. He always knew the right thing to say or do that would just piss Hampton off."

"Interesting. Mr. Hamm didn't mention anything about that when I spoke with him. And we talked about his past."

"I dunno. Maybe he has put it behind him."

"But it still bothers you."

"Well, yeah. It does, Detective. That was my first leading role. It was my big break. All of that drama bleeds into the media. That's all they could talk about. There is nothing about me. I was the star. Not Hampton. Me, Detective. That drama tainted the film. I was the lead in a film ripe with controversy. I can't escape it. I could not get a leading role again for years. It is all commercials and bit parts. Their love squabbling cost me a lot. I had to claw my way back up to where I am now."

"Now, I'm confused. If that cost you so much, why did you accept this new role? You had to know Mr. Peterson was directing it and that Mr. Hamm was the lead."

"Of course I did. My agent told me who was attached to it after I read the script. I flat out refused to take the role. I loved the story, but I did not want a repeat of *Collision Course*.

"Marcus called me up one night. He asks if we could meet the next day and discuss the film over lunch. He assured me it would just be the two of us. I reluctantly accepted."

***

"So, did you read the script?" asks Marcus.

"Yes," says Jacob.

"What did you think?"

Jacob takes a bite of his steak. He says nothing.

"Look," Marcus says. "I know the last project we worked on together was a disaster. I know you see it as tainting your career."

"It didn't just taint my career. It nearly flushed it down the toilet."

"Jacob," Marcus sighs. "You are a talented actor. Blackrock Hill is a personal project for me. I need you on this. You know I wrote the script. I wrote the character of the doctor specifically for you."

"Stop bullshitting me, Marcus. That crap may work on your prima donna husband, but it won't work on me. I know you didn't write this. You were handed the script. You cast your husband as the lead in some attempt to placate him. Marcus, you should be doing sequels. You'd be great at them. That's all this is. A sequel. Well, it's got to be bigger and better than the original. Count me out."

Marcus slams his fist on the table. A few of the patrons turn in their direction. "Dammit, Jacob! Stop being a jackass! That happened over ten years ago! Hampton and I had a long history that led up to those moments you witnessed! He's changed! I've changed! We've both changed each other for the better! You're married! You know damn well how a couple changes each other for the better!"

"I'm sorry," Jacob says. "You're right. I'm judging you guys on the past."

Marcus sits back and relaxed a bit. He starts speaking in a calm tone.

"I gave Hampton that role to help him. His career has been in a spiral lately. This will help him climb back on top again. Sort of a second chance for him."

Jacob smiles and says, "It is a good script."

"Damn good," Marcus says.

"Alright, I'm in."

***

"People do change. And I can assure you, Mr. Wexler, the man I spoke to is definitely not the same man you remember."

Jacob shakes his head. "I know he's not. Hampton is a wonderful human being. And he loved Marcus more than anything. Detective, I honestly do not believe Hampton did this."

"Well," Freddy says, "That is for me to figure out." He does not want to show any of his cards to the man. "Now, let's talk about the day Mr. Peterson was murdered. You were on set that day, correct?"

"Yes. I played Dr. Tengel."

"Did you notice anything odd that day?"

Jacob pauses in thought. He shakes his head. "No. Nothing out of the ordinary."

“Were there any disagreements between Mr. Peterson and anyone else?”

Jacob laughs.

“Did I say something funny, Mr. Wexler?”

“Everybody did.”

“Everybody, except you.”

“Look, Detective, Marcus Peterson was a nice guy off the set. The moment he says ‘action,’ his entire demeanor changed.”

“Oh? How so?”

“Well, don’t get me wrong. Outside of *Collision Course,* I’ve worked with other directors like him. He was passionate and knew what he wanted. But he could push people. Not everybody...appreciated...his passion.”

“Let me guess, you appreciated it.”

“As I said, I have worked with directors like him before. I am used to it.”

“I see. Were there any specific disagreements that went on that night? The shoot went long, correct?”

“Oh, God, yes.” The man sits back in his chair. “That guy that was cast to play opposite Hampton...” He tilts his head slightly up and places his index finger on his lips as if in deep thought. “I can’t think of his name, but there is no way I could forget that smell. It was as if he had been eating out of the garbage or something. I felt so bad for Hampton, though. I only had to deal with the smell during my scenes. Poor Hampton had to deal with it for the entire filming.”

“Richard Olstroski.”

Jacob nods. “That’s it. Richard. Richard and Marcus never got along. Don’t get me wrong. He seemed like a nice guy. He was brought on last minute, though. He and Marcus never saw eye to eye.”

“What do you mean?”

“There were a lot of arguments between those two. Have you spoken with Richard yet?”

Freddy nods. He doesn't mention Richard had run and was still on the loose.

"I know that there were arguments on the set."

Jacob shakes his head. "I don't mean that. I mean personal arguments between those two backstage. I stumbled upon it a few times. There was a lot of yelling between them. I'm not sure what it was about. It isn't my business. I would ignore it the best I could."

"Did they argue often?"

Jacob shakes his head. "Not often, but it was heated. There were a few times I thought it might come to blows."

"No one else noticed these arguments? That's a bit strange. If they were as heated as you say, I would assume multiple people would have heard these arguments."

"I don't know if other people witnessed their arguments. It never happened on set. They were always away from people when these arguments started. In private."

He makes a mental note of this. Something else to ask Hampton about. Or Richard Olstroski, if they ever find him.

"Is there anything else you can tell me about that night?"

Jacob shakes his head.

"Richard Olstroski mentioned that he had been out with a few of the cast members that night. Were you one of them?"

"No. I have a family, Detective. I don't participate in things like that anymore. I came directly home after the shoot."

Freddy pauses and looks through his notes. Mr. Olstroski said he went out for drinks that night. Is there more to it? "According to Mr. Olstroski's testimony, he went out for drinks that night. Family men do go out for drinks."

Jacob laughs. He shakes his head. "Is that what he told you? Perhaps they did go for drinks, but that is not what their ultimate plan was. You see, Mr. Olstroski likes the ladies."

"What do you mean? I know that he's married."

"I don't know about that. I know that he kept hitting on some of the women on the set."

"Oh, really?"

Jacob nods.

"Were any of those women with him that night?"

Jacob shakes his head. "He went out with a few of the guys. They were going to a strip club."

"Do you know who he went with?"

"Of course. There were five of them."

"May I get their names?"

"Of course, Detective. Their names are…"

"Would you mind writing their names down for me?" Freddy hands Jacob his notepad.

"Of course." Jacob grabbed the notepad and wrote the names down.

"Thank you, Mr. Wexler."

"Of course, Detective."

Freddy looks at the list. "Thank you for your time. If you can think of anything else…."

"Of course, Detective. I'll give you a call. Let me show you out."

Freddy shakes his head. "I can let myself out. Have a good day, Mr. Wexler."

He leaves the Wexler home and bolts toward his car. He sits there for a few minutes, looking at the names Jacob Wexler wrote down. There were five names on this list: Adam Greenbriar, Miguel Alvarez, Rodney Cooper, Mitch Blakley, and Aaron Chatsworth.

"Do I have any messages?" he asks his phone.

"There are no new messages. You have one missed call and voicemail from Captain Youngblood. Would you like to hear it?"

"Yes."

"Playing the voicemail from Captain Youngblood."

"Falcon, get back to the Farmhouse ASAP. I want to talk to you about this case."

"End of messages. Would you like to call Captain Youngblood back?"

"No."

"Okay."

The phone goes silent.

"Well, I guess these gentlemen will have to wait. Let's see what the captain wants."

He starts the engine, puts the car in gear, and drives back to the Farmhouse.

Chapter Nine

Chasing Richard

"So, he wants us to track down this Richard Olstroski?" Eddy asks.

"Yup. It appears that way," Shawn replies.

"Why doesn't he just get Oscar to do it? He's the one that screwed up and lost the guy."

"I think you just answered your own question. Would you ask the guy that lost a possible suspect to track said suspect down?"

"I see your point. So, how do we find this guy? Where do we start?"

"We start at the beginning."

"The Peterson-Hamm house?"

"No." Shawn looks at the man as if he had lost his mind. "The place he was last seen. The motel."

Shawn searches his phone contacts for Oscar Ziggler. He taps the call icon. After a few minutes, Oscar answers.

"Yeah?"

"Hey, Oscar. Freddy's got us tracking down Richard Olstroski...."

"Why are you calling me? I don't know where the hell he is."

"I know that," Shawn says with a sigh. He hates talking to this guy. "But you know where he was before...."

"Before what? Before I lost him? Shit, you make one damn mistake, and people don't let you forget it."

"Just give me the address, Oscar."

"It's an old-style motel south of the lake. It's called South Lake Motel."

"I think I know that place. I stopped a drug deal near that place a while back. That's off of South Florida, right?"

"Yeah. Frank and I go back a long way. I can meet with him for ya."

"I don't think Freddy would like that. We'll take this. I'd hate for another...mistake...to happen."

"Screw you, Braxton."

The call ends abruptly. "Well, it looks like we are headed to the south side of the lake."

Eddy rolls his eyes. "This time of day? We'll never get over the bridge in this traffic."

"Yup. Looks like we are going around the lake."

"It will take all day to track this guy."

"You got anything better to do, Eddy?"

Eddy sighs, "I get your point."

Shawn starts the engine, and they drive off toward Congress Ave to make their way around the lake.

Congress Ave travels the circumference of Lake Terra. The road is a giant circle. There are only a few spots along the road that obstruct the view of the lake, a few homes, and Cyan Park. The park is located on the east side of the lake and is divided into several areas. There's a campground, a playground, a place for picnics, and a swimming area. The park also has a spot set up to show movies. The last Saturday night of each month is known as "Saturday Night Movie in the Park." The films are projected onto the backside of an old restroom wall. A concession stand had been built to sell popcorn and soda. Cyan Park is a large part of the town's entertainment.

It's a quiet drive around the lake. They turned off of Congress Ave onto South Florida Blvd. A couple of blocks down, they made a right onto West Jefferson Street. They could see the motel up ahead.

"There it is," Shawn says.

The car pulls into the driveway of South Lake Motel and parks in front of the office. The parking lot is empty. He assumes Frank lives in the house behind the motel and walks to work.

“I know this place,” Eddy says. “There’s a pizza place just a few blocks away on South Illinois. The owner is a bit of an oddball, but the food is good.”

“Yup. I’ve eaten there a couple of times too. Well, let’s go talk to this guy.”

Inside, the office is pretty small. A rack of brochures lie against the wall to the right of the door. There are brochures about the lake, the town’s history, local museums, treasure hunting tours, and various other types of entertainment for the tourists. A small coffee area is set up against the right wall. The left wall has a few chairs and displays pictures of various points in the town’s history. The main desk is near the back of the office. No one is behind the desk.

Shawn approaches the desk and rings the bell sitting on the left side.

“I’ll be with ya in a minute,” a voice says behind the closed door to the left and behind the desk.

They hear a toilet flush and then the sound of running water. The door opens a few moments later, and a tall, thin man, with grey, curly hair walks out.

“I’m sorry to keep ya waitin’. Can I help...oh.” At that moment, the man had turns to see Shawn and Eddy in their uniforms. He sits down behind the desk. “How can I help ya, officers?”

“I’m Officer Braxton, and this is Officer Hickly,” Shawn says with a smile.

Eddy nods at the mention of his name.

Shawn continues, “We’re from the Farmhouse. We’re looking for a suspect who had been held in one of your rooms. Oscar Ziggler says you might know something.”

Frank sits back. He leans over to a mini-fridge near him. “Would ya care for somethin’ to drink?”

“No, thank you.”

Frank nods. He grabs a soda out of the refrigerator. “So,” he says, as he takes a sip of soda, “Oscar tell ya we are old friends? That we go back a ways?”

“Something like that,” Shawn says.

“Well, we ain’t, and we do.”

Shawn looks confused. “Oscar says you would help us. He says that y’all have a history. That he trusts you.”

Frank laughs. “He did, did he? Well, we do go back a ways. But we ain’t friends. We got a history. I ain’t goin’ into it. It ain’t important. There’s bad blood and hurt feelin’s, but he’s a cop now. I ain’t got no reason to steer a cop wrong. I’ll do my duty and help an officer out, but we ain’t friends, and I ‘on’t trust ‘im.”

“Well, Oscar and I are colleagues. We aren’t friends either. Would you mind answering a few questions?”

“Like I says, I’ll do my duty.”

Shawn nods. “Fair enough. Do you recognize this man?”

He takes out a picture of Richard Olstroski and hands it over.

Frank nods. “That’s him. Oscar brought him in late one night. Says he’s a suspect in a murder. I ‘on’t know. He don’t look like the murderin’ type to me.”

He hands the picture back to Shawn.

“Did you notice anything odd about this man?”

“You mean besides the smell?” Frank winces a little when he says that.

“Yeah,” Shawn says with a smile.

“Not really. I only saw ‘im at check-in and when he left.”

“Let’s talk about that. What happened there?”

“Well, Oscar had drove off. A few minutes later, this guy, Richard, you say?”

Shawn nods.

“Yeah, Richard came in. Says Oscar had let ‘im go. I mean, how’s I supposed to know? Anyway, he wanted to borry my phone.

Says he doesn't have his. Says he'd left it at home when the cops picked 'im up. Says he needs a ride."

"Did he call anyone?"

Frank shakes his head. "Naw. He downloaded some confangled app or somethin'. I 'on't know much about these thangs."

"May I see your phone?"

"Sure." The man unlocks his phone and hands it to Shawn.

Shawn starts scrolling through the installed apps. "Do you know what app it is?"

"Naw. I 'on't know much about it. Jest enough to make phone calls. That's all I needs it fer."

"I think I found it." He opens the ride-share app. He fumbles through the options until he finds the trip history. There is only one ride listed. "And you haven't used this app? The last person to use was is the suspect?"

Frank nods. "Yep. Like I said, I 'on't know nu'in' about them confangled thangs. My granddaughter helps me figure this thang out."

Shawn nods. He taps on the driver. There's an option to call as well as a map of the route. He writes down the driver's name, number, and license, as well as the make and model of the car. There's an option to share out the trip route. He shares it with himself. After gathering all of the information he can, Shawn hands the phone back to Frank.

"Can you tell me anything else about that night?"

Frank shakes his head. "Jest that Oscar came in all discombobulated. He's in a panic tryin' to find the guy. I in't know where he went. I jest said he called for a ride."

"Did Oscar ask to look at your phone?"

"Naw, he didn't. He ran out faster than a hawg runin' from a wulf."

"What room was he in?" asks Shawn. He can't resist a giggle from that last statement.

Frank opens a filing cabinet and thumbs through the folders.

"Twalve. Near the end."

"May we look in the room?"

"I 'on't know why. I done cleaned it. Ain't nu'in' in dare."

"Okay, then. Is there anything else you can remember?"

"Naw. Jest that."

"Well, if you see or hear anything…." He hands Frank his name and number.

"I'll let ye know."

"Thank you, sir. Have a good day."

"Y'all do the same. Have a good one."

Both men leave the office and return to their car.

"What now?" asks Eddy.

"We call this…" He looked at the name of the driver. "...Zack Monroe. But first, how about some lunch? Are you hungry?"

Eddy nods. "Yeah. Pizza?"

"You read my mind."

***

Shawn and Eddy walk into *Hold the Anchovies*. Shawn notices the owner jump when they walk in. He realizes it must be the uniforms.

"I gotta pee," Eddy says.

"What do you want? I'll order."

He glances at the menu. "A large chicken Alfredo with a large soda."

"Alright, I got it."

Eddy reaches for his wallet. Shawn shakes his head.

"I said that I have it. You get me next time."

Eddy nods and put his wallet back. He heads for the restroom. Shawn approaches the counter.

"No worries, man."

The owner flinches. "W...wh...what?"

Shawn smiles. “You don’t get many police officers in here, do you?”

The man shakes his head.

He read the name tag. “That’s okay, Mario. We’re just here to grab lunch.”

“Wh...what would you like?”

Shawn looks at the menu board for a few moments. Pizza did sound good.

“I’ll have a medium pineapple pizza and a large soda. My friend wants a large chicken Alfredo with a large soda.”

Mario rings it up. “That will be 22.38.”

Shawn pays in cash. Mario cashes him out. He gives Shawn two large cups and starts making the order.

Shawn walks over to the fountain machine and pours them each a soda. He sits down at a small table and grabs for the note with the driver’s number. He starts fumbling through his pockets. It isn’t there.

“Shit,” he says.

“What?” asks Eddy.

He looks up to see Eddy standing on the other side of the table. The man has his hand on the back of a chair. He had started to pull the chair out when Shawn spoke.

“You snuck up on me.”

“I didn’t mean to scare you.”

He shakes his head. “No. It’s not that. I can’t find the note I wrote that driver’s information on. I must have left it in the car.”

“I’ll go get it.”

“No. You stay and wait on the food. I’ll be back in a second.”

Eddy nods and sits down. He takes a sip of soda.

“Thanks for getting my soda,” he says.

Shawn raises his hand in a wave as he walks out the door. He opens the car door and starts fumbling for the note. There it is, on the dash. He grabs it and goes back inside.

"That didn't take long," Eddy says.

He sits down and dials the number on the note. He takes a sip of soda while the phone rings.

"Hello?" a voice answers. The person on the other end sounds young. Twenty-five or twenty-six, maybe.

"Zack Monroe?"

"Who's this?"

"I'm Officer Braxton. I'm investigating a murder…."

"I didn't kill anyone," he says excitedly.

"I didn't say you did. I think you may have given a ride to one of our suspects."

"Am I under arrest? How am I supposed to know..."

Shawn breaths. "Just listen. We need information. Do you have a moment?"

"Look, cop whatever your name is, I don't know anything about a murder. I didn't give a lift to a murderer."

"If you hang up on me, you will be under arrest."

"For what? Hanging up on a cop isn't illegal."

"But impeding an investigation is," Shawn says matter-of-factly.

There is no response on the other end.

"Good. I have your attention. The other night you picked up a rider at a motel called South Lake Motel. It's on West Jefferson. You remember?"

"Actually, I do. I didn't think I would ever get that smell out of my car."

Shawn smiles. "Good." He put the call on speaker and navigates to where he had the route map saved. "I've got the map of the route you took that day. It doesn't look like you were heading to the airport."

"Airport?"

There is a large crash from behind the counter. He sees Mario picking up a dish. The sudden voice on speaker must have startled the man.

"He didn't go to the airport."

"Meal's up!" Mario says.

"I'll get it," says Eddy.

Shawn nods. Eddy leaves to get the food.

"Where did you take him then?"

There is a long pause.

Eddy returns with their food. Shawn mouths, "Thank you," as Eddy sits down.

"It is an apartment building off of East Lincoln, I think."

"That would make sense with this route. Can you remember anything else? Anything he may have said or done?"

"It is weird. He asked me to stop a block away. I tried to explain I had to reach the destination for the trip to register as complete. He argued with me and demanded I let him out. So, I did. I explained that I still had to reach the destination, or the trip doesn't end. So, I drove up to the place and stopped. I was just waiting in the parking lot for my next trip whenI see him walk up to the front door. I assumed he lived there."

"What happened next?"

"I don't know. I got another ride and left. He was still outside."

"Is there anything else you can remember?"

"No. That's it."

"Save my number. If you think of anything else, give me a call."

"Whatever."

The call ends. Shawn puts the phone away.

"Pineapple pizza?" Eddy looks disgusted as he glances at Shawn's plate. He takes another bite of his pasta.

"Yeah. So?" Shawn bites into a slice of pizza.

"Pineapple doesn't belong on pizza."

"What?" he asks with a mouthful of food. "Of course it does."

"No, it doesn't. It's not traditional."

"What are you talking about? Where are we right now?"

"A pizza restaurant…"

"Look around, Eddy. It's in Italian decor. The menu is American-style Italian. For Christ's sake, the owner's name is Mario. What do you mean it's not traditional?"

"Show me a pineapple that came from Italy."

Shawn just shakes his head. "Eat your damn pasta."

The two men eat as they talk.

Eddy says, "So, I guess we check out this apartment complex."

"Yup."

"But we don't know what apartment."

"Nope."

"So, how do we find this guy?"

"He said there is a front door. There must be a doorman. We ask the doorman."

"Freddy's going to be pissed."

"Yup. At Oscar."

The two men finish their meals and leave. As they are pulling out of the parking lot, they see a car drive past that matches the description of the speeding motorist.

"Run the plates," Shawn says.

"It's a match. That's the man that Oscar stoped."

"Let's see if he knows anything then."

***

Otto sees the cop car in the parking lot of the pizza restaurant. He decides it isn't a good time to go home. He lays low for a while then casually drives past just as the cops are pulling out of the lot.

"Shit!"

He realizes their lights are on, and they want him to pull over. He pulls over, and the cop car stops behind him. He watches as a tall cop with a shaved head and chiseled chin steps out.

"All these young guys look like the cops they see on TV. None of them look average anymore," he says to no one.

The cop approaches the car in a hurry. He had never seen a cop approach him that swiftly. The cop bends over slightly to peer into the window. He holds out a picture of a somewhat unkempt man.

"Have you seen this man?"

"No," Otto replies and speeds off.

The cop starts into a jog as if to chase him and suddenly stops. He had no idea what was going on, and he didn't care. He knows he had never seen that man before.

***

"Shit!" Shawn exclaims. He had almost started into a run before he realized it. He can't chase this guy down. He walks back to the car.

"Well, he claims he didn't see Mr. Olstroski," Shawn says as he gets back into the car.

"Well, what do we do now?"

Shawn places the picture of Richard back over his visor.

"We get back on the trail. What's the name of that apartment complex?"

"Pine Oak."

"Let's check it out."

They pull out and drive East.

***

They pull into the parking lot of Pine Oak Apartments, which is a five-floor complex. It appears to be upper-middle class. He parks next to a fountain, which is a giant dragon with wings spread wide. It is standing atop a precipice looking down. Water spews from its mouth as if it were fire. He isn't sure how that fountain fits the theme of the apartment complex, but who is he to judge? He and Eddy got out of the car and walk inside.

The lobby, inside, looks upscale which makes the dragon fountain seem even more out of place. They approach the front desk.

"May I help you, Officers?"

The woman behind the desk smiles politely.

"What's with the dragon outside?" Shawn asks.

"I'm sorry?"

"The fountain. It's a dragon. It just seems odd and out of place."

"I don't know. I just work here. Is there something I can help you with?"

He decides to forget about the odd fountain for now. "We are investigating a murder."

The woman gasps. "Murder? Here? There must be some mistake."

He shakes his head. "No, no, no. I'm sorry to alarm you. It didn't happen here."

She sighs and then looks confused. "Why are you here?"

"Have you seen this man?" He hands her the picture of Richard Olstroski.

She takes the picture and studies it for a moment.

"One moment."

She steps away. He watches her as she walks over to a man standing by the elevator. The man looks at the photo and nods. They converse for a few minutes. He points to the elevator and then points up. She walks back and returns the photo to him.

"Maxwell remembers him." She points to the man by the elevator. "He says this guy came in early one morning. He asked to see Juliana Martinez."

"May we speak with Maxwell?"

"Of course. This way, Officers."

She leads them over to the man by the elevator. He's a short, thin, balding black man dressed in slacks and a button-up collared dress shirt.

"Maxwell, these two officers would like to speak with you about that picture I showed you."

"Yes, of course. Thank you, Carmen."

She turns and walks back to her station.

Maxwell has a warm, soothing voice. "Officers, how may I help you?"

"First of all," Shawn starts, "What's with the dragon fountain? It's weird and makes no sense. It doesn't fit any of the decor." He motions to various parts of the lobby. Eddy rolls his eyes and lets out a sigh.

"The owner has an affinity for dragons. How can I help you with your case?"

Shawn decides to let it go. "We believe this man," he holds up the picture of Richard Olstroski, "was dropped off here a couple of days ago. Sometime in the early morning. Have you seen him?"

"Yes. As I said to Carmen, he arrived and asked to speak with Ms. Martinez sometime after eight o'clock that morning. He was a little unkempt and seemed to be in a panic. He smelled as if he hadn't bathed in a month. I thought he was a crazy fan. I told him she isn't home. She is out on the set of a new film."

"So, she's an actress?"

Maxwell snorts. "She's not just AN actress, officer. She's one of the highest-paid and sought-after actresses outside of Hollywood. I just hope the controversy over her last film doesn't harm her career."

"You're talking about the Marcus Peterson murder."

He nods.

"That's actually why we are here. We are tracking down a lead for the detective working the case. This man is one of the cast members."

Maxwell snorts again. "They must have reached the bottom of the barrel for that one."

"What happened after you told him she wasn't in?"

"He didn't believe me. He demanded to see her. I had security throw him out."

"Do you know where he went after that?"

"No," Maxwell says matter-of-factly.

"May we speak with Ms. Martinez."

"Officer, as I said, she left. She is working on another project. I was not lying when I told this man that."

"Do you know where? Perhaps we can talk to her."

"Germany."

"Germany? That's fairly quick. The director of a film she is working on is murdered, and she decides to accept a job on a new film and flies off to Europe?"

"The film had wrapped. Principal photography is complete. She flew out the next morning. This is scheduled. How is she to know the man was murdered?"

"It just seems kind of convenient."

"Look, officer, Ms. Martinez is a highly sought-after actress. She has a lot of projects. This one had been scheduled for months. Mr. Peterson's film was running over budget, and filming was taking longer than planned. If they hadn't wrapped when they did, she would have still left. She was doing Mr. Hamm a favor by taking this on. She normally doesn't work so cheap."

"Mr. Hamm? Hampton Hamm? The victim's widower?"

He nods. "Ms. Martinez and Mr. Hamm worked on a television show together a few years back. They had become close friends. He asked her to take the role. He knew her star power would elevate the film."

"So, Ms. Martinez is in Germany, and Mr. Olstroski is MIA. Perfect. Can you tell me anything else about that day?"

"No. I have no idea what he did after security threw him out."

"May we speak to the security officer who was on duty that day?"

"Today is his day off."

"May we get an address? We will pass it along to the detective working the case."

"Of course, officer. One moment."

Maxwell walks over to the front desk. He converses with Carmen for a moment. She types on the computer as if she were pulling up information. Carmen writes something down on a piece of paper and hands it to Maxwell, who walks back over and hands Shawn the paper.

"Stephen McDonald. This is his address."

"Thank you for your assistance."

"My pleasure, officer."

"Have a good one," Shawn says as they turn to leave.

"You do the same, officers."

***

Shawn and Eddy get back in the police car. He places the picture of Richard Olstroski back over his visor. He sits back in exasperation.

"So, do we check this guy out?"

"Let's see what Freddy wants us to do."

He picks up his phone and calls Freddy.

"Did you find out anything?" Freddy says immediately when he answers.

"No 'Hello. How are you doing, Shawn?' Just 'Did you find anything?'"

"I'm driving, Shawn. On my way to the Farmhouse. The captain wants to meet with me. Do you have anything? Did you find him?"

"No, it's all pretty much a dead end."

"Shit! Do you have anything that I can use on the case?"

"Maybe. I spoke with the driver that picked Mr. Olstroski up that morning. That led us to the apartment of a Ms. Juliana Martinez."

"Did you speak with her?"

"Nope. She flew out to Germany the morning of Mr. Peterson's murder."

"Germany?"

"Yeah, apparently she's working on a film over there. This is something she had scheduled before accepting the role in Mr. Peterson's film. According to the person I spoke with at her apartment building, she took the role as a favor to Mr. Hamm."

"A favor to Mr. Hamm? Why?"

"They worked on a television show together. They were good friends."

"Alright. I'll have to ask him about that. Thanks. Now where the hell is Richard Olstroski?"

"We don't know."

"What do you mean you don't know?"

"They thought he was a crazy fan and threw him out."

"Shit!"

"But we have the name and address of the security officer who threw him out. We can't speak to him. He's off of work today."

"Perfect. Send it to me. I'll follow up with this guy. Did you find anything else out?"

"We did see the motorist that Oscar stoped."

"Did he see anything? Did you get his name?"

"No. He sped off in a hurry. I showed him the picture. He said he hadn't seen the man and sped off."

"Did you get a description?"

"He's kind of a stocky fellow. Bad attitude and smoking a cigar."

"Alright. Anything else?"

"That's all we have."

"Thanks, Shawn. I'll take it from here. Bye."

Chapter Ten

All About Richard

Freddy had been back at the Farmhouse for half an hour. The captain was in a meeting when he arrived. He said he'd call when he is ready to meet. Freddy is on his second pot of Mayan coffee he had bought on a trip to Mexico. He knows it is a tourist thing, but he doesn't care. It is still good coffee.

He sits down with the cup and takes a sip.

"This is damn fine coffee," he says.

He is looking through his notes to prepare himself for the captain. He knows he had to have everything in order before meeting with the man. The captain wouldn't take any bumbling.

Captain Youngblood isn't a bad guy. Freddy respects the man. The captain has a calm demeanor, but you don't want to piss him off either. He's firm and fair. He doesn't like excuses and absolutely does not take well to insubordination. The captain has an open-door policy and will listen to all who work under him. Even though all opinions are welcome, the conversation is over once the man makes a decision. Officers must present the facts, though. He doesn't like opinions or conjectures.

His phone rings. He looks at the display. It is the captain's extension. He picks up the receiver.

"Sir?"

"Falcon, I'm ready for you."

"I'll be right there."

"No. I'm heading to your office."

"My office?"

"Yeah, and have some coffee ready."

"Yes, sir."

He hangs up the phone with a smile. He is sure the captain loves coffee almost as much as he does. He looks over at his coffee bar and notices the empty carafe. He rushes over to put on a fresh pot.

Freddy is particular about his coffee. He dumps out the grounds, washes out the mesh filter and the coffee carafe, places fresh coffee in the filter, pours water in the coffee maker, sets the carafe on the warmer plate, and turns it on. He sits back down, takes another sip of coffee, and continues reviewing his notes.

There is something Wexler said that bothers him. He kept referring to how he felt about his wife in the past tense. He assumed it's how the man talks. They were talking about a photo from the past. Most people use words in the wrong tense. He decides to file this tidbit away in his mind for now.

His thoughts keep going back to Richard Olstroski. He is sure the man didn't commit the murder, but how was he this hard to find? It's almost as if he disappeared off the face of the earth. Oscar said the man had called his wife and manager. Has anyone tried contacting them to find out if they have heard from him?

Freddy picks up the phone receiver and dials Oscar's extension.

"What is it, Falcon?" Oscar answers. There is a slight annoyance in his voice. A little more than usual, anyway.

"Hey, Oscar, I'm reviewing my notes before meeting with the captain."

"And?"

"AND I'm going over the disappearance of Richard Olstros...."

"Look, Falcon, I don't know where he is. He didn't tell me he was running. He didn't say anything that would set off an alarm. He didn't email me or send me private messages on social media, alerting me to where he is. We took his phone..."

Freddy takes this moment to interrupt the man. "And that is exactly why I called you. Do you still have his phone?"

"What the hell? I'm not a freaking rookie, Falcon! I've been on the force for thirty-seven freaking years! Of course I don't have the damn thing! It's in evidence!"

Freddy sighs. "Do you know if anyone has tried to follow up with his wife or agent?"

"Now that's a stupid question, Falcon. I thought you were smarter than that. How the hell would I know that?"

"Oscar, just one more question for you."

"Look, Falcon, I don't know anything. All I did is watch a guy. A guy you wanted me to watch. He ran. I have no freaking clue where the damned fool is, and, frankly, I don't give a shit. It's not my problem. It's your case, your problem."

"Dammit, Oscar, just humor me for a moment. Do you remember the name of his wife or his agent?"

"What for?"

"I want to send them a Christmas card. What the hell do you think I want it for? I want to follow up with them. I want to see if he has contacted them."

Oscar sighs. "He kept calling his wife 'Maggie.' His agent is a Mr. Knight. I don't know how much you will get out of them, though."

"What do you mean?"

"He never talked to his agent. He just left a message for the guy to call the phone in the room. And his wife… That's one troubled relation…."

"Wait! What did you say about his agent?"

"What? I didn't. He never talked to the guy."

"He left a message? He gave the number of the hotel room?"

"Yeah, what of it?"

"Thank you, Oscar."

Freddy hangs up the phone. He dials down to the evidence room. A soft-spoken female voice, with a thick southern drawl, answers.

"Evidence. This is Amber."

"Hey, Amber. This is Detective Falcon. How are you?"

He could hear the smile in her voice as she spoke. "Hey, Freddy. I'm good. How are ya?"

"I'm doing well. It's good to hear your voice again. That guy, Jonathan, was a pain to deal with. How was your vacation?"

"It was good. We had a wonderful cruise…."

At that moment, Captain Youngblood walks in. Freddy mouths, "The coffee is fresh and hot." The captain nods and walks over to Freddy's coffee bar. Freddy continues his call while the captain pours himself a cup of coffee. He knows he has a few minutes. Captain Youngblood is particular about the amount of cream, sweetener, and flavoring that goes into his coffee. Freddy continues with his conversation.

"...and we were heading back to our room, or cabin as they call it. Anyway, we actually saw a woman pee in the hall. Can you believe that, Freddy? She opens her room door and just pees right there on the floor. I guess she thought it was a toilet. I dunno. Jasmine says she thought the woman was drunk. I dunno. I never saw a drunk pee on the floor before, but I ain't around that type of people that much. Anyway, so that night we went…."

"Amber…"

"Yes, Freddy. I'm here."

"The captain just walked in. As much as I would love to hear the details about the rest of your trip, I do have to cut this short."

"Oh, okay. What can I help ya with?"

The captain walks over to Freddy's desk. He sets his coffee cup down and motions toward Freddy's empty cup. Freddy hands the man his cup. The captain walks back over to the coffee bar to refill Freddy's cup.

"There is a cell phone that was taken into evidence a few days ago. I believe that Officer Ziggler checked it in."

"One moment. Let me check."

The captain sets Freddy's cup back down in front of him, pulls out the chair on the other side of the desk, and sits down. He takes a sip of coffee while listening to Freddy's side of the conversation.

"Is that Amber?"

Freddy nods.

"How was her vacation?"

"She says she had a good time."

"That's good."

A few moments later, Amber returns to the phone. Freddy lifts his index finger to indicate to the captain to give him a minute. "Yeah. I have it here."

"Perfect. May I come down later and check it out?"

"Of course. But don't worry about coming down. I'll bring it up to ya."

"Thanks, Amber. I need to go. Captain Youngblood would like to meet with me."

"Of course. It's good talking to ya, Freddy. Bye now."

"Bye, Amber."

He hangs up the phone and sits back.

"Thank you for the coffee."

"Don't mention it. She does like to talk. So, her trip went well?"

"I'll give you the short, short version. She had a good time."

Captain Youngblood chuckles. "Better you than me, Falcon."

"She knows better with you, sir," Freddy says with a smile.

"I want to know what you know about this murder. The mayor has been riding my ass. It's starting to hit national headlines."

"National headlines?"

"Yeah. The director of a major Hollywood film is murdered in his home. This isn't exactly a low-profile case, Falcon."

Freddy sighs and sits back. "Jesus…"

"So, I need something to tell the mayor. I need facts, Falcon."

"Well, sir, that's what I am still working on."

"Bullshit. I just heard you on the phone with Amber. You're still on this wild goose chase. Still trying to prove your hunch that Mr. Hamm did not kill his husband."

"He didn't."

"What proof do you have?"

Freddy starts to speak and closes his mouth. He knows the captain would not accept a hunch.

"Look, Falcon, you are one of the best officers I have. You are the best detective. Your hunches and your instincts are what make you good at your job. But I need proof. Right now, we have two suspects. One is downstairs in a cell. The other is MIA."

Freddy opens his mouth to speak. The captain raises his hand. Freddy closes his mouth.

"Let me continue. Right now, all of the evidence you have, points to one person. Do you have anything new that can help exonerate Mr. Hamm?"

He knows this is not the time to mention the insurance policy. That would just be the nail in the coffin for Hampton. "I have a few leads but no new evidence."

"We are going to have to officially charge Mr. Hamm. I want the man arrested for the murder of Marcus Peterson."

Freddy sits up straight. "What the hell? He didn't do this! The man watched his husband die!"

"Falcon! If you talk to me like that one more time, you are off this case!"

"Yes, sir."

The captain leans forward, hands cupped on Freddy's desk. "Look, I need to know. Are you taking this personally? Is Mr. Hamm's situation bringing back memories for you? Is it clouding your judgment on this case?"

Freddy shakes his head. "No, sir. I am able to separate myself."

The captain sits back and takes a sip of coffee. "Good. The first time it does, you are off of this case."

"Yes, sir."

"Now, outside of consoling Mr. Hamm and this Richard Olstroski wild goose chase, do you have any solid leads?"

"I spoke to a Mr. Jacob Wexler. He gave me a few names of possible suspects."

"Oh? How so?"

"Here's what bothers me about that night. Mr. Olstroski went out for drinks and never returned home. Who all may have known that Mr. Olstroski is staying at the home of the victim?"

"Probably the entire cast and crew."

"And out of those people, who knows that Mr. Olstroski would not be returning that night?"

"Well, whoever it is he went out with."

"Did they? Mr. Olstroski claims he was too drunk to drive back. He claims he slept it off in his car."

"So, what are you saying?"

"Whoever murdered Mr. Peterson knew that Richard Olstroski was staying with him and his husband. They also knew that Mr. Olstroski was not returning home that night and that the screen door to the pool enclosure would be left unlocked."

"Which points us to Mr. Hamm."

"Sir."

The captain raises his hand again. Freddy closes his mouth.

"Falcon, where is your evidence folder?"

Freddy slides his evidence folder over to the captain. Captain Youngblood starts thumbing through it.

"Alright, I want to interview Mr. Hamm."

"But, sir! I should be the one to interview him."

The captain shakes his head. "No. You've been his therapist long enough. I will speak with Mr. Hamm. If he did not do this, as you suspect, then I want to know who did. I want answers. I want this case solved. I will interview Mr. Hamm. You are welcome to listen in."

"But..."

"Falcon, don't make me take you off of this case. I am beginning to think this case is getting to you."

"I can assure you that it's not."

"Then act like it. Show me the Freddy Falcon that annoys us all. Show me the Freddy Falcon who thinks he's never wrong and loves to explain how he's the smartest man in the room. Show me the sarcastic, egotistical, logic-minded Freddy Falcon that I hired."

The captain stood to leave. Freddy starts to respond, but he thinks better of it.

"Falcon, I will be reading him his rights shortly. Thank you for the coffee."

The captain places his empty cup on the counter by Freddy's sink. He walks out the door, closing it behind him.

Freddy sits back in his chair, exasperated. He knows they are making a mistake. They are charging an innocent man. He knows he has to get to the bottom of this as soon as possible. However, this may help him in tracking down the actual killer. If Hampton is charged for the murder of his husband, then the real killer may relax. This person may let their guard down just enough. He knows that's not what the captain is thinking, but this may be enough to open the door to solving this case. He would listen in on that interview. The captain will be tough with Hampton. He may be able to get more out of the man than Freddy ever could.

There is a knock at his office door.

"Come," Freddy says.

The door opens, and in walks a short, chubby curly haired red-headed woman with a smile on her face.

"Amber!" Freddy says with a smile. "It's good to see you."

"Hey, Freddy. Here's the phone you asked for."

She holds up a plastic bag with a smartphone inside.

"Thanks, Amber."

He reaches out for the bag. She pulls it away.

"Not so fast, Freddy. You know the rules. You have to sign for it."

She reveals a printed-out piece of paper with the heading "TPS-47 Evidence Report Form". Everyone who checked out any piece of evidence had to sign a TPS-47 form to release it. This is a form of record keeping. This way, if a piece of evidence went missing, they knew who last had it in their possession.

"Of course."

He grabs a pen from his drawer and signs the form. He hands the paper back to Amber, and she gives him the plastic bag.

"Thank you, Freddy."

He places the pen back and closes the drawer.

"So," she says, "you and I are gonna have to go out sometime and catch up. I've missed a full month on this vacation."

He smiles. "I'm still single, but I'd love to go out for trivia or karaoke with you and Travis sometime."

She playfully slaps him on the arm. "Silly, I'm not thinking of double datin' again. Just old friends catchin' up."

"It sounds like fun. You know what? We will set something up."

"Perfect," she says. "Just let me know when ya have some free time."

"It may be after this case, though."

Her smile fades, and her demeanor takes a more serious stance. "Freddy, we've known each other since the academy. I'm always here to listen."

He looks puzzled. "What do you mean?"

"I've read the file on this...Mr. Hamm…"

He sits back and rolls his eyes. "First the captain, and now you?" He shakes his head. "It's not what you think. I am not letting my past cloud my judgment. I listen to Mr. Hamm for two reasons. It's what he needs right now, and I'm hoping he will reveal something."

"Freddy, you know what he's goin' through. You know he's not thinkin' clearly."

"Exactly why I have to be the one to work this case. I KNOW what it's like to lose someone you love. That's why…"

He starts to choke up. Tears run down his cheek. He shakes his head and clears his throat. Her look of concern turns to sympathy.

"No. He didn't do this, and I am going to prove it." He looks at the clock on his desk. It reads four-thirty. "If you will excuse me, Amber. I'm going to see what I can get off of this phone before the captain arrests Mr. Hamm."

She returns to her usual jovial self. "Of course. I have to get back, anyway. It is good talkin' to ya, Freddy."

She turns to leave.

"It's good to have you back, Amber."

She leaves and closes the door behind her.

Freddy gets up and goes over to his coffee bar. He starts washing the captain's coffee cup. He pours the last of the coffee in his empty coffee cup and washes out the coffee carafe, filter, and basket. He sits back down at his desk.

"Let's see if we can get into this phone."

He grabs a pair of gloves and put them on. He did not want to contaminate the evidence. He opens the plastic bag and removes the phone. Freddy powers on the phone and waits for it to boot up. The passcode screen appears.

"Well, Mr. Olstroski, let's see just how secure you are."

He tries "password." The phone does not unlock. He tries "Richard." Still, no access. "Olstroski," "Maggie," "actor."

"Damn! Think, Freddy, think. What the hell…"

He types in "12345". The phone let him in. Up pops Richard Olstroski's home screen.

Freddy is taken aback. "Really? 1,2,3,4,5? I can't believe that actually worked."

He shrugs it off and opens the man's contacts. Freddy knows he can not look into the phone any further than the two contact numbers he is looking for. He finds "Maggie" listed in the contacts. Freddy writes down the phone number. He continues through Richard's contacts. There it is. "Cecil Knight." He writes Mr. Knight's number down. Freddy closes out of the contacts and powers off the phone. He places the phone back in the plastic bag and removes his gloves.

"Let's start with Mr. Knight."

He dials the number. A young-sounding male voice answers.

"Red Wolf Talent Agency."

"Yes, this is Detective Freddy Falcon. I'm investigating the Murder of Mr. Marcus Peterson."

Freddy waits for a response. There is silence. He waits. After a long silence, the person responds.

"We don't represent a Marcus Peterson."

"But you do represent a Richard Olstroski."

There is another long pause. One of the tricks Freddy liked to use is to let the other person break the silence. He never broke long pauses of silence. The person responded.

"We do represent Mr. Olstroski."

"Is his agent available to talk?"

"One moment."

He hears a series of three beeps, a click, and the phone ringing again. After a couple of rings, he hears a firm male voice answer.

"Cecil Knight."

"Mr. Knight. This is Detective Freddy Falcon. I'm investigating the Murder of Marcus Peterson here in Terra Loch."

"How may I help you, Detective?"

"I understand that you represent one of our suspects: A Richard Olstroski."

"That is correct. Richard is one of our...newer...clients. I haven't spoken with him in weeks."

"He didn't call you the other night?"

"He called. Thomas, a member of my messaging service, says that he called a few days ago. I called the number he left. It went to a motel."

"So, you have not spoken with Mr. Olstroski at all in the past few days?"

"Did I stutter, Detective? No."

"Do you know if he made it back to L.A.?"

"How the hell would I know that?"

"Doesn't he have another film he is starting?"

"Detective, Mr. Olstroski is a joke. Mr. Peterson's film is the first time he has had real work in years. He mainly gets work in commercials. He's lucky to get one movie, much less two."

"Wait a minute. Now I am confused. He didn't have to rush back to film another movie?"

"English isn't your first language, is it, Detective? Richard Olstroski had no other work after Mr. Peterson's film. None."

"Can you tell me anything else?"

"No."

"Do you expect to hear from him soon?"

"No."

"Do you know where he may be?"

"No."

"Why does this feel like an adventure game where I have run out of conversation options?"

"What?"

He shakes his head. "Never mind. This conversation has been quite illuminating, Mr. Knight. Thank you for your time."

"Detective."

"Yes?"

"If you do find Mr. Olstroski, tell him to find another agent."

Freddy hears a "click" and silence. He places the receiver back on the hook. He knows he did not want to have any part of Hollywood if this is the type of jerk he would have to deal with. So, Richard Olstroski lied. He had no other work. That confuses him even more. Why did he run? Why did he insist on getting back to L.A.?

"Maybe Maggie Olstroski can help shed some light on this mystery."

He reads the number for "Maggie" that he had written down. He picks up his phone receiver and dials her number. After a few moments of ringing, he hears a woman answer in a stern voice.

"Hello?"

He looks at his clock. It is still morning in California. Freddy breaks nto his natural smile. "Good morning. I'm Detective Freddy Falcon. May I speak with Maggie Olstroski?"

"This is Margaret Slythe. It's afternoon. Your watch may be off. How may I help you, Detective?" She had no emotion when she spoke. This woman is all business.

Afternoon? He looks at the clock again. Dammit, she is correct. It's a three-hour time difference. What was he thinking?

"I'm sorry, ma'am…"

"Dr. Slythe," she emphasized.

"My apologies, Dr."

"How may I help you, Detective?"

"I want to make sure I have the correct person before I continue. You are married to Richard Olstroski, correct?"

"Richard is my husband." He heard a sigh in her voice before she continued. "What did he do now?"

Freddy shakes his head as if she were in the same room. "No, no, no. It's nothing like that. I'm investigating a murder. We are trying…"

"Marcus Peterson. I don't know where Richard is, Detective."

He decides to get down to business. There were no pleasantries with this lady.

"When was the last time you spoke with your husband?"

"He called me one morning. I don't remember when it was. I remember it was early. He woke me up. I was pissed at him. I was up late grading papers and had to be up early to get to class. I need my rest…"

"Class? You're a teacher then? I misunderstood. I thought you said you were a doctor?"

She sighs again. "I am, Detective. I have a doctorate in psychology. I teach at the university three days a week. I am also a practicing therapist."

"I see. My apologies, Dr. Did Mr. Olstroski say anything else to you?"

"He said that he is a suspect in a murder investigation. He swore he is innocent. I haven't spoken with him after that."

"He hasn't tried to reach out to you anymore?"

"Detective...Falkor...is it?"

"Falcon. Falkor is the luck dragon in *The Neverending Story*."

"Excuse me?"

He shakes his head, again, to no one. "Never mind. Here's the thing. Your husband is a suspect only because he is part of the cast. We are investigating everyone. No one has been officially charged. Your husband decided to run the morning he spoke with you. He claimed he needed to be back in L.A. for a new movie."

"Richard doesn't have another movie project. He is lucky to get this one."

"What do you mean?"

"Look, Detective, our marriage is more of convenience. There is no 'love' here."

He thinks that is sad. He thinks it wise to keep that thought to himself. He didn't understand this concept, but he understands that all relationships are different. Whatever worked for the couple.

"Richard is my ticket into Hollywood. He may be a horrible actor, but he knows people. He is my key to being a therapist to the stars. And I keep food on his table. That's it. No, I don't know where he is. I know he's not back in L.A."

"How do you know that?"

"I track him, Detective."

"We have his phone."

"No, Detective. Not his phone. Him."

"I don't understand. What do you mean 'him'?"

" He is chipped."

"You mean like a dog?"

"Very similar. It's an experimental GPS chip. So, Detective, I can say, without a doubt, that Richard Olstroski is still in Terra Loch."

"May I get access to that?"

"Access to what?"

"His tracker."

"You want to track him?"

"We want to find him, Dr. We think he may know who murdered Mr. Peterson."

"I can send you the information so that you can track him."

"Can you email it?"

"Yes."

He gave her his email address. "Is there anything else you can tell me?"

"No."

"Well, thank you for your time. Have a wonderful day Dr."

He hangs up the phone and sits back. He is a little excited. They finally may have a break in this case. Richard Olstroski can be tracked by GPS. This is important information the captain needs to know. He grabs the phone and dials the captain's extension.

"Yeah, Falcon?"

"Captain, we may have…"

"Falcon, this will have to wait. I'm speaking with Mr. Hamm soon. If you would like to listen, it will be in interrogation room three in a half-hour."

"But sir…"

"Goodbye, Falcon."

Freddy heard a click and silence.

“Shit!” Hampton is about to be charged for a murder he didn’t commit.

Chapter Eleven

Youngblood and Hamm

Hampton sits on the edge of the bed in his cell. He has been using this time to think about the days after he lost Marcus. Time has been passing slowly for him. He has no clue how long he has been locked away in this cell nor how much longer he will be in here. How much time has passed since Marcus had...had…? He felt the pain again. He still could not bring himself to say the rest of it.

He still can't understand why he is here. It's bad enough he's trapped in his own prison that his mind has constructed for him. He has been and will continue to replay those events in his head. It's as if it's a recording set on repeat. It's more than that, though. It's more like a simulation on repeat. He can still see, hear, feel, and smell everything that happened in the moments of that tragic night. Some part of him still blames himself. What if he had been awake? What if he hadn't been so angry at Marcus? What if he had suggested they go to bed?

The reality is that it did happen. He had been angry at Marcus. He did want to be alone. He didn't want to go in the house to be with his husband. He knows he acted like a child that night. Marcus had been right. They needed to get that scene finished while they still had the location.

There are no windows in his cell. He is surrounded by walls and, of course, the cell bars. His bed, if you call it that, lays against the back wall. It is more of a metal slab with a mattress than a bed. Hampton sits on the edge, facing the bars. That is the only way he can look out onto the world. His only glimpse of freedom. His only bastion of hope. Hope that someone will come running up and tell him this is all a terrible joke.

He hadn't been arrested yet, but no one spoke with him either. The only visitor he has had is the officer bringing him his meals. He hasn't seen another soul. Freddy hasn't even stopped by to discuss the case. He hates this feeling. He is not in control. He hadn't been since that night.

Freddy had given him a chance to talk. Why didn't he? All he could do was cry and blather on about Marcus. Why had he been crying so much? Why didn't he go into details about the film set? Why did he allow himself to sit in misery? There is so much more that he could have said. More that could have, possibly, saved him from this predicament.

Freddy had been there to listen. The detective was right there. He had asked Hampton to talk. He realizes that he had squandered his time. Every chance he had to go into any details is now lost. There was so much he could have said. The arguments between Marcus and Richard. Granted, those were mainly about how Richard's housekeeping and hygiene conflicted with their own. The controversy with Jacob. The fact that Jacob blamed Hampton and Marcus for his career taking a dive. Then there was Adam. Why didn't he mention Adam? What was he thinking? Adam is the one person who has a larger motive than anyone else. Adam despised Marcus for years. Hampton still isn't sure why the man accepted. He did appear to have changed. Not his lifestyle, but his personality.

He shakes his head. It doesn't matter now. He is in a cell. All of the current evidence points to him. No one is talking to him. No one is coming. Not even Juliana.

He wonders if she had heard the news. He had been so consumed with his grief that he didn't think to call her. She had flown out to Germany that night. He never had a chance to say goodbye. Did Miguel see her off? And there is Miguel. Did he know? He would get the word to Juliana. She would fly back immediately, wouldn't she? He didn't know anymore. All he knows is someone he and Marcus trusted did the unthinkable, and there would be no coming back from that.

Then there's Freddy. The detective claimed he is doing all of this to help Hampton. He can't fathom why this detective is so positive he didn't do this. He's ecstatic that the man does believe him, but he is right to be a suspect. That is one thing Hampton does understand. Hampton had watched and guest-starred in enough television police shows to know they cannot rule out the grieving spouse. This detective doesn't even know him. All he knows are the stories he had heard and the characters he had played on TV and in film. Why does this guy even care, outside of just solving a case? A case that Hampton should be a prime suspect in.

At this point, he is convinced the detective only listened as a way to get him to talk. Is he faking it? Is it all a ruse just for information? Is he placating a grieving widower just to gather information from this possible suspect? Hampton is determined not to be so "open" with any of these cops moving forward.

He hears the sound of footsteps. He isn't sure of the time, but he knows it is too early for a meal. Is someone coming to talk? Could it be the detective? Could it be Juliana? No, they wouldn't let her down here. Perhaps she came to bail him out. Perhaps he will be told they caught the person responsible. Perhaps they are here to arrest him. That feeling of dread rises up, like bile, in him again. Would he be convicted of something he didn't do?

An officer he doesn't recognize approaches his cell. He is short, like Hampton, and speaks with a gruff voice.

"Mr. Hamm, the captain would like to speak with you about the murder of your husband."

***

Freddy isn't sure what to do. He had to do everything he could to prevent this murder charge. He picks up the receiver of his desk phone to call down to the holding area.

"Hey, Freddy. What's up?"

"Murphy? Where's Oscar?"

"He had to run an errand for the captain. What's up?"

Freddy is taken aback by this. Is he too late?

"What do you mean?"

"The captain asked Oscar to take Mr. Hamm to interrogation room three, a few minutes ago. What do you…"?

"Thanks, Murphy. Bye."

Freddy hung up and immediately dials Oscar's cell.

"What now, Falcon?" He hears the gruff voice ask.

"Oscar, is Mr. Hamm with you?"

He hears the man sigh. "Yeah. What of it?"

"I need to speak with him for a minute."

"Look, Falcon, I am in the process of taking this suspect to an interrogation. The captain wants a confession about how he murdered his husband."

"Allegedly. Oscar that has yet to be proven. He's only a suspect."

"A suspect that's about to be charged with murder."

"Just ask the man a question for me."

Oscar sighs again. Freddy could imagine the man rolling his eyes. "Fine."

"Ask Mr. Hamm if Richard Olstroski mentioned where he was going the night of the murder."

He hears the two men converse. After a few moments, Oscar replies. "As far as he knows, Mr. Olstroski went out for drinks. Falcon, we know all of this already. Stop hovering around this guy."

"Just humor me, Oscar. Ask Mr. Hamm if Mr. Olstroski hit on anyone on the set."

"What? What the hell kind of question is that? The man is married!"

"Just ask."

Oscar and Hampton converse again. When Oscar speaks again, his tone was changed. He sounds a little confused.

"He says 'yes.' Mr. Olstroski had been getting close to a few of the single women on set. He had tried to hit on a few of the married ones too, but their husbands put a quick stop to that. What the hell's going on here?"

"I'm honestly not sure yet. I think there is more to Mr. Olstroski than any of us know." Freddy hears his cell phone vibrate on his desk. He glances down at it. It is an email from Margaret Slythe. He smiles. "And I think I know how to find him. Oscar, thanks for your help. Tell Mr. Hamm that I truly believe he did not do this. Bye."

"Of course he did, Fa…"

Freddy hangs up the phone. He sucks down the remains of his coffee, sets the empty cup in the basin of the sink, and heads out the door.

***

The officer leads Hampton down the hall to the foot of a set of stairs leading up. This was the first time he had seen these stairs since Freddy lead him down them. That seemed as if it were eons ago. At this point, he just wants to see a calendar. He needs to know how long he had been in that cell. They claim he isn't arrested. They have not read him his rights. They claim he is being detained. It doesn't feel that way to him. This phone call had been the first time he heard the name Freddy Falcon since he arrived at his cell. If this is the person working hard to prove he did not do this, why had he not heard a word from the detective until now?

He shrugs it off as the officer leads him up the stairs. At this point, he no longer cared. As far as he was concerned, his life ended when he found Marcus lying on the rug. He could care less what happens to him moving forward.

The officer opens the door at the top of the stairs. He motions for Hampton to walk through. He walks through and realizes where he is. The detective's office is up ahead on the left. They are not heading in that direction. The officer leads him right. They are heading toward the opposite side of the building.

They arrive at one of the interrogation rooms. The officer opens the door and motions for him to enter. The room is small. No decorations on any of the white walls. The wall on the right does have a large mirror on it. He had seen enough television to know this is no ordinary mirror. This is a two-way mirror. There would be people on the other side watching the interrogation. Possibly even recording it with a camera.

A small, rectangular table sits in the center of the room. Two sets of chairs are on either side of the long ends of the table. The officer motions for him to sit on the opposite side of the table, facing the door.

"You haven't been charged. Yet."

"It sure does feel like it," he replies.

"Trust me," the officer says, "I would not be this gentile if you were. Just relax, Mr. Hamm. The captain will arrive shortly."

The officer leaves the room, closing the door behind him.

Relax? How could he relax? His husband is murdered. He is being detained, possibly arrested. The cops think he either did this or knows what happened. The only officer who claims to believe him hasn't spoken with him in... however long he has been here. How could he relax?

***

Captain Youngblood stands in front of the glass, looking into interrogation room three. He watches Oscar lead the suspect into the room. His eyes are more on the suspect than anything else. How far could he push this guy to get answers out of him? How far would this man take his ruse? How long would he deny what he did? How long could he keep it up with all of the evidence pointing directly at him? Freddy wants facts? The facts are, the only person at the scene is this man. The one person the victim trusted most had just been lead into this interrogation room. All of the facts are there. What more could Freddy want?

The door behind him opens. He glances back to see Freddy's red hair. The detective closes the door and walks over to stand beside him.

"You believe he didn't do this?" The captain asks.

"There is no doubt in my mind."

He understands Freddy is capable of separating himself from his cases. He needs to be sure the man isn't personalizing this particular case.

"Falcon, I have to ask…"

"It's not, Captain. It has nothing to do with what happened to Harry. I know I can't prove it yet, but I know this man did not murder his husband."

How could he know? There is no proof. The captain prefers facts and evidence. He knows Freddy relies a lot on his hunches and feelings. He also knows that Freddy is almost always correct to do so. But he can't release this man on a hunch.

"How the hell can you know? You weren't there to witness it. Aren't you the one who loves to point out that a person can't know something for a fact unless they see it first hand?"

"Call it a feeling. An intuition. I dunno. Psychic powers or some shit. I know, for a fact, that this man did not murder his husband. I can feel it."

"Falcon, I trust you. I trust your intuition. It has never failed you. You know things and can figure things out before the evidence is there to back you up. And it's always there. It always appears at the right time to back up your intuition."

"Then why fight me on this, sir?"

"Because this is getting bigger than you and I. I need proof to present to the mayor and, possibly, the media. I can't go to the mayor and say, 'My lead detective believes Mr. Hamm did not kill his husband because of a feeling.' I would be thrown out on the spot."

"I understand that Captain."

"Do you?"

They both are watching Hampton while they talk. The man looks uncomfortable and nervous. He sits back. He folds his hands on the table. After a moment, he crosses his arms. He sits forward again. He keeps looking at the mirror. The man repositions himself a few times. He sits forward again, laying his arms on the table with his right hand resting on his left arm. He stays that way for a while before sitting back and crossing his arms again.

"Does that look like an innocent man to you?"

"It looks like a man who has no idea what is going on and is afraid he is going to be charged with a murder he did not commit."

Captain Youngblood smiles. "That, Falcon, we agree on. Well, we have kept Mr. Hamm waiting long enough."

Captain Youngblood turns toward the door. He glances at the camera facing the glass. He flips the switch to start the recording.

"Falcon, I do hope you are correct."

The captain closes the door behind him, leaving the fiery redhead to watch the show.

***

Hampton keeps fidgeting. He can't figure out what to do with his hands. He continually swaps between folding his hands on the table and folding his arms. He keeps looking at the mirror on the wall, wondering who is on the other side. Is Freddy over there? He almost wants to wave but decides against it.

He finally settles on resting his arms on the table. He places his right hand on his left arm. He wonders what he will say. It almost feels like a job interview. Is he supposed to say what is on his mind? Is he supposed to say what they want him to say? He finally decides. He has nothing to hide. He will speak his mind. He sits back and folds his arms. He sits like that as he waits.

The door opens a few minutes later. In walks a tall, thin black man with a bald head. He smiles as he closes the door and walks toward the table. The man is not dressed as an officer. He is wearing a button-up collared shirt and dress pants. His clothes look neatly pressed. There are no wrinkles. Nothing is out of place. He walks with authority. Hampton can see the confidence in the man's stature. This must be the captain.

"Hello, Mr. Hamm. I am Captain Youngblood."

The captain is soft-spoken, but there is a sternness to his voice. The man sits down across from him. Hampton does not say a word.

"I want to start by saying that I am deeply sorry for your loss...."

***

Freddy stands on the other side of the glass, watching. He shakes his head.

"That's the last thing he wants to hear."

***

Hampton raises his right hand. "Please don't give me false sentiment."

The captain pauses. He sees the confusion on the man's face.

"I'm sorry?"

He sits back a moment in thought. He chose his next words carefully.

"Have you ever lost anyone, Captain?"

"Of course I have. I am a police captain. What does that..."

He shakes his head. "No. I mean, have you ever lost a spouse? A wife? A husband? A girlfriend? A boyfriend? Perhaps even one of your children? Have you had to watch the person you cherish more than anything else die in front of your eyes? Do you know that pain? Do you know that feeling?"

***

Freddy smiles. He says to no one in particular, "Careful with this. The captain will crush you if you are not careful. But keep going."

***

The captain shakes his head. "No. I can't say that I have."

"Trust me when I say this; nobody wants to hear that 'I'm sorry for your loss' crap. It's a false sentiment that people say when they don't know what else to say."

"We are not here to talk about me or the emotional state of someone in grief. We are here to discuss the events leading up to your husband's murder."

Hampton freezes for a moment. That statement hit him to the core. It brought back the memory of that night for a second. He shakes it off. He hoped the captain didn't notice.

***

"Shake it off," Freddy says. "He's trying to get a reaction out of you."

Freddy notices Hampton's reaction at the mention of his husband's murder. He notes that the captain sees it as well, and as a true professional, Captain Youngblood plays it off as if he didn't notice.

***

Captain Youngblood sits back in his chair. He keeps his face emotionless.

"I've read Detective Falcon's report of the events of that night. Now, rest assured that we are working hard at bringing his murderer to justice. Detective Falcon has been following up on a few leads to track this person down…."

"Then why am I the one behind bars?" Hampton asks.

"It comes down to the evidence. As of right now, the only evidence we have points to you."

He observes Mr. Hamm carefully. The man repositions himself. He could see the man getting a little nervous. It wouldn't be much longer before he would get his confession.

"Mr. Hamm, I would like to know, in your own words, what happened that night."

***

Freddy watches Hampton explain the events of that night. This is illuminating for him as well. He is learning details that never came up during his conversations with Hampton. Perhaps the captain is correct. Perhaps he is getting too close.

***

"So, you two had an argument that night?"

"I wouldn't call it an argument," Hampton says.

"Then what would you call it?"

"I was angry at him. I was furious."

"Because he told you to shut up? That sounds a little extreme, to react the way you did. Don't you think?"

Hampton shakes his head. This guy doesn't understand. "No. It had nothing to do with that, exactly."

"Then what is it, exactly?" the captain asks.

"Look, Marcus and I loved each other more than words could express. We had our differences. Everybody does. We've known each other for twenty-five years. During that time, we have had our rough patches. Marcus is passionate about his work. I enjoy working with him, but sometimes he can be harder on me than any other cast member. I had my butt on my shoulders that night. I'll admit that. I was angry with him for no reason."

"Angry enough to kill him?"

***

"What the hell kind of question is that?" Freddy asks no one. He could feel his temperature rise. He breaths slowly and composes himself.

***

Captain Youngblood let the suspect see his smile. He wanted to see the man's reactions. The captain knows the man will deny it. There is a slight chance the guilt would be too much for him.

He observes the man carefully. He can see drops of sweat form on the man's forehead and roll down his cheeks. His hands and arms start to shake slightly. The suspect repositions himself again in the chair. He had him. The guilt is gnawing at him.

"I loved my husband. I still love my husband. My soul died that night. I cannot express in words what I am going through. I did not. I could not. I...I…"

The man hangs his head and starts to cry. The captain sits there, stoic. He watches the suspect. After a few minutes, the man wipes the tears away with his arm and composes himself.

"Am I under arrest?"

The captain shakes his head. "No."

"Then I am leaving."

He watches as the man stands. Mr. Hamm walks around the table toward the door. He waits until the man's hand is on the doorknob.

"There's just one more thing I don't understand."

***

"Oh shit," Freddy says. "What does he have? Here it comes."

***

Hampton removes his hand from the doorknob. He turns around to face the captain. What else could this man possibly have to say?

"What?" Hampton asks.

The captain motioned toward the chair Hampton had been sitting in.

"Would you mind having a seat for a moment?"

***

Freddy shakes his head. "Don't do it. You're almost there. Just leave. You aren't under arrest. You don't have to say a damn word. Just leave."

***

Hampton exhales and reluctantly returns to the chair he had been sitting in. He watches as the captain pulls out his phone and calls someone.

"Bring it in."

The door opens a few minutes later. In walks the short, gruff officer who had brought him into the interrogation room. Hampton immediately recognizes the folder in the man's hand. The officer hands Detective Falcon's folder to the captain and durns to leave.

"Oscar," the captain says. "Stay a moment."

The officer nods. He stands next to the closed door with his arms folded.

"Thank you," the captain says.

The captain opens up the folder and starts thumbing through it.

"Do you know what this is?"

Hampton nods. "This is Detective Falcon's evidence folder."

"Correct. This folder contains everything that we know, so far, about this case."

This got him a little excited. He knows they would have been speaking with everyone who is involved with the film. Perhaps they talked to Adam. Maybe they talked to Jacob. Maybe they called Juliana. She would shed some light on this.

"So, you spoke with Juliana then?"

The captain looks up in genuine surprise.

"Juliana?" He looks through the folder. "Ah, Juliana Martinez. She was a member of thc cast, correct?"

Hampton shakes his head. "No. I mean, yeah, she is…"

"No. It says here that she is in Germany filming a movie."

"She is."

"Then why would we speak with her? She isn't here. She didn't do it."

"But she can clarify things."

"How?"

"A character witness."

The captain smiles. "A character witness?"

Hampton nods.

"So, I take it you are admitting guilt then?"

Hampton shakes his head. Panic shows all over his face.

"I mean as a way to defend my character in this matter. To help clear things up."

"Mr. Hamm, the only time you should need your character defended is if you are on trial for murder. Should you be?"

Hampton shakes his head. He takes a breath before speaking again.

"Has anyone spoken with Adam?"

The captain thumbs through the folder again. "Adam Greenbriar?"

Hampton nods.

"No. Not yet." The captain sits back. "Why?"

"This was one of the things we argued about. You need to speak with Adam."

"Why?"

"It's a long story."

"Humor me. We have plenty of time."

The captain folds his hands behind his head and leans back.

"Marcus and Adam were best friends at one time."

"Were?" the captain asks.

Hampton nods.

***

"Oh my God…" At that moment, Freddy knows exactly what Hampton is about to say. The memories of this exact conversation come flooding back.

***

The captain is a little confused. "So, he hired his best friend. I mean, I'm not from Hollywood, but I do watch movies. I know that directors do have actors they enjoy working with. Alfred Hitchcock, Mel Brooks, Quinton Tarantino, Kevin Smith. It happens all the time."

"No, you don't understand."

"Then help me understand."

"They were best friends. Something happened years ago that ruptured that friendship."

He watches as the man hangs his head again. This time there is no crying. This is actual guilt the man is feeling. Guilt for what? His husband's murder or something else? He listens as the suspect continues. His head down and his tone somber.

"There has only been one time in the past twenty-five years that I honestly thought I was going to lose Marcus. One time that I hurt and betrayed him deeply. He would have had every right to leave me. I mean, it did cause us to split up. He didn't speak to me for a full year after that. It killed his friendship with Adam."

"You cheated on your husband with his best friend."

Hampton nods. "We weren't married then. He chased me for ten years. We dated for a year after finally got together. Then I...I...I'm sorry, Marcus."

The captain leans forward, folding his hands on the table.

"Then why would he hire this guy for his movie?"

"Marcus always believed in second chances. It is the same with Jacob."

"Jacob Wexler?"

Mr. Hamm nods. "Marcus always felt guilty for what happened to Jacob's career."

The captain thumbs through Freddy's notes until he finds the notes on his interview with Wexler.

"You're talking about what happened on the set of *Collision Course*."

The man nods. "We argued a lot back then. Jacob blamed the media's coverage of our bickering on his failed career. He was partially correct. He was 'poison' in Hollywood after that. No film studio wanted him. His agent fired him. He was the lead in a movie surrounded by a scandal. Nobody wanted him tainting their projects."

“I will never understand the film industry. I remember the media’s coverage of that. You and your husband were the center of that. Your careers should have been in jeopardy. Not his.”

“We didn’t come out of that unscathed. We had to borrow money to fund any projects we attempted to work on. It took us years before any studio would speak with us. And they wouldn’t work with us together. We worked separately. In fact, this is the first project we have been engaged in together since then.

“We worked ourselves back, Captain. Jacob, on the other hand, wallowed in self-pity for years. Like a phoenix rising from the ashes, he finally emerged to the greatness he once was. Marcus gave him a second chance and an apology.”

“So, he asked Adam Greenbriar to work on the film after you both betrayed him? That doesn’t make sense.”

“As I said, Marcus is extremely forgiving. He had gotten past that years ago. Actually, Marcus didn’t ask Adam. Adam auditioned.”

“Oh? And you were fine with this? It doesn’t bring back any old feelings? You didn’t want to leave your husband for Mr. Greenbriar? Perhaps rekindle some lost fling?”

“I love my husband, Captain. I did tell Marcus I didn’t think this was a good idea. It wasn’t because I thought I would commit adultery or anything. It is because I didn’t trust Adam. I told Marcus that I refused to be on set during any scene with Adam in it. I wanted to be as far from him as I could be. Marcus trusted him. I did not.”

“So, you loved your husband and would never harm him?”

“I love my husband. Present tense. I still love him. And no, I don’t have it in me.”

“Not even for money?”

***

“Shit! He found the damn insurance policy,” Freddy says.

***

Hampton freezes. He is confused. What is this man talking about?

"Money? I don't understand. What money?"

The captain thumbs through the folder and stops on a page. The document's title is upside down, but Hampton knows this is the insurance policy he had on Marcus.

The document is in a transparent sleeve. The captain removes it and places it in front of Hampton.

"Do you recognize this?" he asks.

Hampton nods. "This is a life insurance policy on Marcus."

"Naming you as the sole beneficiary in the event of his death."

"I don't understand. It's normal for couples to take out life insurance policies on each other. He had one for me in case I died."

"Is it normal for it to be a five million dollar policy?"

Hampton freezes. Five million? It is only a million. Enough to pay off the house, bury Marcus and give Hampton a cushion to get back on his feet. They had the same for Marcus.

"It's only a million."

The captain grabs the policy and reads it. "It is for five million. It was modified one week before filming began," he says.

"Modified? That's not possible. I would have to have…"

"You did sign it." He turns the signature page around to where Hampton can see his name. "Is that your signature?"

"Yes, but I didn't…"

The captain places the document back in the sleeve and closes the folder. He turns to the officer at the door.

"Oscar, read him his rights."

***

"Shit!"

Freddy runs out the door and bursts into the interrogation room.

"Falcon, what the hell are you doing here?" Oscar asks.

"Freddy?" Hampton looked confused.

"He didn't do this, Captain. You're holding him based on an insurance policy? What about the other folks he mentioned? What about Adam Greenbriar? Richard Olstroski is still out there, thanks to incompetence..."

Oscar's face turns red. Freddy could see Oscar about to speak. The captain raised his hand.

"Enough! Falcon, get out."

Freddy steps between Oscar and Hampton.

"Falcon, move before I have you moved. Let Oscar do his job."

"The hell I will! You're wrong on this, dammit! He didn't commit the damn murder!"

The captain speaks in a calm tone. "If you ever speak to me like that again, I'll have you busted down to traffic cop faster than you can blink. Move, and let Oscar arrest the man."

Freddy backs away. He watches as Oscar asks Hampton to place his hands on his head. Oscar put each of the man's arms behind his back and cuffed his wrists. Oscar read Hampton his rights. He watches as Oscar escorts Hampton out of the interrogation room. The door closed shut with a "thud."

Freddy just stood there in silence. The captain walks over and places his hand on Freddy's shoulder.

"Do I need to remove you from this case?"

He shakes his head.

"I have to ask. Is this too personal? Are you too close?"

He shakes his head.

"Don't ever talk to me like that again. Especially in front of a suspect or a fellow officer. Understand?"

He nods.

"Do you honestly believe this man did not murder his husband?"

He nods.

"Alright. Prove it then. That's the only reason you still have your position after that stunt. I promise you this. If you ever pull another stunt like this again, I will have your badge. Do you understand?"

He nods.

The captain left him alone in the interrogation room.

Chapter Twelve

Better Call Sal

The captain is wrong. Freddy isn't too close. He isn't making it personal. He is defeated. He had been from the beginning. The moment Hampton was arrested is the moment it all sinks in. It all hit him like a ton of bricks. He had been going so fast down one track that he didn't stop to think if it was the right track. It is time for this train of thoughts to switch tracks.

He had been down this road once before. It was the day he took Hampton in. He had promised himself, then, he would slow down and look at other avenues. Everything keeps bringing him back to Richard Olstroski. What is his connection to all of this? Why had he lied? Why did he run? Where is he? All of these questions, and more, will be answered on the next episode of *Freddy Doesn't Have a Freaking Clue*.

This thought helped him remember the email from Margaret Slythe. He opens his email on his phone and pulls up the message.

Detective Fallon,

Below is the link to the website I use to track Richard. I created a personalized link just for you. This should give you enough access to locate his exact position.

"My last name is in my email address. Whatever. At least she is cooperating."

He will never understand why this woman is with someone like Richard Olstroski. She is not just out of his league but in a completely different sport with her education and stature. It isn't for him to judge, and, frankly, he doesn't care. Whatever worked for them.

This will be a good follow-up for Shawn and Eddy. They are familiar with this part of the case. This will free him up to follow other leads. He is more concerned with this Adam Greenbriar. Also, he thinks it is time he reviewed all of the evidence found in the house. That's one rookie move he should not have made. All this time, and he had yet to review the evidence found or speak with the damn coroner.

He reaches into his pocket to grab his phone. There is nothing there.

"Not again."

He pats himself down. Nothing. No wallet. No phone. No keys. How could he have no keys? He looks around and does not recognize his surroundings. He had his phone a second ago. He was reading the email. Did he drop it? Where is his car? He remembers standing by his car outside of a coffee shop. Where is the coffee? Wait a damn minute, he thinks. He had a cup of coffee in one hand as he was reading the email from Margaret Slythe. What's going on?

He realizes he is walking through a forest. Where did the buildings go? He looks up at the sky. It is pitch black. No stars or moon in sight. He knows that is odd. The sun was out a moment ago. Freddy keeps moving forward. He can not see anything except trees. Hundreds of trees. He thinks he can hear voices. They aren't clear, but they are voices. He strains to listen.

"Don't go that way."

He freezes. It sounds like. It can't be. He moves forward.

"You're going the wrong way."

The voice is clearer this time. Closer. He keep walking.

"Are ya deaf, son? I said not to go down that path."

It is him. There is no denying it is his voice.

"Papa?" Freddy asks.

"Choose a different path."

"Papa, I can't see a thing. Just these trees. This is the only path I can see."

"Step back, son. Look at the entire forest. Look at all of the paths before you."

"Papa, I've failed."

"Close your eyes and trust your instincts, Freddy."

"What?"

"Don't sass me, boy! Do it."

Freddy does just that. He closes his eyes and stands there. Freddy feels his body relax. He clears his mind. After a moment, he opens his eyes. There it is. A small path to the right. It wasn't there before. He shrugs and decides to follow it. There is a clearing up ahead. This isn't a clearing in the woods. It is...

"Hampton Hamm's living room?"

Now he is confused. He looked behind him. The forest is gone. All he sees is Hampton's kitchen. He looks out the sliding glass door. It is still pitch-black outside. At his feet lay…

"A wine bottle?"

There is an empty wine bottle on the exact spot where Marcus Peterson's body had been found. Red wine puddles on the rug matching the pattern of the victim's blood. He picks up the wine bottle to get a closer look. Instead of the bottle, he is now holding a shoe. Not just any shoe. This is the smelly shoe that Shawn had found in the house.

***

Freddy's alarm startles him awake. He rolls over and turns it off. He sits up on the side of his bed. That is one messed-up dream. One thing is clear. He needs to concentrate on the evidence.

He had read Margaret Slythe's email earlier. Somehow it had made it into his dream. Why can't he dream that she got his name correct? The forest he understood. What the hell was up with the wine bottle? Had they found a wine bottle in the house? Had Marcus Peterson been drinking that night? Hampton hadn't said anything about that. And what does that have to do with the shoe?

One thing is obvious. He needs to call Shawn. He walks over to his desk and grabs his phone from the charger. He finds Shawn's contact and calls.

"Hello? Freddy? What time is it? Shit! Eight o'clock! Whatcha got for me?"

"Well, good morning to you too," Freddy says with a smile. "Can you do me a favor?"

"Shoot."

"You will never believe this. I spoke with Richard Olstroski's wife. She has a GPS tracker on him."

"You're yanking my chain? Wait. You serious?"

Freddy grins. "Yup." He pops the "P" on the word for effect. "So, I would like for you and Eddy to track him down for me. I'm forwarding you the email she sent me. All you should have to do is click the link. It's supposed to open a map or something. Whatever it does, it allows you to track him."

"You haven't tried it yet?"

"I still use pen and paper for all of my notes. You know me and electronics."

"Yep. Like oil and water. Sure, Freddy. We'll find him for ya."

"Thanks, Shawn. Later."

He ends the call. He opens the email that Margaret Slythe sent him and forwards it to Shawn. His message reads:

Shawn,

This is Freddy. Here's the link that Ms. Slythe sent me. I'm not sure how this works, but you can use it to track Mr. Olstroski. I want him brought in for questioning the moment you find him.

Thanks,

Freddy Falcon

He throws his phone on his bed. He grabs a blue golf shirt and slacks from his closet and lays them on the bed. He grabs a fresh towel and heads for the bathroom for a nice warm shower.

The warm water flows over his body. He can feel all of his muscles relax. He starts thinking about his dream. He understands the forest. Perhaps his subconscious told him he could not see the entire picture because he is focuses on specific minute details. What is with the wine bottle? Is his mind giving him clues?

He starts to chuckle. "Clues," he says as he does his best imitation of Scooby-Dum. He never cared for that character, but he finds the moment funny. He shakes it off and continues his thinking on the case.

He doesn't remember seeing a wine bottle in the house. He didn't check the liquor cabinet either. Is there a liquor cabinet? Is there something more to this smelly shoe? He assumed it is a red herring.

He shrugs it all off. It's just a dream, after all. Just his mind sorting out the details of the case. The most he takes from it is that he needs to focus more on the entire case.

He finishes his shower and gets dressed.

"No better time to call the coroner," he says as he grabbed his phone.

"Terra Loch Coroner," a voice answers.

"This is Detective Falcon. I'm investigating the murder of Marcus Peterson."

"Freddy!" the voice says excitedly. "It's Sal. How are ya?"

Freddy recognizes the voice now. It is Salvador Cantino. Sal did the autopsy on Freddy's first few murder cases. He and Sal were about the same age. Sal is divorced with three children. Heather would be about seventeen now. The twins, Marc and Jeffrey, would be around twelve.

Sal stands about 5-5. The last time Freddy saw him, the man weighed 460 pounds and had short, black hair. It is good to hear a friendly voice. Sal knows how he works. He will be willing to assist in any capacity he is able to help.

"Sal! It's been a few years. I'm well, my friend. How are you?"

"I'm good. Still single."

"Are you dating?"

"Nope. Kids come first. Cheryl and I agreed not to date anyone until the kids were grown and out. It is hard enough on them bouncing between the two of us. We don't want to make it harder."

Sal and Cheryl separated on good terms. They both stayed friends after the divorce. They never could make the marriage work. There is no animosity between the two. They both still love each other. Both realized they work better as friends then as a couple.

"So, you two still keep in touch?"

"All the time. We talk once a week on the phone, and we still have our morning breakfast together the first Saturday of every month."

"I will never understand why you two divorced. You get along so well."

"Freddy, trust me. We work better as friends."

He decided not to press it and to change the subject.

"How are the kids?" Freddy asks.

"They're good. Heather is a senior this year. She wants to study computer programming in college. The twins are a handful, though. Marc plays baseball. I coach his team. I can't keep Jeffrey off of the video games. He'd rather stay in his room on those damn video games than do anything outside. I think he's allergic to the sunlight." He chuckles at that.

"None of them want to join the police force?"

"Nah. Not dealing with dead bodies either."

"I don't blame them there," Freddy says with a smile.

He hears Sal laugh on the other end of the line. "So, how can I help ya, Freddy?"

"Do you know who did the autopsy for Marcus Peterson?"

"The dead director?"

"Yup."

"That was me. Whatcha need?"

"Do you still have his body?"

"Yup. He's in cold storage. We aren't allowed to release him due to the ongoing investigation."

"Good. I'll be there shortly. I want to talk to you about this, and I want to see his body for myself."

"I'll be here."

"Perfect. I'll see you in a few."

"Have a good one, my friend."

Freddy ends the call. He receives an email notification from Shawn that reads:

You don't have to tell me the email is from you, Freddy. I can clearly see it is sent from your email. Oil and water, my friend :) We're on it for you, though.

He places his phone in his pants pocket. He grabs his wallet, keys, and notebook as he heads out the door.

***

The coroner is a few blocks away from The Farmhouse on North Carolina Boulevard. Carolina Boulevard and Dakota Avenue are the only streets in town named directly for the states. North Carolina stops at Congress north of the lake. South Carolina is a separate road, south of the lake. Sal's father originally opened the business as a mortuary. He started working with the police as an official coroner in the

1990's. He kept the mortuary running as a side business. Sal started out working in the mortuary for his dad. He took over the entire business when his father retired ten years ago.

Freddy walks in and smiles at the man behind the counter. He starts to introduce himself when the man interrupts.

"Freddy! It's good to see you, my friend!"

He is the right height for Sal. He has short, black hair. The voice is correct for the man he knows. But it looks as if Sal had switched bodies with a completely different person. This man looked no more than 160 pounds soaking wet.

"Sal?" he inquired.

The man with Sal's voice hesitates for a second. He can see the man work out the confusion and finally realizes why Freddy is confused.

"Ah. You haven't seen me in, what, three years? I had weight loss surgery two years ago."

"Wow. You look like a completely different person."

"You should see me with my shirt off. That would change your opinion."

"What do you mean?"

"I can't afford to have the plastic surgery that would take care of the excess skin. Insurance won't pay for it. They see it as cosmetic or some bullshit. I don't know. So, I have a skin flap."

"Like Adam Sandler in *Click*?"

Sal shakes his head and chuckles. "No. That is exaggerated. It's not as pronounced."

"Ah. Well, I want to say that you look good, but you never looked bad. You've always been cute."

Sal blushed and quickly changed the subject. "How can I help you, Freddy?"

He waits a moment before responding. Realization shows on the man's face.

"That's right." He shakes his head. "I'm sorry. It's been one of those days. I completely forgot we spoke earlier. Marcus Peterson, right?"

Freddy nods. "That's right."

"This way."

Sal leads Freddy through the building and to a back room. The man pulls a chain hanging from the ceiling. A single light bulb illuminates the small room. Along the far wall stands the cold lockers. Sal puts on a pair of gloves and hands Freddy a pair. He slips on the gloves Sal gave him.

Sal opens one of the lockers, numbered forty-seven. He slides out the table the body is lying on. Freddy realizes this is the first time he has viewed Marcus Peterson. The body had already been extracted from the house before his arrival. He is taller than Freddy expected. He takes into account the natural process a body goes through hours after death. Based on the look of the cadaver in front of him, he could tell that in life, Mr. Peterson would have been an entire foot taller than Mr. Hamm. The man had been exceptionally fit as well. He could imagine this man's physique in life. Mr. Peterson would have been tall, thin, and muscular. He understands why Mr. Hamm found the man attractive.

He remembers Hampton saying he found his husband holding his side. He checks both sides of the body. There it is. A small puncture wound. It looks as if the man had been stabbed with something fairly dull. It appears as if the assailant was possibly aiming for his appendix but did not have the general knowledge of human anatomy. The wound looks to be a few inches deep. He does not recognize the type of object that could cause this.

"What could cause a wound like this? It isn't a knife. I don't think anything in the house would have causes it."

Sal is on the other side of the cadaver, leaning in as well. "We aren't sure, actually. I have a wild hypothesis, though."

"A hypothesis? What is it?"

"It's a supposition or proposed explanation made on the basis of limited evidence, as a starting point for further investigation."

Freddy rolls his eyes and let out a sigh. "I know what a hypothesis is. What is your hypothesis?"

Sal replies, "No. It's too ridiculous to be true. It's the kind of thing you would see in a novel."

"Humor me."

"It's impossible to be the case."

"Nothing's impossible, Sal. Improbable. Unlikely. Never impossible."

The man sighs and reluctantly replies. "Cheryl used to read a lot of those romance novels. A few of them were murder mysteries. I knew you would think this was stupid."

He realizes the man saw his eye roll. He shakes his head as he speaks. "No. It's not that. I'm interested in your hypothesis. The eye roll is because I never took Cheryl as the romance novel type."

He chuckles. "Yeah. She used to read them for a while. Anyway, one of these books will always stand out to me. She was always telling me the plots, and I pretended to care. But this one just seemed too ridiculous. As a mortician, it always stuck with me."

Freddy is a little annoyed the man is not getting to the point. "Well? What is it?"

"A stiletto."

"A what?"

"It's a high-heeled shoe. The heels come in varying sizes…."

"I know what a stiletto is. I'm just surprised."

He leans down to examine the hole. "It's possible. But…why would...where would...how? You don't happen to have a stiletto heel, do you?"

"I'm a divorced man with three kids. What the hell would I do with a stiletto? Dress in drag and do the hula?"

He let out a laugh. Sal glares at him. He shakes it off and composes himself.

"You never tested your hypothesis?"

Sal shakes his head. "What the hell? Do you think this is my first day on the job? Why would I? It's a silly thought from a ridiculous romance novel. No person in their right mind would try to…."

"I never exclude anything without testing it. Doesn't matter how insane the hypothesis sounds. It may be the correct outcome. Anyway, is there anything out of the ordinary found in his body?"

"Well, there were large amounts of arsenic found in his blood."

"Arsenic? What the hell? Why didn't you lead with that?"

"Well, arsenic in the body is normal. Several types of food or drink naturally contain arsenic. Vegetables, fruits, rice, grains, juices. It seeps into them from the ground. I didn't think it was out of the ordinary. It could have come from his diet."

Freddy's dream flashes back to him. The picture of the empty wine bottle on the rug. "Grapes. Can grapes or wine contain arsenic?"

"Absolutely. Arsenic is found in all types of wine. It's natural. Gets into the grapes from the ground. Why do you ask?"

"Call it a wild hunch, but I think Mr. Peterson was poisoned."

Sal lets out a hearty laugh.

"What's so funny?" Freddy asks.

Sal shakes his head. "There isn't enough arsenic in his system to account for poisoning. Sure, it's there, but to actually murder someone…."

"How much are we talking about then?"

"It would have to be a slow poisoning over time. Certainly, more than a bottle of wine would contain. If someone could die from arsenic poisoning from wine, we would have a hell of a lot of drunks dead from arsenic poisoning."

"Well, from your experience, what do you think killed him?"

"Simple. He bled to death."

"From what?" he asks in an annoyed tone. No shit the man bled to death.

Sal points to the wound.

"I mean, what caused the wound?"

The man shakes his head. "We don't know."

Freddy sighs. "That wound did cause problems and a lot of blood loss, but I don't believe that is the cause of death. Thank you, Sal. I'm not sure who yet, but I do believe I know how."

The man still looked confused. "Didn't y'all arrest his husband?"

Freddy shakes his head. "He didn't do it, Sal. Anyway, did you find traces of wine in his system?"

Sal nods. "Actually, we did. No excessive amounts. It appears as if he had been drinking shortly before the time of death."

"What do you mean? Mr. Hamm found him around three o'clock in the morning. He was still alive when he was found."

"I'm telling you, the amount of wine that is in his system, he had to have downed an entire bottle no more than a half-hour before death."

"Wait. So, he decided to get drunk after he was brutally attacked, or…."

"Or he was drunk when he was murdered. That's my assumption."

"Attempted murder. It's obvious the wound did not kill him. I honestly think it was arsenic."

"It wasn't arsenic. He showed no symptoms of arsenic poisoning. This isn't some sort of a murder mystery novel, Freddy. This is real life. Arsenic poisoning isn't a quick death. It's a long, drawn-out process over time. Plus, he would have had other symptoms."

"Such as?"

"Abdominal pain. Nausea. Vomiting. Diarrhea. Vertigo. Cardiac issues. Mr. Peterson had no records of any of this. If it is arsenic, as you suspect, then there is only one person that was around him long enough to do it."

"He didn't do it, Sal! Was there still enough alcohol in his system to show he was drunk at the time of death?"

Sal nods. “Yeah. He was definitely drunk. As I said, that is my conclusion.”

“Well, he certainly didn’t get drunk after he was attacked. That leaves one conclusion. He was murdered shortly before Mr. Hamm woke up. The killer was still in the area, possibly watching the house when Mr. Hamm found him.”

“Or Mr. Hamm murdered his husband and is lying about the entire thing.”

Freddy looked annoyed. “He didn’t do it, Sal. Anyway, I think I have learned all I can. Thank you.”

Both men remove their gloves and dispose of them. Freddy shakes Sal’s hand and leaves.

***

Back in his office, he desperately searches his desk for the smelly shoe found at the crime scene. He remembers checking it out of evidence before the Richard Olstroski interview. He had decided not to worry about the shoe after speaking with Mr. Olstroski. He concluded the shoe belonged to the wretched smelling man. Once Freddy deduced the man could not have murdered Mr. Peterson, he had disregarded the shoe completely.

Had he been wrong about Richard Olstroski? Did this shoe play more of a part in this mystery? It is a man’s dress shoe. There wouldn’t be a high heel on it. But, there is something about that shoe that Freddy can’t place. Something odd about it. Where is that shoe?

He searches every nook and cranny of his desk. There is no sign of the shoe. Had he returned it to evidence? He doesn’t remember doing that. So much has happened since this case began. It is hard to tell what he had and hadn’t done. He sits down at his desk to call down to evidence. That’s when he sees it. The plastic evidence bag behind his chair.

He grabs a pair of gloves and places them on his hands. He puts the bag on his desk. Before opening this bag, he decides on grabbing a nose plug. That stench is probably permeating that bag by now. He wants to ensure it would not knock him unconscious.

"Where am I going to get a nose plug?"

That's when he remembers the chip clip on one of the bags of chips in his pantry. It had been opened by Shawn the last time the man had been in his office. He grabs the clip off of the bag and sits back down at his desk. The clip is a clothespin. He had purchased a few clothespins when his chip clips had suddenly "disappeared."

"Why does this suddenly feel like the solution to a puzzle in a point-and-click adventure game from the '90s?"

He places the clothespin on his nose and winces at the pain. He could withstand the pain. Better a little pain than to be knocked unconscious from the stench inside this bag. He carefully opens the bag and removes the shoe.

It is a brown men's dress shoe. There are laces to lace it up. Nothing out of the ordinary. It appears to be a size ten or eleven. It is a left shoe. They never did find the right one.

Freddy turns the shoe over for a closer examination. That's when he notices it. The heel of the shoe is raised, but it isn't the standard large block style. This heel is thinner. It isn't as thin as a woman's heel would be. This heel is more of a slim square shape. He grabs a ruler from his desk drawer and measures the heel. It is exactly three inches.

"Sal, my good friend, you may be onto something here."

He places the shoe back and seals the bag. He removes his gloves and the clothespin and throws them all in the garbage. That is not going back on the bag of chips after being on his nose.

He makes a cup of coffee from one of the pods he had and sits back down at his desk. He sits back and starts munching on the chips. He pulls out his phone and looks up the number for a nearby men's clothing store.

"Tailored by Taylor. This is Malcolm. How may I help you?". It sounds like an older gentleman. He is a little soft-spoken as well.

"Hello, Malcolm. This is Freddy Falcon. I am a detective with The Farmhouse. Do you have a moment for a question or two?"

"The Farmhouse?" The voice on the other end sounds hesitant.

Freddy chuckles. "Yeah, that's what we call our station on the northeast side of town. It is built on the site of an old farmhouse. I sometimes forget that not everyone in town is familiar with it.

"How may I be of assistance, Detective?"

"How familiar are you with a men's dress shoe?"

"I started this business over forty years ago, Detective. I would say I am an expert in men's fashion. Well, real fashion, that is. Not this tripe these young kids call fashion."

"I see." Freddy knows fashion is constantly changing. He doesn't share the man's beliefs that there is only one "correct" style. He is wearing a golf shirt with a breast pocket, a pair of blue jeans, and tennis shoes. "Have you heard of a men's dress shoe with a three-inch square heel?"

"Are you sure you aren't mistaking this for a woman's shoe, Detective?" Freddy could hear the disdain in his voice.

"Does a woman's heel typically look like a man's lace-up dress shoe?" Freddy asks, annoyed.

"Not typically, Detective. I am no expert on women's shoes."

"Is something like this mass-produced, or would these be more custom made?"

"I would assume the shoes you have would be custom made. No manufacturer mass produces shoes with heels as you describe them. Perhaps talk to a cobbler."

"Thank you, sir. Have a wonderful day."

He hears the receiver on the other end hang up. He hears the "click" of a landline phone. Freddy hung up the phone and sits back. He folds his hands on his chest and leans back in his chair in thought.

A cobbler? There's no point in speaking with a cobbler. He has all of the information he needs to confirm this shoe is custom-made. Here's what he knows so far. We have a missing right dress shoe. It's a size…He sits up and grabs the bag with the shoe in it. He takes his ruler and measures the shoe still inside the bag. Size eleven. He leans back, with his hands folded across his chest, and continues in thought. It's a size eleven brown dress shoe with black laces. The shoe has a square three-inch heel. The wound on the victim has to match that heel. Sal found traces of arsenic in his system, as well as enough alcohol to suspect Mr. Peterson was drunk at the time of death. One last thing to check.

He leans up and calls down to evidence.

"Hey, Freddy!"

It is the bubbly voice of Amber on the other end.

"Amber! Just the woman I want to talk to!"

"Freddy." He could tell by her voice she is blushing on the other end. "Saying things like that makes a woman say, 'Too bad he's gay,' ya know."

Freddy chuckles. He knows that Amber had always had a crush on him. She tried to hit on him once at one of the Christmas parties early in his career. He remembered the look of embarrassment on her face when he told her he was gay. He had taken her out for drinks later, and they quickly became good friends.

"Amber, was a wine bottle brought into evidence from the Peterson house?"

"Right to business, hey? You men are all alike." She said that statement with a playful smile. "Let me check."

He hears tapping on a keyboard. After a few minutes, she replies. "Actually, yes. It appears Shawn found an empty wine bottle and glass sitting on the kitchen counter."

"Interesting. Were either of them broken?"

"No. It's a perfectly intact wine glass and empty wine bottle. One moment and let me grab them real quick."

After a few minutes, he hears her back on the line. "I have them both right here. It's a blue wine glass with a long stem. It's a glass for drinking red wine, specifically."

"How do you know that?" he asks.

"Red wine glasses are typically taller than white wine glasses. They also have a wider opening at the top. Anyway, this is weird."

"What?"

"Well, it's a white wine."

"How is that weird?"

"Obviously, he is drinking a white wine from a glass meant for red wine."

"What does that matter? I drink wine and never pay attention to the glass."

"Freddy, sweetie, that means he's a casual wine drinker."

"I don't see how that fits, but okay."

"It's just an observation."

"Anything else out of the ordinary with the bottle?"

"No. Nor with the glass."

"Thank you, Amber. Goodbye."

He hangs up the phone and leans back. He has everything he needs to confront Hampton with. He knows what he has to do. He did not like the thought of doing it. This is the only way he can prove, without a doubt, that Hampton Hamm did not murder his husband. Freddy hated himself for what he is about to put this man through.

With a sigh, he dials Oscar's extension.

"Yeah."

"Oscar, you on duty?"

"I answered my phone, didn't I? Great deductive skills you have, Detective."

He ignores the sarcasm. "Bring Mr. Hamm to interrogation room three. I want to speak with him."

"Why? You already think he's innocent?"

"New developments have arisen. And Oscar…"

"What?"

"Will you run the camera and observe for me?"

"Why me?"

"Because you have the most experience, and I trust your objective, open-minded opinion."

"Cut the bullshit."

"Just do it, Oscar."

"Whatever."

"Thanks, Oscar."

He hangs up the phone, grabs his evidence folder, and heads out the door. A moment later, he returns. He snatches the full coffee cup on his desk.

"Can't forget that," he says as he leaves.

Chapter Thirteen

Where in the City is Richard Olstroski?

It is nine forty-five in the morning, and Shawn is finally leaving his apartment. He hopes Eddy doesn't let it slip that he overslept. He shakes the thought off. He knows better than that... Eddy wouldn't care. The man isn't that petty. Besides, Freddy gets lost in his cases and will forget that he was still sleeping when he called. All he will want to hear is that they found Richard Olstroski.

He calls Eddy as he pulls out of the apartment complex.

"You're late," the man says when he answers.

"I'm on my way now. We are helping Freddy again today."

"Chasing the guy Oscar lost?"

"Yeah. I'll be there in an hour."

"Alright. I'll be waiting."

Shawn ends the call as he turns onto the road.

***

He pulls into the parking lot of East Lake Apartments precisely one hour and thirty minutes after he ended his call with Eddy. Eddy's apartment is on the second floor of Building G, located at the back of the complex. He parks in a spot directly below Eddy's apartment and lets out three short honks of his horn. He allows a smile form on his face as he does that. Eddy has an angry look as he comes down the stairs.

"I hate it when you do that," the man says as he gets in the car.

"I know. That's why I did it."

"You're late," he says as he buckles up.

"There is traffic on Congress. Took me longer than I expected."

Shawn pulls out of the parking spot and drives toward the exit.

"So, how are we supposed to find this guy?"

Shawn hands the man his phone.

"We're going to call him?"

"There's an email from Freddy. Open it and tap the link."

Eddy grabs the phone. He opens the email from Freddy.

"He had to specify the email is from him? You know he does that in his text messages too."

"Yeah, I know," Shawn says with a chuckle. "The man is technologically impaired. Good thing he's a great detective."

Eddy focuses back on the phone. He taps the link in the email.

"Wait, these things can do that these days?"

"Do what?" Shawn asks.

"I tapped the link. It opened a web browser for a couple of seconds. I guess to get the account information or something. I dunno. It then opened your navigation software and starts navigating us to the location on the map."

"That's cool," Shawn says. 'Well, where are we headed?"

"Looks like we are heading to the south side of town," Eddy says. "This is weird."

Shawn turns onto the street and drives toward Congress. "What's weird?" he asks.

"We're tracking Richard Olstroski, right?"

Shawn nods. "Yeah. Why?"

"Well, there's a red dot and a green dot. The green dot is not moving. The red dot just turned out of my apartment complex. I think we're the red dot."

Shawn sighs. "What's your point?"

"That's just it. The red dot is moving. Not the green one. I'm assuming he's the green dot."

Shawn shakes his head. "Eddy, he's probably asleep or watching TV or something. Just navigate us there."

"Alright, head south around the lake once you hit Congress. Then turn south onto South Dakota."

"South Dakota? Isn't that near the place that Juliana Martinez lives?"

"Actually, yeah. About three blocks from it."

"We know he didn't get too far then,"

"I watched *The Ordeal* last night," Eddy says.

"What's that?"

"That's the new Raymond Scott movie."

"Oh, yeah. I remember the previews for that. How was that? It looked kind of 'artsy.'"

Eddy nods. "It is. You wouldn't care for it. And the actual 'ordeal'...You remember how *The Happening* never actually explained what happened?"

Shawn sighs. "We've had this discussion, Eddy."

"Okay, you know how it is never explained to 'my' satisfaction? Well, they never actually explain what 'the ordeal' is."

"Isn't it a kidnapping or a drug deal gone wrong or something? That is in the previews."

Eddy shakes his head. "No. That's how it all starts. It is weird and convoluted. I started watching something else before it was over."

"You never finished it?" Shawn asks. "What the? You can't judge a movie without watching the entire thing." Shawn shakes his head. "What did you end up watching?"

"Vader Maid."

They are coming up to a stoplight. Shawn stops a bit too fast. The tires screech to a halt. Shawn rolls his eyes as he looks at Eddy. The man did not say a word. This revelation doesn't surprise him.

That movie is about the ghost of a dead cleaning lady who had worked for a church. She always wore a Darth Vader mask and never spoke a word. She fell from the stage and broke her neck when she was cleaning the pulpit. The youth group is having a church lock-in and is being terrorized by the ghost of the maid. The gimmick is she would kill them by sucking them up in her vacuum.

Eddy loved that schlocky crap. The light turned green, and Shawn drives on.

"Where to?"

"Congress."

"'I'm on Congress." He emphasizes the first two words.

Eddy looks up for the first time. He had been focused on the phone.

"Oh, so we are. There's the lake. Hello, lake. I love this city. I love how Congress wraps around the lake. The fact the city refuses to clutter the view with developments."

"Yeah, it's great. Where do I turn."

"You keep that attitude up, and I'm going to call you Oscar," Eddy says with a smile.

"You do, and you will be walking the rest of the way."

"How will you find it without the tracker?"

"It's my phone."

"It's in my hand," he replies with a smile.

Shawn smiles at that comment. He likes Eddy. The guy is a good guy. He has a heart of gold, and he's good at his job. He could be a bit of a Barney Fife, at times, but he means well.

"Turn onto South Dakota."

"That's right. I forgot you mentioned that earlier."

They continue around the lake in silence. Shawn sees South Dakota Avenue up ahead. He turns on his left blinker and prepared for the turn.

As they turn onto South Dakota Avenue, Shawn asks, "Where do we go now?"

"That building on the right. The four-story red building."

"Okay."

He pulls into the empty lot in front of the abandoned building. It looks as if it were an uncompleted office building of some sort. Why would he be here?

"He's in there?" Shawn pointed to the building.

"That's what this thing says."

"Okay," he says as he shrugs. "Let's go."

The men close the car doors quietly as they exit.

"This way," Eddy says. The man starts to walk toward the building.

"Eddy," Shawn says. The man stops and turns to look at him. "Over here."

Shawn walks around to the back of the car. He opens up the back and grabs his gun. He places it on his hip. He makes sure his body cam is working correctly as well.

"Why are we taking our guns? Freddy says this guy's not dangerous."

"Call it a hunch," Shawn replies. "I have a bad feeling about this."

"Okay."

Eddy follows suit. After testing his body cam, he is ready.

"Now, let's go," Shawn says. "Lead the way."

Eddy has Shawn's phone out. Shawn thinks they must look silly walking toward the building. He imagined onlookers thinking they looked like they were busting ghosts with a make-shift PKE meter, or they had some kind of tricorder from *Star Trek*. Either way, he assumes this would be an odd sight to see.

They approach the building and pause. The men look around.

"Where are the doors?" Eddy asks.

Shawn is looking up. There are windows lining the walls on all of the floors. He looks left and right. Windows along the entire front-facing wall.

"I'm not sure," he says.

"I'll head right," Eddy says.

The man starts to walk off. Shawn grabs his shoulder.

"No. We stay together."

This must be how Freddy feels when he gets those "hunches" of his. Shawn did not like that feeling. He knows nothing good would come out of this.

"Wouldn't it be easier to split up?" Eddy asks.

"And that's exactly how the killer picks people off in a horror film. We stay together."

"This isn't a horror film."

Shawn sighs and rolls his eyes.

"That's not the point. We stay together."

Eddy nods.

"We head left," Shawn says.

"Okay," Eddy reluctantly replies.

The men walk around the left side of the building. Shawn's "spidey-sense," if he had it, is off the chart right now. He has never read Spider-Man or watched any of those movies. He assumed it is the same as when the hair stood up on the back of his neck. That is the feeling he has now.

They turn the corner and see a black metal door. No windows at all on this side of the building. Shawn surveys the area as the men slowly creep toward the door. Eddy turns the knob. The door opens with a creak.

"That's not creepy," Eddy whispers with a hint of sarcasm.

The men enter the building. The door closes with a loud "thud." Both men jump at the noise. The building looks like an empty warehouse on the inside. Windows stretch along both of the long sides of the building. The side with the door, where they entered, as well as the far side, has no windows. Sunlight illuminates the entire floor. There are stairs on the left wall leading up.

"What now?" Shawn asks. "Up, I assume."

Eddy shakes his head. "Straight back."

"Straight back? Along the wall?"

"I think so. I think that's how it reads."

"That makes no sense. We would be able to see him."

"That's what this thing says."

"Let me see that."

Eddy hands Shawn the phone. He looks at the navigation app. That's odd, Shawn thinks. He looks up at the back wall. He looks down at the phone. He looks at the back wall again.

"I don't think this building is as open as we think it is."

Eddy looks confused.

Shawn clarifies, "I think there's another part of this building on the other side of that wall. Come on. Let's check out the perimeter. Perhaps there's another entrance on the other side."

They exit the building. Shawn makes a point to close the door instead of letting it slam shut. The men walk the entire perimeter of the building and back to the door they originally entered.

"I guess that's the only door. That's weird."

Eddy just shrugs.

"We go in," Shawn says.

They enter the building a second time.

"What do we do now?" Eddy asks.

Shawn points to the stairs. "We go up."

The men walk up the stairs. Shawn hears the metal steps "cling" with each step they take. The second floor looks like the first. Another staircase on the left.

"Now what?" Eddy asks.

"We go up."

The men climb the stairs to the third floor. This floor is different. This floor has long hallways with empty, uncompleted offices on either side. They walk down the hall to the other end. There is a staircase going up and one heading down.

"Which way?" Eddy asks.

"We go down."

The men head down the stairs to the second floor. This side looks like a mirror of the opposite side.

"We go down," Shawn says.

The two men head down to the first floor. This is not a mirror image of the other side. Shawn thinks it is a strange design. Perhaps the building was abandoned before it was completed. This looks more like the third floor. Hallways and empty offices. They walk down the hall. Shawn is looking at the navigation app.

"Left," he whispers.

The men go down the hall. No doors or windows.

"Right."

The men turn right.

"Left."

Down another hall.

"Right."

Shawn sees their dot pass Richards.

"Back-up."

They stop in front of a wooden door. No windows along this wall. The men have their hands on their guns. Shawn slowly places his hand on the doorknob and turns. He pushes until the door is slightly ajar.

"Advance," Shawn says with a smile.

He peers into the room. White empty walls on all sides. The room is empty, except…

He bursts in and bolts toward the body like a torpedo. The man is lying on his stomach. Shawn carefully turns the body over.

"It looks like we found him," Eddy says.

Shawn grabs the man's wrist and feels for a pulse.

"Shit."

He lays the arm back down and leans over the man's face. The man isn't breathing.

"Shit!"

He stands and grabs his phone to call Freddy. He notices Eddy grabbing his radio to call it in.

"Not yet. Let me talk to Freddy first. This is his case. Let's see how he wants us to handle it."

Eddy nods and puts the radio away. Shawn calls Freddy. He hears it ring a few times. Freddy finally answers.

"Did you find him?" Freddy asks.

"We found him," Shawn replies.

"Bring him in. I want to talk to him."

"That's going to be difficult."

"What do you mean?"

"Well, we will need a medium if you want to talk to him."

"A what?"

"It's a person who can channel the spirits of the dead. Most people confuse them with psychics…."

"I know what a medium is, Shawn. Why would we need…?" There is a long silence before Freddy speaks again. "He's dead, isn't he?"

Shawn nods as he replies. "It appears that way."

"Son of a...Okay."

He hears Freddy sigh.

Freddy continues, "Alright. I'm on my way to speak with Mr. Hamm now. There are a few new developments in the case that I need to get more insight on."

"What do you want us to do with the body?"

"Have you called it in yet?"

He shakes his head as if Freddy could see it. "No. It's your case, Freddy. I wanted to wait for your word on that."

"Good. I would have been pissed if you had. Alight. Call it in, but don't give any names. The only people that I want knowing who this person is are the two of you, me, and Sal."

"Sal?"

"The coroner. He and I go back aways. I trust Sal to keep this quiet."

"Understood."

"This is important, Shawn. I don't want this getting out just yet. Not until we know more. I want the killer thinking we believe Mr. Hamm did this."

Shawn is confused. "But didn't he do this? I mean, obviously, he didn't murder Mr. Olstroski, but…."

"He didn't murder his husband either, Shawn." He could hear the irritation in Freddy's voice. "So, where are you, anyway? I'll call Sal as soon as I am off the phone with you."

"We're on South Dakota. It's a four-story large, rectangular building. Not sure of the address. You can't miss it. It's a large, red building."

"Gotcha. Anything else?"

"We're on the bottom floor, but this building is laid out weird."

"What do you mean?"

"Okay, when you first arrive, there are no doors in front. There is only one door. It's on the left side. There's a trick to getting here."

"A trick? What trick?"

"The building is unfinished or appears to be. Doors and windows have not been cut out of walls. It appears to be an open warehouse at first glance. Stairs on the left wall. First and second floors have the warehouse design on half of the floor. The other half appears to be unfinished office space. Third floor is all unfinished office space."

"And the fourth floor?"

"I dunno. We didn't go to the fourth floor. Anyway, we are on the other side of the wall that separates the two halves of the first floor. Here is how you get to us."

"Alright. I'm writing all of this down."

"Go up, up, down, down, left, right, left, right. Be a good man and tell Sal not to let the metal door slam shut. That makes such a loud noise."

"Got it. You do realize those directions make no sense?"

"Well, there are hallways to go down to get to the next set of stairs, but that is the general direction."

Freddy sighs. "Alright. Let me call Sal. You guys call it in. Say you have it under control, and the coroner is on his way. Do not mention any names of who this is."

"Roger."

"Good." Freddy changes his tone to a more sincere one. "Thanks, Shawn. After this clean-up, you guys are done with the case. I greatly appreciate it."

"No problem, Freddy. Later."

Shawn ends the call and looks at Eddy. "Call it in. Do not mention any names. Say we have the coroner on his way. Stress that we do not need backup. I'm going to search the rest of this building. Stay with the body. I want to make sure there is no one else in this building."

"I'll go," Eddy says.

Shawn shakes his head.

"Let me," Eddy says.

"I'm the experienced officer here."

"That's why you need to stay," Eddy says. "When the coroner arrives, he needs an experienced officer here."

Shawn knows the man is correct. He nods and waves Eddy on. "Go."

Eddy leaves and heads down the hall.

"What the hell happened to you?" he asks Richard's body. He reaches for his radio to call it in.

***

Freddy ended the call with Shawn. He assumes this has to be a comical sight. His phone is in his left hand. He has his coffee in his right. The folder he always uses is under his chin. He was already on his way to interrogation room three when Shawn called. This can't have happened at the most inappropriate time. He shrugs the thought away and calls the number for the coroner.

"Terra Loch…"

"Sal, it's Freddy."

"Hey, Freddy. You miss me already?"

He hears the smile in the man's voice. He is not in a jovial mood at the moment.

"Sal, what I am about to say needs to be kept between us."

"Freddy, you know that…"

"Please, Sal. The success of my investigation and case depends on this staying quiet."

"Okay, Freddy. What do you need?"

He explains the entire story to Sal. Once he is finished, he waits for the man's response. Sal remains quiet.

"Sal? You there?"

"Yeah, I'm here. That's such a fantastical story. I'm letting it all sink in. Alright. I'm on my way, and I won't say a word…for now."

"Thanks, Sal. Once I'm done with Mr. Hamm, I'll be over there to speak with you. I want to know what this man died of."

"I'll be here. Later, Freddy."

Freddy ends the call. He knows he has to keep this revelation from Hampton as well. Oscar would be listening, and the camera would be recording. What happens next is solely meant to prove the man's innocence.

***

It feels as if an eternity had passed. Shawn is pacing the floor of the small room. Eddy hasn't made it back yet. Where is the coroner? There are only so many games he can play on his phone. He knows he should have gone in Eddy's stead. What if he ran into trouble? What if there is someone still inside the building? He didn't hear any gunshots. Perhaps that's a good thing.

"Shawn," The voice makes Shawn jump. His back is to the door. He is lost in his thoughts. He turns around, his hand on his gun. He relaxes when he sees Eddy.

"I'm sorry. I didn't mean to startle you," the man says. "I searched the entire building. Every floor. Every room. Every nook and cranny, you could say."

"You find anything at all?"

Eddy shakes his head. "Nothing. The only people here, living or dead, are in this room. No signs that anyone else is or has been here. Whoever did this left no traces."

Shawn hopes the disappointment does not show on his face. "I was hoping to have something concrete for Freddy."

"I'm still confused about how this happened."

"Me too, Eddy. We know that Mr. Olstroski eluded Oscar in the early morning. In fact, it was the same day Freddy asked us to take the prints from that door at the crime scene, remember?"

Eddy nods.

"We know he took a ride share to meet with Ms. Martinez."

"But she's in Germany."

"Right. Would he have known that? He would have had to. I wonder…" It is almost as if a lightbulb lit up in his mind. "Mr. Olstroski knew she was leaving after the shoot. He wasn't sure as to when. Maybe she knows something about the murder of Mr. Peterson. Or maybe he thinks she does. Maybe he was being watched."

He realizes he is starting to think like Freddy. He unconsciously had his index finger on his lips as he is saying this. He moves his hand back down to his side.

"We're not done here," he says.

Eddy nods. "I know. We are waiting for the coroner."

Shawn shakes his head. "No. I mean, we are not done with our part in this investigation."

"We're not?"

"Nope. We're going to continue to follow this trail of breadcrumbs. Mr. Olstroski may end up being a MacGuffin, but he's our MacGuffin. We are going to see this part of Freddy's case to the end."

"MacGuffin?" Eddy asks.

"You ever watch a Hitchcock film?"

"I've seen *Psycho* and *The Birds*."

"*Psycho*. Perfect example. Remember the entire first half of that movie? Janet Leigh stole the money from her boss and skipped town?"

Eddy nods. "Of course. But she ended up being murdered by Norman Bates."

"Yeah. The money is the MacGuffin. Think of it as a 'wild goose chase.' For the entire first half of the film, we are following the money. Is she going to be caught? Will it be discovered? What ends up happening to the money in that film?"

Eddy pauses a moment in thought. "She had it hidden away. After she was murdered, he cleaned the room. Removed all of her belongings, including the money. Placed it all in her car, along with her body. Drove the car into the lake. As far as the film, I don't know what happened to it after that."

"Exactly. And you aren't meant to. The money wasn't the point. It was a misdirection. The MacGuffin is the thing you have the audience focus on. You make them think it's important to the story. In the end, it never matters at all."

"So, you think that Mr. Olstroski may be our MacGuffin?"

"Perhaps. Perhaps not. Did someone want him dead? Is it the same someone who murdered Mr. Peterson? Is it an accomplice if the murderer is sitting in jail right now? Is it not related at all? Is Mr. Olstroski in the wrong place at the wrong time? That is for us to discover. You and I will follow this to its conclusion. Let Freddy do his investigations. Perhaps the twain shall meet. Perhaps not."

At that moment, a skinny man with short, black hair enters. He is panting as if he were out of breath.

"I'm...Sal...Sal...Salvador..." The man is panting as he is saying this.

"You must be Sal," Shawn says. "The coroner."

The man nods, still panting.

"Take your time. No rush. Catch your breath," Shawn says.

After a few minutes, the man composes himself. A look of annoyance forms on his face.

"Who the hell thinks it is a good idea to design a building like this?" he says. "Moreover, who the hell would leave a body in the most remote part of this screwed-up design of a building?"

Shawn chuckles. The man looks more annoyed at that.

"Whatever. Let me look at the body."

Sal walks over to Mr. Olstroski's body and kneels over it. He scans the body without touching it. He looks up at Shawn after a moment.

"Is this how you found him? Did you touch him?"

Shawn walks over to the body and kneels as well.

"We found him face down. I turned him over. I wasn't sure if he was deceased. I checked his pulse on his left wrist. Outside of that, I haven't touched him."

"How did you turn him over?"

Shawn reaches out to grab the body to show the man. The coroner slaps his hand away.

"Don't touch him again," he still sounds annoyed. "Explain it. I don't want his body contaminated even more."

Shawn nods. He should have known better. This body is considered evidence.

"I grabbed his left side and flipped him over. His entire left arm and shoulder may have my prints. Perhaps even the left side of his torso. Outside of that, I have not touched him."

"Okay," he says.

The man pulls out two pairs of gloves. He hands a pair to Shawn. He slides his hands into the second pair.

“Put those on,” the coroner says.

Shawn slips the gloves over his hands as well.

“Now,” the coroner says, “feel free to touch away.”

The coroner starts to examine the body. Salvador unbuttoned the man’s shirt to reveal his chest. There were no signs of foul play. Shawn watched as the man examined Richard’s arms, legs, and face. He watched the man maneuver the body. He assumed he is checking for a cause of death. After a few minutes, Salvador let the body rest. He stood, removed his gloves, and places them in a plastic bag. Shawn followed suit.

“I noticed you were able to control your impulse to fondle the man once you had the gloves on,” the coroner says as Shawn places his gloves in the same plastic bag. “Too bad you can’t control yourself before placing the gloves on your hands.”

Shawn glared at the man.

“Anyway, I need to get this man back for a complete examination. I was hoping for similar signs.”

“Similar signs?”

The man nods. “Similar to the wound found on Mr. Peterson. This man shows no signs of foul play. That’s the one thing both bodies have in common. No sign of a struggle. No marks of any kind. I’m beginning to think Freddy may be correct.”

“What do you mean?”

The man shakes his head. “Nothing. Freddy seems to think Mr. Peterson was poisoned. I couldn’t understand it until now. But from what I see here...Perhaps he is correct.”

“Or perhaps not. It’s possible that Mr. Olstroski here just may have been in the wrong place at the wrong time.”

“But where are the wounds? If he is a victim of coincidental foul play, where is the evidence? No bullet wounds. No stab wounds. No marks from strangulation. Not even signs of drowning. No. Something else happened to this man.”

"Eddy and I are going to continue this trail. We started this part of the investigation and have a few leads on how to find out where he was before his murder."

"Whatever you need to do. My job is to examine the body and find out what killed the man. Look," his tone suddenly changed, "I'm sorry for the way I have been speaking to you. I know you are doing your job. You guys go ahead. I'll handle the transporting of the corpse back to my office."

Shawn shakes his head. "No need to apologize. I made a stupid mistake here. I hope I didn't screw up your examination."

"You're fine. You guys did good work here. Go on. Get back on your search. I'll finish up here."

Shawn nods. He reaches out to shake the man's hand. The coroner acknowledges and reciprocates. The two men leave the coroner alone in the building. Shawn hears the man talking on the phone as they are leaving the room.

"Well, let's pick up where we left off. It's time to talk to that security guard."

Chapter Fourteen

A View to an Interrogation

Oscar can't understand why Falcon wants him to observe the interview. He doesn't even want to be here. All he wants is to sit at his desk and play solitaire on his computer. His job is simple. He spends his days sitting at a desk and watching the jail cells. There is very little paperwork and even less action. Occasionally, he will have to walk a suspect to or from an interrogation room. He is never asked to observe. What is Falcon planning?

Everybody assumes he's a jerk. He understands that is how he comes across. He has been an officer for far too long. He wants to show up, do his job, and go home. He isn't interested in, what he refers to as, the bullshit that everyone usually gets caught up in. He finds the pleasantries that people feel they always have to say are pointless and stupid. Just get to the point and do your job. Most people misunderstand this as him being a jackass. He doesn't care. He makes no apologies for who he is.

He has a lot of respect for Falcon and the job the man does. He can not understand the man's methods, though. There is no doubt that he is excellent at his job. As long as he's known Falcon, the man has never been wrong. He always solves his case and leaves no loose ends. He would never let Falcon know just how much he respected the man. There's no need to have the man's already overinflated ego cause his head to explode. However, it might improve his looks. He smiles at the joke as he thinks it.

This is why he can't understand why Falcon insisted the suspect is innocent. All of the evidence is pointing to Mr. Hamm. The only prints in the house are his. No evidence shows anyone else is in that house. They had been arguing that day. His career is on a downturn. Perhaps this is his way of getting himself noticed. The poor widower of the murdered director. This case should be over.

Oscar shakes his head while watching the man in the other room. He has been in the interrogation room for five minutes now. How could anyone observing this man come to any different conclusion? This man is showing all of the signs of a guilty person. His nervous tendencies. His fidgeting. Even the look of panic on his face. This man can even cry on demand. He's an actor, after all. That's his job, and he's doing it well. That is the one thing people appear to be missing. Hampton Hamm is an actor. Hampton Hamm is playing us all. There is no question about this. There is no doubt in his mind this man murdered his husband.

Why won't he just sit still? Oscar watches through the glass as Hampton keeps repositioning himself in the chair. It is as if he kept slouching and is repositioning to sit up straighter. If he sits any straighter, he would be standing up.

He averts his attention to the camera. He looks through the viewfinder to verify the camera is looking dead-on in the room. He could see the entire room from the door to the chair the suspect is sitting in. The camera is plugged in, and everything appears to be connected properly. All that is left is for Falcon to arrive and for all of this to get rolling.

At that moment, the door to the observation room opens. Oscar looks up to see the tall redhead walk in. Speak of the devil, he thinks.

"Alright, let's get this over with," Oscar says.

"Well, hello to you too," Freddy replies.

"Look, Falcon, this is a waste of time. I don't even know why we are doing this. I don't know what you can pull out of him that the captain already hasn't. He's guilty, Falcon."

Freddy sighs. "Oscar, trust me. New evidence has come to light."

"What evidence?"

"You'll see."

Freddy grins as he says that. Oscar hates it when he does that. It is as if he knows something that no one else could figure out. Almost as if he were pointing out that he is the smartest man in the room.

"Whatever. I'm just here to operate the camera."

"And observe. I need a witness, Oscar. You know how this works."

"Yeah, yeah. Look, Falcon, anybody can do this. Hell, Norman could have been the one…."

"I want you," Freddy emphasized the last word of that statement. "Oscar, you misunderstand me. You think I don't understand you. You think that I think of you the way everyone else does. You're wrong. There's a soft, gooey center to that hard candy shell."

"What the hell are you talking about?"

"You care. You want to make sure every person you take to a cell is guilty. You want to make sure the right person is caught, and the innocent are protected. This gruff exterior is all a facade."

Oscar sighs and shakes his head. The man is far more perceptive than he gave him credit for. He opens his mouth to retort but thinks better of it. He knows the man is right. It's best to leave it alone.

Freddy just smiles.

"So," Freddy changes the subject, "is the camera ready?"

Oscar nods. "Yeah. It has a full view of the room. Everything is connected. It can see and hear that room with no issues. All that's left is to start the recording."

"Perfect."

He notices Freddy change his focus to the suspect. Oscar shakes his head. The man can not figure out what to do with his hands. He keeps swapping between folding his hands on the table to separating them and laying them flat on the table's surface.

"I don't get it. I don't see what you see. This is obviously the sign of someone who is nervous and guilty."

"Or scared," Freddy replies.

"Either way, guilty," Oscar says.

Freddy opens his mouth to retort and closes it again. The man lets out a heavy sigh.

"I trust you, Oscar. That's why I specifically asked you to do this. Whatever happens in that room, I trust you to stay here. I trust you will keep this between us. No matter what happens in that room, do not let anyone in there. Do not let a soul interrupt this."

"What the hell are you talking about?"

Freddy remains silent with a grin on his face.

"Falcon, don't ask me to stand by if you are planning to do something illegal or help him escape."

"What the hell, Oscar? When have I ever?" Freddy sighs. "I am going to ask questions and say things that are going to upset Mr. Hamm. I've been too soft on him. I need to push him to get answers."

"It's about damn time."

"Oscar, just watch. Once it's over, I think we will have enough proof of how Mr. Peterson was murdered. And, we may have a clue as to who murdered him."

Freddy heads for the door as he is saying that.

"We already know 'who.' Falcon."

"Do we?" Freddy never turns to look at Oscar when he says that. He walks out the door and closes it behind him. That's the kind of shit Oscar hates. The man is too smug. He loves leaving people hanging and loves showing he is the most intelligent person in the room.

Oscar turns his attention back to the glass. He flips the switch on the camera as soon as Freddy walks in.

***

Freddy opens the door to interrogation room three and walks in. He sees Hampton's face light up when he enters.

"How are you, Mr. Hamm?"

Freddy sits his folder and coffee down on the table. He closes the door behind him and sits down. The expression on the man's face has changed to irritation.

"How am I?"

Freddy nods. "Yes. Are you doing well?"

"How am I? My husband was murdered. I watched him die. I've been accused of the murder. I've been interrogated, arrested, and jailed. I haven't had a good meal since the day you brought me in. I haven't been able to plan my husband's funeral. No one seems to believe I'm innocent. My entire world crumbled the day Marcus died. I've lost my husband, my home, my career, my life. I am alone and have no one standing beside me. Ask yourself, Detective, how would you be? Would you be doing well?"

The man could be a little overdramatic, but he is correct. That is a stupid question. Freddy imagines that Oscar is laughing on the other side of the glass. He decides to change his approach.

"A few interesting new developments have come to light. I need to ask you a few questions for clarity. Mr. Hamm, believe it or not, I am on your side. My goal is not to convict an innocent man. My goal is to solve this case and tie up any loose ends associated with it. Do you understand?"

Hampton nods. The man is still on edge. He doesn't speak.

"Okay. Do you remember the night I stoped by? The night I asked you about that screen door on your lanai?"

Hampton nods.

"Good."

Freddy sits back in his chair and grins at the man. He is doing his best to disarm him. He wants the man to relax and work with him instead of fighting him.

"Mr. Hamm, you offered me a glass of wine that night."

Hampton nods.

"Now, I'm not much of a wine drinker. I don't usually drink it. I'm more of a coffee man, myself. I'm not sure if you've noticed my coffee habit."

He observes a slight smile on Hampton's face with that comment. Good. The man is relaxing.

"Is that red wine? White wine?"

Hampton shakes his head. "I have no idea. Marcus and I drink wine at night to relax. I don't know red wine from white wine. I just know what I like."

"Yeah, me too. It's the same with the glasses. When I drink wine, I just grab a glass. Did you know there are glasses for drinking red wine as well as glasses for drinking white wine?"

Hampton shakes his head.

"Neither did I. I just grab a glass. I learned recently that red wine glasses are the ones with the long stems and wider mouths. I don't know why. Perhaps it's for the taste. Who knows?"

"I didn't know that either. I always thought it was just varieties of wine glasses. You know, like with tall drinking glasses versus small ones."

"Yeah. Same here. Apparently not. Apparently, it's more like juice glasses versus milk glasses. The average person may use them interchangeably, but there are those who only use them for the purpose intended."

"Well, I don't even remember what type of wine glasses we used that night. I just grabbed a couple. We had one bottle of wine left. That's the one we drank that night."

"One bottle left? How many bottles did y'all have?"

"Well, we had been drinking off of one. We always bought a second once we opened a bottle. It is weird, though."

"What is?"

Well, Marcus was given a bottle of wine as a gift a while back. When we first started shooting this film."

"Oh? Who was it from?"

Hampton shakes his head. “I have no idea. After the first day of shooting, there was a gift basket on the hood of the car. It had candies and a bottle of wine. There was a typed note directed to Marcus. The person thanked him for the job and was looking forward to working with him.”

“And you don’t know who it was from?”

Hampton shakes his head. “No. It wasn’t signed. Marcus asked everyone involved with the film, cast, and crew. Everyone denied sending the gift. Nobody saw anyone leave it either. We just assumed the person wanted to remain anonymous.”

“Is there anything else you can tell me?”

“It became a nightly occurrence.”

“What did?”

“The gift baskets.”

“Y’all received a gift basket every night?”

He nods. “It was always the same. Wine for Marcus and candies for me.”

“Was there always a note attached?”

Hampton nods.

“The bottle you are speaking about, is that the last of the ones from the gift baskets?”

Hampton nods.

“When did you receive that one?”

“The night of...That night.”

Freddy doesn’t have to ask. He knows what night the man is referencing.

“What was weird about the bottle?”

“Well, that night you were over at my house, the bottle was missing.”

“Missing? What do you mean?’

“Just that. Missing. Gone. I don’t know where it went. I just assumed the person who murdered Marcus stole it.”

“I think I may have an answer to that mystery.”

"You found it? Did I just misplace it?"

"Not exactly. We found the bottle."

Hampton looked confused. Freddy decides to elaborate.

"Had your husband been drinking the night of his murder?"

"Drinking? No. He never drinks when he's working. We returned home late that night. We had a small argument. He went into the house to watch TV."

"As far as you know, your husband had nothing to drink that night?"

"That's right. Why? Was alcohol found in his system?"

Freddy nods. "And an empty wine bottle and glass were found in the house."

"What?" Hampton has a look of horror on his face. The man lowered his head. "It's all my fault. I hurt him badly that night. What I said cut him to the quick. I should have…"

"Mr. Hamm," Freddy says. Hampton does not look up. "Mr. Hamm, knock it off. I need answers right now. You can feel sorry for yourself later."

Hampton looks up. Freddy can see tears in the man's eyes.

Freddy sighs. He hated himself for this. "I need you to focus. I need facts right now. Do you understand?"

Hampton nods.

"Good. Now, did that bottle have a cork, or was it a screw-on cap?"

"It had a cork, I believe."

"Had it been tampered with in any way?"

"What do you mean?"

"Were there any signs the cork had been removed and reinserted? Any signs of a hole in it? Any signs of tampering?"

Hampton shakes his head. "Not to my knowledge. There is tape over the top of it."

"Tape?"

"Yeah. The card is taped to the bottle. The tape is over the cork."

"What type of tape? Packing tape?"

"No. It looked more like duct tape. It is as if a thin piece of duct tape had been cut and used. We just assumed the person wanted to make sure the note stuck to the bottle."

"You don't think it is weird that duct tape was used? Most people would use gift wrap tape or just sit the card in the gift basket."

"Not at all. You have to understand something, Detective. Most of these people flew out from either California or New York. Very few of them live here. Whoever it was probably used duct tape because that's all they had. We just assumed that the tape was left over from a box the person had packed. It's not that unusual."

"I see. Are you aware that arsenic is in wine?"

Hampton shakes his head.

"Neither was I. Arsenic was found in your husband's body as well."

"Arsenic!" Hampton exclaims.

Freddy raises his hand. "Don't get excited, Mr. Hamm. It's normal."

"Normal? You found arsenic in Marcus's body! Proof he was murdered! And you think that's normal?"

Freddy exhales. "Mr. Hamm, please."

Hampton keeps on as if he can't hear Freddy.

"Well, that's it. Find out who poisoned him. Whoever it is was the person who stabbed him. Maybe the poison didn't work. Maybe the stab wound isn't deep enough. Why are you talking to me? Why aren't you out there? Why aren't you finding him?"

"Mr. Hamm, shut up!"

Hampton immediately stops talking. Freddy can feel the awkward silence between the two of them. He hates letting someone cause a reaction like that from him. He needs this man to listen, and this is the only reaction he could think of to get him to stop talking.

"I'm sorry, but I need you to listen. Arsenic is normal in wine. It gets into the grapes from the ground. All wine has arsenic. The amount of arsenic in his body is as if he had drunk an entire bottle of wine at one time. That's why I was asking about the wine."

Freddy watches the man carefully. There is no visible reaction from him. Hampton sits there like he is frozen in stone. He can not read the man.

"Now, had your husband complained of any type of abdominal pain? Any diarrhea? Heart issues? Anything like that?

Hampton shakes his head.

"These are all signs of arsenic poisoning. Now, I have another question for you. I want to know more about the insurance policy you have on your husband."

"What do you mean? I explained this to your captain already. It is normal. He had one on me."

"Five million dollars is normal?"

"No!" He can tell that Hampton is getting frustrated. "I've already been through this! We both had a one-million-dollar insurance policy on each other! It is enough to pay off the house, bury one of us, and live off of it! There is no five million dollar policy!"

Freddy hates himself for what he is about to do next. He knows the man in front of him is innocent. He knows the man is in pain. He knows the man is still suffering. He has to do it. He has to hurt this man. He has to break him. He needs the man in front of him to break down enough that it would prove he did not murder his husband.

Freddy opens his folder and takes out the insurance policy for Marcus Peterson. He lays it in front of Hampton.

"Read it."

Hampton looks down at the policy. He looks back up at Freddy.

"I don't have to read it. This is the insurance policy on Marcus."

"Read it," Freddy is firm when he says that. The smile had left his face.

"No. I already know what it says."

"I'm only going to say this one more time. Pick up the damn paper and read the policy."

Hampton grabs the papers and starts reading. Freddy watched the man's face. He watches confidence descend into confusion. This is it. Here it comes.

"What in the world?"

"What do you mean?"

"It does say five million dollars. That doesn't make sense."

"Look at the date."

"No. That's not possible. These were drawn up a year after we were married."

Freddy sighs. He had to stay strong. He could not waver. This man had to believe this is real. Everything depends on it.

"Cut the shit, Mr. Hamm."

Hampton jumps. He looks up at Freddy with confusion.

"What?"

"Cut the shit. This insurance policy was amended one week prior to Mr. Peterson's death. Look at the date. Look at the signature."

Hampton stares at him.

"Look at it. Or do you already know what it says?"

Hampton looks at the date and the signature.

"That's not possible," he says.

"Is that your signature?"

"No. Yes. I mean…"

"Is that your signature?"

Hampton nods. "It is but I…"

"Here's what I think happened. Your career was floundering. Your husband's was taking off. You were jealous and tired of riding his coattails. You hated that he asked Jacob Wexler to take a role in the movie. This was your chance. Your break. Not his, but yours."

He can see panic set in on the man's face. Hampton slowly realizes the gravity of the situation. The man is buying it. He truly believed that Freddy believed he is guilty. He has to keep it up.

"You slowly poisoned him with the wine. You were the one who pretended it was a gift. You were the one who argued with him on the set. You were the one who argued with him that particular night. You still hated Jacob Wexler. You decided to frame the man for your husband's murder. You stabbed your husband with the heel of a man's dress shoe. When that didn't kill him, you poured the entire bottle of wine down his throat. You made up the story that you fell asleep."

Hampton is shaking his head.

"Don't deny it. You told me the entire story of how you guys met. You cheated on him with Adam Greenbriar. When Mr. Greenbriar was brought back into your life, it brought up old feelings. You wanted your husband out of the way to forward your career and to get Mr. Greenbriar back. You murdered your husband. His last thought was that of betrayal. Watching the man he loved, the man he thinks loved him, murder him. What is it like looking into those eyes as you poured the poison down his throat? How did you feel knowing you were betraying him? Did you care? Do you care? His last thoughts are that of horror. How does that make you feel, Mr. Hamm? Do you feel good? Do you feel happy? Do you feel relieved? How do you feel knowing his last thoughts are that the man he loved betrayed and murdered him. How did you feel when you looked into those eyes?"

"How do I feel? How the fuck do you think I feel? I love Marcus with every fiber of my being! Yes, we've had our differences! Yes, we've argued! Yes, I cheated on him with Adam! I was a fool! It was a minor slip! It was a lustful moment! I have regretted that every day of my life! I treasure Marcus! He forgave me for that long ago, but I have never forgiven myself! That was my betrayal to him! Not this!"

He shakes the papers as he says that. He throws the papers down on the desk as he continues. Hampton's voice changes to more of a calm tone.

"You're a son of a bitch, Detective. You made me think you were helping me. You let me open up to you. The entire time, you were building a case against me. I don't know what this is. Yes, that looks like my signature. I didn't sign this. I didn't amend anything. I was happy for Marcus. I was excited his career was taking off. He was still my world. I enjoyed staying home while he worked. He had to convince me to take this role. I didn't want it. He wanted it for me.

"I didn't murder my husband, Detective. Everything I told you about that night is true. I don't know who did it, but I know who didn't. Go ahead and try me. Convict me. Lock me up and throw away the key. I don't care. My life ended the day Marcus died. My world shattered that day. Nothing else matters. I've been going through the motions. The things people expect you to do. I want my husband back. Every night I fall asleep, I tell myself this is all a nightmare. I tell myself when I wake up, Marcus will be there. His shining face staring at me. All I want is to be with my husband. I want Marcus back! I want him to walk through that fucking door right now and tell me this has all been a joke!"

Hampton slumps down in his chair and bursts out crying. Freddy feels a heavy pressure come over him. The guilt is too much for him. He hates himself for what he did to this man. After a few minutes, Hampton speaks.

"But he won't. It's not. My husband is gone. I will never feel his arms around me again. I'll never hear his voice. Never clean up his mess. My last memory of him is holding his hand as he is dying. My last words to him were not 'I love you' but 'leave me alone.' That's the burden I carry."

Freddy doesn't say a word. He places the insurance policy back in his folder. He stands, grabs his folder and coffee, and leaves the room.

***

Oscar watches Freddy leave. A few minutes later, the man enters the observation room. Oscar is still watching Hampton through the glass. He could feel Freddy standing beside him.

"And they tell me I am heartless," he says to Freddy. "Did you have to do that to him? Take it that far?"

"I had to break him."

"That is cruel. You didn't break him. You destroyed him. Look at him."

"I don't have to. I know what I did."

"Well, you accomplished one thing," Oscar says as he stops the recording. "You convinced me he's innocent."

"That was my goal. Do you think this will convince the captain?"

"This will convince him that you have no soul."

"As long as it convinces him the killer is still out there. I want this man in protection as well. One more thing, Oscar. After I leave here, I am heading back over to the coroner."

"What for?"

"This stays between us. There are only three other people that know what I am about to tell you."

"What?"

"Richard Olstroski was found. Shawn and Eddy found him."

Oscar sighs. What a relief. He still kicked himself for letting the man get away.

"Want me to bring him to an interrogation room?"

Freddy shakes his head. "There's no need. He's dead. I'm going to the coroner to find out how he was killed."

Oscar feels like someone had just punched him in the gut. If he hadn't left. If he hadn't chased down that speeder. Perhaps this man would still be alive.

"It's not your fault, Oscar."

"Freddy, I screwed up. Look, you are right. I have this rough exterior. But I…"

"Oscar, you made a mistake. You trusted the man would stay. Don't blame yourself. That speeder you stoped, do you have his name?"

"Yeah. Well, I can get it for you. Why?"

"I want to talk to him. I want to know if he knows anything about Mr. Olstroski's death. Perhaps he saw the man that night."

"Alright. I'll get it for you. I'll pull up the record of the ticket I wrote him. Go on to the coroner. I'll text it to you. What do you want me to do with him?"

Oscar points to the man in the other room. He is still sobbing.

"Show the recording to the Captain. I want to know if I have permission to place him in protective custody. This is enough proof that Mr. Hamm is innocent. He cannot return home to the crime scene. I also don't want the media to know. I want everyone to think we believe we have the right person. Also, I want him watched. The killer may try to tie up loose ends. The man in that room is a loose end."

"Roger. I'm on it. You have me at your disposal."

Freddy nods and turns to leave. Coffee cup in one hand and his folder under his arm. Freddy opens the door and starts to walk out.

"And Oscar," Freddy says. He does not turn. His back is still to Oscar.

"Yeah?"

"You called me Freddy." He closes the door behind him.

***

Freddy holds his composure as he walks through the Farmhouse back to his office. He has to keep a stoic face as long as possible. What he did to Hampton is eating him up inside. Just a little longer. Stay strong. Don't let them see you lose it.

He enters his office and heads for his coffee bar. He pours the remaining coffee into a thermal mug to carry with him. He fills it the rest of the way with the remaining coffee from an earlier brew. Freddy washes out the coffee carafe, empty cup, and filter basket. He was working hard to hold back tears as he washed up.

He double-checks to make sure he has his phone. Grabs the thermal mug and his folder, he leaves his office.

He doesn't say a word to anyone as he walks through the Farmhouse. The emotion is swelling inside of him. He barely held it together when he was talking with Oscar. One word and tears would start flowing.

Norman waves as he walks past. He nods to the man but doesn't say a word. He grabs his wallet, keys, and gun from the basket Norman hands him. He walks out of the door and bolts for his car. Unlocking the car and opening the door, he throws his folder in the passenger's seat. He gets in the car, places the mug in the plastic cup holder hanging on the door, closes the door, and starts sobbing.

Chapter Fifteen

McDonald and Me

"Remind me why we are doing this again?"

Shawn rolls his eyes. They had been over this multiple times. Yes, he agrees, on the surface, this may appear pointless. Perhaps this is just his need for closure. Whatever the reason, he feels they need to tie up this thread. Worst-case scenario, Mr. Olstroski was in the wrong place at the wrong time. Best case, this could help Freddy find his suspect. They need to follow this to the end.

The car turns off of Congress. They are on their way to Pine Oak Apartments. He understands Eddy's frustration. If this ends up being fruitless, then he will make it up to the man later. They are the ones hunting down Mr. Olstroski for Freddy. They are the ones who discovered his body. They are the ones responsible for following up on this. There is a slim possibility this could blow Freddy's case wide open.

"We've been over this multiple times," Shawn replies.

"I know. It just seems pointless."

"Eddy…"

"The man is dead, Shawn. Mr. Hamm is in custody. What are we even looking for?"

"I don't know," Shawn says. He could see the frustration in Eddy's face as he said that.

"You don't know?"

"I get it. Were the roles reversed, I would be just as frustrated."

"You'd tell me I'm acting like a fool on a wild goose chase."

Shawn chuckles. "Yeah, I probably would. Perhaps this is just that. You remember our discussion about the MacGuffin?"

"Yeah. That's what this is."

"Perhaps. What if it isn't? Eddy, I get it. I don't believe Mr. Hamm is innocent. All of the evidence points to him."

Eddy opens his mouth to speak. Shawn shakes his head.

"But Freddy believes he's innocent. It's not a hunch. It's a belief. You're no longer a rookie, but you're still a bit green when it comes to the Farmhouse. Freddy's good. Real good. I mean, he almost has a sixth sense about these things. If he believes Mr. Hamm did not murder his husband, then Freddy will stop at nothing to prove it. For as long as I have known him, the man has never been wrong. His methods can be a little unorthodox, but he always solves his case. If Freddy believes Mr. Hamm is innocent, we have to pursue this as if he is. And if he is, the real murderer is still out there."

"But that doesn't explain what we are doing."

"Doesn't it? Think about it, Eddy. If you murdered someone and left no evidence. The person's spouse was charged with the murder. You want to make sure you don't get caught. You will do everything possible to tie up all loose ends. Mr. Olstroski was a loose end."

"How?"

"Perhaps he knew something he shouldn't. Perhaps the murderer thinks he did, at least."

"Or perhaps his murder is unrelated."

"That's a possibility as well. But there is only one way to know for sure. And that is what we are doing now."

Eddy sighs. "Alright," he says, "I'll go along with it. If anything, just to rub it in your face when we reach the dead end."

Shawn smiles. "Or to rub it in your face if it does lead to something. I'll make you a deal. If I'm right, lunch is on you for the next three months. And you're right, lunch is on you for the next three months."

"Deal," Eddy says.

They turn into the drive at Pine Oak Apartments. Shawn parks the car next to the dragon fountain. They both exit the vehicle. Shawn looks at the dragon atop the precipice. Water pouring out of its mouth into the basin below.

"You are looking at it as if you expect it to come to life."

Shawn jumps at the sound of Eddy's voice. He didn't notice Eddy standing beside him.

He grins, "Yeah, we just need to raise the entire complex above the clouds to see if it breaks the spell."

"What?"

Shawn shakes his head. "Never mind. Just making a joke. Come on. Let's see what Mr. McDonald can tell us."

They both entered the front door into the main lobby. The lobby appears to be bustling today. The last time they were here, it was like a ghost town. Today, people are going to and fro. He could see people checking in and checking out. Shawn is confused. Isn't this an apartment complex? He knows of Pine Oak Apartments. He had driven by multiple times while on patrol. This is the second time he has been in the place.

He notices the same woman behind the front desk. What is her name again? Carrie? Camille? Carmen, that is it. She is busy assisting guests, and she did not notice them. Shawn and Eddy step in line and wait their turn at the counter. They are in no hurry.

"I thought this is an apartment complex."

"So did I," Shawn replies. "It appears to work more like a hotel."

"Perhaps it's one of those extended stay places. Maybe they just call it 'apartments' because people do live here."

"Perhaps."

They are moving fairly quickly. There were only two people in front of them now. Shawn watches the people walking in and out of the lobby. He is decent at reading people. He's not as good as Freddy, but he could at least tell if someone looked suspicious. Not that he expected anything to happen, but he could never let his guard down when on duty.

Just one person ahead of them. She is a tall, thin African American woman. She is wearing expensive clothes and jewelry. The woman appears to be an executive, based on how she is dressed. She seems to be a woman of power and high stature. She walks off and they step up to the counter.

"May I," Carmen starts to say as she looks up at them. He notices that she recognizes them. "Officers? You're back. How can I assist?"

"Hello, Carmen, is it?" Shawn asks.

She nods. "Yes. How may I assist you again? Ms. Martinez is still away."

Shawn shakes his head. "We aren't here to speak with her. We are here to speak with Stephen McDonald."

She looks puzzled. "Mac? May I ask why you need to speak with Mac?"

"Mac?"

"Oh, I'm sorry. Everybody here knows him as Mac."

"Oh, I see. It's because his last name is McDonald?"

She nods.

"Is he here? May we speak with him? One of our suspects was last seen here."

"Oh, the unkempt man who smells as if he needs a bath."

Shawn nods. He remembers Freddy saying to keep Richard Olstroski's death quiet. "He's one of our suspects for the murder of Marcus Peterson. Our trail stops at Mr. McDonald. We would like to speak with him to find out what he may know."

"I see," she says. "Mac is the head of security here. He's in his office. I'll take you to him."

"Thank you."

"One moment while I ask someone to cover the front desk."

She picks up the phone receiver and dials an extension.

"Hello, Tyler. Would you mind covering the front desk for me? There are two officers here who would like to speak with Mac. I won't be long. I'm going to take them to his office. Thank you, Tyler."

She hangs up the phone. A few minutes later, a tall blonde-haired man walks in. He appears to be in his twenties. He nods to Shawn and Eddy as he steps behind the desk.

"Tyler, this is Officers…"

"Braxton and Hickly," Shawn finishes. He can see she is struggling to remember their names.

"Nice to meet you both," Tyler says with a smile.

"Watch the front desk for me. I'll be back in a moment." She turns to Shawn and Eddy. "This way, Officers."

She leads them down the hall, past the elevator where they spoke with Maxwell. A few more turns, and they stop in front of an office. The sign on the door reads "Security." Carmen knocks on the door.

"Enter."

Carmen opens the door, and the three enter.

It is a small office. A desk sits in the middle of the room. There are two chairs on one side of the desk. The man behind the desk reminds him of Freddy in a way. There are rows of filing cabinets behind him. It is apparent he isn't comfortable with computers.

The man they call Mac is of average height. He looks to be in his mid-fifties. He is balding with dirty blonde hair and glasses. He speaks with a loud, jolly voice.

"Hi, Carmen. How can I help you?"

Mac, this is Officer Braxton and Officer Hickly. They would like to ask you a few questions."

He shakes his head and holds out his hands to either side. "I'm an open book. I'll be happy to help in any way I can. Come on in and sit down, gentlemen." He glances at Carmen. "Thank you, Carmen."

She nods and leaves, closing the door behind her. Shawn and Eddy sit down.

The jolly man sits back and rests his arms on the arms of his chair. "How may I help y'all?"

"Well, Mr. McDonald," Shawn starts.

The man holds up a hand. “Please, call me Mac. Everybody does.”

Shawn smiles. “I gotta know, what’s with the dragon fountain outside?”

Eddy glances at him. “You are still on this?”

Shawn brushes the comment off.

Mac laughs. “I’ll admit it’s a strange sight. An upscale place like this having a fountain like that. I understand how you think it’s out of place. I had the same question when I first started. The owner has this fascination with dragons. He had the dragon fountain erected when he bought this place.”

“Wait. It was added later?”

“Yeah. He wanted dragons throughout the lobby. Thankfully, his business partner urged against it.”

“That was a good idea,” Eddy says.

“I agree,” Mac says.

“Well,” Shawn says, “this place operates more like a hotel.”

Mac laughs. “Ah, everyone asks about the name. Why is it called ‘Pine Oak Apartments’?”

Shawn nods.

“This was originally an apartment complex. When Max bought it…”

“Max? You are referring to the gentleman named Maxwell?”

Mac nods. “He’s the owner. You’ve met him?”

Shawn nods. “We spoke with him the other day. Funny, he never mentioned he owns this place. I even asked him about the dragon fountain. His response was, ‘The owner has an affinity for dragons.’”

“And he does,” Mac says.

“But why doesn’t he just tell us he owns this place?”

“Max is an odd individual. He is a bit closed off to strangers. Anyway, Max and Geoff purchased this place when it was an apartment complex.”

"Geoff is his business partner?" Shawn asks.

"Yes. The apartments were a failing business. They converted it into a live-in hotel. All of the apartments remain full apartments. They are rented on a temporary basis. Think of it similar to a timeshare, but no one actually buys their room. They left the name because the business has been well established in town for decades."

"I see. What can you tell me about Juliana Martinez?"

"Ms. Martinez? She was working on Mr. Peterson's film. She's in Germany on a new project at the moment. Ms. Martinez has a standing room here. She pays for it annually."

"Is that normal?"

"For most people, no. But Ms. Martinez is a good friend to Mr. Peterson and his husband. She flies down from New York once a year to visit with them."

"She does?"

"Yes. Mr. Hamm, Mr. Peterson's husband, and Ms. Martinez are old friends. They've been over a few times to play cards and have a few drinks."

"Has anyone else visited Ms. Martinez lately?" Shawn asks.

"Not really. I mean, she has a string of crazy fans that like to pretend they know her. But none of them do. Mr. Peterson and Mr. Hamm visited her the night before Mr. Peterson's murder."

Shawn's ears perk up with that last statement. "Was it a social visit?"

"You would have to ask Mr. Hamm that question. I just know they were here."

Eddy places the photo of Richard Olstroski on the desk in front of Mac. "Has this man stoped by to visit Ms. Martinez?"

Mac picks up the photo to examine it. He nods.

"He stopped by early one morning. He was a bit frantic. Talking about how he needs to see Ms. Martinez. The man stunk as if he had been in the garbage. His hair and clothes were unkempt as well. Is he a suspect?"

Mac hands the photo back to Eddy. Eddy put it away.

"He's one of the cast members on the film," Shawn says.

Mac looks startled. "You're pullin' my leg?"

Shawn shakes his head.

"I thought he was another crazy fan of hers. He certainly doesn't look the type that goes around in her social circles. Don't get me wrong. Ms. Martinez is extremely generous. She is always giving her time and money to those in need. She came from nothing. She got to where she is with hard work. Definitely not a silver spoon brat. She has never forgotten where she came from. At the same time, you know this industry. The average Joe would not move around in her social circles."

"Well, what can you tell me about this man's visit?"

"Not much, actually. He was screaming about how he needs to talk to her now. He refused to leave until he did. The front desk tried explaining she had already left for Germany. He refused to listen. He kept on asking to speak with her. Saying her life is in danger. He wanted to make sure she is safe."

"Wait, what?" Eddy asks. "He said her life is in danger?"

Mac nods. "At the time, I thought he was a crazy fan. Front desk called security. I escorted him out. He tried to resist. A skinny little guy like that, I could have thrown him a mile." The man chuckles as he says that.

"So, what happened?"

"I dunno. I made sure he left the premises. Last I saw, he was walking down the road."

"Did he mention any other names?"

Mac sits back in thought. He places his right hand under his chin, resting his elbow on the arm of the chair. After a moment, he shakes his head.

"Not that I recall. Just kept saying her life is in danger. He has proof who killed Marcus. Is he talking about Marcus Peterson? The director?"

Shawn wanted to say, *Who else? What do you think we are investigating?* He quickly decides against it. Shawn glances at Eddy. He sees the man open his mouth and promptly close it. Perhaps they both had the same thought.

Shawn nods and replies, "Yes. He is talking about Marcus Peterson."

The man leans forward. He folds his hands together, resting his elbows on his desk. "So, this man claims to know who killed our local celebrity director?"

"So you say," Shawn replies. "Can you tell me anything else, at all, about that morning?"

He shakes his head as he sits back in his chair. "No, Officer. That's all I know."

The two men stand. Shawn reaches out to shake Mac's hand.

"Thank you for your time."

Mac nods. "My pleasure, Officers. You gentlemen, have a wonderful day."

"Thank you. You do the same," Shawn replies.

They both leaves Mac's office. Eddy starts to speak.

"Not now. Wait until we're in the car."

They walk back to the lobby. As they pass by the front desk, Carmen says, "Have a good day, Officers."

Shawn smiles. "Thank you. You do the same. And thank you for your kind hospitality."

She smiles. "Only the best service here."

They both exit the building and get back in the car.

"Now we can talk," Shawn says.

"Did he say that Mr. Olstroski claimed to know who murdered Mr. Peterson?"

Shawn nods. "And that Mr. Olstroski believed that Ms. Martinez's life is also in danger."

"Good thing she's in Germany."

"So everybody claims."

Eddy looks puzzled. "What do you mean?"

"Everybody here claims she is in Germany. And they may believe she is. Mr. Olstroski believed that her life is also in danger. Why? We need to find out if she is in Germany. I'm beginning to think there is more to Mr. Olstroski's death than being at the wrong place at the wrong time."

Shawn picks up his phone.

"Who you gonna call?"

"Ghostbusters," Shawn replies with a smile. "Who do you think? Freddy, of course."

Shawn calls Freddy's number. It rang a few times. He heard it switch over to Freddy's voice mail.

"This is Freddy. Leave a message, and I will get back as soon as I can."

He heard the 'beep.' "Hey Freddy," he starts. He sees an incoming call From Freddy. "Never mind. You are calling me back." He ended the call and answered the incoming call.

"Hey, Freddy. I was just leaving you a voicemail."

"What do you have?"

Freddy sounded a little shaken. His voice is breaking up.

"You okay?"

"I'm fine. What do you have for me?"

"So, I don't think Mr. Olstroski's death is circumstantial. I think he was murdered. Possibly by the same person who murdered Mr. Peterson."

"What did you find out?"

"Mr. Olstroski claims to have known who murdered Mr. Peterson."

"What?"

"There's more," Shawn says. "He also claimed that Ms. Martinez's life is also in danger."

"So, he believes someone is murdering the folks on the set?"

"That's my take-away."

"Shit. And I just tore into Mr. Hamm."

"What?"

He heard Freddy sigh. "It is a tactic I was using. Trying to prove Mr. Hamm did not murder his husband. I think it worked too well. Oscar, of all people, told me I have no soul."

"Freddy, you know he…"

"He didn't do it! Wait until you see the tape. You'll understand."

"Video."

"What?"

"Video. We stopped using tapes a long time ago, old man."

"Whatever."

He could feel the eye roll. He decides to get back on topic. "Well, if it is enough to convince Oscar…."

"As long as it convinces the Captain. Anyway, I am on my way to the coroner now. I want to find out what killed Mr. Olstroski. With this information you guys found out, I am sure the cause of death will be similar. Though I don't think the killer is murdering the entire film crew. I think Mr. Olstroski watches too many slasher flicks. Thanks for your help in this."

"One more thing." Shawn raises his right index finger as he says this.

"What's that?"

"Mr. Hamm and Mr. Peterson visited Ms. Martinez the night before the murder."

"That is interesting. I'll have to ponder that later. Alright, guys, get back to the Farmhouse. If Mr. Olstroski is correct, and I don't believe he is, then Mr. Hamm's life may be in danger. I'm going to speak with Sal. After that, we need to find a safe place for Mr. Hamm."

"What would you like for us to do?"

"Talk to Oscar. Make sure the Captain watches my interview with Mr. Hamm. You guys take Oscar as a witness. Update the Captain on everything we know. Explain everything, including Mr. Olstroski's death. This new information changes the nature of the case."

"Will do."

"When I get back, we all need to get together and figure out what to do with Mr. Hamm. That man needs to be protected."

"Gotcha. We're on it."

"Thanks, guys. You guys have been a huge help on this case."

"Meh," Shawn says as he waves his hand in the air. "Don't mention it. That's what we do. We are there for each other."

"Alright. Bye."

The call ended. Shawn places his phone back in his shirt pocket.

"Well, back to the Farmhouse."

Shawn starts the engine. They pull out of the drive and head back to the Farmhouse.

Chapter Sixteen

Six Feet Under

Freddy's Mustang is flying down the highway. He is heading north, out of town. He can't remember the last time he visited his grandparents. Life has been moving too fast the past few years. Losing his mom at such an early age and never knowing his dad, his grandparents were more like parents to him. It's long past time since he visited them.

Red Ridge Cemetery is just a few miles away. How long had it been since he last visited them? Is it two years? Three? He had lost track after becoming a detective. It had nothing to do with him loving them or caring about them any less. He lost focus on what is important in his life. There is no changing his mind once he has it set on something. Right now, his mind is set on making these recurring visits again.

The Mustang turns left off of the road at the sign that reads *Red Ridge Cemetery* and drives down the red dirt road. Trees are on either side for the first few minutes. The path opens up to a large green field of grass. The cemetery is small. Only a few dozen plots are there.

Like most cemeteries of the area, Red Ridge used to be on church property. The church burned down about ten years before Freddy's birth. It was re-built on the other side of town. The property still belongs to the church.

He parks the mustang next to a small hill. His grandparents rest atop the hill. He leaves the car and walks up the side of the hill. There they are, two solitary gravestones, away from the rest. Behind them is a small, white picket fence. Freddy stands facing them. The wide-open grassy field looks like a picturesque landscape behind him.

The headstones read:

Arthur Noah Miller

Born November 12, 1928
Died July 26, 2010

Lois Jolene Miller
Born November 30, 1928
Died January 17, 2005

He stands there in silence. All of the guilt rushed in at that moment. The guilt of losing contact. The guilt of not being there when they passed. The guilt of not visiting their gravesite until now. Tears run down his cheeks.

After a few moments, he finally speaks. "Papa, Granny, I love you. I'm sorry I haven't been by to visit. I'm sorry I never tried to reconnect before either of you passed. That last argument we had...I didn't mean what I said. I understand why you said what you did. It isn't because I'm gay. It is because you were trying to protect me.

"You knew what I was getting into. I mean, it leads to…"

He pauses for a minute before continuing. He is reliving Harry's death. He shakes it off and continues.

"Papa, you and I both know what it's like to watch the person you love die."

Freddy shakes his head as if to shake off the depressing thoughts. He looks down at the Mustang and back at the graves.

"I've taken good care of her. You'd be proud. She still runs like new. I'm still taking care of the old homestead. You know I'm not a farmer. I rent out the fields to Russ Conger's son. You remember little Tommy Conger? Well, he's in his twenties now. He's married with two kids. Anyway, Tommy farms the land now.

"I still live at the house. In fact, I'm in my old bedroom." He smiles as he says that. "Your bedroom is off-limits. It remains well kept, but nobody, other than me, goes in there. That will always be your room.

"I've started gardening. I'm using your old garden. Those two field rows are the only ones Tommy is not allowed to use."

He pauses again before he speaks. "After Harry's death, I entered the police academy. I'm a detective now. A damn good one too." He smiles again. "You guys would be proud of me.

"This current case has brought back so many memories. See, Hampton Hamm, I still can't get over that name.

"Anyway, Mr. Hamm's husband was murdered. He is the only person who can be pinned at the scene of the crime. I know in my gut that he did not do this."

He shakes his head before continuing.

"I had to prove it to the captain. In doing so, I think I pushed it too far. I broke that man hard. Too hard. I need the captain to see that this man did not murder his husband."

Freddy sighs.

"Papa, Granny, I took it too far. Now, another man is dead. He possibly knew information about the case. I'm not sure if he is another victim or if it is a coincidence. I'm going to talk to Sal after I leave here.

"As if you know who I'm talking about. Sal is the coroner. He's investigating the body to find out the cause of death. We need to find out if his death is related to Mr. Hamm's husband's murder."

At that moment his phone buzzes. It is a text from Oscar.

"Falcon, I know I'm late getting this to you. My computer is on the fritz. It takes Devon a while to get it back. Anyway, the guy I stoped is named Otto Von Snaut. Hope that helps."

"Son of a…" He sighs again. "Like a bad penny."

He places his phone back in his pocket and focuses on his grandparents.

"Remember Otto Von Snaut? Of course, you do. We were always hanging around each other growing up. Anyway, our paths went separate ways after the incident. Lately, he keeps showing back up in my life. I can't shake him. Now, I just found out that Otto may have information on this case. That's what the text is. See, the officer who was guarding Richard. Richard is the possible witness who was possibly murdered. That's a lot of possibly's, and this is a lot of information. I hope you can follow this. Anyway, the officer guarding Richard stops a guy the morning Richard escaped.

"To make a long story short...too late...Otto is the motorist he stopped. So, it appears I need to follow up with Otto. I'm hoping he has seen something or knows someone who did."

He pauses for a moment before continuing.

"I know what you are thinking, Granny. You would see this as a sign from God. A sign that it is meant for Otto and me to rekindle our friendship, or at least come to peace with each other. Perhaps it is time. Perhaps we will. You know my thinking on superstitious hocus pocus. It's just coincidences converging. But we shall see.

"Anyway, I love you guys. I'm off to the coroner. I will find Mr. Peterson's murderer and bring that person to justice."

He turns to leave and stops mid-stride. "I'll be back more often to pay my respects. I promise."

He walks back down the hill to his car. He looks back at the two graves atop the hill and smiles. An overwhelming sensation of peace fills his entire body. This is a promise he will keep.

***

Freddy walks into the coroner's office. Sal is nowhere to be seen. He walks up to the desk in the small room. There is a bell with a sign that read *Ring only once*. Freddy shrugs and presses his hand down on the silver-colored bell in four repeated strokes.

DING
DING

DING
DING

He hears sounds from the back. Sounds of someone putting something down and rushing to the front. There is a loud *thud* followed by a familiar voice.

"Son of a…"

After a few more moments, the door behind the counter opens. Out steps Sal holding his head.

"Are you okay?" Freddy asks.

Sal rolls his eyes. "Damn wall."

Freddy chuckles. "You ran into the wall? How the hell…?"

"Well, if you wouldn't ring the damn bell so many times. Can't you read?"

Sal walks up to the bell and slams the sign down right in front of Freddy. This starts Freddy a bit, and he shrinks back.

"Ring only once, Freddy! I thought it was a damn emergency!"

Freddy shakes his head. "I'm sorry, Sal. I didn't mean to..."

Sal put a hand up and shakes his head.

"Bah. Don't worry about it. In the future, ring that thing only once if I am not up here. I thought it was a damn emergency or something."

"Well, you have a nice goose egg on the side of your forehead."

Sal felt the spot on his head that made first contact with the wall.

"Damn knot's the size of a football."

He walks over to a freezer in the corner and pulls out an ice pack. He holds it up to the spot on his head. Sal walks back over to Freddy.

"You here to get my results?"

Freddy nods.

"You came at the right time. I've just finished the examination. C'mon."

Sal motioned for Freddy to follow. They walk through the doorway leading to the back.

"Watch your head," Freddy says with a smile.

"Is that supposed to be a joke?" Sal turns to look at Freddy.

Freddy nods.

"Well, don't quit your day job."

Sal turns back around to face forward. He starts walking before he could complete the rotation. Freddy barely got out the words, "Sal. Look out!"

THUD

"Dammit!" Sal exclaims. Sal sighs and motions, "Come on."

They continued the trek to the back room.

"So, as I said, I just finished the examination of the body."

"What did you find?"

"Well, it isn't arsenic or a stiletto." He rolls his eyes when he says the last part of that sentence.

"What is it?"

"See for yourself."

They enter the back room. Richard's body lay on the examining table. Freddy could smell the familiar stench of whatever causes Richard Olstroski's repugnant body odor. He recoils and pinches his nose.

"Yeah," Sal says, "I have no idea where that smell emanates from. I've examined a lot of cadavers over the years. It takes a while for rigor mortis to set in. I ain't ever smelled one that reeks as bad as this guy."

"This is how he smelled when he was alive," Freddy says.

"You're joking?"

Freddy shakes his head.

"This guy ever heard of taking a shower?"

"He did," replies Freddy. "The first time he was brought down to the Farmhouse to talk about the case. I made him shower then." Freddy shakes his head. "Didn't help."

"It makes me wonder why your fellow officer wanted to fondle him so desperately."

Freddy is taken aback at that. "What?"

Sal shakes his head. "Nothin'. It's just, the damn fool poked, prodded, felt, and moved the body so much...It's a wonder he didn't contaminate it. They don't teach you how to use gloves in the academy?"

"Of course they do."

"Well, he suddenly wanted to stop fondling this guy once I made him put on gloves."

Freddy sighs. "What did you find, Sal?"

"This."

Sal holds up a pair of tweezers to Freddy's face. Freddy shakes his head in confusion.

"What? Tweezers? In his body?"

Sal sighs. "No," he says sharply, "Not the tweezers."

"What then?"

"This." He holds the tweezers closer.

"What?"

Sal sighs again. "Look closer at them."

He holds the tweezers so close that Freddy thinks the man might puncture his eyeball with them. Freddy instinctively jerks back. He opens his mouth to speak. That's when he sees it. It is almost microscopic. Some sort of black material.

"What is it?"

Sal sits the tweezers down on a nearby table. "A glove," he says matter of factly. "Well, fibers from one anyway. A black glove, to be exact. I found it in his mouth."

Sal walks behind Richard's head and points to the right side of his mouth.

A lightbulb went off in Freddy's head. "Interesting," is all he says. He places his index finger and middle finger of his right hand together and laid them over his lips. This is a signal that he is in deep thought.

"Suffocation."

Sal nods.

"But the murderer wore a glove. It doesn't fit with the MO of the person who killed Mr. Peterson. But we can't ignore the fact that Mr. Olstroski's murderer was wearing gloves. That shows intent. That also shows this was planned. This is no accident. He wasn't in the wrong place at the wrong time. No. We find Mr. Olstroski's killer, and we find Mr. Peterson's."

Freddy pauses for a moment. Was this planned? Are the murders connected? He needs to be sure.

"Or, perhaps not. Sal, did you find anything else?"

Sal glares at him as if to say, "I know how to do my job."

Freddy shakes his head. "I'm not doubting your ability to do your job. I need to be sure. Is there anything, I don't care how insignificant, that you found on either body that could connect them?"

Sal shakes his head. "No. Nothing. There is nothing that connects the murders."

"No. There are three things that connect them."

"No, there aren't," Sal insists.

Freddy smiles. "Perhaps not that you can find. But there are three things." He holds up a finger as he mentions each point as if counting each one out. "First, we have the gloves. No prints outside of Mr. Hamm's were found at the Peterson crime scene. Second, Richard Olstroski was staying with the Peterson-Hamm's and never returned the night of the murder. Third, Richard Olstroski insisted that others on the set might be in danger. That shows that he may have known more than he was letting on. Perhaps he was scared."

Sal interrupts Freddy in mid-thought. "Do you honestly believe there is someone out there killing off everyone involved in the film? This isn't a slasher flick, Freddy. It's real life. That shit only happens in the movies."

Freddy shakes his head. "No. That's not what I'm saying. I don't believe that all of their lives are in danger. I think Mr. Olstroski found out something he shouldn't have. I think he assumed this is greater than what it is. I believe Mr. Peterson is the only intended target. Perhaps this is revenge. Perhaps a robbery. Perhaps something else.

"Here's what I think. I believe Mr. Peterson is the sole target. His murder is pre-meditated. His killer knows what they were doing. Mr. Olstroski found out something. I don't know what, but it is enough to scare the killer. Enough to cause the killer to get rid of him.

"Which means if Mr. Peterson's killer is tying up loose ends…."

"Mr. Hamm," Sal answered.

"Exactly."

***

The screen goes black. Oscar closes the laptop lid. The captain sits back in his chair. Shawn sits there, waiting for the captain to speak. No one says a word for a couple of minutes.

The captain finally speaks. "What the hell is he thinking?"

"Sir?" Shawn asks.

"Freddy. What is he thinking? And you," he looks over at Oscar, "You let this go on?"

"Falcon told me not to interrupt. No matter what."

"Use a little common sense, Oscar!"

"Sir," Shawn interrupts.

The captain glares at Shawn.

"Freddy is trying to prove that Mr. Hamm did not murder his husband. He was pushing Mr. Hamm to get that reaction."

"This is a place of law and order, Braxton! Yes, we do push suspects to get a confession! But, Jesus, what the hell?" The captain shakes his head. "That is too far!"

"That's what I told Falcon," Oscar says.

"If you knew he was going too far, why the hell didn't you stop it?"

"But…"

Shawn interrupts, "Sir, it does prove Mr. Hamm did not murder his husband."

The captain looked at Shawn. "Yes, it does. It also shows that Freddy willingly harassed a grieving husband. It shows that Freddy knows Mt. Hamm did not murder his husband. It shows that Freddy willingly traumatized this man."

"But, sir," Shawn interrupts, "Freddy thought he had no other way. He knew we had an innocent man."

"Then let the law work, Braxton! We are law officers! We have a duty to the law! We aren't vigilantes! What we have here is a possible lawsuit against the department! Dammit!"

No one says a word for a few moments. Shawn knows the captain is correct. He looks over at Oscar. The man sits there, expressionless. Shawn could not read the man's body language. He looks back at the captain. The captain leans back in his chair and is staring at the ceiling. He knows the captain is correct. He knows this could be bad for the Farmhouse, the entire department, the city, and possibly Freddy himself.

It is common knowledge that Freddy believes the man is innocent. The man had already been arrested for the crime. It is time for the damn lawyers to have their turn. He knows why the captain is upset. Freddy went around the law to harass this man even further, just to prove he is correct. It is all about Freddy's ego. Nothing more.

"Well," the captain says in a calm voice. "We know one thing for sure. This is proof we have an innocent man behind bars."

He sits up and looks at Shawn. "Where's Freddy?"

"The last time I talked to him, he was on his way to the coroner."

"The coroner? Why?"

Shawn sighs. "There is one more thing you need to know."

The captain glares at Shawn. No word is spoken. Shawn looks at Oscar. Oscar's face remains expressionless, but he did hang his head ever so slightly. Did the man already know?

"There is another murder."

"What? Who?" the captain asks.

Shawn looks at Oscar. He knows that Mr. Olstroski's murder is, ultimately, because Oscar screwed up. He keeps his eyes on Oscar as he speaks.

"Richard Olstroski."

Oscar does not say a word. He can see the guilt in the man's expression. He knows what the man must be thinking. Shawn never liked the man. He always thought of Oscar as a jackass. But, he feels terrible for the man at this moment. Oscar may be a lot of things, but he is a good officer. He believes in following the law. He doesn't want to drag the moment on. Shawn turns his attention back to the captain.

The captain is glaring at Oscar. No one says a word. The silence is broken by the ringing of Shawn's phone. Shawn glances at the display.

"It's Freddy."

The captain nods. Shawn answers the phone.

"Hey, Freddy. What's up?"

"Where are you?"

"In the captain's office. Oscar and I…"

"Oscar's there too?

"Yeah."

"Good. The captain knows?"

Shawn looks at the captain as he speaks. He nods. "He saw the video. He's pissed, Freddy."

"I went too far, and I didn't have to."

"Yeah, Richard Olstroski…"

"Richard was smothered to death."

"What? How?"

"Sal found a small piece of black fabric in his mouth."

"Black fabric?"

"Yeah, from a glove."

A lightbulb went off in Shawn's head. "That explains why there were no prints."

"Exactly."

"That also means you put Mr. Hamm through hell for nothing."

"Yeah." Freddy's tone became more sombre.

The captain is glaring at Shawn after hearing that statement.

"Where is he?" the captain asks.

"Where are you?" Shawn asks Freddy.

"At the coroner. I'm finishing up now."

"You're finishing up with the coroner?"

Freddy sighs. "Shawn, I'm not an idiot. You don't have to repeat what I am saying. You can just tell the captain. I know he is the one asking."

"Tell him I want to see him now."

"Freddy," Shawn says, "the captain…."

"Wants me back at the Farmhouse," Freddy finishes. "I'm heading there as soon as I leave here."

"And Freddy, he's pissed."

"Alright. Later."

Shawn ends the call and places his phone back in his pocket.

"He's on his way back now."

The captain nods.

"Alright, gentlemen. You are dismissed."

Both men stand and walk toward the office door.

"But," the captain says, "if anything like this ever happens again, I will have your badges. Understood?"

"Both men nod. "Understood," they both say in unison.

The men leave the office and close the door behind them. They both walk down the catwalk to the stairs, talking as they go.

"Do you think he is serious?" Oscar asks.

"About what? Taking our badges? Hell yeah. He is pissed, Oscar."

"I only have a few more years before retirement."

"Look, it's no secret that I don't like you. I think you are a rude jackass. But I do respect you as an officer."

"I'm frank, Braxton. I cut through the bullshit and get to the point. You guys these days are too soft. Yeah, I'm a hardass. I need to be. You guys do too. What you see as being rude is me being honest. I don't sugarcoat anything. We are all adults, and all have a job to do. This isn't daycare. We aren't babysitters. We are here to do a job. Some of these folks have done some bad shit."

"Then there is Mr. Hamm."

"Yeah. Falcon did cross the line though. You and I both know he did. Falcon knows it too."

"And it all seems pointless now."

"Yup. Look, Braxton, what happened, happened. What is, is."

The men reached the bottom of the staircase. Shawn heads for his desk. Oscar is heading for the holding area.

"Oscar," Shawn turns and says.

Oscar stops but does not turn. "What?"

"Don't tell Mr. Hamm yet."

"What the hell, Braxton? This isn't my first day on the job."

With that, Oscar walks off. Shawn sits down at his desk. Eddy is busy working on reports. Shawn opens up his computer and types in his password.

shiloh6A54559C

It is a stupid password, but it is one that he would never forget. Part of it came from a football video game he used to play as a kid. He can't remember what game it was or what team he was playing in the video game. He just remembers he had been over at a friend's house. They had rented the game and stayed up late playing it. They were in the middle of a season play when it was time for bed. The only way to save their progress is by a password. He committed the password, *6A54559C*, to memory and has never forgotten it.

This was before save features were commonplace in video games. These days, any video game has some way to save your progress. Back then, a few games had a save feature. The cartridges used a battery backup to save the data. This could be expensive for most developers. Society didn't have the big-budget development and production houses that they have today. Most video games were developed by a small team of one to two people. Sometimes a group of ten or so. It was nothing like it is today. They were the equivalent of the independent developer scene that we have today.

The other part of his password, *shiloh*, came from another video game. This was a password needed to access a computer in an old point-and-click adventure game. It was years later when he found out the word is Hebrew for *God's gift* or *peace*.

"So, what did the captain say?" Eddy asks.

"He's pissed."

Eddy nods. "But what about Mr. Hamm?"

"Freddy's theatrics proves Mr. Hamm's innocence. But so does Mr. Olstroski's murder. Eddy, the captain is pissed. I mean, pissed. Mr. Hamm could sue the city over what Freddy did. Freddy could lose his job over this."

"But he was just…"

Shawn shakes his head. "It doesn't matter. Freddy crossed the line. He needs to let justice work. Look what happened. Mr. Olstroski was murdered while Mr. Hamm is behind bars. We know, for a fact, Mr. Hamm could not have done that."

"Right, but Freddy doesn't...."

"It doesn't matter," Shawn says matter of factly. "Freddy met with the coroner. We have proof, now, the murders are be related."

"Proof? How?"

"They found a small piece of fabric from a black glove in Mr. Olstroski's mouth. He was suffocated."

"But how does that?"

Shawn interrupted him, "The only prints found at the Peterson crime scene were of Mr. Hamm."

Eddy nods.

"So, the murderer was wearing gloves. This is something Freddy suspected back then, but now we have proof. This exonerates Mr. Hamm. All Freddy had to do was be patient."

"So, where's Freddy now?"

"On his way back here to have a 'come to Jesus' meeting with the captain."

Chapter Seventeen

It's Raining, Man

Freddy knows what is about to happen the moment he parks his car. He dreads the meeting with the Captain.

"I'm going to get my ass chewed."

It is storming outside. The rain is falling so fast and heavy that he can't see anything out of the windshield. He grabs his umbrella from the back. He pauses for a moment. This is not going to be fun. It doesn't matter how swift he is in evacuating the car. He will get soaked.

"Well, no time like the present."

He pushes open the car door. He can feel the heavy wind blowing in on him. The torrential downpour soaks his body. He opens the umbrella, gets out of the car, closes and locks the car behind him in a rapid motion. The entire time, he could feel the rain and wind fighting against the umbrella.

A sharp flash of lightning, followed by a loud "crash" of thunder, makes him jump. He walks as fast as he can toward the front door of the Farmhouse.

He learned a hard lesson as a teenager about running in the rain. The incident had taught him to be more cautious and less anxious. It had been a heavy storm like this one. He stopped at a convenience store to pick up a soda. He didn't have an umbrella with him at the time. He decided to run into the store to avoid as much rain as possible. He lost his footing on a water puddle and fell fast. His face kissed the concrete hard. He will never forget the pain he felt that day. He had scraped up the side of his face and his knees. He twisted his foot in the process. His foot and face recovered, but his knees were never the same.

That lesson also taught him to carry an umbrella. From that day forth, he always ensured he had an umbrella within reach in the car. He never knows when he would need an umbrella.

Freddy reaches the door of the Farmhouse and slings it open with vigor and tenacity. He runs inside and closes the umbrella. He looks up and notices Norman's startled face.

"What the hell, Freddy?" the man says in his deep voice. "I was about to come over this counter and tackle you. I thought someone was rushing in to take us by surprise or something."

Freddy shakes the water off of his umbrella. "Sorry about that. I wanted to get in as fast as possible."

"And you are cleaning that up too."

Freddy's eyes follow the invisible line that ran from the end of Norman's outstretched index finger to the puddle of water at his feet.

"Sorry about that, too."

Norman opens a nearby supply closet and hands Freddy a towel and a mop. Freddy uses the towel to dry himself off. He then mops up the puddle of water caused by his umbrella.

"What's with you, Freddy?" Norman asks.

"What do you mean?"

"I mean this case. You're never this sloppy."

Freddy shakes his head. "It's not what you think."

"Isn't it?"

Freddy shakes his head. Norman hands him a bucket. Freddy wrings out the mop in the bucket.

"I mean," Norman says, "I think you are personalizing this case. It's reminding you of what happened to Harry."

Freddy shakes his head. "It's not the same. Harry was part of a deal that went bad. This is different."

"It's not directly the same. Mr. Hamm was present when his husband was murdered. I think you are suffering from PTSD. It's impairing your judgment on this case."

"I don't see a therapist's degree on that wall."

Norman nods. "Understood. Consider it dropped. Now, don't you ever startle me like that, again. You're lucky I didn't jump over this counter and break your arms."

"Understood." Freddy hands the mop, bucket, and towel back to Norman.

Norman raises his hands and shakes his head. "Towel goes to laundry. Water goes down the drain. Mop and empty bucket go to the janitorial closet. I ain't your maid."

"Understood."

"The captain wants to see you."

"I know."

"He says to tell you he will call your phone when he's ready for you. He's on the phone with the chief and the mayor now."

Freddy sighs. "Thanks, Norman."

Freddy struggles with the mop, umbrella, and mop bucket as he walks toward the door leading into the station proper. The light is still red. He turns his head to look over at Norman.

"Nor…"

That's when he sees it. Without saying a word, Norman is holding out an empty tray. He knows Norman's rules. But can't the man let it slide this once? Freddy is struggling to carry everything, and Norman expected him to empty his pockets.

"Can't you let it slide this once? I'm in a predicament here."

"I don't make the rules, Freddy."

"Actually, you did. They're 'Norman's Rules.'"

"You got me there," he says with a smile. "Now, how's it gonna look if I let you slide? I'll have to let everybody slide. Then what? Anarchy in the streets. Cats and dogs living together. Total chaos." He shakes his head. "Freddy, these rules are here for a reason. You know that."

"Cats and dogs living together…." Freddy rolls his eyes at that statement.

"Okay, so I exaggerate a little."

"A little," he says with raised eyebrows.

"You get my point, Freddy. Everybody follows the rules here. No exceptions."

Freddy sighs. "Yeah, yeah."

He places the umbrella and mop under his left arm. The mop bucket in his left hand and the towel over his shoulder. Freddy struggles with his right pocket, almost dropping the mop and umbrella. His hand emerges with his wallet and keys. He places them on the tray.

"You could have just set them down. Sometimes you're too smart for your own good. No common sense."

"Just open the door."

Norman shakes his head. He points to Freddy's gun.

Freddy sighs. "Shit." He places his gun on the tray. "Is that it?"

Norman pushes the button behind his desk. The red light next to the door leading into the station turns green. Freddy thinks he must look like a clown. He struggles with the mop, bucket, towel, and umbrella as he attempts to open the door. The light turns red before he can open the door. Norman pushes the button again. Freddy is finally able to turn the knob and push the door open. He goes into the station proper, letting the door swing closed behind him.

***

Meg walks through the rows of cubicles. She is on her way out. As she turns to walk toward the exit leading to the reception area, she sees a sight that almost makes her burst into laughter. Freddy Falcon, famous ace detective, is carrying a mop bucket.

She waits, with arms folded, to see how long it would take him to notice her. She watches as he almost drops the bucket, then almost drops an umbrella while trying to catch the bucket. Is this real life or television? She almost thinks Freddy should quit his day job for a comedy act.

After a few moments, she approaches him with a smile. "Need any help?"

Meg takes Freddy so much by surprise that he drops the mop and umbrella with a loud "CLANG." She grabs both off of the floor.

"Thanks," he says.

"No worries. I'm Meg. You must be the new janitor," she says with a smile.

Freddy glares at her. "Not funny, Meg."

"I dunno, Fred. I think it's funny," came a nearby voice.

"No, it isn't, Barney. And it's Freddy. Not Fred," Freddy replies.

"Sorry, pal," Barney apologizes. The man turns back to his work.

"So, where are you headed?" Meg asks.

"Well, I have been tasked with taking the wet towel to the laundry, dumping the water down the drain, and returning the mop and bucket to the janitor's closet."

"I'll walk with you."

"Aren't you heading out?"

"I am. I want to talk a minute."

"About what?"

They carry on the conversation as they walk.

"The Captain's pissed Freddy."

He shrugs. "So. He's been pissed before."

She shakes her head. "Not like this. You really did it this time."

"He knows my methods are unorthodox. I always solve my case."

"Freddy, Mr. Hamm could sue over this."

"What? Why?"

They made it to the laundry area. Freddy dumps the wet towel in the laundry. They head for a sink next to dump the dirty water.

"Freddy, this is a high-profile case. The director of a major motion picture is murdered. The media and tabloids are all over this. The mayor's involved. It's huge."

"I know, Meg. That's why I need to solve this. Mr. Hamm is innocent."

"And thanks to your theatrics, the entire department knows it."

Freddy dumps out the water.

"Look. I know I went too far. Even Oscar told me I have no soul."

"Oscar?"

Freddy nods," Hard to believe."

Meg nods.

Lastly, they head for the janitor's closet last.

"Look, Meg, I know I screwed up. And the Captain will probably threaten to take my badge. It's always just that. A threat. He never follows through with it. You know why?"

He pauses. She assumes he is waiting for a response. Well, she had none to give. She knows how pissed off the Captain is. Freddy may lose more than his badge this time.

"Because I'm the best detective in this city. Hell, in the entire state. He can't afford to lose me."

"And there's the famous ego we all know so well. The overconfident Freddy Falcon. You may be wrong this time."

They reach the janitor's closet. Freddy stores the mop and mop bucket away. He closes the door.

"Freddy," Meg says, "everybody's expendable."

She turns and walks away, leaving Freddy to ponder what she said.

***

Freddy finishes frothing the milk for his espresso. He pours the espresso into a mug and pours the milk in it. He takes a spoon and scoops the froth on top. Freddy takes a sip and smiles. He always made great cappuccinos.

He sits the mug down and proceeds to clean the espresso machine. He washes out the carafe. He dumps the pressed grounds into the trash and cleans each piece of the espresso maker. This includes the steam wand. He could tell the steam is struggling to exit on this last use. It's time the wand is cleaned thoroughly. Milk can clog it up if one is not careful.

Freddy had been thinking about what Meg said. There is truth in what she is saying. And he was a pompous ass. Everyone's expendable. Even the great Freddy Falcon can't escape it. Would the Captain suspend him over this? Or worse? Fire him?

That thought doesn't sit well with him. He shrugs it off. He knows the murders have to be connected. He knows the real suspect is taking out loose ends. What about Hampton? What would happen when the suspect realizes Hampton isn't our target any longer? What would happen to Hampton? Is he another "loose end" that needs to be expunged?

He shakes off that thought as well. He knows Hampton didn't witness anything. The killer has to know that too. Hampton said nothing could wake him. Surely, the killer knows Hampton was there. Why was Hampton left alive? It would have been easy to kill them both.

But Marcus Peterson wasn't dead when the killer left. Or was he? Had the killer left when Hampton found his husband? Hampton was too overtaken with grief to have noticed. Mr. Peterson was still alive when Hampton found him. What if the commotion did wake Hampton? What if Hampton interrupted the murder? What if the murderer escaped when Hampton's attention was turned toward his husband dying in his arms?

But why? Why not just kill both men then and there? Freddy shakes his head. That part doesn't make any sense. There had to be a reason Hampton was left alive. The killer would not have left knowing there was a chance his victim would live. Mr. Peterson was the only person who could identify his attacker. No. The killer would have stayed. Would have watched to make sure Mr. Peterson died.

That means whoever murdered Mr. Peterson watched as Hampton held his dying husband. Watched a grieving widower suffer as his husband gasped his last breath. No. This is revenge for something. Whoever did this wanted Hampton to suffer. Mr. Peterson isn't the target. Hampton is. But why?

At that moment, Freddy's phone rang. He dried off his hands and sprinted to his desk.

"Hello," he answers.

"Falcon," replies an irritated, stern voice.

"Captain."

"Come to my office."

"On my way, sir."

"And Falcon."

"Yes, sir?"

"Don't bring any coffee."

"Yes, sir."

Freddy hears the captain hang up. He places the receiver back on the hook.

"Well," he says with a sigh. "Let's get this over with."

***

Freddy knocks on the Captain's door.

"It's open."

He opens the door and pops his head inside.

"Come in, Falcon. Act like you work here. Don't be shy."

"Yes, sir."

He closes the door and approaches the captain's desk. He pulls out a chair and sits down. He sits back in the chair, folds his arms, and waits for the captain to speak.

The silence is finally broken.

"Falcon," the captain says. "Do you know why I asked you to come to my office?"

Freddy nods. "Because you saw the video."

The captain nods.

"Sir," Freddy starts. The captain holds up a hand. Freddy closes his mouth.

"How long have you been on the force?"

"Sir?"

"Did I stutter?"

Freddy shakes his head.

"How long?"

"Ten years, sir."

"Ten years," the captain repeats. "During those ten years, how long have you been a detective?"

"Seven, sir."

"And before you were a detective?"

"Sir?"

"What was your position before you were a detective, Falcon?"

"I was an officer, sir."

"You were two years out of rookie status when you were promoted to detective. It takes most people years, sometimes decades, to get where you are now. Falcon, do you know why we promoted you so quickly?"

"Sir, I don't understand what this has to do with anything."

"Answer the question, Falcon. Understanding and clarity will come later."

"Because I am good at detective work."

"Wrong."

Freddy is taken aback at that. The captain ignored his confused look.

"You are exceptional at detective work. The best this city, no, this state has ever seen. You show remarkable promise, Falcon. Your perceptive and deductive skills are unmatched by anyone else."

“Thank you, sir, however I feel a ‘but’ coming on.”

The captain smiles. “Good. Now that’s the deductive skill I am talking about. Why the hell did you act like a damned idiot in the interrogation room with Mr. Hamm?”

“Sir,” Freddy starts.

“Don’t ‘sir’ me! Listen, Falcon! Your little stunt could cost this city! If Mr. Hamm knows what you pulled….”

“He doesn’t know? Good.”

“Hell no, he doesn’t know! Not the fact this is a damned stunt! You better be glad he thinks that was real! I ought ’a have your badge for this!”

“Captain…”

The captain ignores that statement and continues. “I got the mayor breathing down my neck! The damned entertainment media keeps calling! I’m getting calls from Hollywood, newspapers, national news channels, you name it! And you have to pull a stunt like this! Are you trying to get us sued?”

“I’m trying to solve a case, sir,” Freddy says calmly.

“You’re trying to get yourself fired!”

“Sir, I know my methods are unorthodox at times….”

“Unorthodox? This is damn insane!”

“You’re just upset because you are under so much pressure. It has nothing to do with me.”

“It has everything to do with you!”

“Sir, my job is to solve this case. You can be the mayor’s puppet all you want. At the end of the day, this case is no different than any other.”

There is dead silence in the room. You could cut the tension with a knife. The captain finally speaks.

“What did you say?”

“Forgive me, sir. You are better than this. This case has you acting like you are the mayor’s puppet. You aren’t thinking rationally.”

“You’re suspended!”

"Sir?"

"You are off this case! You will not investigate the murder of Marcus Peterson any longer!"

"Sir, you need me," Freddy replied. "You said yourself that I am the best person for the job."

The captain nods. "You are, but I will not tolerate insubordination. Not from you. Not from anyone."

"But, sir," Freddy feels panic building up inside of him. This is real. This is happening. The captain had never followed through with these threats before.

"You 'sir' me one more time, and I will fire you."

Freddy nods.

The captain picked up the phone and dials. "Norman. Detective Falcon will be leaving soon. He will be leaving without his gun and badge. Give him everything else."

He hangs up the phone and addresses Freddy.

"One week without pay. Go home, Falcon. Your job and office will be waiting when you return."

Freddy nods. He stands and heads for the door.

"Falcon," the captain says as Freddy reaches for the doorknob.

"Yes, sir?"

"Relax and forget about this case for a week."

"Yes, sir."

Freddy leaves the office, closing the door behind him.

***

Freddy reaches the bottom of the stairs. He does not head for his office. Instead, he bolts for the door leading down to the holding cells. He flings the door open and briskly walks down the stairs. He sees Oscar's desk up ahead. He walks past Oscar without a word.

"Falcon," Oscar says.

Freddy grabs Oscar's cell keys off of his desk and keeps walking.

"What the hell, Falcon!"

Freddy keeps walking.

"Falcon," Oscar says again. This time the man grabs Freddy's arm.

Freddy jerks his arm away and keeps walking.

"Not now. I won't be long."

He feels like the Terminator homing in on Sarah Connor. He has one mission down here. The man deserves to know. It is the right thing to do.

"Mr. Hamm," Freddy says as he approaches Hampton's cell.

Silence.

"Mr. Hamm," he says again.

Nothing.

He looks into the cell. Hampton is sitting on the edge of the cot, looking out at him. No expression on his face.

"Mr. Hamm."

Not a word. Not a motion. He can read the man. It doesn't take a genius detective to know the man is pissed at him.

Freddy opens the door to Hampton's cell. He steps inside, closing the door behind him. He walks over to the cot and sits down beside the man. Hampton sits there, motionless.

"What I'm about to tell you will not make you happy. In fact, if the captain knew I was down here, it could cost me my job. I never lied to you. I do know you did not murder your husband. What I did, what I said to you, is all to set you free. Your reaction is exactly what I wanted. The captain saw the videotape of your interview. You're going to be a free man. Anyway, I'm sorry."

Freddy reaches out his hand to touch Hampton's arm. Hampton jerks his arm away. Freddy feels the ice coming from the man. A shock of fear comes over him. Fear that he had damaged this relationship beyond repair. He shakes it off.

"I deserve that," is all he says.

Freddy stands and walks toward the cell door. He exits the cell, closing and locking it behind him.

"Oscar," he says as he walks by the man's desk.

Oscar looks up from his computer. He holds out the man's keys. Oscar reaches out and grabs them.

"You won't see me for a week. I'm suspended for my little stunt."

Oscar starts to speak. Freddy interrupts him.

"I told him, and I apologized for it."

"Falcon, if the captain finds out…."

"You can tell him if you want. I don't give a shit. The man deserved to know. I needed to apologize."

He notices Oscar is looking into his eyes, reading him. For the first time, since knowing the man, he sees a smile on that stern face.

"Falcon, I've never liked your smug attitude. You're a conceited smart-ass with delusions of grandeur. You never shy away from letting everyone in the room know you are smarter than them. It's annoying."

Freddy opens his mouth to speak. Oscar keeps going.

"Don't interrupt me. But what you did for the man in that cell… You put your job on the line to prove his innocence. Yes, it is a dumbass thing to do. There are other ways you could have done it. Other ways without cutting the man to his core. What you did a moment ago...I respect that. That is humble. That is honest."

Oscar shakes his head, "No, I have nothing to tell the captain. I'm just down here playing solitaire on my computer. I never saw you."

"Thanks, Oscar."

"Enough emotion. Go before someone does see you."

Freddy nods and starts for the stairs.

"One last thing," Oscar says. Freddy pauses and turns to face the man.

"What?"

"I can't speak for the captain. I can only tell you how I see it. The country hates us right now. They have for decades. The office, the badge, none of it has been respected for years. There are bad cops out there that have taken center stage. Their stupid, hateful antics have soured what we stand for in the public eye.

"You know, as well as I do, that's the minority. The majority of cops are good people who want to uphold the law. You're one of the good ones. That stunt you pulled doesn't reflect that. The media is already on this case because of its nature. We don't need your little stunts magnifying it any more than it already is.

"Where the hell is the Falcon we all love to hate? You've gotten soft after you started this case. Even at the beginning of the case, you were on point. Perceptive. Logical. Professional. Brilliant. All of that is still there, but it's clouded by your emotions. Use this week to go find that Freddy Falcon. The one that doesn't allow his emotions to get in the way of his professionalism. Come back with a clear head, Falcon. Show me the Freddy Falcon that annoys the hell out of me."

Freddy smiles. "I thought you said 'no more emotion.'"

Oscar flipped him off. "Get the hell out."

"Now that's the Oscar I know and love."

Freddy turns and walks up the stairs. He opens the door at the top and exits into the station proper.

***

It is still raining when Freddy steps outside. It isn't as heavy as it was when he arrived. He walks fast to his car, unlocks it, and swiftly gets inside. He sits there for a moment while the rain beats down on the roof.

"Why did I do that?" he asks himself. "Why did I have that reaction?"

As a flash of lightning streaks across the sky, the answer hits him. He shakes his head. "No. I can't consider him a friend. He's part of a case. I need to step away. The captain is right. Oscar is right. They are all correct. I've got to find myself again. Find my focus."

He puts the key in the ignition and starts the engine. He backs out of his parking space and drives toward the highway. Stopping at the mouth of the drive, he waits for the traffic to give an opening.

"I can't promise I will stop thinking about the case, but I will come back with a fresh start and a clear head. First things first, though. I need to visit an old friend."

He sees the opening in the traffic. The Mustang turns onto the highway and drives off.

Chapter Eighteen

My Dinner With Otto

It is about eight-thirty-five in the evening when Freddy finally sees Otto's car in the parking lot of *Hold the Anchovies*. He had been driving around the south side of town for hours, waiting for Otto to return home. Freddy had filled his tank up twice because of that. He is also on his eighth cup of coffee.

"Why does everyone and their uncle sell some type of coffee these days? Don't they know I have an addiction?"

He parks the Mustang next to Otto's car. He steps out of the car and locks the door. Just to be sure, he checks Otto's plate against the one Oscar pulled. As he thought, it is a match. He shakes his head and starts for the front door.

The bell attached to the front door makes a "DING" as Freddy opens it. The small, chubby man behind the counter looks up with a smile when he hears the sound. The smile quickly fades when he sees Freddy.

"Detective?"

Freddy shakes his head. "I'm here to see Otto, Mario."

The man fakes confusion. "O...Otto?"

"Look. I know Otto's downstairs. I know he rents the basement from you. I know that's his car outside. I don't give a shit about whatever arrangement you two have. Otto and I go way back. It's sort of a love-hate relationship. Now, I'm going down those stairs, and I am going to have a chat with Otto. Understand?"

The man just nods.

"Good."

Freddy walks toward the back door that reads "Employees Only." He can see the light at the bottom of the stairs when he opens the door. He closes the door behind him and heads down the stairs.

Reaching the bottom of the stairs, he sees Otto hunched over a computer. The man is too engrossed in whatever he's doing to notice the red-heads intrusion. The detective walks up and stands behind Otto. He wonders how long it will take the man to notice he is there. After a moment of silence, Freddy finally speaks.

"You know, just anyone could have murdered Mario, snuck down the stairs, and robbed you without you noticing."

The man almost jumped out of his skin at the sound of Freddy's voice. He quickly locked the computer and rotated his head to glance over at the man.

"Freddy...," Otto says with that stupid grin.

"Cut the crap, Otto. I'm not here to arrest you."

"You're not? Good. I mean, of course, you ain't. What do I owe this surprise visit to?"

"Look, Otto, I just want to talk." Freddy rolls his eyes. "Unfortunately, you are the only person still alive that knows me well."

Otto still has that stupid grin on his face. His cigar bounces on the right side of his mouth as he speaks.

"Of course, old friend."

"We aren't friends. Not anymore. You just happen to be the only person I have left to turn to right now. Can we sit down?"

"Of course, Freddy. Anything for an old frenemy. C'mon, pal."

Otto stands and walks into his living area. Fredy follows. He remembers the first time he was down here. It was a few days before the Peterson murder case had started. He was out for one of his Sunday drives. Coming back into town, he decided to stop for pizza. That's when he discovered Otto's little hideout. And Otto's little...

"Hey, what happened to the lady you had tied up down here?"

"What lady?"

Otto sits down in one of the chairs in the living area. He motions for Freddy to sit in the other chair.

"The lady you had tied up on the pool table. What happened?" Freddy points to the pool table. It lay uncovered. The balls racked at one end.

"Oh, that lady," Otto says with a grin. "I let her go."

"Just like that?"

"Look, Freddy. I may be a lot of things, but I ain't no killer. I found out she is in on what happened to Harry. I needed information."

Freddy sits down. "Well, did you get it?"

Otto shakes his head. "She punched me in the gut and ran off after you left."

Freddy chuckles.

"It's not funny, Freddy," the man says with an annoyed look.

"Yes, it is," Freddy replies. "You've always seen yourself more like Wilson Fisk or Tony Soprano. You're more like a cartoon villain."

Otto just glares at the man. "If you are going to insult me, then you can just leave."

Freddy shakes his head. "Look, Otto, we need to talk. This case I'm on, it's brought back memories. There are issues I never resolved."

"You and me?"

Freddy gave him an irritated look as if to say, 'that is a dumb statement.' "No. Harry."

Otto nods. "That."

Freddy nods.

"You ate yet?"

Freddy shakes his head. He hears his stomach rumble. How long has it been since he had anything to eat? Had he eaten today?

"I'm hungry. I can tell you are too." He points to Freddy's stomach as it rumbles again. "I'm going to place an order with Mario. I'll be back."

Freddy reaches for his wallet. Otto shakes his head.

"One of the perks living in a restaurant," Otto says with a grin. "Besides, Mario owes me."

Otto stands and heads up the stairs. Freddy leans back in the chair. He looks up at the ceiling and folds his hands across his chest. Closing his eyes, he let the silence consume him.

***

BAM! BAM! BAM!

Freddy jumped at the sound. He stands with his hand where his gun should be. He reached for it out of instinct, forgetting that the captain had taken it from him. He surveys the room. Otto is holding a gavel, standing in front of the table.

"What the hell!" Freddy exclaims. "Are you trying to get yourself killed?"

"I'm trying to wake your ass up. Food's here."

"I wasn't asleep. I was thinking."

"Do you usually snore when you think?"

Freddy glares at Otto. "I don't snore."

Otto laughs. "Freddy, pal, you've been snoring for as long as I've known ya. Your snores can raise the dead. Mario thought there was a wild animal down here."

Freddy rolls his eyes. "Let's eat."

They approach the bar in Otto's make-shift kitchen. It appears as if Otto has one type of each menu item laid out. Freddy's eyes skim the counter: pizza, calzones, soup, salad, garlic knots, breadsticks.

"What? No soda?" He grabs a plate and begins to help himself to some food. "You drink soda the way I drink coffee."

Otto follows suit. "Not anymore. Can't."

Freddy grabs a couple of slices of supreme pizza, a few breadsticks, and a few garlic knots. Otto went right for the salad and soup.

"What happened?"

"Heart attack."

Freddy pauses and glances at Otto. "What?" When?"

Otto smiles and replies, "So you do care."

"Not if you are going to gloat."

Freddy turns his attention back to his plate. He reaches for one last garlic knot and turns toward the table. He sets his plate down. Otto follows.

"I'm off caffeine, but I did ask Mario to make you something special."

Otto sets a large cup of steaming coffee down on the table in front of Freddy.

"It's a peppermint mocha. I remember how much you love 'em."

"He doesn't serve coffee."

Otto smiles. "Not to the public. This is from his private stash."

Freddy nods. "Thanks. What are you drinking?"

"Apple juice."

The two men sit and start to partake of the meals in front of them.

"So, heart attack?" Freddy asks as he takes a bite of pizza.

Otto nods. "It was about three years ago. I was in an...altercation...with a...colleague."

"Alright. So, you were fighting with a fellow crook. Go on."

Otto glares at Freddy. "If you're gonna be a smartass about it, I'll stop now."

Freddy nods. "I'm sorry. Old habits, I guess. Go on."

"Where was I? Oh yeah. So, Three Finger Travis…"

Freddy is taking a sip of coffee when Otto says the name 'Three Finger Travis.' He sits the cup down and exclaims, "Travis Herbert! What the hell were you doing with that psychotic?"

"Look, I know Travis hasn't always played nice with the cops..."

"He blew up a police station!"

"Nobody was hurt."

"That's only because they were celebrating their captain's birthday. They were down the block at Nate's Donuts."

"What is it with you cops and donuts anyway?"

Freddy shakes his head. "I dunno. I can't stand them."

"He was justified."

"How?" Freddy says with disgust. "How could anyone be justified to do that?"

"He thought the captain was sleeping with his wife."

Freddy rolls his eyes. "Was he?" He remembers this case and already knows the answer to the question. This was meant more as sarcasm.

Otto shakes his head. "No. It was a case of mistaken identity."

"Mistaken identity! He tried to murder an entire police force!"

"How could he know it was the captain of a tugboat and not a police station?"

"Really," is all Freddy says.

"Besides, happens to you cops all the time."

"Yeah, but we don't blow up buildings when we mistake someone's identity."

"No. But you do break into homes of innocent people, and you do profile and entrap."

Freddy just sits there. He knows Otto is right. Unfortunately, that does go on. Not as often as the media likes to portray, but it does go on.

Freddy's voice is calmer now. "It breaks my heart every time I hear about a fellow officer gunning down innocence. Yes, it's true there are bad officers out there. Anytime an officer stops anyone these days, the officer is automatically guilty before the facts are known. A few bad apples have made it so much harder on the rest of us trying to do our jobs."

"Look," Otto says, "I know Three Finger Travis has had a checkered past, and I am not defending him. He and I had a...business arrangement...you could say."

Otto pauses. Freddy assumes he is waiting for a smartass remark to follow. He has none to give.

"Go on," he says. "I'm listening."

"We were in the middle of our altercation when I felt this sudden pain in my chest. I can't breathe. I started getting lightheaded and collapsed. I remember waking up with three men hovering over me."

"Travis's henchmen?"

Otto shakes his head. "Paramedics."

"He called 911?"

"No. He left me for dead. See, we were in the parking lot of an abandoned building. I found out later that some old farts out for a Sunday drive found me layin' there."

"These people save your life, and you call them 'old farts'?"

"Well, they were in their seventies."

Freddy glares at him.

"Okay, older couple then. Anyway, to make a long story short...."

"Too late," Freddy replies.

"You still make that reference? Freddy, that movie's over thirty years old. Get with the times, man. And frankly, it never was that good."

"You're crazy! That's a cult classic!"

"When's the last time you saw it?"

"I dunno. It's been fifteen or twenty years."

"Go back and watch it. You remember the acting. The story is shit."

"We'll table this for later. Get on with your story."

"That's it. Doc says I had a heart attack. Caused by too much caffeine. I had to get off caffeine immediately. Let me tell ya, Freddy, comin' off caffeine ain't no fun. Stick with your addiction or wean yourself off of it. I stoped cold turkey."

"You what?"

"Yeah. So, I had a massive headache for the first few weeks. After that, all I did is sleep for a few more weeks. It was hell."

Freddy nods. "I understand."

Otto takes a bite of salad. He points the prongs of his fork at Freddy. "What about you? What's with this case?"

"You remember Mr. Hamm?"

Otto stares at Freddy blankly.

"The guy in the burger place," Freddy adds.

Otto still had a blank stare on his face.

"The guy you tried to rob inside *Burger Palace* a while back."

He sees the lightbulb go off in Otto's head.

"Oh, right. The fat loser you were sitting with."

Freddy's voice became stern. "Mr. Hamm," he starts, "is grieving. His husband was murdered the night prior."

"Marcus Peterson?"

"So, you have heard of the case."

"How can you not? A Hollywood director from a small town is murdered in his own home."

Freddy nods. "Yeah, not the typical case you find around these parts. Anyway, Mr. Hamm is one of two possible suspects."

"Only two? Freddy, you're losin' your touch if you can't solve this."

Freddy ignored that. "We arrested Mr. Hamm for the murder."

"See, solved."

"Mr. Olstroski…"

"Who?"

Freddy sighs. "The other suspect. Do you want to hear the details or not?"

"Go on," Otto says with a mouthful of food.

"Mr. Olstroski is one of the leads in the movie. He had been staying with the Peterson-Hamm's for the duration of the shoot. Anyway, Mr. Olstroski never returned home that night."

"Sounds suspicious."

"Not really," Freddy says. "He has an alibi and witnesses. He was out partying that night."

"So, the fat guy did it. He murdered his husband."

"No!" Freddy exclaims. He pounds the table with his fist. The tableware shakes at the force of his fist. "Mr. Hamm did not murder his husband, dammit!"

Otto doesn't budge. He acts as if this temper doesn't surprise him. A smile creeps upon his face.

"What?" Freddy asks in a sharp tone.

"Now that's the Freddy I know. The passion. The drive. The conviction. I'm listening."

"Look, perhaps my judgment has been impaired on this case. I acknowledge that. It's brought back a lot of old feelings and memories. A lot of pain."

"Harry."

Freddy nods. "But Mr. Hamm did not do this. I know it with every fiber of my being."

"Freddy, you've always had some type of sixth sense about this stuff. That's part of what makes you good at your job. You know things, man. You always have. Call it psychic. Call it supernatural."

"I'm not Harry Dresden."

"Who?"

"Fictional detective with magical and supernatural abilities."

"I don't follow fantasy."

"Anyway, to make a long story short. Too late. Richard…"

"Really? You do that to yourself too?" Otto shakes his head. "Just stop."

Freddy pretends to ignore that. "Richard is found dead while we had Hampton locked up."

"Who and who?"

"Richard Olstroski and Hampton Hamm. Try to keep up, will you, Otto?"

"Wait. The man's actual name is Hampton Hamm? What? Was he bitten by a radioactive pig?"

"That reference you know? You've never read a comic book in your life."

"I see movies."

"Yeah, don't get me started on that one. My opinion is not the popular one."

"You didn't like *Into the Spider-Verse*? That is a great film, Freddy."

Freddy sighs. "I loved the Miles Morales stuff. I never read any Spider-Man comics after the '90s. I know nothing about Miles's story. That is a breath of fresh air. Peter Parker had been done to death in film and TV. If I have to see Uncle Ben die one more time… Anyway, I loved the Miles story. I find Miles Morales more compelling than Peter Parker. That should have been the movie. That would have held without the alternate universe Parker or Spider-Man Noir. And don't get me started on Spider-Ham."

"What's the matter with Spider-Ham?" Otto asks.

"Nothing," Freddy replies. "He was created as a parody of Spider-Man and the Marvel universe. Saying Spider-Ham is part of the Spider-Verse is like saying Dark Helmet belongs in the Star Wars universe."

"Well, I liked it."

"That's fine," Freddy says. "It's not a bad movie. It's just not for me. Now, where is I? You made me lose my train of thought. Oh yeah. So, Richard is dead, and there is no possible way Hampton could have murdered him."

"So, what other suspects do you have?"

Freddy looked puzzled. "What do you mean? I just told you."

Otto takes a sip of his juice. Freddy is munching on the garlic knots.

"You can't tell me the great Freddy Falcon has absolutely no leads. Haven't you spoken with people? There are no other possible suspects? What about the cast and crew?"

"Juliana Martinez flew out to Germany for another movie. Jacob Wexler is a dead end."

"And?" Otto asks.

"And what?" Freddy takes another sip of coffee.

"The rest."

"What rest? What are you talking about?"

Otto leans back in his chair. "Look, Freddy, I'm not the smartest cookie in the pack, but I know you. Freddy Falcon is meticulous. You got it all figured out. You are the smartest person in the room, and you let everyone know it. You can't tell me you have no other leads. That's not the Freddy I know."

Freddy shakes his head as he takes his last bite.

"I don't know what to say. There just isn't anything else."

"Alright. Go sit down. I'll clean up. We will finish this discussion in the living room."

Freddy gets up, grabs his coffee, and goes into the living area. Otto throws away the paper plates they were using and places everything else in a plastic tub.

"What are you doing? Don't tell me. Mario does your dishes."

Otto smiles, "Now that's the perceptive Freddy I know. I'll take 'em up there later."

Otto grabs his juice and sits down in his chair. He takes a sip and nods for Freddy to continue.

"Look. There were no prints. No signs of a struggle. No one was found in the house. The only possible witness was asleep on the lanai. We have nothing."

"One of two things are true," Otto says. "Somethin's clouding your judgment, or you've lost your edge."

"I haven't lost my edge," Freddy says.

"Let's go back to the day Ms. Atworth was visiting."

"Held in captivity," Freddy says.

"Toe-may-toe, toe-ma-toe," Otto says. "Anyway, why did you stop by?"

"I heard a noise down here."

Otto shakes his head. "No. I mean Mario's. Why did you stop by Mario's?"

"I was hungry."

"You were on your normal drive that day?"

Freddy nods.

"So, you were coming from the south?"

Freddy nods again. "Where is this going?"

Otto raises a hand. "Just follow me."

"Yes, I was driving north. I turned onto West Jefferson and then onto South Illinois."

"Well, there are a thousand restaurants going that way. Why did you stop here?"

"I was craving pizza."

Otto raises his eyebrows. "Were you?"

"Yes." Freddy pauses for a moment. "Something told me to stop here."

"That sixth sense of yours. That's the Freddy we need to get back. That fiery redhead genius that has it all figured out. You knew what is going on. You read her. You read me. You knew."

"I remember."

"So, what's got you blocked?"

"I don't…"

"Don't say you don't know. Think. Use that damn brain you claim is smarter than the rest of us."

The two men sit there in silence for what felt like hours. Freddy glances at the clock on the wall. Only a half-hour had passed. What is Otto getting at? He can not figure out what it is. Or could he?

"Harry."

"What about him?" Otto asks.

"Talking to Mr. Hamm brought back memories. It brought back emotions and the pain of losing Harry. I think that was a fork in the road. The crime, booze, gambling. We thought it was the time of our lives. That part of my life died along with Harry. My life is better now.

"You know, that's why I don't like you now. You remind me of a past I left behind. You never changed, Otto."

"That's where you're wrong."

"Otto, the first time I came here, you had a woman tied up."

"I was trying to get information from her."

"She was being tortured."

"Look, Freddy, we both have our methods. We have the same goal. To solve a case. Methods may differ. Goal is the same."

"Look, we aren't having this discussion now. Bottom line is this case did bring back everything I remembered and felt after his murder. It all came rushing back. Everyone tried to tell me. I wouldn't listen."

Freddy sits back, hands folded across his chest. "You know, I was on top of my game at the beginning of this case. I was firing on all cylinders. Perhaps it's a good thing I was suspended."

Freddy sits up in a sudden motion. "The list!"

"What list?"

"Wexler's list."

"What are you talking about?"

"The other leads."

He can tell Otto is confused. "Jacob Wexler gave me a few names of people to talk to. I was so distracted by the Richard Olstroski/Hampton Ham thing that I never followed up. I completely forgot about that list."

Otto's face lights up. "Now there's the Freddy I know."

Freddy sighs. "Otto, when this case is over, I'll help you. I need to know too."

"With what?"

"Your investigation into Harry's murder. I'll help."

Otto nods.

"I may not agree with everything you do. You absolutely annoy the hell out of me most of the time. But you're the only family I have. You're like a brother to me."

"Don't go gettin' sappy on me."

"Otto, I have a few questions for you though. About this case."

"I don't know nothin' about that murder."

"But you may know something about Richard Olstroski that can help us."

Otto starts to argue. Freddy raises his hand.

"Don't argue. Just listen. We had Richard Olstroski in custody. The morning he got away, the officer watching him abandoned his post to go after a speeding motorist. The plates and description match you."

"I remember that guy. Short guy, bad attitude."

Freddy nods.

"I paid that ticket!"

"I'm not here to press you about the speeding ticket. I want information. What do you remember about that morning? This is your turf. Did you see anything unusual?"

Otto shakes his head. "No. I'm sorry, Freddy. I was on my way home from a...business negotiation...is all."

"No unusual cars or people that seemed out of place."

Otto shakes his head. He pauses. "Wait. Now that I think about it. There is this one car. Too rich for this area."

"Oh? Go on," Freddy presses.

"It is one of those electric cars."

"Electric? How do you know?"

"It is quiet. No sound from a combustion engine."

Freddy nods.

"Nobody around here can afford anything like that."

Freddy thinks for a moment. What type of car did Wexler drive? Prius, he believes.

"Is it a Prius?"

Otto shakes his head. "No. One of those expensive ones. You know, the company owned by the guy who wants to go to Mars. The guy that owns SpaceX."

"Elon Musk? It is a Tesla?"

"Yeah."

"Interesting."

"Freddy, you serious about helping me?"

"Yes, as long as you promise no stupid criminal activity. You're better than that."

Otto rolls his eyes. "Fine."

Freddy sits there a moment, reading the man. "You're telling the truth."

Otto smiles. "Now that's the Freddy we need to see."

"Alright, Otto, you have a deal. One more thing, though. I may need you again."

"What do you mean?"

"If what I suspect is true, then we may need a place to hide Mr. Hamm. A place nobody will think to look."

"Freddy, I ain't got the room."

Freddy looked around the basement. The area is huge. He sees Otto's bedroom to onc side. He sees a California king bed in the room.

"What about there?"

"That's my bed!" Otto protested.

"It's a California king. Big enough for an entire family."

"No man is sleeping with me!"

"Really Otto. Now, I thought you were more forward-thinking than that," he says with a smile.

"I ain't gay."

Freddy rolls his eyes. "I'm not asking you to sleep with the man. Just give him a place to stay. You can sleep on the floor or a cot for all I care."

"It's my home!"

"And Mr. Hamm would be your guest. You don't treat a guest like a servant. You treat them like royalty. Otto, it may not come to this. If it does, I want to know Mr. Hamm is in a safe place. I trust you."

Otto nods. "If it comes to it."

Freddy smiles. "Alright, I'm out of here. It's getting late. Thanks for the food and for getting me back on track."

Both men stand. Otto opens up his arms to hug Freddy. Freddy pauses for a moment, reading the man. He smiles and embraces the man.

"I do love you, brother," Freddy says.

"Yeah, me too, I guess. Now stop with the mushy shit."

Freddy turns to leave. He pauses mid-step.

"And Otto."

"Yeah?"

"Not every gay man wants to sleep with you. Don't be so conceited."

With that, Freddy turns and leaves.

Chapter Nineteen

How Freddy Got His Groove Back

Freddy is four days in on his seven-day suspension. The night he left Otto's, he had no idea what he would do for seven days. A week of not working on any case seems more like an eternity to him. He was so sure that he would do nothing except think about this case.

His visit with Otto had been extremely illuminating. He took the time to think about everything that had happened since this case began. He used this time to allow his colleagues' wise words to permeate his thoughts. Even the comments from Otto made a huge difference. He is sure about one thing. This week off allowed him to regain his focus.

"This is what, the third time I've decided that I am back on course since this case began? Or is it the fourth? This time is different, though."

Freddy had been spending most of his time in the garden these past four days. It has been an illuminating experience. He has been able to forget the world out here on the farm. He allows himself to soak in the energy of the nature that surrounds him.

He had read *The Celestine Prophecy* years ago. He was never sure if any of that is real, but he loved the idea of it. He never understood the scope of what the book is saying. It is a great fictional story. He loved the idea of gaining positive energy from being around nature. But all of that hocus pocus aura crap is a bit too much.

"That should do it," he says as he pats down the soil around a freshly planted Cranberry Hibiscus bush. The leaves will go well in a salad or just to snack on. Freddy also read that you can dry out the leaves and use them for tea. He doesn't care about any of that. He just thinks they are pretty.

He stands and brushes the dirt off of his clothes. His arms and legs are black from playing in the garden. He wipes the dirt from his legs and arms the best he can. His arms still have patches of black on them. It will have to do until he can shower.

He pulls his phone from his pocket and looks at the time. "Five-thirty? Where has the day gone?" he says to no one in particular.

He enters the house and heads for the shower.

***

Hampton sits there in his cell with his head hung. His usual daily routine is to wake up, wash his face, and sit on the edge of his bed. The thinks of his interrogation by Freddy and Freddy's last visit keeps running through his head. Burning rage swells within him. Hampton has never felt this much rage toward anyone before.

"How could he lead me on like that?" he says. "I trusted him. I believed him. I opened my heart and soul to that jerk. What he did is just evil."

He slams his fist into the mattress of his bed. He is too gullible. Why did he let this man lead him on like that? Claiming he believed Hampton. Gaining his total trust. He shakes his head. And then the visit in his cell. The fake apology. Trying to lay his hand on Hampton's arm precisely the way Marcus did the night he was...

"It is all an act. His dead boyfriend is probably just a figment of the lie." He says out loud.

"No, he isn't," comes a voice.

He looks up and sees Officer Braxton standing on the opposite side of the bars. He had been engulfed in his pity party so much that he never heard the man approach.

"Harry is very real, as are Freddy's feelings toward him."

He just sits there staring at the man.

Officer Braxton shakes his head. "I saw the video of the interview Freddy had with you. You have no idea how much Freddy deeply regrets what he did. I won't say any more about that. That's for Freddy to talk to you about if he chooses to.

"What I will say is the captain saw the video. Because of that video, you are a free man. No more jail cells. No more shitty food. No more isolation. You are free, Mr. Hamm."

Hampton sits in silence. It still doesn't justify what he did, the man thinks.

"Look, Freddy caused you a lot of unnecessary pain. He is a jackass for it, and that stunt got him suspended. Right now, it is about you. When's the last time you had a hot shower?"

Hampton shrugs. He honestly can't remember.

"I'm not sure," he says. "Before my arrest is all I know. I had a shower that morning."

Officer Braxton smiles. "How about a hot shower and some food? Then we will discharge you and let you go home."

Hampton nods. "Sounds good," he says.

The officer opens the cell and steps aside so Hampton can exit. The two men walk down past the jailor's desk. Shawn lay the keys on the desk as they pass. They walk up the stairs and through the door.

"We've got you some clean clothes. An officer dropped by your house and grabbed some."

Hampton nods.

"Once you have showered, come and find me. My desk is over there."

His eyes follow the invisible line from the officer's finger to the man's desk. He nods.

"Good," the officer says with a smile. He leads Hampton into the shower area. There is a duffle bag sitting on a bench. A towel and facecloth were neatly folded on top.

The officer moves the towel and facecloth to the side. He opens the duffle bag and takes out a clean shirt, pants, underwear, socks, and shoes. He sits them on the bench beside the bag.

"Once you are done, take the towel and facecloth to the laundry over there." He pointed to a door off to the side.

Hampton nods.

"I'll leave you to it then."

The officer turns and walks off. Hampton grabs the towel and facecloth and heads toward the showers.

***

Norman had been working the front desk at the Farmhouse for the past 25 years. He had seen a lot of changes during that time. Though the filing cabinets along the back wall are still there, they had been long since repurposed. After everything had been digitized on the computer, there is no need for paper copies of anything.

He had repurposed them into a make-shift pantry. They were filled with all types of non-perishable foods. He had bread, condiments, cookies, chips, and cereals, just to name a few. Atop the cabinets sits a microwave oven, a convection oven, and a single cup coffee maker. A mini fridge sits to one side. This houses sandwich meat, eggs, milk, and cold drinks. It also has a freezer, where he keeps frozen foods, ice cream, and a couple of ice trays.

Every time Freddy sees Norman with a cup of fresh coffee, he reminds the man about his coffee bar in his office. Norman appreciates the offer, but he enjoyed his one cup a day. He thinks Freddy drinks too much coffee.

"There's no such thing as 'too much coffee,'" Freddy would always reply.

Norman is fumbling around with the top drawer of one of the filing cabinets. He is craving cereal. Just as he opens the drawer, he feels something slam into his body. He is thrust forward into the filing cabinets. The momentum slams the drawer shut on his fingers.

He can feel the pain creep slowly from his fingertips up to his knuckles. Whatever force is holding him against the cabinet has a tight grip on him. Struggling is useless. The weight against him tightens the more he struggles. A black-gloved hand wrapped itself around his mouth in a tight grip. A piece of paper is thrust in front of his face. The pain is so intense that his vision is a little blurry. He can barely make out the writing.

GIVE MEHAN TONS OF HAM

What the hell kind of message is that? Who's Mehan? he thinks.

He feels his body jerk. His pelvis slams forward as his head jerks back. The paper in front of him shakes in annoyance. How is he supposed to know where the ham is or what this person is referring to?

Another push into the cabinet. And another. Norman has had enough. His fingers are writhing in pain, and he is starting to get whiplash.

He decides to take this moment to introduce the black-gloved hand to his teeth. He chomps down hard on what he assumes is a finger. The hand loosened enough that he could force the body off of him. It is enough to release his fingers from the drawer.

He takes this opportunity to elbow the person in the gut. He hears the man wince in pain. The hand releases entirely now. Norman turns around to see a man dressed all in black hunched over, holding his gut.

He is not exaggerating about the garb. Black shirt, pants, shoes, gloves, and a black ski mask hiding his face. This man does not want them to know who he is.

The man stumbles backward, dropping the paper. He regains his composure after a moment. A fist met square with Norman's jaw. Norman returned the gesture. His aim is not so generous. Norman aimed low and hit his target head-on.

The man winces in agony as he cups his hands over his groin. Norman imagined the pain to be almost unbearable. He swings again.

This time, he knocks the man backward as his fist met with the man's nose.

The man backs out of the office enough to make his escape. He runs out the main door, and Norman gives chase. He bursts through the main door into the wide-open air of the environment outside. He sees the man running toward a Tesla.

Norman is too slow. By the time he catches up with the man, the car is already in gear and ready to make its escape. He has to jump out of the way as the car races past.

"What the hell was that about?" he says to no one in particular.

He heads back inside. His vision is clear now. He picks up the paper and takes a second look at it.

"That doesn't say 'Give Mehan tons of ham." It says, 'Give me Hampton Hamm'. I gotta get this to the captain."

***

Hampton lets the water pour over his naked body. He lets it fill every crevasse from his armpits to his crotch. He stands under the rushing water spewing down from the shower head, letting the hot water consume him.

He lays his hands against the wall of the shower and buries his head in the rush of water. The warm water flows like a river down the back of his neck. As his muscles relax, the water rushes through the tributaries in his skin made by the grooves of his muscles and joints. It is an intoxicating experience. He found his Zen moment. This is the first time he showered since his arrest, and he is taking full advantage of it.

He starts to chuckle to himself. The thought of the only time he and Marcus had decided to shower together. It's not as exhilarating of an experience as people are lead to believe. Both partners' bodies have to be built for it, he guessed. All he knows is he is too fat, and Marcus is too broad and tall. They did more bumping into each other and the shower wall for it to be romantic. It is more cumbersome than anything. They decided to keep the romance in the bedroom.

"I miss you," he directed that to Marcus.

Tears start welling up in his eyes. He rests his arm against the wall of the shower and his face on his arm. The heat from the warm water radiates his arm. It feels good against his forehead and eyes. He stands there, allowing his tears to mix with the water on his arm. He can feel the water flow down his arm. The mixture of hot water and salty tears travel down his arm toward his elbow. It makes a turn and travels down the side of his arm at the bend in his elbow.

He stands there, letting the tears flow. All he can think about is how much he misses Marcus and how much he still loves his husband. He could "feel" Marcus's presence, or what his mind told him is Marcus's presence. His mind imagined Marcus wrapping his arms tight around him.

"It's going to be okay," he hears Marcus say in his mind.

"No, it's not," Hampton says. "It will never be okay. This is my life now. My penance. My suffering. I'll never be held by you again. Never feel your body against mine. What happens when I forget your voice? Forget what you look like?"

With that, the feeling is gone. No answer came. Just the rushing water upon his body. Hampton awakes from the trance with a shiver. He realizes the once-hot water is now cold. He looks at his pruning fingertips. The skin has risen so much it looked like a washboard.

It's time to get out, he thinks.

He turns off the water and stands there for a few seconds. Would these moments ever end? Would it ever get easier? He hated when this happened. A sudden thought or action would trigger these emotions or memories. It is torture, and he wishes it would all just be over. Times like this made him wish he could just forget Marcus completely. Perhaps that would make things easier.

The logical part of him knows he is wrong. He knows that only time will heal this. That thought doesn't make it easier in the here and now. All he knows now is this constant despair and these flashes of what felt like pain and torture. This has to be what soldiers who deal with PTSD go through. He now understood exactly what people mean when they say they re-live incidents in the past. It's more than just a memory. It's the sights, sounds, smells, and emotions of that memory. Your brain is literally in that moment as if you had traveled back in time to live it again.

He slides the shower curtain aside and grabs the towel from the rack. He is freezing now. The rush of cold air hit his wet body. A feeling of numbness consumed him for a second as if he had stepped into a freezer.

As he dries off, he hears noises coming from outside. He can't make it out. It sounds as if the entire Farmhouse is scurrying like ants. He finishes drying off and grabs his clothes from a nearby table. He throws on his clothes and shoes. He walks out of the shower area to the laundry. He tosses the wet towel and facecloth in the laundry. The sounds of people scrambling grows louder as he approaches the door leading out. He opens the door and heads into the fray.

***

Freddy is standing in front of his closet wearing only his underwear. He grabs a clean shirt and slips it over his head. He no longer feels dirty and grimy. The shower is a breath of fresh air.

He walks into the kitchen and powers on the single-cup coffee pot. He misses his office. He spent more time in his office than at home. This is why his office had more options for coffee than his own house did. He keeps a single cup coffee pot on his counter. It is enough for that first jolt of coffee in the mornings.

"Just a few more days," he says to himself. "I'll be back in my office soon. Then I'll have my entire arsenal of coffee at my disposal. Until then…"

He lets out a sigh as he opens a cabinet above the coffee pot. He pulls out a large can of generic supermarket coffee. He scoops up some coffee grounds and dumps them into the mesh filter. He scoops up three times the recommended amount, trying to make it as strong as possible.

"That should do it," he says.

He shuts the lid on the filter and fills the water reservoir. He places a coffee mug underneath and flips on the switch.

He grabs a bagel and places each half in the toaster. He opens the refrigerator and extracts the container of cream cheese. The coffee finishes as he sets the cream cheese on the counter. He grabs the coffee mug and takes a sip. He instinctively makes a face as if to say, "It's mediocre, but it will have to do."

The toaster pops up the bagel halves as he sets the coffee down on the counter. He takes a plate from the cabinet and places the bagel halves on it. He spread the cream cheese over each half and returns the container to the refrigerator.

He sits down with his breakfast as the sun sets in the sky. There is no wrong time for breakfast. It has always been a firm belief of his.

He notices his phone light up as he takes a sip of coffee. He sets the cup down and picks up his phone. A new voicemail and a missed call from Captain Youngblood. He unlocks his phone and listens to the voicemail.

"Falcon, call me ASAP."

"What the hell? I still have three days left." A light goes on in his brain. "Something happened. Shit!"

He calls the captain back immediately.

"Falcon!"

"What happened?"

"Get your ass in here now!"

"I still have three days left."

"Not anymore. Get your ass here now."

"What happened?"

"Mr. Hamm."

Freddy freezes. "What about him?"

"He's fine. Just get here now. There is an attack on the Farmhouse."

"What? Alright. I'm on my way."

He ends the call and places the phone in his shirt pocket. He wolfs down his bagel and the coffee as quickly as possible. He places the empty dishes in the sink, puts on pants and shoes, grabs his wallet and keys, and races out the door.

***

Hampton opens the door to utter chaos. Officers are at their desks on the phones. Others were in the side rooms talking. He races through the central area of the Farmhouse, looking for Officer Braxton.

He hurries in the direction of the officer's desk. He can see an empty chair behind it. There is no sign of Officer Braxton. Perhaps the officer is in one of the side rooms? He focuses his attention on the offices and meeting rooms along the wall. Men and women are gathered in a few of the offices. None of them are Officer Braxton.

"Mr. Hamm," he hears a voice call.

Hampton looks around.

"Mr. Hamm," the voice calls again.

"Y, yes," he answers.

"Up here. Look up," the voice says.

He looks up to see Officer Braxton on the catwalk above.

"Take the stairs. Meet me in the captain's office."

He follows the man's gaze to the large glass office in the back. He nods and heads for the stairs. Arm guards are stationed on either side of the staircase. As he reaches the top, he notice two more. What is going on, he wonders. He scurries down the catwalk to the office in the back.

"Have a seat," the captain says. The man motions toward an empty chair. "It's good to see you again, Mr. Hamm."

Hampton nods as he sits. Officer Braxton and his partner, he could not remember his name, sits beside him.

"I bet you feel refreshed after that shower," Officer Braxton says.

"I do. And call me Hampton, officers."

"Please, call me Shawn."

"And call me Eddy," the other officer says.

"You can call me Captain," the captain says matter of factly. "You'll forgive me, Mr. Hamm, but I am not in the habit of calling people by their first names in an official capacity."

Hampton nods. "Yes, sir."

"You have probably noticed the commotion downstairs," the captain says.

"And the armed guards," Hampton replies. "I don't remember seeing armed guards before."

"There weren't," another voice says.

Hampton turned to see the officer who works the front desk walk in.

"How are your fingers, Norman?" Shawn asks.

"They are better," he replies. "Thanks for asking."

"Show Mr. Hamm the note," the captain says.

Norman hands Hampton a piece of paper. He grabs it and read the words. He freezes as he reads:

GIVE ME HAMPTON HAMM

"It can't be," he says. "That's not possible."

"You recognize the handwriting style?" asks the captain.

He did not take his eyes off of the paper. "Yes," he replies.

"But how?" asks Eddy. "It's in all caps."

"Marcus," Hampton replies.

The four men were taken aback at that.

"It can't be. I know it isn't. But this is Marcus's style. It's exactly what his handwriting would be."

"Interesting," says a familiar voice. "May I see the note?"

Hampton turns to see a tall, skinny redhead standing at the door. The man looks different somehow. He looks refreshed and filled with vigor. This is not the same redhead that came to visit him in his cell. No. This is the redhead who first offered him a glass of water in his home.

"Glad you could join us, Falcon."

"How are you?" Freddy asks Hampton.

He doesn't say a word. He isn't angry with the man any longer, but it would be a while before he would be comfortable with Freddy again. He hands Freddy the paper.

"Give me Hampton Hamm," he reads aloud.

Freddy looks directly at Hampton. "And this is an exact match of your husband's printing?"

Hampton nods.

"Who knows you are here. Scratch that. Everybody in the damn world knows you are here, thanks to the media. Is there anyone else who knows your husband's style of writing well enough to replicate it?"

He doesn't say a word. He just glares at the man.

"Mr. Hamm?" The captain asks.

He addressed the captain and starts to shake his head.

"Don't answer so quickly," Freddy says. "Think."

"Does he have to be here?"

The captain sits back. He lets out a sigh before he speaks. "Mr. Hamm, we all understand Freddy acted like an ass. Please, just for the moment, answer his questions. You can go back to hating him after we all leave the room."

He nods and addresses Freddy. "Well, there is no one outside of myself."

"No one?" Freddy asks. "No one on this planet besides you?"

"You have to understand something, Detective. Marcus was not an open person. He was extremely private. He rarely hand-wrote anything. Anything public was always typed. The only times Marcus hand wrote was letters and cards to me."

"Why those particular things?" Freddy asks.

"You claim you've been in love," he says. Freddy opens his mouth to retort. Hampton continues, "So you told me when you were gathering information from me. Anyway, if that were true, and Officer Braxton here," he says as he motions to Shawn, "claims it is, then you would know the intimacy of a relationship. Marcus always felt handwriting to be personal, intimate. Private letters to me were handwritten because he loved me deeply. As I still love him. Yes, typing it would convey the same message, but not the meaning. It's the physical act of writing a letter on paper that showed how much he loved me. It is Marcus's way."

"So, nothing else he wrote was ever handwritten?" Freddy asks. "Not to anyone, anywhere?"

Hampton shakes his head. "Not since his mother passed away."

"What do you mean?" asks the captain.

"Marcus wrote to his mother every year on her birthday. In fact, he still wrote to her every year after her passing. He never mailed those letters, of course. But he still wrote her."

"Where are these letters now?" asks Freddy.

"I assume they are still in his dresser drawer in our bedroom."

"Shawn, did you find any letters in the bedroom dressers?" asks Freddy.

"No. I didn't. Eddy?"

Eddy shakes his head.

"That's not possible," Hampton says. "They are there. Top drawer. Left-hand side. Under his underwear."

"I'm sorry, Mr. Hamm," Eddy says. "I thoroughly checked your bedroom. There were no letters."

"Now we have a larger mystery," Freddy says. "Who, besides Mr. Hamm, would know that Mr. Peterson writes to his mother? And would also know where the letters are kept?"

"There is no one that would know that. No one besides me," Hampton says.

"Think, Mr. Hamm."

The thought suddenly hit him. He shakes his head as to shake it from his memory. "No. It can't be him. True, there was the falling out, but no."

"Who, Mr. Hamm?" asks the captain.

"Adam Greenbriar," Freddy says. "That's the only logical explanation."

Hampton nods.

"Who?" asks the captain.

"Mr. Hamm, it's your personal story to share. I understand if you wish to keep it private."

"No. I've come to terms with it. The only time I almost lost Marcus is over my own stupidity. I cheated on him with his best friend, Adam Greenbriar. It was the end of their friendship and almost the end of our relationship. Adam is the only other person who would know Marcus writes his mother...wrote his mother."

"They had more than a friendship, too, didn't they?" Freddy asks.

Hampton nods. "How did you...?"

Freddy grins, "Because I am good at my job, Mr. Hamm."

"Yes. They tried a relationship a few times. It never worked out. Marcus always said it was because they were too much alike. I just don't think Adam was into black men."

"And you are?" the captain asks.

"I married a black man," Hampton replies.

"Marcus Peterson was African-American, sir," Eddy interjects.

"Look, I don't care if Marcus is black, white, red, or purple. That's the man I fell in love with. The man I still dream about. The fact is he loved me deeply, and now he's dead. I miss him every day. I keep expecting him to walk through the door, arms open wide. He's never coming back. Someone took him from me. I want to know who, and I want them brought to justice."

"And we will," Freddy says. "Every person in this room is dedicated to solving this."

"You have the lead on this, Falcon. What do you want to do?"

"Okay, first I will take Mr. Hamm to a safe-house."

The captain opens his mouth to reply.

"Not one of ours. I have a place no one knows about. No one would suspect to look there for him."

"Who?" asks Shawn. "Where?"

"An old friend. We go back a long way."

Hampton sees Freddy look directly at him when saying this. He is confused for a moment. It is as if Freddy is expecting him to know this person. That's when the memory hit him. That day in the hamburger restaurant.

"Burger Palace," Hampton says.

Freddy nods. The other men looked confused.

"But you said you guys were no longer friends," Hampton says.

Freddy smiles. "I wouldn't say we recently made up. What I would say is, I trust him."

Hampton nods.

"Who are you talking about, Falcon?" the captain asks in frustration.

"I'm sorry, sir. For Mr. Hamm's protection, I cannot say."

"Cannot, or will not?"

"Will not."

"So, what do you want us to do?" asks Shawn.

"You two are going back to the building where you found Richard Olstroski's corpse."

"Richard's corpse?" Hampton exclaims. "Richard's dead?"

Freddy sighs. "Oh my God. You don't know."

"Know what?"

"We tracked Mr. Olstroski down," Eddy says. "We found his body in an abandoned building south of the lake."

He doesn't know what to think. First Marcus. Now Richard. What about the others? Were they safe? What about…

"Juliana!" Hampton exclaims.

"As far as we know, she is still in Germany," Freddy says.

"What about the rest of the cast and crew?"

"The only other person I have spoken with is Jacob Wexler," Freddy says.

"Jacob," Hampton says.

"What about him?"

"He can't have."

"Can't have what?" asks Freddy.

"I never trusted Jacob. Not after the falling out we had with him. He never forgave us. Always blamed us for his career falling apart. Even his marriage to Shelly. He blamed that on us too."

"What do you mean? He's no longer married?"

"No. I mean, yes. I mean…"

"Which is it, Mr. Hamm," says Freddy. The man is glaring at him. "This is extremely important. Is Jacob Wexler still married?"

"He's on his fourth wife."

"Fourth?" Freddy asks in surprise. The man's eyes grow large as he says the word.

Hampton nods. "Shelly was the love of his life. She couldn't take it anymore. All he could talk about was how we ruined his career. She left him. He never forgave us for that. After Shelly, he married Rita."

"What happened there?" asks Freddy.

"Rita's dead," says Hampton. "She drowned in a swimming pool."

"And his third wife?"

"Shark attack."

"Wait," says Freddy, "Are you telling me his second and third wives are dead?"

"And Shelly is too," Hampton says as he nods.

"You said she left him," Freddy says.

"She did. She and her boyfriend were found dead in their home. Carbon monoxide poisoning."

"So, this man who had a grudge against you and your husband has three dead wives?" says the captain. "What about the fourth?"

"She's alive. Or at least she was when I interviewed him," says Freddy.

"How do you know? Did you speak with her?" asks the captain.

Freddy shakes his head. "She was asleep."

"How do you know that?"

"Their son. The boy said his mom was asleep."

"He's a good kid," says Hampton. "Lots of energy. Extremely polite. He's actually Shelly's. Tina officially adopted him when they married."

"You're telling me that this man went through four wives in six years?"

Hampton nods. Freddy just shrugs.

"Here's the plan," Freddy says. "Shawn and Eddy, check out that abandoned building. Search it thoroughly. Leave no stone unturned. Find any type of camera that may have captured the person who murdered him."

They nod.

"And you?" asks the captain.

"After I drop Mr. Hamm off, I am going to have another chat with Mr. Wexler. Then I am going to speak with everyone on this list."

Freddy holds up a piece of paper.

"What's that?" asks the captain.

"A list of names given to me by Jacob Wexler. People he claims Richard Olstroski was out with the night Marcus Peterson was murdered."

The captain nods. "Okay, anything else, guys?"

The two officers shake their heads.

"Nothing from me," says Freddy.

"I don't even know why I am still here," Norman says.

"Alright, gentleman. Let's get this murderer found and this case solved," says the captain. "Dismissed."

The two officers stand and nod. They both pat Hampton on the shoulder as they pass him. Norman follows them out. Freddy walks over to Hampton and puts his arm around Hampton's shoulders.

"Well, Mr. Hamm. Let's get you someplace safe."

Chapter Twenty

Living in a Basement With Otto Von Snaut

They are crossing the bridge over the lake. Neither says a word to the other. The moon illuminates the night sky. It carries with it its entourage of shining stars. It is a beautiful night with no clouds in the sky.

"Full moon tonight. Isn't it gorgeous?" Freddy finally breaks the silence.

Hampton just sits there, gazing out the window.

"The stars too. Not a cloud in the sky to obscure them," Freddy continues.

Hampton sits there. Not even a minuscule amount of motion from the man. Freddy sighs. It doesn't take a crack detective to deduce how this man feels about him at the moment. He expects the man to be upset. He has no expectations of a friendship from the man. He needs Hampton to at least work with him on a professional level.

"Look," Freddy starts. "No, scratch that. Mr. Hamm, have you had to work with anyone you can't stand to be around? Of course you have. I forgot for a moment. Anyway, that's what this situation is. You don't like me. You are forced to work with me. It's uncomfortable for you. I understand where you are coming from. Were I in your shoes, I would be uncomfortable working with me too."

"Do you realize what you put me through?" Hampton does not turn to look at Freddy as he speaks.

He nods. "I do now."

"Then understand that I don't want to speak to you. Not until you apologize."

"Is that what you want? An apology?"

"It's a start. Show some remorse."

He rolls his eyes. "If we are going to work together, then you need to understand something about me. I am a firm believer in knowing the difference between actions and words. I could say 'I'm sorry' until I am blue in the face. That won't change a damn thing. It's the actions, Mr. Hamm. The actions are what show change. The actions are what show genuine remorse. I am sorry for what I did to you in that interrogation room. It was a stupid stunt. Regardless of the intentions, the end result is hurtful. Saying that I am sorry won't make things right. It's my actions now and my actions yet to come that will start to, hopefully, build that bridge back.

"I don't expect us to become best friends after this is over. Hell, I don't even expect to see you outside of the TV or movie screen after all of this. I have a case with a murdered director. There were no witnesses, and there is, so far, no real evidence pointing to anyone. My goal is simple. I'm solving a case and bringing a murderer to justice.

"Your life is hard enough as it is, and it will get harder before it gets easier. Don't add this to it. Use this time to build happy memories that you can draw on when times do get tough for you. And they will get tough."

He looks over at Hampton. The man turns his head the second he sees Freddy look. Freddy smiles. He is getting through.

"So, 'grow up, Mr. Hamm,'" Hampton replies.

Freddy shakes his head. "I never said that."

"You didn't have to."

He glances over again and sees the man relaxing.

"Detective, I don't hate you."

"That's good. Hate is a strong word. You shouldn't hate anybody," Freddy says with a smile.

"I hate the person who took Marcus from me," Hampton replies.

"How can you? You have no idea who that person is. For all you know, he could have done it to himself."

Hampton glares at Freddy. "Don't you dare!"

He shakes his head. “What I mean is, the evidence, so far, points to an accident. There is an abundant amount of arsenic in his system, and the wound….”

“Yeah. I remember you telling me.”

“What is surprising is that wound. It’s possible it could have been self-inflicted. He was drunk. Mr. Hamm, I have to look at all possibilities. It is possible that your husband died by his own hand.”

“But…”

“I’m not saying that’s what happened. In fact, I don’t even believe that’s what happened. I have to look at all possibilities. As Sir. Arthur Conan Doyle is famous for writing, ‘When you eliminate the possible. Whatever remains, no matter how improbable, must be the truth.’”

“So, you are comparing yourself to Sherlock Holmes now? Freddy Falcon, you may be a lot of things, but you are no Sherlock Holmes.”

Freddy sees a smile on the man’s face. He returns the gesture.

“I have failed you. I need to keep you more involved in my findings on the case.”

“I was in jail. It’s not like you could have just stoped by my house.”

“Actually, I could have. Not your house, of course. But I could have visited you at the Farmhouse. It’s not like it’s out of my way. It’s not that hard to schedule interview time with you.”

“Why didn’t you?”

“I had demons I needed to take care of. I wasn’t in the correct headspace.”

“And you are now?”

Freddy just nods.

“I can tell. You look refreshed and full of vigor. You are more like the Freddy I first met and less like the emotional wreck who tried to make out with me in a jail cell.”

He glares at Hampton. "I did not try to make out with you," he says sternly.

Hampton smiles.

"Mr. Hamm, do you remember what I said at Burger Palace? About keeping this professional?"

Hampton nods.

"I lost that for a moment. I started to care for you, as a friend, and less on a professional level. That's what the visit in the cell was. A loss of judgment. Nothing more. Understand?"

Hampton nods.

"Good," he says. "Now, let's talk about this case."

Hampton sits there as Freddy relays the details of the case, as he knows them thus far. He explains Richard's escape, as well as where his body was found. He explains the details of all of the evidence found at Hampton's home and the lack of evidence found at the second crime scene.

Hampton sits there, taking it all in. Freddy is having a hard time reading the man. He is sitting there stoically. Is he comprehending what he is hearing? Why doesn't he have any reaction at all?

Freddy starts talking about the wine glass. That's when Hampton begins to react. It isn't much. The untrained eye would not have caught it, but it is there. A microscopic fidget.

"What do you know about that wine glass?"

"Cobalt blue?" Hampton asks.

Freddy nods.

"The night you stopped by my place, and we had wine."

"The night I figured out the suspect might have come in through the pool deck."

Hampton nods. "Well, that glass was missing. I tore the house apart looking for it."

"What's so special about that glass?"

"That's Marcus's glass. See, Marcus knows wine. He is...is a bit of a connoisseur. He had two cobalt blue wine glasses. One for red wine and one for white wine. Marcus knows the difference."

"Are you telling me that your husband never would have drunk white wine from a glass meant for red wine?"

"Yes," Hampton nods. "That alone tells me my husband was murdered."

"Interesting…" Freddy motions for Hampton to continue. "Go on. I'm listening."

"I couldn't find that glass. The other one is in its place, but that one is missing." He shakes his head, "I wouldn't have grabbed it anyway. Nobody but Marcus touches those glasses. You said you found it. Is it safe?"

"Freddy nods. "We have it in evidence."

Hampton lets out a sigh of relief.

"How well do you know Juliana Martinez?"

He shakes his head again. "She didn't do this."

"That's not what I asked. How well do you know her?"

"No," Hampton says, shaking his head. "She wouldn't. Can't."

Freddy gives a stern look. "Mr. Hamm," he says matter of factly. "Do you remember what I said earlier? About eliminating the possible?"

Hampton nods.

"Good. Now, how well do you know her?"

The man sits back, relaxing his shoulders as he speaks. "We met on the set of *Cube*. I was cast, as you know, to play Jason Andrews. He is your typical sarcastic, arrogant gen-xer."

"I've seen the show," Freddy says.

"Anyway, Juliana was cast as Elaine."

"Ah, the lady who worked in HR."

Hampton nods. "We were both up and coming. We would do read-throughs together every night. We became the best of friends. Juliana has a good heart. She's had a rough time with men and relationships. She is one of the nicest people you will ever meet."

"Mr. Hamm, the case."

"So, that starts our weekly get-togethers. We would keep in touch. Every time we were both working on the same project or in the same city, we would get together once a week for the duration. Play cards. Watch a movie. Talk about the men in our lives." That last part, he says with a smile. "She liked Marcus a lot. She knew we would be together before I did. Juliana is the reason we ended up together."

Freddy is confused. The timeline doesn't add up. That show is in the mid-2000s. Maybe it did. "She is the reason you two started dating?"

Hampton shakes his head. "No. I didn't say that. She is the reason we married. Juliana saved our relationship. Do you remember me telling you how I almost lost Marcus?"

"Adam Greenbriar," Freddy says.

Hampton nods. "Juliana worked hard on Marcus to get him to talk to me. I opened up to her completely about all of it."

"Did she know that Mr. Greenbriar would be working on the film when she accepted?"

Hampton shakes his head. "She found out when she arrived at the set. She was furious with Marcus about that."

"Furious?"

Hampton nods. "They argued about that in private. She couldn't believe he cast Adam after our past. As I said, Marcus is a peacemaker. Don't get me wrong, he does have a temper. But he believes in peaceful resolutions. Marcus believes in giving people second chances. Marcus doesn't look at people and judge them based on their past. He looks at the person for who they are today, not who they were."

"He sounds like an amazing man."

"He is. Trust me, Detective. Juliana loves us."

"How long will she be in Germany?"

"The entirety of the shoot. Probably a few months."

"When did she fly out?"

"The day after Marcus…" The man stops. It is apparent he could not finish that statement.

Freddy nods in understanding. "The day I met you," he says.

Hampton nods.

"Take a look at this list." Freddy turns on the cabin light and hands him the list of names he got from Wexler.

Hampton read over the names. He looked up at Freddy. "What's this?"

"A list of names that Wexler gave me. These, according to him, are the people who were out with Richard Olstroski that night."

Hampton read over the list again. "Miguel wasn't there."

"What?" Freddy says with surprise.

"Miguel Alvarez. He wasn't there."

The car swerves for a second as Freddy jumps with surprise. "What? How do you know that?"

Hampton composed himself. "I didn't mean to startle you."

"Never mind that. This could be important. How do you know that?"

"He's dating Juliana. He was with her that night." Hampton looks at the list again. "Maybe Jacob is mistaken. Miguel and Aaron are friends. Perhaps he just assumed Miguel was there."

"Perhaps," Freddy says. "Perhaps not." It's possible Jacob Wexler could have been mistaken. Perhaps he should speak with the man again. He knows he needs to talk with the men on that list. It's odd, though. There is something about Wexler that bothers him. He can't pinpoint it, though.

"Watch out!"

Freddy jerks back into reality and out of his thoughts. He swerves back in his lane right before he hit a truck head-on. Both men take a deep breath.

"You okay?" he asks Hampton.

"Me?" The man raised his eyebrows in surprise as he says the word. "Are you okay?"

"I'm fine. Just drifted off in thought."

"Next time, try not to drift into oncoming traffic. I'm not that anxious to join Marcus."

Freddy nods. "Enough talk about the case for now. We are almost there. Just a few blocks away."

"What are you going to do after the case is over?"

Freddy glances over at Hampton with a puzzled look. "What do you mean?"

"What do you do when a case is over? Do you relax? Do you move on to another one?"

"There's always another case."

"That's sad."

"How so?"

"It's like this case. I understand how you are the way you are. I could never be that way."

"Now I am curious. What does that mean?"

"How you come across as being cold to the situation."

"You think I'm cold? Now, that does concern me."

Hampton shakes his head. "No. I see you as a kind and caring person. You have the ability to shut off your emotions when on a case. You are callus to the death."

"Is that what you think? That I'm callus to it?"

Hampton nods.

Freddy sighs. "I didn't realize I came across that way."

Hampton shakes his head. "I didn't mean…"

"Yes, you did," Freddy says bluntly. "I'm not upset. That's how you see me. It's not that I'm callus, or heartless, or whatever else people perceive me as. Oscar will even tell you that he thinks I'm a conceited jackass."

"I don't…," Hampton starts to say. Freddy shakes his head.

"Let me finish. I am very aware of how people perceive me. I've gotten it my entire life."

He turns on his blinker to make a left-hand turn.

"I've always been the smartest kid in the class. That's not ego. That's a fact."

The car turns left. The streetlights are the only things illuminating the way. No other cars on the road. No businesses are open.

"I've always been able to read the room. My perception is spot on. I guess you could say I am a lot like Jupiter Jones." He smiles as he says that.

"Who?" Hampton asks.

"Jupiter Jones. One of *The Three Investigators*."

Hampton looks confused.

"*The Three Investigators*? Jupiter Jones, Pete Crenshaw, and Bob Andrews?"

"Are those colleagues of yours?"

Freddy smiles. "I'm honestly not surprised you've never heard of them. Most people are familiar with *Nancy Drew* or *The Hardy Boys*. These younger kids, probably *Goosebumps*."

Hampton nods.

"Well, I read *The Three Investigators* growing up. Three kids who solved mysteries and crimes. The operation was run out of a trailer that sits in a junkyard run by...I can't remember if it is Jupiter's dad or uncle or what... Anyway, just three kids who solved mysteries. That's also how I was introduced to Hitchcock."

"Alfred Hitchcock?. The director?"

Freddy nods. "The original books I read, which were probably 20 years old when I read them in the '80s, were titled *Alfred Hitchcock and the Three Investigators*. Granted, the director did not help them in their cases. Think of it more like a debrief. The last chapter of each book involved them summarizing their case to Hitchcock.

"I learned later that it was the author's idea of popularizing the books. According to what I have read, the author believed he needed to tie the books to a famous person to gain notoriety. I never got that as a kid. I cared more about the mysteries. I enjoyed the three boys solving the case and less about Hitchcock.

"I never knew Hitchcock was a real person until later."

"Really?"

"Yeah. I saw my first Hitchcock film in the '90s. Never saw *Alfred Hitchcock Presents* until I was older, either. I just had no exposure to it at the time."

"I see. So, how do you keep yourself separated from the case?"

"I didn't on this one. I failed."

"What do you mean?"

"Harry."

"Your former boyfriend?"

Freddy nods. "I'll just say, your particular situation brought back memories."

"Marcus."

"You see, Mr. Hamm, this is not my first murder case. It's not even my first murder case where a spouse is murdered. I can't pinpoint it, though. There is just something about this case or your particular situation. I dunno." Freddy shakes his head. "I just know I can't let it go this time."

Freddy looks over at Hampton as they come to a stop at a red light.

"It's not callus or being able to shut off my feelings that makes me good at this. I can separate myself from the situation. Think of it as watching a television show. You get invested in it, but you are not part of it. Once it's over, you're done. Back to real life."

The light turns green. Freddy drives on.

"You think the cases you are on aren't real?" Hampton asks.

"No. Not at all. It's very real while I am working it. The people are real and have real feelings. I can just separate myself from it, similar to how you separate yourself from a TV show or movie. Once it's over, it's done. I don't carry it with me. Does that make sense?"

"I think so."

Freddy sighs. "I'm extremely introverted. I'm not good with people or explaining my thoughts and emotions. Just know that I care deeply about every case I work on and the people involved in each one. I may not show it or express it. It is there. I promise you."

The two men sit in silence for a moment before Freddy speaks again. "I care too much. If I didn't have this ability, I would explode with emotions. Each case would be reckless. The same recklessness you witnessed."

"So, you're more like Mr. Spock?"

Freddy smiles. "Accurate. That's an apt way of putting it."

"You never really answered my question, though. What are you doing after this case? Is there a queue of sorts?"

Freddy shakes his head. "No. Not a queue. Some type of case will just pop up, though. But, I am going to take a vacation after this case. I have a promise to keep."

"That's nice," Hampton says. "Are you going out of town, or is it a staycation?"

"Actually," Freddy says with a smile, "it's a case of sorts."

"Wait. Your idea of a vacation is another case?"

"It's a promise to Otto. See, I let the circumstances around Harry's death go a long time ago. Otto never has. He needs that closure."

"Based on your reactions in my case, you do too."

Freddy smiles and glances over at Hampton. "Perhaps you are right."

"You're an interesting character, Detective."

"As are you, Mr. Hamm."

***

The car pulls into a parking spot in front of *Hold the Anchovies*. Hampton is confused. He thought they were going to the home of this guy Otto.

"I'm not hungry," the man says.
"Neither am I," Freddy replies.
"Why are we at a pizza restaurant?"
"We're not."
"Where are we?"
"We're here."
"Where?"
"Here."
"Where's 'here'"?
"Where you are staying."
"The pizza restaurant?"
"No."
"Where?"
"Otto's."
"Here?"
"Otto lives in the basement of this pizza restaurant."

Hampton is taken aback. Shock and disbelief had to be showing based on Freddy's next comment.

"What's wrong?" Freddy asks.

"You're joking. Please tell me this is a joke."

Freddy shakes his head. "No. This is where you will be staying for the duration of the case."

"Hampton Hamm does not live in a basement," Hampton says in a firm tone.

"He does now," Freddy replies. "Now, come on. We don't want to keep Mario. It's late. He closed hours ago. The man is kind enough to wait until we arrived."

"Mario?"

"Yeah. Now come on."

Freddy gets out of the car, closing the door behind him. Hampton, reluctantly, follows suit. What have I gotten myself into? he thinks as he follows Freddy inside.

The place is small. Just a few tables. A chubby older man is cleaning off the countertop. He looks up when the two men walk in.

"Hey, Mario. Thanks for staying," Freddy says.

"No problem, Detective. This must be Mr…"

Freddy smiles. "Mr. Hamm. Yes."

"Pleasure to meet you," Hampton says. He reaches out to shake the man's hand. Mario returns the shake. "It's a nice place you have here. Quant."

Mario nods with a smile. "Thank you. I purchased it years ago. I converted it into a restaurant."

"Converted? What was it before?" Hampton asks.

"A bar." The man pauses. "Well," Mario continues, "let me back up. Originally, this place was built as a bar. When prohibition came along, the bar was converted into a restaurant. The basement was built as a speakeasy. After prohibition was abolished, the restaurant was converted back to a bar. The basement was converted into a living area. The bar never did that well. The owner rented out the basement.

"After my brother passed…."

"I'm so sorry," Hampton says.

"Why? You didn't kill him," Mario replied.

Hampton shakes his head. He understands where the man is coming from. He would have had the same response if the man had said that about Marcus. "No. I mean, it saddens me to hear of the loss."

The man throws up a hand as if to brush the statement off. "That was years ago. Decades now. Besides, it was a freak accident," the man says. "He was a plumber working atop a new building being built. The area he was working in still had open walls. He lost his balance and fell to his death. Broke his neck. Died instantly."

"What was his name? Luigi?"

Mario shakes his head as if not getting the reference. "No. Sam. His name was Sam. Look, kid…"

Hampton glares at the man. "Kid?"

"I was working full-time jobs and living on my own when you were in diapers. So, yes, kid. Look, not every Italian is named Vito, Tony, Vince, or Luigi. You come into my place of business and insult me with stereotypes?"

Hampton is a little embarrassed. "I'm sorry," he says.

"Eh, don't be. Just don't do it again." He directs his attention to Freddy. "Lock up when you leave. Otto has his own key."

Mario neatly folds the washrag he is using to clean off the counter. He laid it on the edge of the counter. The man grabbed his keys off of a hook in the back and starts to leave. He walks past the men and out the door.

"I didn't mean to…"

"I think it is funny. Just inappropriate," Freddy says. "Come on."

Hampton follows Freddy through a door in the back. The sign on the door reads "Employees Only." They go down a small staircase. At the bottom, it opens up into a large basement. He can tell the basement is sectioned off into rooms. There is an office area, a kitchen, and even a bedroom. The main living area is open and spacious.

Otto is behind a computer in the office. He looks up as the men arrive.

"Freddy…" he says with a smile. A cigar bounces in the corner of his mouth.

"Hey Otto. I believe you know Mr. Hamm."

"Hey pal," Otto says with the same smile. "Make yourself at home." He pointes toward the chairs in the living area. "I'll be done in a few minutes."

"Thank you," Hampton replies. He looks around and only sees one bedroom. "Where do I sleep? I'm a bit tired. You want me in one of the chairs?"

Freddy smiles. "No need, Mr. Hamm. Otto has graciously offered you his bed."

"The pig ain't takin' my bed," Otto says with a gruff tone.

"Hey!" Hampton says. Where does he get off? Hampton is ready to explode.

Otto smiles. "Well, you kinda do look like one. You're short and chubby."

Hampton glares at the man. He starts toward Otto in a bit of a rage. Freddy grabs his arm to hold him back.

"Enough, Otto!" Freddy yells. Hampton is taken aback. He has never heard Freddy get so loud.

"What?"

"Enough with the fat jokes. Mr. Hamm is your guest. Besides, you aren't exactly thin yourself."

"What do ya mean? This is mostly muscle. Besides, I'm big boned."

"Big boned? Right." Freddy rolls his eyes. "You look like a rhinoceros. How would you feel if I called you a 'rhino'?"

Otto is taken aback at that. "Hey now…"

Hampton can't contain himself. He lets out a hearty laugh.

"What's so funny?" Otto asks. He glares at the man.

"Well, you kinda do," Hampton replies.

Freddy let out a laugh.

"Hardy, har, har," Otto says. "And what about you, Freddy Falcon? Tall and lanky like a giraffe."

Freddy smiles and replies, "I'm as sly as a fox, my friend. Sly as a fox."

With that, Freddy pats Hampton on the shoulder. "Good luck," he says. He turns and walks up the stairs, leaving the two men alone.

"I can take one of the chairs," Hampton says.

Otto shakes his head. "Nah, you can take my bed."

"Thank you," Hampton replies. He starts walking toward the bedroom. "Goodnight."

"Mr. Hamm!"

He turns around to see Freddy at the bottom of the stairs. He holds up the duffle bag that contains Hampton's things from home.

"You forgot this."

"Thank you." Hampton walks over to the bottom of the stairs and takes the bag from the man.

"Call me if you need anything."

Hampton nods. "I'm going to bed now."

He carries the bag to the bedroom. He turns on a lamp on the bedside table and places the bag in a chair.

"No door?"

Otto shakes his head. "Is that a problem?"

"Nope. I'm not shy. I hope you don't mind seeing a grown man naked."

"I ain't gay!"

"I never said you were."

***

Freddy rolls his eyes at that comment. "Grow up Otto."

"What?"

Freddy sighs. "You are far from homophobic. Stop acting like a jackass."

"What? I'm not gay, and I ain't sleepin' with no man."

"I know that. Again, stop acting like a jackass. Not every gay man wants to sleep with you. You grew up with me and Harry. You know damn well the stereotypes aren't true. Mr. Hamm has been through a lot. The loss of his husband. The loss of his home. The loss of his privacy. He has gone from having everything to living in the basement of a restaurant. Cut the man some slack. He's still grieving."

'I ain't a babysitter either."

"What the hell, Otto? I'm not asking you to be. I'm not even asking you to be his friend."

Freddy looks across the room toward the bedroom. He sees Hampton getting ready for bed, oblivious to the conversation between the two men. He turns his attention back to Otto.

"Just give the man a place to stay until the case is over. His life may be in danger, and this is the only place I know of that nobody would think to look."

"Danger? You never said anything about this being dangerous."

Freddy sighs. "He's the closest thing there is to a witness to a murder. So much so, he is still considered a possible suspect."

He knows the look on Otto's face. He quickly needs to say something to appease the man.

"He didn't do it. He's not a murderer. We just have no other suspects and very few leads at the moment. Someone tried to kidnap him at the Farmhouse…."

"What? If he ain't safe at a police station…."

"That's why he's here. There are only four people who know Mr. Hamm is here. I didn't even tell the captain."

Otto looks confuses. Freddy can tell the man is counting in his head, trying to figure out the fourth person.

"Mario," Freddy says.

"I know that," is his only reply. It is clear by his body language that he didn't.

"Just keep him safe, alright."

Otto nods.

"Thanks."

"Goodnight, Mr. Hamm," he yells across the room.

Hampton is lying on top of the covers, naked. He sees the man reaching for the pull string on the lamp.

"Goodnight."

He pulls the string, and the room goes dark.

"Goodnight Otto. I hope you find that chair comfortable."

"What's that supposed to mean?"

Freddy shakes his head. "Wingback chairs are not comfortable to sleep in."

"I ain't sleepin' in the bed."

"I know you, Otto. Perhaps not in the beginning. At some point in the night, your back will be hurting too bad."

With that, Freddy turns to walk up the stairs. He hears Otto reply, "He's naked."

Freddy doesn't turn around. He smiles as he says, "Goodnight, Otto."

He turns out all of the lights in the restaurant. Locking and closing the door behind him, he steps out into the night air.

Chapter Twenty-One

There's Something About Adam

It is your typical suburban neighborhood. All of the homes on either side look like they were produced from the same mold. He had always heard this referred to as "cookie-cutter homes." They aren't all the same. Each one has slight differences. This one has the garage on the front. That one has the garage on the side. Every fourth house looks exactly the same.

Sidewalks line either side of the street. Children are out playing. Some are shooting hoops, while others ride bikes. Still, others are playing the types of outdoor games he played as a child.

All of the lawns are nicely manicured. They all are mirror images of one another. The grass is the same length. Even the mulch around the flowerbeds is all the same color and thickness. It is apparent this is an HOA community.

Freddy pulls up alongside one of the homes. He looks at the address and compares it to the address next to one of the names on the list.

"Six-zero-five North Virginia Boulevard," he reads. "This is the place."

He looks at the names on the list Wexler had given him:

Adam Greenbriar
Miguel Alverez
Rodney Cooper
Mitch Blakely
Aaron Chatsworth

He can not understand why Adam Greenbriar is on this list. Didn't Wexler say these men went to a strip club that night? As far as he knows, Mr. Greenbriar is gay. That's why he decided to put this man first on the list. Well, that and the other reasons Hampton had given. Mr. Greenbriar would be the perfect place to start.

He places the list back above the visor and leaves the car. Walking up to the door, he sees a neighbor watering the garden at the house next door. The woman is too engrossed in what she is doing to notice him.

"Hey, mister."

He turns around to see a young girl tugging on his shirt. She appears to be five or six.

"Yes?" He says with a smile.

"Are you here to visit Mr. Greenbriar?"

"Yes, I am, actually. How did you know?"

Obviously, he knows the answer to that. He decided to play along with her.

"He lives here."

"Yes, he does. Is he home?"

She shrugs her shoulders. "Mama doesn't like him."

"Why is that?"

She shrugs. "I think he's a nice man. Want some lemonade?"

"What?"

She pointed. His eyes followed her point to a small table across the street. Two boys, about the same age as her, sit at the table. The sign reads "Lemonade 50 cents".

"Maybe when I leave."

She hung her head.

"What's wrong? I promise I'll buy some when I leave."

"That will be tomorrow."

"Tomorrow?" He shakes his head. "No. I'm only visiting for a few minutes."

"Mr. Greenbriar always has visitors."

"He does?" He thinks that this is an interesting statement.

She nods. "They always come during the day and leave the next day. They never leave on the same day."

"Are his visitors always men, or are some of them women?"

She shakes her head. "Always men. His friends. Mr. Greenbriar is very popular. He has a lot of friends who sleep over. I've never seen a woman go in there."

"Well, thank you, Ms…"

"Huh? I ain't no Ms. I'm Carol," she says in a sharp tone.

He smiles, "Well, Carol, I promise you I will only be a little while. When I leave, I will buy some lemonade. Okay?"

"You better, Mister," she says. She turns and trots off across the street.

Freddy can't help but smile. He liked kids, but he never had intentions of having any of his own. It is the same with animals. He is great with them as well, but he would rather enjoy other people's pets than have any for himself.

He walks up to the front door and rings the doorbell.

"Yes?" he hears a voice answer.

"Hello?" he says. He looks around but sees nobody. He presses the button again.

"What do you want?" the voice says.

"Uh, hello?"

"Look, I can see you standing there. Don't keep pressing the button. You're annoying me. What do you want?"

Freddy looks around. He sees no sign of a camera on the house.

"It's the doorbell," the voice says. "It's one of those video doorbells."

"That's cool," he replies. He is not good with technology. He heard of these, but he has never seen one in person. Well, none he knows of that is.

"Yes, it is," the voice is getting annoyed. "Tell me what you want or leave my property. I don't want to have to call the cops."

"I am the cops."

"You are the cops?"

"Well, I'm a detective. Freddy Falcon. I'm investigating the murder of Marcus Peterson."

"Marcus's murder? One moment."

He hears the frantic rustling of paper. Then, what sounded like a toilet flush.

"Shit! Forgot to turn this damn thing off. How do you…?"

Silence. Well, when you gotta go, he guessed.

After a few minutes, he hears a commotion on the other side of the door. The door opens to a short, chubby man. Is he even five feet? He looked about four feet, nine inches...maybe ten. He's clean-shaven, brown eyes and balding. It is one of those horseshoe-type patterns on the top of his head.

If he didn't know better, he would think that Mr. Peterson had a type. Perhaps he did. Hampton did say they had tried a relationship at one point. He shrugs it off.

"Mr. Greenbriar?" he asks.

The man nods. "Please, come in, Detective."

The man steps aside for Freddy to enter. Greenbriar closes the door behind them.

"This way, Detective."

The house is not what Freddy expected. He expected to see expensive paintings on the walls, perhaps high-end carpeting. Sure, there were a few items that spoke of money. The kitchen had all stainless-steel appliances and real granite countertops. The living room had a set of three electric theatre chairs and an eighty-inch television hanging on the wall. True, none of this represented extravagant living. It is clear that Mr. Greenbriar did enjoy high-end items and a relatively modest living.

Mr. Greenbriar motions for Freddy to take the rightmost theatre chair.

"Would you care for anything to drink? I have a fresh pot of coffee that should be ready."

Freddy smiles, "A man after my own heart."

The man returns the smile. “One moment.”

Adam steps into the kitchen. There is a breakfast bar that separates the kitchen from the living room. Freddy sits back in the chair and relaxes. The man looks as if he were right at home.

“Are you from Terra Loch?” Freddy asks.

“No. I’m from Texas originally.”

“How long have you lived here?”

“Ten years. What about you, Detective?”

“I’m a native. Born and raised.”

“That’s not surprising.”

“Oh? Why is that?”

“Your accent.”

Now, this surprised him. He worked hard to work his accent out of his speech pattern. He isn’t embarrassed by it. On the contrary, he is proud of his heritage. As sad as he thinks it is, he had learned that people assume a certain lower intelligence when they hear a southern accent.

“Interesting,” is his only response.

“Now, that is an interesting response. How do you take it?”

“Black. Why do you say that?”

“Any sweetener? The usual response I receive when I detect someone’s accent is more ‘I have an accent?’.”

“No. Just black coffee. I know I have an accent. Everyone does. Why pretend I don’t?”

“Then why hide it?” the man asks as he walks back with a cup of coffee in each hand.

“Why answer my question with a question?”

The man smiles as he hands Freddy one of the coffee cups. Freddy takes the cup and sips. Adam sits down in the far-left chair, leaving a theatre chair between the two men empty.

“There is a tray inside the right arm of your chair. You’ll find it has a little peg that fits in the slot in the arm.” Adam is making the motions as he is explaining. Freddy follows suit.

"Most people are proud of their heritage. Why hide yours?"

"I'm not hiding my heritage. On the contrary. I'm extremely proud of it."

"Then why lose your accent? And why are you avoiding this simple question?"

Freddy smiles, "I think I am the one who is supposed to be doing the interrogating."

The man returns the smile as he sips his coffee. "Only curious. As you can tell, I have not lost mine. You, at least, picked up on my southern accent."

"Let's just say that there are times a detective needs to speak on television or to politicians. Sometimes even in court. People tend to take you seriously when you speak without a southern accent. As sad as this sounds, they assume your intelligence is higher. There is a certain stigma with the southern accent. People believe you are an ignorant hick or some such. So, I worked hard on working it out of my vernacular."

"Interesting," the man replies.

"I find it curious you picked up on it. You have a keen ear, Mr. Greenbriar. Most people I grew up with can't hear it anymore."

"Perhaps it is part of what makes me good at my job."

"Your job?"

"Acting, Detective. I am, after all, a thespian."

"Did you always want to act?"

A slight grin formed on the man's face. "Believe it or not, I wanted to be a police officer."

"Like most children, I assume. Police officer, firefighter, or astronaut."

"No. I did go to the police academy."

"Oh?" Freddy's ears perk up. "In Texas?"

Greenbriar nods. "I realized it isn't for me."

"You never made it out of the academy?"

The man shakes his head. "No. I did. I did very well. Top of the class, you might say. Let me back up a little. My best friend in high school was found dead."

"Found dead? What happened?"

"Chris and I were great friends. We did everything together. It was our sophomore year. No longer Freshmen. The year is bright. I was the last person to ever see Chris alive. Well, besides the killer, that is."

Freddy is intrigued by this revelation. He doesn't show it. He still gives the illusion he is relaxed and chatting with a friend.

"It was a Saturday night. We went to a movie and dinner."

"What movie?"

"How is that relevant?"

"It's not," Freddy says with a shrug. "I'm just curious. Making conversation."

"Independence Day."

"Good movie."

"We enjoyed it."

"Where did you eat?"

"Pizza Hut. It was within walking distance from the theatre and on our way home."

"Dine in?"

The man nods. "Still had the jukebox and a tabletop Pac-Man arcade."

Freddy smiles. "Pizza Hut was the place to be at one time. So, what happened after you left?"

"We walked for a mile before reaching my street. We said our goodbyes and parted ways. I was home for about two hours when mom ran upstairs. She said that Chris's dad was on the phone. Chris never made it home."

"Did they catch the person?"

The man shakes his head. "Still unsolved."

"How did they clear you?"

"Excuse me?"

"Your friend's murder. You were the last to see him alive. How did they clear you? You would have been the prime suspect."

"They did question me. I guess they decided I wasn't involved."

"You guess? I would be questioning that, to be honest."

"What do you mean?"

Freddy shakes his head. "Not that you did it. I mean, the fact that the last person to see a murder victim alive is just questioned and let go? There's no wonder it's still unsolved."

Greenbriar leans in. "That was my thought as well. I decided to join the police force after high school. I wanted to solve that case."

He sits back and sips his coffee.

"So, what happened your rookie year?"

"I didn't make the cut."

"You didn't make the cut? It's not an audition."

"Too much paperwork. I didn't expect that."

"What did you expect?"

"You know...fast cars, chases, action, shootouts. That sort of thing."

"You watch too much TV."

Greenbriar nods. "So, I joined a community theatre. A friend mentioned someone from Hollywood was auditioning for a hit movie. The rest is history." He raises his right hand in the air as he says the last sentence as if to brush it off.

"What movie?"

"Excuse me?"

"You said it was a hit movie. What was it?"

"*Water Falls*. The movie about Alfred Water's fall from grace."

"Ah. Yes. The politician who is convicted of murdering that prostitute."

He nods.

"I didn't realize you were in that."

"I played Water's assistant."

"How did you meet Marcus Peterson?"

"That's a long story. Marcus and I go back a long way."

"As in a relationship?"

Greenbriar smiles. "Perceptive. I see why they say you are the best. Yes. We attempted a relationship. That's how we met. In a bar. We discovered we were better as friends. We had too much in common. Hampton thinks there is more to it than that." He shakes his head. "He's too paranoid. The truth is, Marcus and I just aren't compatible as a couple. A relationship works better when both parties are more different than the same. Would you agree?"

"I'm not qualified to answer that. I'm not a relationship kind of guy."

"More married to your work then. As am I."

"I'm not going to ask you what happened between Mr. Peterson and yourself. I already know the basic story. Mr. Hamm was generous enough to explain it."

"It was a mistake. Neither of us should have made it. A moment of weakness for both."

Freddy shakes his head. "I don't care. Your business is your business. The past is the past. I care more about now. What happened the night Mr. Peterson was murdered? Where were you?"

"My alibi?" He smiles and raises his eyebrows as he says it. "I went out for drinks after the shoot that night."

"Anyone go with you?"

He nods. "Rodney Cooper, Mitch Blakely, Aaron Chatsworth, and Richard Olstroski."

"Miguel Alvarez wasn't with you?"

He laughs.

"Did I say something funny?"

"Detective, you need to do your homework."

"How so?" Freddy leans in now.

"Miguel had other interests."

"Juliana Martinez."

He smiles. "You did do your homework. Good. Miguel and Juliana went back to her place that night. One last night together. She flew out to Germany the next morning."

"Did anything out of the ordinary happen that night?"

"No. We all talked. Laughed. Got drunk. Richard was so drunk he could not drive home. When I left, he is still asleep in his car."

"What about the other three?"

"They decided to take the party to a strip club. Definitely not what I am into. Well, if the strippers were more masculine…." He smiles as he says that.

Freddy shows no expression. He never could understand that need. It never was his idea of a good time.

"Then what? You returned home and fell asleep?"

"Pretty much. I found out about Marcus's murder the next morning."

"How?"

"I called Miguel to let him know I was going to be late."

"Late?"

"Detective, we still had one more scene to shoot."

"Miguel Alvarez informed you of Mr. Peterson's death?"

"Not immediately. I reached his voicemail. He called me back half an hour later. Maybe forty-five minutes."

"About what time?"

"Well, we were supposed to be on set at ten o'clock that morning. I don't remember the exact time he called me back. It was fairly early, though."

"Early?"

"Yes. You see, I had a friend over that night. He didn't want to leave that morning." He says this with a knowing grin on his face.

Freddy kept his straight face. "Interesting. Is there anything else you can tell me about that night?"

"Nothing relevant to your case."

"I see." Freddy gulps down the rest of his coffee and sets the cup down on the tray table. "Thank you for your time."

"It has been a pleasure."

Freddy stands and reaches for the empty cup.

"No need, Detective. I will get it. Let me see you out."

"No need. I can see myself out."

Freddy turns to leave. He gets as far as the foyer and turns around. Adam Greenbriar is taking the coffee cups to the sink.

"One thing still bothers me."

"What's that?"

"My understanding is that you and Marcus Peterson had a huge falling out. This was a rift that destroyed your friendship. What made him decide to come to you for this film?"

"Perhaps you should ask his husband. Detective, Marcus came to me. He apologized to me."

"He apologized to you? For what? You betrayed him."

"What I mean is, Marcus had forgiven Hampton and myself a long time ago. He regretted not healing this rift earlier. It is Hampton who refuses."

"Mr. Hamm?"

He nods. "Hampton convinced Marcus that I was a horrible friend for what happened. He took no responsibility for it. Hampton convinced Marcus that he was the innocent victim, and he was the unwilling party. I did lead him on. I did make advances toward him. Hampton went along with it. He returned my advances. I swear to you, Detective, it was consensual."

"And Mr. Peterson divulged all of that to you?"

"He did. Hampton had no idea we spoke. See, Marcus is a man of peace. He never liked to hold grudges. He always felt any conflict could be worked out with communication."

"He sounds like a brilliant man."

"He was."

"Thank you for your time."

"My pleasure."

Freddy closes the door as he leaves. He walks down the walkway toward the street. The children are still out there. He walks across the street and approaches the lemonade stand.

"How much?" he asks.

"You came!" the little girl exclaims.

"I always keep my word. How much for a glass?"

"Fifty cents," replies one of the boys, pointing to the sign.

He feels in his pockets for change. His pockets contain only his wallet, phone, and car keys. Freddy looks in his wallet for a one-dollar bill. He has two twenty-dollar bills and one five-dollar bill. He pulls out the five and hands it to the boy.

"I said fifty cents."

Freddy smiles. "Call it a tip. For all of Mr. Greenbriar's guests who leave without buying anything."

The three children smile with joy.

"Thank you!" they exclaim.

The boy takes the five and pours Freddy a glass. Freddy takes a sip and smiles.

"This is amazing. The best I have ever had."

"Thank you!" they exclaim again.

Freddy finishes the glass. He throws the empty cup in a nearby trash can the children had sitting next to the stand. He waves and walks back to his car.

"Goodbye, sir!" he hears them say.

He gets back in his car and closes the door. He grabs his phone and calls Shawn.

"What's up?"

"Shawn, I have a question. What time was Mr. Peterson's death called in?"

"Did you learn something interesting?"

"Perhaps. What time?"

"Around seven-thirty that morning. Why?"

"Perhaps nothing. Thank you."

He ends the call. He is looking at the entrance to Mr. Greenbriar's home. His focus changes to the list. He grabs it from the visor. Reading through the names again, he crosses out the name of Adam Greenbriar.

"Let's see what Mr. Alvarez has to tell us."

He starts the engine, and the Mustang drives off.

Chapter Twenty-Two

Stuck in a Drive-Thru

Where the hell is he supposed to find Miguel Alvarez? The man's address nor phone number is listed anywhere within the case file. Does he even live locally, or is he part of the folks who flew in from California?

Freddy has been pouring over the evidence for hours now. He stoped at *Filled to the Brim*, his favorite local spot for coffee. He isn't big on these national coffee chains. They never made the coffee quite right. It either isn't appropriately stirred, or it is too bitter. Local is always the way to go for good coffee.

"Would you care for anything else, Freddy?"

He looks up to see Helen standing there. Freddy makes a point to always sit at one of her tables. He had helped her out on another case a few years back. It was an arson case. Her husband had been killed in the fire. James, her husband, worked in real estate. He found out his business partner had been embezzling from the company for years. James threatened to press charges on the man. Poor guy never expected what happened.

After the case was over and the man was convicted, Freddy helped Helen get back on her feet. He found her this job and made sure she located a place to live. She's still recovering and will never be the same. He's glad to see her smiling and happy again. This is where he knows Hampton can be one day. Healthy and moving on, but never actually "over" it all.

He smiles at her and holds up his empty cup.

She returns the smile. "Freddy, you realize that if this were a bar, you'd be cut off by now? What is that? Your sixth? Seventh?"

"Tenth, but who's counting?"

"Jesus Freddy, you ever think about Coffee-holics Anonymous or something?"

"No such thing."

"The way you drink coffee, there should be. Trevor could retire off of you alone. I'll be back."

"And make it to go."

"Gotcha."

She walks off toward the back. He engulfed himself back in his work.

There isn't much on this guy. At least not much that he doesn't already know. Mr. Alvarez had been dating Ms. Martinez for five years now. They always tried to work on projects together. There is absolutely nothing on this guy. His record is clean.

"Shit!" Freddy closes the folder in frustration. He sits back in the chair and exhales.

"Maybe this will help. I put a little extra espresso in it this time."

She sets the cup down in front of him. He takes a sip.

"Always topping yourself, Helen. Thanks."

"Anything else?"

He shakes his head. "Just the check."

She hands him the check. He looks at the total.

"Keep the change," he says as he hands her cash.

He grabs his folder and coffee and walks out the door. He still has no idea where to start. The thought finally occurs to him as he reaches his car.

"Of course. How could I be so stupid? It's been staring me right in the face."

He gets in the car and calls Shawn. The call goes to voicemail. He tries Eddy. That call goes to voicemail as well.

"So much for the lazy route."

He opens his folder and finds what he is looking for. He enters the address into his phone's GPS and drives off.

***

The Mustang turns into the parking lot of Pine Oak Apartments. He pulls around and parks next to the giant dragon fountain. The man glances at the dragon atop the precipice as he leaves the car to enter the building.

"I bet you Shawn obsessed about that damn thing," he says as he enters the building.

"Good morning. How may I help you?" a young woman says as he approaches the front counter.

He glances at her name tag. "Good morning, Carmen. I am Detective Falcon. I'm investigating…"

"The murder of Marcus Peterson."

Freddy jumps and whips around to see a security guard standing behind him.

"Exactly, Mr…"

"Mac," the man replies.

"Mr. Mac," Freddy finishes.

The man shakes his head. "Just Mac. You are waisting your time, Detective. I told the officers, I don't know anything that happened after I threw the guy out."

It takes Freddy a minute to realize the man is talking about Richard Olstroski.

"No. I'm not here about him. You actually may be the best person to talk to about this."

"Oh? Why is that?" Mac says with a particular curiosity.

Freddy nods. "You work security here."

"I'm head of security. How can I help?"

"I'm here to ask about Miguel Alvarez."

The man's face shows he knows the name well.

"He's not here. He should be back tonight."

"Tonight?"

He didn't expect that response. Is the man living here? Is he taking care of her apartment while she is away? Shawn didn't think to ask if anyone was in her apartment?

The man nods. "He owns the same apartment as Ms. Martinez."

"They own it together? I understand they are dating, but…."

The man shakes his head. "No, Detective. They own it separately."

It doesn't take a detective of Freddy's caliber to tell that this man is aware of his confusion.

"Detective," he starts with a smile, "you ain't aware of how this place works, are ya?"

He shakes his head.

"It's similar to a timeshare."

He still isn't quite sure how timeshares work. He had even been on those timeshare tours as a kid. You may leave with some type of prize they are giving away. The hope is that you bought into it. His grandparents went a few times. They never bought into it, though. He just remembered how boring it was. He doesn't remember much of the details.

"Multiple people can own the same apartment. They may stay for a week or a month or so. It depends on the buy-in."

"The buy-in?"

He nods. "Think of it like a hotel room you own. Yes, you own it, but so do other people. You have a deed to it, as you would a house. You can pay for a week stay, a month stay, or several months stay. It all depends on what you can afford."

"A week? Are you telling me that someone can own a timeshare and only have access to it one week out of the year?"

He nods.

"What do you do with it for the other 51 weeks?"

"Well, I will use the one in question as an example. Mr. Alvarez and Ms. Martinez own the same apartment. Normally, an apartment has multiple owners throughout the year. In this case, they both pay for six months at a time. When it's vacant, we rent it out like a hotel."

"You rent it out? I thought they owned it?"

"They own the right to live here. The place still has to keep running. So, on weeks or months that a guest is not here, we rent out their apartment to someone else. Be it a family member from out of town or a tourist or whomever.

"You aren't guaranteed the same apartment either, Detective. If the one you have the deed to is rented, we put you in another apartment for the time you are here."

"What does someone pay for the 'privilege' of living here?"

"It varies. Anywhere from eighty to a couple hundred."

"Thousand?"

He nods.

Freddy shakes his head. "It seems like a waste of money to me. You could just buy a house for that."

"Most of these people live elsewhere. We handle the upkeep for them."

"And I'm assuming there is a charge for that 'privilege' as well...."

He nods.

"Most of the people you have here could afford a second home as well as staff who live on-site."

He could tell the man is about to argue. Mac is taking a defensive posture.

"Look, I'm not here to argue over the merits of a timeshare. Who am I to judge how people choose to spend their money? I'm here to talk with Miguel Alvarez, about the murder of Marcus Peterson."

"As I said, he will return this evening."

"I may return later to talk with him."

The man nods. "Just mention it to the front desk when you arrive." He motions to the desk where Carmen stands. "Carmen won't be here, and neither will I."

"Carmen," he directed that to the lady behind the front desk.

She looks up from her computer. "Yes, Mac?"

"Who's in tonight?"

"Behind the desk?"

He nods.

She made a few clicks with the mouse on her computer.

"Ian. He relieves me at six."

"Good. Would you give Ian a message?"

She nods and produces a pen and pad.

"Let him know that Detective Falcon will return this evening to speak with Mr. Alvarez."

She wrote the message down. "Anything else?"

Mac glances at Freddy. Freddy shakes his head.

"That will be it," Mac replies.

She nods, puts away the pad and pen, and returns to her work. Mac returns his attention to Freddy.

"There ya go. Just come in and speak with Ian. He's a tall, lanky fella. In his 20's. Short hair. Glasses. Good kid."

"Thank you so much for your time, sir."

Freddy holds out his hand to the man. Mac gripped it in a firm shake.

"Mac," he replies.

"Mac," Freddy says with a smile. "Thank you, Mac."

"My pleasure, Detective. Have a good one."

Freddy leaves and returns to his car. He can't understand why someone would buy a timeshare. Perhaps it is just easier. They know they have a place to stay when coming into town. They don't have to worry about finding a hotel. Everything is set up for them. They don't have to worry about cleaning or yard work. Perhaps it's not a bad idea for someone who frequents this city and doesn't want to deal with the hassles of a house or condo. But he still believes it is more economical to just buy a second home here and hire staff with the upkeep. The folks that purchased these things could afford that. He decides to let it go. It isn't any of his business.

He pulls out the list of names when he returns to his car. Sitting in the driver's seat, he makes a dash mark next to "Miguel Alvarez" and writes, "Return tonight."

"I've spoken with two of the four priorities on this case, Wexler and Greenbriar, and I'll speak with the third, Alvarez, tonight. Perhaps he can shed some light on the fourth, Martinez. I still want to find a way to talk to her."

He peruses the names on the list again as he thinks.

"I haven't spoken with Rodney Cooper, Mitch Blakely, or Aaron Chatsworth. They seem like low priorities. Always investigate all possible leads."

Wexler's lie still bothers him. Is it a lie or an oversight? He isn't sure. Either way, the man turned out to give more misinformation than anything. He may have to pay another visit to Mr. Wexler. But now is not the time for that.

At least no one else has been killed. Which leads to a more profound puzzle. Why Richard Olstroski? He understands the attack on Hampton Hamm. The man was there when his husband was murdered. He had been sleeping on the lanai, but he was there. Why Richard Olstroski? He never returned that night. It's confirmed he was drunk and slept it off in his car. Did he know something, or does the killer think he knew something? And what made him escape the hotel that night? He knew he wasn't being charged. He knew it was just a precaution. It is apparent, by his route, he wasn't heading for the airport.

"I'll have to return to that later. Right now," he says as he gulps down the last drops from his coffee cup, "I need more coffee."

***

The drive-through at *Boomer's Coffee House* is packed. He is the last in a line that is wrapped around the building. The Mustang inches forward.

"Oh, the things I do for coffee." He lets out a sigh. "Is this what I have been reduced to? Fast food coffee from a drive-through?"

The line moves, and Freddy moves with it. He never understood the appeal of drive-through coffee. They never get it right. If a person uses flavoring, they never have the flavoring that's wanted. The prices are too high for what is served. And it's never appropriately stirred.

He lowers his hands to his sides and leans his head back on the seat. "All I want is a cappuccino. Espresso with frothed milk on top. The largest they have. That's all."

His mind begins to wonder about the case. What about the arsenic? Granted, Marcus Peterson was drinking that night, and arsenic does occur naturally in wine. Was Mr. Peterson showing signs of arsenic poisoning before that night? They were ending the film shoot. This is a project they had been working on for months. It is possible that someone could have been slowly poisoning the man. He would need to talk to…

The car behind him let out a blaring honk. He jumps at the sound. He is lost in his own thoughts again. He never realized the line was moving. He never realized a car pulled in behind him. Placing his foot on the gas, he pulls up to the vehicle in front of him.

At that moment, his phone rings. It is Shawn.

"Thank God," he says as he answers.

"You're...welcome…?" Shawn replies as if he were unsure what to say.

"I'm in the drive-through and bored out of my mind."

"Drive-through? Since when do you eat at a drive-through?"

"Coffee. I'm at *Boomer's*."

“Since when do you order coffee from a drive-through? I always thought ‘The Great Freddy Falcon’ is too good for a drive-through.”

“There’s a first time for everything. Now cut the shit. What do you have?”

“That building we found the Olstroski corpse in.”

“What about it?”

“It’s a set.”

“A set? Do you mean?”

“Yup. A set for an upcoming movie.”

“Not the Peterson film then?”

“Yes and no.”

“Could you be more vague?”

“Not THIS Peterson film.”

“Marcus Peterson was working on another project?”

“Starting to.”

“Interesting. So, why would Richard Olstroski head there?”

“This might give a slight clue. It’s owned by Marsly Productions.”

“Not ringing a bell.”

“Marsly Productions is owned by Margaret Slythe.”

He sits up straight when he hears the name. “What the hell?”

“I thought that would get your attention.” He can hear the smile in Shawn's voice. He bet the man is ecstatic that he got one over on “The Great Freddy Falcon", as Shawn liked to put it.

“Wait a minute. Isn’t she a therapist?”

“Apparently, she is into a lot of things. She owns a production house that is funding the next three pictures our murdered director is involved in.”

“Three? Wow, the man’s career was on the upswing. His husband confirmed as much.”

“And she owns the talent agency that Juliana Martinez and Miguel Alvarez work out of.”

"Now that is interesting."

"Welcome to *Boomer's Coffee House*. May I take your order?" came a sound from the loudspeaker.

"One moment Shawn."

"Order when you are ready."

"Not you," he says with annoyance. "I'm on the phone."

"Take your time, sir. Order when you are ready."

"I'm ready now." He knows the man on the headset can hear his frustration. "I want a cappuccino."

"Hot or iced?"

Freddy is taken aback at that. An iced cappuccino?

"Hot. Who the hell orders an iced cappuccino?"

"We sell both hot and iced coffee, sir. What size?"

"But cappuccino? There is no such thing as an iced cappuccino."

"Sir, what size?"

"Large."

"We don't have large."

"You don't have large?"

"No, sir."

He heard Shawn chuckle.

"Shut up," he says to Shawn.

"I'm sorry, sir. Continue when you are ready."

"Not you!" He is ready to explode. "I'm on the phone."

"I'm sorry. Continue when you are ready."

"I'm ready now!"

"What size, sir?"

He breaths deep and exhales slowly.

"What sizes do you have?" he asks in a calm tone.

"We have micro, mini, tiny, super, and jumbo."

"So, the jumbo is the large?"

"We don't have large. We have micro.."

"What I mean is, the jumbo is the equivalent of a large?"

"No, that's the super."

"Then what's a small?"

"We don't have small."

Freddy takes another breath.

"What's the equivalent of a small?"

"The mini."

"What's the micro equivalent to?"

"Extra-small."

"So, what's the jumbo equivalent to?"

"Extra large."

"Give me that then."

"We don't offer a cappuccino in jumbo."

"Son of a bitch!"

Shawn is laughing hysterically now.

"Please watch your language, sir. This is a family establishment."

"What sizes do you offer for a cappuccino?

"Mini, tiny and super."

"So small, medium, and large."

"We don't have…"

"I know. Just give me a super cappuccino then."

"What flavor?"

"What?"

"What flavor would you like? We have pumpkin spice if you would like it."

"What do you mean? It's espresso and milk?"

"Correct. We also offer flavors."

"First, it's a cappuccino. You don't flavor it."

"We do."

"Second, it's May, and pumpkin spice is a holiday flavor."

"Memorial Day is coming up."

"Third, and most importantly, pumpkin spice should be banned. It's disgusting and not meant for human consumption."

"It's a popular flavor, sir."

"No flavor. Just a plain, large cappuccino."

"We don't have…"

"Give me the largest damn cappuccino you sell!"

"That would be the super. And again, sir, language, please. What type of milk?"

"I don't know. The kind that comes from a cow."

"Skim, two percent, or whole?"

"Whole milk, please."

"Thank you, sir. Look at the screen. Is your order correct?"

He looked at the display. It had a picture of a cup of coffee. Beside the picture were four lines of text:

Cappuccino
Super
Whole Milk
No Flavoring

"Yes, that's correct."

"That will be eight dollars and thirty-four cents. Pull around, please."

"Eight dollars for a cappuccino?"

"Yes, sir. Pull around, please."

"That's highway robbery. Jesus."

"Language, sir. Pull around, please."

"I will when the damn car in front of me moves!"

"Thank you, sir. Remember, language."

Shawn is still laughing on the other end of the phone.

"Laugh it up," he says as he rolls his eyes.

"You really do hate drive-throughs."

"No, I hate stupid drive-throughs. That dumbass knows what I meant when I ordered a large."

"You ever work fast food, Freddy?"

"No. I was on the farm throughout high school. Why?"

"They have a certain order they have to do things. Give the kid a break. He's just doing his job."

"He knows what I meant."

"Freddy, this place obviously has a certain brand. He may know what you mean, but he can't call it that. He has to stick to the branding."

"All I want is a cappuccino."

"And you got it. It's not his fault. He's just doing his job."

Freddy shakes his head. "Alright. What else did you find?"

"Cameras."

"Perfect!"

He hears the smile in Shawn's voice again. This is a smile of unbridled enthusiasm. "And we have the footage."

"You have the tape? Perfect!"

"What century are you from? We have the footage on a thumb drive."

"Either way, that's great! From the time frame in question?"

"I'm not a rookie. Yes. I watched part of it to make sure. It clearly shows Richard Olstroski entering the building."

"Too bad we don't have…"

"We do."

"There were cameras inside?"

"Like I said. A movie set. They want to make sure it doesn't get vandalized."

"Shawn, I could kiss you right now."

"That will be eight dollars and thirty-four cents."

Freddy had just pulled up to the window. The kid looked to be about sixteen. He handed the teen his debit card.

"And I'm sorry about earlier."

"Sir?" the teen asks.

"When I was ordering. I'm sorry I got so frustrated."

The teen looks confused. "I just work the window. I didn't take your order."

"Oh, well, I'm sorry anyway."

The teen runs the card and hands it and the receipt to Freddy. He places both in his wallet. The window closes again.

"You aren't my type," Shawn says.

"Cut the shit. You know what I mean."

"When do you want to see it?"

"I was going to speak with a few more folks from the production. I can change my plans. This is more important. I'm free until tonight in any case."

"Tonight?"

"Yeah. I meet with Miguel Alvarez later tonight."

The window opens.

"Your cappuccino."

Freddy looks at the cup in the teen's hand. It is the size of a small soda.

"I ordered a large."

"We don't have lar…"

"Super. I ordered a super."

"This is a super."

"That's a super?"

Shawn starts laughing again.

"Yes, sir. It's a super cappuccino."

Freddy sighs and takes the cup.

"Thank you."

"My pleasure, sir. Have a wonder..."

He rolls up the window and drives off.

"For eight dollars, this had better be amazing," he says as he takes a sip.

Surprisingly, it is. This is the best-made cappuccino he had ever tasted. Better than anything he could get at *Filled to the Brim*. He has to admit this is a damn good cappuccino.

"Damn fine cappuccino," he says as he places it in the plastic cup holder on the door.

The Mustang did not have the built-in cup holders that modern cars have. He purchased one of those plastic cup holders that fits onto the door. He remembered how popular those things were in his childhood.

"Glad you approve," Shawn says. "So, you heading back to the Farmhouse?"

"I wasn't, but I can be. We will watch the tape."

"Recording."

"Whatever."

"Can we do it tomorrow?"

"Why? I want to get this solved, Shawn."

"So do I, but all I have is the footage from the outside."

"Where's the rest of it?"

"I pick it up tomorrow."

"Pick it up? I thought it was on a thumb drive?"

"The footage I have is. The cameras all record to a central hard drive. The footages had to be extracted and placed on a thumb drive. The rest of the footage will be ready tomorrow."

"Alright. Tomorrow then."

"You still headed back to the Farmhouse?"

"No. I have time. Looks like I can interview a few more people."

"Alright. Later."

The call ends. He takes another sip of coffee. Pulling out the list again, he looks it over.

"Let's see what Mr. Chatsworth has to say."

Chapter Twenty-Three

Wexler's List

He is on his way to the home of Aaron Chatsworth when his phone rings. A number he doesn't recognize is showing on the display. It is an area code he doesn't recognize either. On the off chance it dealt with the case, he decides to answer it.

"This is Detective Falcon. How can I help you?"

"Good afternoon, Detective. This is Miguel Alvarez. How are you this afternoon?"

"Mr. Alvarez," he says with a smile. "I am well. How are you today?"

"I'm well, sir."

"If you don't mind me asking, how did you get my number? Don't get me wrong. I do want to speak with you. I don't remember giving my number out to anyone."

"Of course. I stopped by the apartment early. Carmen informed me that you stopped by. A pleasant gentleman at your precinct gave me your number."

"Good ole Norman."

"Yes. I Believe that is the gentleman."

"I am on my way to speak with Aaron Chatsworth at the moment."

"Aaron. He is a wonderful man. A bit eccentric, but wonderful."

"When would be a good time for you and me to speak?"

"Are you free tonight, Detective?"

"Sure."

"I will be at the golf club tonight. Are you familiar with Shelby Lakes?"

"I am. Golfing? At night?"

"It will be at the driving range. They have it illuminated in the evenings. For those members who do not have time during the day."

"I see. Sure. I'll meet you there."

"How does nine o'clock sound?"

"That's perfect. I can grab a bite to eat, and I will be on my way."

"Wonderful. I will see you tonight."

"I'm looking forward to it."

"As am I, Detective. Thank you for your time. And inform Aaron that I said 'hello'."

"I will. And thank you, Mr. Alvarez.."

The call ends. He seems like a pleasant man. That is a first for Freddy. No one had ever gone to such lengths to speak with him. This man is either hiding his true intentions, or he has valuable information to share. Either way, he would find out tonight.

He had been reviewing Mr. Chatsworth's file before the drive over. There isn't much information on the man. He is a virtual unknown. Mr. Chatsworth is up and coming. He's not an actor. The man works in some type of sound design. He worked on a few low-budget, direct-to-streaming projects. Nothing major and nothing out of Hollywood until now. Based on the facts, this man wouldn't damage a promising career in such a way. But you always follow every lead. You never know how crazy people may be.

He arrives at five-twenty-eight North Colorado Avenue a few minutes later and parks the car on the side of the road in front of the house. This is a simple, two-story home. The lawn is well manicured. A single oak tree stands in the front yard.

He knocks on the door. He hears footsteps a few seconds later. The door opens, and he is taken aback. Towering over him is a giant. The man stands about seven feet tall. He has to weigh about two-hundred-fifty pounds. He has dirty blonde hair, a receding hairline, blue eyes, and glasses.

"May I help you?" He speaks in a deep, friendly voice.

"I'm looking for a goose that lays golden eggs," Freddy says with a smile.

"Funny. I've never heard that before," he says in a sarcastic tone.

"I'm sorry, sir. I'm Freddy Falcon. I'm…"

"Ah! Of course. Come on in, Detective. I was wondering when you would stop by."

"You were?"

Now, this confuses Freddy. He hadn't called ahead of time.

The man nods. "You've spoken with Jacob, Adam, and Hampton. And you are meeting with Miguel tonight."

"Word travels fast, I guess."

The man nods. "It does."

He stood aside and motioned with his hand for Freddy to enter.

"Just as long as you don't grind my bones and bake me into bread," he says with a smile.

"Real comedian we have here. Don't quit your day job," Chatsworth says.

Freddy acknowledges the gesture. The man closes the door behind him.

"I hope the drive treated you well," the man says as he leads Freddy through the house.

"It was peaceful," he replies.

"Glad to hear it. I'm not exactly in the city. Yes, it's on North Colorado, but it's almost out of the city."

"Yeah. I thought, for a moment, I was heading into the county."

"You almost are. And I prefer it that way."

He leads Freddy through the kitchen and dining area. The man opens a sliding glass door and motions for Freddy to step through. Freddy can't believe his eyes when he steps out. If he had not known better, he would have thought he had stepped into a luscious paradise.

The most magnificent garden he has ever seen surrounds him. Dozens of flowers with colored petals: red, blue, purple, yellow. Gorgeous to look at. An awning of green plants with red petals made an archway they were walking under. It is the most magnificent landscape he has experienced in his entire life. A feeling of calm and peace embraces him. He half expects to see butterflies flutter by.

Chatsworth leads him to a patio table under the flora awning. Both men sit on either side. Chatsworth sits back in his chair with his arms resting on the arms of the chair. Freddy is still busy looking around at the garden he finds himself in.

"Amazing, isn't it," Chatsworth says.

"It is," he replies without looking at the man. He is still in awe of the display.

"Do you garden?"

He laughs at that.

"Obviously not," Chatsworth says with a smile.

"I do tend my grandparents' farm. Well, I rent out the fields. I dabble a little in gardening, but I am not good at it. I pick things to plant based on what they look like. I have no idea how to do anything like this. The last thing I planted is a cranberry hibiscus."

"You planted that in your garden?"

"Yes."

"You might want to move that."

"Why? Do they get big?"

The man just smiles. He turns his attention to his garden.

"It took me years to get it looking like this. I guess you could say this is my legacy."

"And one to be proud of."

"That I am. Honestly, if something happened to it, I'd move on."

That did get Freddy to notice the man. He turned to look at Chatsworth.

"You wouldn't be upset? You said it took you years."

"Detective. May I call you Freddy?"

Freddy shakes his head. "No. Please forgive me. When I am on a case, it is strictly formalities."

"Understood. I can respect that. Detective, I'm fifty-five years old. I've seen my fair share of loss and tragedy. Probably more than my fair share. I've been through times where I have lost absolutely everything. I've started over. I've rebuilt. I won't lie. I would be disappointed and hurt. But these are just things. Things can be replaced. Life cannot."

"They're plants. They're living creatures."

"No," he says, shaking his head. "You misunderstand me. Plants can be planted again. I can take a tiny piece of all of this," he waves his hand as he speaks to indicate the entire awning overhead, "and plant it to have it all grow again. Plants are magnificent creatures, Detective.

"What I mean is that human life is precious and cannot be replaced. It broke my heart when I learned what happened to Marcus. My heart broke for my loss and for poor Hampton's as well. How is he holding up?"

"As well as can be expected. To be honest, he's been through hell. Part of that is my fault."

"You're just doing your job."

"Perhaps. Perhaps not."

He still feels guilty for what he had put Hampton through. His mind starts to drift off again. He shakes himself back.

"Hampton has a beautiful soul. His aura shines bright."

"Aura?" Freddy asks. Alvarez did say he is a bit eccentric.

The man smiles. "I'm sorry, Detective. I have a bit of a sixth sense. I can see auras. I can predict things."

Freddy thinks that he must look puzzled based on the man's next statement. But, in all honesty, he believes the man believes what he is saying. He detects no exaggerations or embellishments.

"It's not what you think. No crystal balls or hocus pocus. And it's not an exact science. Sometimes it's dreams. Sometimes it's just a feeling. I can't explain it. You see, we all can have it. Some more than others. Most of us just choose to block it out. You probably have a little of it and just don't realize it. It's, most likely, what makes you a great detective."

"You flatter me. Good, perhaps. Not great."

The man smiles. "When I found out the name of the person working the case, I decided to read all about this man. I wanted to know who, exactly, would be working on the murder case of a dear friend. I wanted to be sure this person would not pin it on poor Hampton. To that event, I read up on all of your cases. Your mind is extraordinary. The deductions you make. These aren't just hunches or guesses. You can read people. You watch the body language. You listen to every word. You're doing it now. At this moment. With me."

Freddy smiles. "And I see nothing but pure honesty and a large heart. You want to do the right thing."

"That's part of what drives me. I would burst through the gates of Hell to right a wrong if I could. You see. Even you have it. Do you mind me asking if you have discovered any evidence of how Marcus was murdered?"

"I can't discuss specifics."

"I'm not asking for specifics. Is there anything you found due to a hunch or a feeling?"

"Just a dream."

"Interesting. So, you found the evidence in a dream?"

Freddy nods. He starts recalling the dream in his mind. How he is lost in the forest. He hears his papa's voice. That did show him the way to the murder scene. That's where he found the wine bottle. Of course, he isn't going to tell this man all of that. He doesn't care how pure his intentions may be.

"I would say, the dream showed me the way."

Chatsworth smiles. "Well, there you go. Now you understand."

"No," Freddy says in an irritated tone. He sees shock in the man for the first time. His face shows a tent of surprise for half a second. How could Chatsworth not be surprised that Freddy would have this reaction? How could Chatsworth think this mysticism would magically solve everything?

"It's not magic or psychic powers or even a revelation from God, Himself. It's logic. It's obvious I'd been mulling over this case. My thoughts had been clouded. That I do admit. But I've seen the evidence for myself. I've been reviewing the case. My brain takes all of that information and sorts it out for me. The bottom line is, there is no mysticism or magic. Pure logic and deduction from a brain that is always working. That's it."

The man sits there in silence for what feels like an eternity. It is as if Chatsworth had been turned to stone. He could not read the man.

"I didn't mean to insult you in your home. Please forgive me. I don't believe what you believe. I appreciate that you believe it, and I respect that. I just…"

Chatsworth raises a hand as if to say, ``Enough talking". Freddy stops talking.

"No offense taken at all. We all have faith in something. Yours is your logic. Mine is more spiritual. Hold tight to your logic. It serves you well, Detective."

The smile returns to his face.

"Enough about me and my 'hocus pocus.'. You came here to discuss a murder investigation. I don't know what I can tell you, but I will tell you all I know."

Freddy feels his shoulders relax. He sits back and lets his mouth form that charming smile he is known for.

"Mr. Chatsworth…"

"Call me Aaron."

"No," he replies, shaking his head. "Forgive me, but I do things a certain way. I prefer to keep things on a professional level when working a case. It helps me keep my distance."

"I understand," he says knowingly.

Freddy can tell that he truly did understand.

"You don't want to seem too familiar or get too emotionally involved," Chatsworth says with a smile. "It helps you keep your distance. Smart man. Very well then. Mr. Chatsworth will be fine."

Freddy nods and continues, "Mr. Chatsworth, what is your work on the movie?"

"Sound Engineer. I'm responsible for the sound equipment, sound set-up, etc."

"Sound set-up?"

Chatsworth nods. "I arrive with all of my equipment for recording sound on set. All ambient noise, foley work, etc. I am responsible for it all. I hire the boom mic operators. I ensure the mics are set properly, and the sound is perfect on set."

"So, you are like a Sound Director?"

"I am in charge of how the sound is captured on set. I don't handle sound editing."

"I see. How long have you been doing this?"

"About twenty years now. I got my start in radio."

"Oh?"

Chatsworth nods enthusiastically. "Radio is my passion. I love the medium. There is something magical about telling a story auditorily. It's similar to reading a book. You let your brain and imagination fill in the pictures."

Freddy nods. "I can see the similarities. What made you decide to get into filmmaking?"

"I'm from Atlanta. There was a call looking for anyone who knows anything about sound for a local television station. I got the call. Someone there loved my work. As you know, shows such as *The Walking Dead* and movies such as *The Avengers* brought Atlanta to the forefront of the film industry. Hollywood loves filming here in Georgia. My job afforded me the ability to move out of the city. I love the water, so I moved down here. I must say that I love this town."

"I can understand that," he says with a smile. "But you are in the country north of town. The lake is at the center of town. Why not buy near the lake?"

"Flooding."

"Flooding?"

Chatsworth nods. "Granted, it doesn't rain here as it does in Florida. Have you ever been to Florida?"

He shakes his head.

"Well, they have two seasons: Hot and Hotter than Hell. And the rain. Let me tell you. You have never seen more bi-polar weather than Florida. When they say you can set your watch by the afternoon showers, they are not joking. The joke about Florida weather is, 'If you don't like the weather, just wait thirty minutes'. I have seen it rain on one side of someone's yard and the other side dry as a bone."

He isn't sure how much of that he believes, but what did he know? He's never been outside of Georgia. Who is he to doubt the man? "Wow," is his response.

The man nods enthusiastically. "Don't get me wrong. I love visiting that state. I certainly would not want to live there."

"Let's talk more about that night."

"What night?"

"The night Marcus Peterson was murdered." What night? What night did he think he is talking about?

"Oh. I was here."

"At home?"

He nods.

"Are you sure?"

"Yes, Detective. I was working in my garden."

"Multiple people confirmed you were out that night?"

"Now I am concerned." The man sits up straight as if in alarm. "Detective, I promise you, I was here."

"You didn't go out that night?"

"No," he shakes his head frantically.

"Interesting. So, you weren't out at a bar with Richard Olstroski?"

"Richard?" He says the name in disgust. "First of all, I don't drink. Second, I would never be anywhere with that man. Are you aware of how he talks to the women on set? Whatever Richard says isn't true."

"I heard that you were drinking that night with Richard Olstroski, Adam Greenbriar, Rodney Cooper, and Mitch Blakely. Miguel Alvarez may or may not have been there."

The man shakes his head as each name is said. "No. I swear to you, Detective, I was here. I left the set late. I had to pack up all of the sound equipment. The last people left were Hampton and Marcus. Hampton was angry with Marcus."

"Angry?"

"It's not as bad as you think. Marcus can be rough on set. He's harder on Hampton than anyone else. He's conscious about not showing favoritism."

"I can respect that. Go on."

"That's it. I packed up my things and left. I came straight home."

"Can anyone corroborate that?"

"Besides Hampton?"

"Yes. Did you stop anywhere? See anyone?"

"I stopped for gas on the way home."

"Do you have a receipt?"

The man nods. He stands up and turns to walk inside the house. "One moment."

Freddy knows someone is lying. Why would Wexler and Greenbriar both say Chatsworth was there that night if he wasn't? Wexler also said Alvarez was there. Greenbriar states otherwise. He can't put his finger on it but getting to the bottom of this puzzle may be the key to solving the case.

Chatsworth reappears, holding out a receipt.

"Here it is. Proof I was getting gas."

Freddy looks at the receipt. "That's just a block before heading out of town."

Chatsworth nods. "Last gas station heading this way."

"That it is."

Freddy hands the receipt back to the man. Chatsworth places it in his pocket and sits back down.

"So, you have no idea what happened after you left?"

Chatsworth shakes his head. "All I know is that I received a call from Miguel the next morning."

"Miguel Alvarez?" Now, this got his attention.

Chatsworth nods. "He informed me that Marcus had been murdered."

"What time was the call?"

"Around eight o'clock that next morning."

"Are you sure?" Freddy presses.

"Pretty sure."

"This is important. Are you absolutely sure that Miguel Alvarez called you at eight o'clock on the morning of Marcus Peterson's death to tell you the man had been murdered?"

Chatsworth pulls out his cell phone and looks at the recent calls. He scrolls to the date in question.

"There."

He hands Freddy the phone. There it is, plain as day. Miguel Alvarez is listed as an incoming call at 8:05 in the morning.

"Son of a bitch!" is all Freddy says.

He hands the phone back to Chatsworth.

"Just when I think I have a handle on this mystery. Did Mr. Alvarez tell you how he found out?"

He shakes his head. "I didn't think to ask."

"Is there anything else you can tell me that may be relevant?"

He shakes his head.

"Well, thank you for your time."

"It has been a pleasure, Detective. Let me show you out."

"I can find my way."

Freddy stands and starts for the door that leads inside. Chatsworth grabs his arm and nudged it the opposite way.

"No. This way is quicker."

He leads Freddy through another path to a gate. Chatsworth opens the gate to reveal the side yard. Freddy could see the street around the corner.

"Follow the path around. It will lead you to the front of the house."

Chatsworth holds out his hand. Freddy grabbed it in a firm embrace.

"Thank you again," he says.

"It's been a pleasure, Detective."

He follows the cobblestone path around the side of the house. He can see his car as he approaches the front. He grabs the list of names when he returned to his car.

Adam Greenbriar
Miguel Alverez
Rodney Cooper
Mitch Blakely
Aaron Chatsworth

Aaron Chatsworth joins Adam Greenbriar as people he has spoken with. He will talk with Miguel Alvarez tonight. That should be an interesting conversation, he thinks. That leaves two people on the list Wexler gave him.

"Let's see what Rodney Cooper has to say."

***

Rodney Cooper lives in apartment 217 in Kingstan Overlook Apartments. It isn't on the lake, but it is across from it. The complex does get its name because it overlooks the lake. Kingstan Overlook is located at 237 South Colorado Avenue. Even though it overlooks the lake, it is still only a small two-story apartment complex. There are no elevators. Metal stairs lead up to the second story from either side. The bottom floor apartments have a small patio, while those on the second floor has a small balcony.

"What are the odds that two people on this list would live on the same road? One north of the lake. The other one south," he says as he approaches the building.

The clanging sound of each footstep can be heard as he walks up the stairs. There are apartments on either side. The long catwalk that serves as a hallway stretches to the far end. He walks down the catwalk, looking at the apartment numbers. The even numbers are on the left, and the odd numbers are on the right. He passes 209, 211,215. That is odd 213 is skipped. He assumes the owner is superstitious. Standing in front of apartment 217, he knocks. There is no answer. He knocks again. Still no answer.

"What the hell?"

Knocking harder, he calls out, "Mr. Cooper! This is Freddy Falcon! Mr. Cooper! I am a police detective! I want to ask you a few questions!"

No answer.

"Mr. Cooper!" he exclaims while knocking one last time.

No answer.

He shrugs. Perhaps the man isn't home? Freddy decided to return later. He turns to leave. That's when he hears footsteps and a voice.

"Give me a damn minute! Dammit! Can't a guy take a shit in peace anymore?"

The door flings open to reveal a middle-aged man about average height. The man has a sour look on his face.

"What the hell do you want?"

He sees the man sizing him up. There is no detection of hostility. Freddy assumes the grouchy attitude is due to him disturbing the man's daily constitutional.

"I'm Freddy Falcon, a detecti…."

"You said that already. It was loud enough to wake the dead. What do ya want?"

"I am investigating the murder of Marcus Peterson."

"I didn't do it. I don't know who did."

"Perhaps you may have some insight about that night?"

"I already said I don't know nothin'. Can't ya hear?"

Freddy holds steadfast. He doesn't show any sign the man is getting to him.

"Mr. Cooper, I understand that you went out for drinks that night."

"Ain't no law against that."

"No, there isn't."

"Then why pester me?"

Cooper starts to close the door. Freddy catches it with his hand.

"What the hell?" the man exclaims.

Freddy places his face so close to the other man's that he could smell the alcohol on his breath.

"Look. I am in the middle of a murder investigation. You can either answer my questions here or back at the station. Your choice."

"Bah," is all the man says.

He moves out of the way to allows Freddy to enter.

The inside of the apartment is immaculate. Everything is clean and well kept. Not even a speck of dust could be found.

"What's so surprising? I'm not white trash." The man says. "Stop standing there lookin' like a deer in the headlights. Sit down and stay awhile, or leave. What do I care?"

He obviously noticed Freddy's surprised look. It had nothing to do with any prejudices he had. It is more due to experience. Most places such as this were not that hospitable.

"Of course not. I am taking in the sight. It's amazing what you have done with the place."

"Well, take it in while sitting. Yer making me nervous."

Freddy nods and sits down on the leather couch.

"Real leather? Very nice."

"What the hell else would it be? Definitely not that fake shit. That shit falls apart too quick."

He decides to forgo the small talk and concentrate on the reason he is here.

"Do you remember what happened that last day of filming?"

"Of course I do. I ain't got dementia."

"Did you come straight home that night?"

"What's that got to do with anything? I told ye I don't know nothin'."

He sighs before continuing.

"I was informed you went out for drinks that night. You and possibly five others."

"Five? What others?"

"I was told that you, Adam Greenbriar, Miguel Alvarez, Mitch Blakely, Aaron Chatsworth and Richard Olstroski all went out for drinks and then to a strip club that night."

The man lets out a hardy laugh. "A strip club? Adam and Aaron? Maybe Adam if they are naked men. But never Aaron. Yeah, I was out drinkin'. Me, Rich, Mitch, and Adam all went to a bar. Adam left early. Says he had a 'friend' coming over."

He says the word "friend" in air quotes. Freddy doesn't have to ask what he means.

"What happened after that?"

"Well, we'd talked about goin' to a strip club. After Adam left, we were all too wasted. Rich fell asleep in his car. Me and Mitch came over here for more drinking. Mitch passed out on that couch yer sittin' on, and I passed out in my bed."

"What about Aaron Chatsworth and Miguel Alvarez?"

"What about 'em?"

"I heard they may have gone out with you."

"Ye heard wrong. Who told ye that nonsense? Jacob?"

Freddy nods.

"Thought so. See, Jacob was there when we were talkin' about it. It was me, Jacob, Aaron, Adam, Rich, Mitch, and Miguel. Jacob had to get home. Somethin' about the wife. Shit, I'm glad I ain't married. Damn ball and chain. You married Detective?"

Freddy shakes his head.

"Ah, yer better off for it. Ain't no woman gonna be a noose around my neck. Anyway, where was I? Oh yeah, Jacob. He left. Aaron was there packin' up his shit. I'm glad he's there. It's an important job. Glad it ain't me. Too much work settin' up and breakin' down. Shit. I do my damn job and get my ass home. Call it a nine to five in the film industry if there's such a thing."

"What about Miguel? You said he didn't join you."

"I'm gettin' there. Stop chompin' my ass. So, Miguel had a woman too."

"Juliana Martinez."

"Well, if ye know, why'd ye ask?" he inquired in frustration.

"I need to hear the details from you."

"Eh," he grunts as he waves his hand. "So, yeah, Miguel met with Juliana that night. Says they had some lines to go over. I bet he went over lines alright. Every line of her body. Have ye seen her, detective? She's a fine-ass woman. Miguel is one lucky son of a bitch."

Freddy chose to ignore that. "So, that leaves you, Greenbriar, Olstroski, and Blakely going out?"

He nods.

"Was anyone still on set when you left?"

"Yeah. Aaron was packin' up. Like I said, it's a lot of work. Other than that…" He pauses a moment and thinks. "Just Hampton and Marcus. They were the last ones."

"And what were they doing?"

"Waitin' for us all to leave. Marcus had to be the last one out. He secured the location."

"Is that normal for a director to do?"

He shakes his head. "Normally, we have scouts that go out lookin' for locations. Marcus says he found this one while out for a drive one day."

"What happened after that?"

"Nothin'. Just what I said. I mean, Hampton was pissed at Marcus. That was normal."

"What do you mean?"

"Eh, there was always somethin'. Don't get me wrong. They adore each other. But they ain't good workin' together. Marcus was a hardass on set and even harder on Hampton. Don't like to play favorites."

"So, I've heard. Is there anything else you can tell me about that night? Did Marcus have any arguments with anyone else?"

He shakes his head. "Naw. Wait. Now that I think about it, yeah. He and Rich got into it. I thought it was gonna come to blows."

"What happened?"

"Rich was bein' a dick is what happened."

"How so?"

"The dumbass called Hampton a flaimin' fag is what happened." His tone softens when he speaks next. "Look, Detective, I ain't gay. I ain't never thought about bein' gay. But, shit, we're all people. Don't make a damn difference to me if ye gay, straight, black, white, man or woman. Just don't be a dick, and we'll get along fine."

There was a lot about the man that Freddy disagrees with. He is a foul-mouthed, sex-crazed drunk. But this, they both could agree on.

He does find this a little hard to believe. His understanding is that Richard Olstroski had no issues staying at the Peterson-Hamm house.

"My understanding is Richard Olstroski had no issues with Marcus Peterson or Hampton Hamm. Mr. Hamm and Mr. Olstroski both informed me that Mr. Olstroski was happy to stay with them. Mr. Olstroski was a lot of things, but he was not homophobic."

The man shakes his head. "No. He ain't homophobic. Look, he hung with Mitch and me. He was happy to have a free place to stay, but he was getting frustrated. Rich hated their rules. Hampton made a comment about a mess Rich didn't clean. Apparently, Rich made a mess in the kitchen. That was the last straw. He went off on Hampton. Called him all sorts of names. That's one of the reasons Rich didn't go back that night."

Freddy nods. "Anything else?"

"Other than that, nothin' else happened."

"I see. Well, I have spoken with your entire group except for Mitch Blakely."

"Mitch? Ya won't get much more outta Mitch."

"Why is that?"

"He was with me the whole time."

"The entire day?"

The man nods. "See, me and Mitch are a team. We are camera operators."

"And you work together?"

He nods again. "So, Mitch won't be able to tell ye more than I can."

"I would prefer to ask him myself."

"Whatever floats ya boat, I guess."

"Well, thank you for your time, Mr. Cooper."

"What about the others?"

"What others?"

"Rich, Aaron, Adam, and Miguel? You speak with them then?"

"I have spoken with them all."

This isn't a total lie. He had spoken with Miguel Alvarez, be it briefly, to nail down a time and place to talk about the case. Mr. Cooper doesn't need to know that.

"Well, thank you for your time. I can see myself out."

"No shit. The door's right in front of you."

"It's been a pleasure."

Freddy leaves and starts down the long catwalk of a hallway. His phone rings as he approaches the stairs. He glances at the display. It is Shawn.

"What's up?" Freddy answers.

"Hey. Where are you?"

"Just leaving the home of one of the crew members. About to head to one more. What's up?"

"We found a cell phone."

"And?"

"It belongs to Juliana Martinez."

"So, she left her phone. That's odd, but not unusual."

"The last call is from Marcus Peterson at 6:45 on the morning of his death."

Freddy pauses at the bottom of the stairs. "Son of a bitch."

"I thought that would get your attention. What do you want us to do?"

"Nothing. At least not yet. Alight, this changes things. I'll still meet with Miguel Alvarez tonight. See what he has to say. Shawn, this may be the break we need. I would kiss you if I could."

"Nah, you aren't my type. If I were gay, I'd be more into guys with muscles. You're too skinny."

"You have no sense," he says with a smile.

"So, what's the plan?"

"Nothing changes, save one. I think I can skip talking to the last person on Wexler's List. I'm going to meet with Alvarez tonight as planned. We will watch the tapes…."

"Video."

He continues as if he didn't hear Shawn. ``...from that film set where Olstroski's body was found. Perhaps that, plus this new evidence, will be enough for us to catch this son of a bitch."

"Alright. Well, I'm going to see what prints I can lift from this phone."

"Why?"

"To see what I can find. Perhaps that will..."

"I mean, what's the point? We know that phone belongs to Juliana Martinez. We know that she was, or is, depending on the living state of her body, dating Miguel Alvarez. We also know that Richard Olstroski's killer was wearing gloves. The person who broke into the Farmhouse was also wearing gloves. No prints, save Mr. Hamm's, were found at the Peterson crime scene. I am willing to bet you will either find Ms. Martinez's prints, Mr. Alvarez's, a combination of both, or none."

"None?"

"If she were murdered, then her killer might have wiped the prints."

"I see."

"What I want to know is where is Marcus Peterson's phone and who has possession of it."

"Want us on it?"

"No. You guys have done enough. I'll take it from here."

He ends the call and continues to his car. Once he is in his car, he takes out the list of names that Jacob Wexler gave him. He sits there transfixed on the name of Miguel Alvarez.

"What are you hiding? Do you know the secret to solving this case? I'll find out tonight."

He starts the engine and pulls out of the parking lot. The car turned onto South Colorado Avenue in the direction of the lake.

"I hope he doesn't expect me to play. I've never touched a golf club in my life."

Chapter Twenty-Four

Golfing with Suspects

Hampton is in the middle of brushing his teeth when he heard a phone ring from upstairs. That is one thing he doesn't think he would get uses to. The thin floor made it easy to hear everything upstairs in the restaurant. He can't believe how busy that small place gets during lunch. Afternoon naps were impossible. He doesn't understand how Otto could stand it.

Now that is a man he thought he'd never get used to being around. He wanted to kill the man that first night. Hampton doesn't want the man in bed with him any more than Otto wanted to be there. He awoke in the middle of the night to find Otto cuddled up to him like a baby to a blanket. It startled him so bad that he let out a scream. This causes Otto to jump what seemed like ten feet. Both men found themselves standing on either side of the bed, Otto apologizing and Hampton furious.

That's when Hampton decided to sleep on a blanket on the floor. Otto could have the bed for all he cared. Hampton just wanted rest. For the rest of that first night, he slept on the floor and gave the bed to Otto.

What happened next astonished him beyond belief. It seemed entirely out of character for Otto, or at least what he knows of the man. The next day, Otto brought in a cot and moved it into the office area. He rearranged his office to make room for it. He turned the bedroom over to Hampton, and he slept on the cot the next night.

This one simple act changed Hampton's entire perspective of the man. Yes, Otto is still Otto. Yes, the man still got on his last nerve at times. The man did have a big heart. He is starting to understand the friendship Otto and Freddy shared.

"Yes. He's here," he heard Mario speaking above. "Let me give you his number."

It is apparent to Hampton that the person on the other line knows Otto lived here but did not know his number. Whatever this is about involved Otto and not Hampton. He finished brushing his teeth and steps into the shower.

***

"Thanks, Mario," Freddy says. "I'll give Otto a call now."

He ended the call and called the number Mario had given him. He heard it ring three or four times, then the click over.

"Great. Doesn't recognize the number, so he is letting it go to voicemail."

A couple of more rings, and then he heard Otto's message.

"It's Otto. You know the drill."

A small beep after that.

"Hey, Otto, it's Freddy. Call me back. I need to ask Mr. Hamm a few questions. And save this damn number. I don't want you to send me to voicemail again."

He ended the call and looked at the time. It is 8:10 PM. It had been storming all day. Overcast and nothing but heavy rain. He still had some time before he had to meet with Mr. Alvarez. There is a convenience store nearby. He could use some coffee.

The parking lot of the store is empty. There were only two people pumping gas. He parked in front of the door. The sign above the store read "Echolson's." This is one of the last locally owned convenience stores in town. All of the rest were part of national chains. Sunny Echolston has owned and operated this place for over 30 years.

He reached for his umbrella and prepared himself for the heavy downpour. He exited the car and approached the front door. Sunny is behind the register waiting on a customer when Freddy entered.

"Have a wonderful night, ma'am," he says with a smile.

The woman returned the smile. Freddy holds the door open for her as she left.

"Thank you, sir."

"You're welcome. Have a good night."

He approached the counter.

"Good evening," he says.

"Good evening to you, sir," Echolston replied.

He scanned the store, looking for the coffee.

"Can I help you?"

Freddy smiles. "I'm actually looking for coffee. Do you have a fresh pot?"

"It's after eight o'clock at night. I've already washed up the coffee pots."

"I understand. It's a pain to clean that stuff thoroughly."

"Then you'll understand that I don't want to make another pot tonight."

Freddy nods and turned to leave. He stops mid-stride.

"I normally don't drink it, but do you sell the cold, prepackaged bottles of coffee?"

"In the back of the store, to the right," he says as he pointed.

"Thanks."

Freddy walks down one of the aisles toward the back of the store. Against the back, right corner is a refrigerator cooler. He found a large bottle of cold coffee on one of the shelves.

He turned to walk back to the counter. The door opens and a white man of average height enters the store. He is wearing jeans and a t-shirt.

"Good evening, sir," Sunny says.

He watched the man carefully. It appeared as if the man were casing out the front of the store. It is apparent the man did not see him.

"How can I help you?" Sunny asks the man.

The man pulled out a gun and pointed it at Sunny.

"Give me what you got in the register."

Freddy snapped to attention. His instincts kicked in. He starts to sneak toward the front of the store.

"Open the register. Put the money on the counter."

He starts down the candy aisle. This is perfect. It is directly behind the robber. Freddy will be able to sneak up on the robber as long as he doesn't turn around. He slowly creeps down the aisle. He is almost there. Right on top of the man. Just a few more steps, and he would have the jump on the man. He drew his gun slowly. When he did, the gun accidentally clanged on the glass bottle of coffee.

Shit. I never put that back? He thinks.

"What the hell?" the man says as he turned around.

He pointed his gun at Freddy.

"Drop it."

Freddy froze, gun drawn.

"Are you deaf or just stupid? Don't be a hero. Drop it. Now!"

Freddy dropped his gun. It is apparent this is the first time this man had robbed anyone. Sweat is on his forehead. The gun is slightly shaking in his hand.

"Don't move! Hands up!" the man says.

Freddy slowly raised his hands above his head. "Can I at least put the coffee down?"

"Shut up!"

He turned his attention back to Sunny. Freddy followed the man's gaze. Sunny had started to reach for a gun behind the counter. The man fired a warning shot in the air. Sunny jumped and backed away.

"Don't be a hero, dumbass! All I want is your money."

"Do what he asks," Freddy says.

"I said shut the hell up!" The man starts breathing hard.

"You don't want to shoot anybody. I can tell. My name's Freddy. What's yours?"

"Shut the hell up! You don't know what you are talking about!"

"I may know more than you think."

"Mr," Sunny says, "just be quiet. I don't want to die."

"Yeah, and you don't know a damn thing about me!"

"I know your type."

"My what?"

Freddy allowed his face to form that smile he is known for. "I'm a detective." The man looked frightened at that. He reassured the man by saying, "Don't worry. I'm off duty. All I want to do is talk. Can we talk?"

The man nods.

"Good. My name is Freddy. As I said, I'm a detective. What's your name?"

"Scott. My name's Scott."

"Is there anyone in your life you care about, Scott? A girlfriend? A child?"

"Yeah. I got a little boy." He starts to choke up as he says the words. "Peter. His name's Peter."

"Ask yourself, what would Peter think if he were here now? If he were watching this? What would happen to him if this went bad?"

Scott stood there in silence for a moment. Freddy takes this chance to lower his hands. He could read that the man is thinking about what he had says.

"I lost my job today. Layoff. They said they had to close the entire plant. Not enough revenue, my ass. Those fat cats sit up in their ivory towers while us grunts do all the work for what? Minimum wage? Then to close without notice? It ain't right. I'm a single dad tryin' to raise my kid the best I can. What am I supposed to do now?"

"I wish I had an answer for you. This isn't the way, though. It's easy to be confident when times are easy. It's when life gets hard that we see what we are made of. That's when you need to be strong. That's when you need to be the example your son needs to see."

He could see he had broken through to the man. Scott understood and nods.

"Now, why don't you put the gun down and quietly walk out? You don't want to do this, and I don't want the paperwork. Call it a second chance."

Scott looked at Sunny and back at Freddy. He quietly backed toward the door, lowering his gun. The man put his gun back in his pocket.

Freddy shakes his head. "That, you leave with me."

Scott nods. He handed the gun to Freddy.

"Take care of your son. Here." He wrote down the address of a local food kitchen and temp agency and handed the man the paper.

"What's this?"

"In case you need it. It's a food kitchen and a temp agency nearby. Take care of your son. Do your best to give him a good life."

Scott takes the paper and nods. He opens the door and walks out.

Sunny let out a sigh of relief. "I don't know what would have happened if you hadn't been here."

"I'm just doing my job. Most people like that are good people. They're just hurting or struggling. They want to do the right thing for their families. Sometimes people feel they have no other choice. We never know what someone's situation is."

Freddy turned to leave and stops.

"Oh, I almost forgot," he says.

He places the glass bottle of coffee on the counter. The man shakes his head.

"Call it a 'thank you' detective."

"Thank you," Freddy says with a smile.

He starts to walk out the door and stops himself. He turned toward the man one last time.

"Next time, don't try to be a hero. You could end up dead."

The man nods. "Thank you again, sir."

"Have a good evening."

He left the store and got back in his car. He noticed a missed call and a voicemail on his phone.

"Freddy, it's Otto. Call me."

***

"Hey Freddy," he heard Otto answer.

Freddy? Why would Freddy be calling this late? Is there a break in his case?

Hampton is relaxing in one of the chairs in the living room. He is leaning back with his eyes closed. Otto is in his office doing whatever he did on his computer.

His eyes were closed. He could hear Otto approaching.

"Hey," Otto says. He felt the man nudge his shoulder.

He opens his eyes. The man is holding his phone directly in front of Hampton's face.

"Freddy wants to talk to you."

"Me?"

"Yeah. Some sort of questions about the case."

Hampton nods and takes the phone. Otto walks back to his computer.

"Hello," he says.

"I have a few questions for you. Do you have a moment, Mr. Hamm?"

"Yes, Detective. How can I help?"

"You didn't happen to take your husband's phone, did you?"

"Marcus's phone?" He shakes his head. "No."

He is confused. Why would they ask him about Marcus's phone? They are the ones who removed all of the evidence. Don't they have it? He assumed as much. He never found it after cleaning up the house.

"Interesting."

"Why do you ask?"

"We found a phone."

"Marcus's phone?"

No, dummy, he thinks. Why would they ask you if they already have it?

"Of course not," Hampton says. "That's a stupid question."

"No worries," Freddy replied with a slight smile. "You've been through a lot."

"I just assumed your officers took it. I never found it in the house."

"Interesting."

That frustrated him. His husband is murdered. He is hidden away. Why won't they tell him what's going on?

"You keep saying that. Look, what's going on? What have you found?"

"I'm sorry, Mr. Hamm. I cannot tell you."

"It's my husband! He was murdered! I watched him die!"

"Mr. Hamm…"

"Don't you dare say you understand."

"Mr. Hamm, I want to tell you. You deserve to know what's going on. Please understand that I can't."

"I don't care about the law. Please, detective."

"It's not about the law." He heard the change in Freddy's voice. It had become lower and softer. "It's about the integrity of the case. We are close to solving this. I have to keep what I know quiet. Richard Olstroski has been murdered. The Farmhouse was broken into. Norman was attacked. You were almost kidnapped. This person, whoever they are, is panicking and cleaning up. I risk jeopardizing the case if I say any more. Ask yourself, Mr. Hamm, what would your husband want?"

Hampton knows the answer to that. Marcus would burst through the gates of Hell to make sure this person is caught, had he been the one who was murdered. But, he would work with the police. Do what they ask.

He sighs and nods. "He would trust you and let you work."

"Then let me work. I will keep you updated."

"Okay."

"I have a few more questions for you, Mr. Hamm."

"Okay. I'll answer what I can."

"How well do you know Juliana Martinez?"

"Juliana?" He shakes his head. "No. I can assure you she had nothing to do with this. I am positive."

"Mr. Hamm, the only thing you can say for sure is that you know whether or not YOU murdered your husband. Anyone else, myself included, you cannot say you know for a fact. I ask you again, how well do you know her?"

How well does he know her? Pretty well, actually. They first met on the set of *Cube*. The two of them went out to grab lunch together and became instant friends. Both of them are open books to each other. He knows everything about her. Neither of them holds any secrets from the other.

"We have no secrets."

"Mr. Hamm, everyone has secrets."

He shakes his head. "You don't understand. Juliana and I are that close. Outside of anything personal between Marcus and myself, we tell each other everything."

"I doubt that very much, Mr. Hamm. Everyone has secrets they do not share."

"I never discussed my personal life with Marcus. Outside of that…"

"Mr. Hamm, you may not want to believe it, but there are things people are too embarrassed to share. I'm sure that if you think about it, there are some things you do in private that you don't want anyone, including your late husband, to know about."

He thinks for a moment and shakes his head. There is absolutely nothing that Marcus did not know about him. Juliana, perhaps, but not Marcus. They had no secrets. He decided to let it go and pretend he agreed with the detective.

"I see what you are saying. I guess none of us are truly an open book."

"No, we are not. So, it is obvious you knows her extremely well. How often do you get together?"

"That's easy. Every time she's in town."

"How often is that?"

"Once a month, maybe."

"Has she ever given you any gifts?"

He nods. "All the time. She's always sending us something. She's a huge star. World-famous."

"I'm familiar with her work."

"So, she's always traveling to different countries. Either for publicity or due to filming locations or even just for a vacation."

"What types of things would she send you?"

"I dunno. The usual. Postcards. Candies. Different teas. Wines…"

"Wine? She would send you wine?"

He shakes his head. "Not me. Marcus is the wine connoisseur. She would send him wine."

"How often?"

"I dunno. Whenever she is in a different location."

"Think. This actually could be important. How often and how much?"

"Once a month, maybe. It is a lot too. It is almost as if he were a member of a wine of the month club or something."

"Interesting. One more question for you."

"Detective, I don't know where this is going, but Juliana can't have."

"Mr. Hamm, I am just asking questions. My job is to investigate everything, regardless of how small the possibility. Understand?"

He nods. "Yes."

"Okay, so one more question. I don't want you to answer right away. I want you to think hard. I'm going to list out a few symptoms. Did your husband have any of the following?"

"Symptoms? He isn't sick?"

"Mr. Hamm, just listen."

Hampton listened as Freddy listed out different types of medical symptoms. He doesn't know what would cause this, but he doesn't want to catch whatever it is.

"Diarrhea. Thickening of skin. Discoloration of skin. Small corns or warts on his palms or soles of his feet. Nausea. Abnormal heart rhythm. Numbness in his hands or feet. Partial paralysis. Blindness. Drowsiness. Seizures."

"What the? Drowsiness? Nausea? Yeah, he is drowsy. Marcus worked hard. When he isn't working on a film project, he is always doing something at the house. And yeah, he would get nauseous. Who doesn't sometimes?"

"Mr. Hamm, think for me. Please."

"Well, he had started to get calluses on his feet. There is one right under the little toe on both feet. Also, another on the side of both big toes. Marcus always, he would kill me if he knew I was about to say this, had a hard time going to the bathroom. Please forgive me for this, sweetie. There were times he would get so impacted that it felt as if he were being ripped open when he would go. Except for the past few months. He's been going regularly, and it's been loose. I wouldn't say diarrhea per se, but it's been a lot looser than it ever has been for him. He has been a lot more drowsy than normal. Sure, he's tired. But he's starting to fall asleep at the oddest of times. He has been feeling tired and sluggish. He has been getting sick to his stomach lately. A little nausea and lightheadedness."

"Anything else?"

He shakes his head. "That's it. He hasn't had any of the other things you stated."

"And none of those are normal for him?"

"No. In fact, that all starts a few months ago."

"How long exactly?"

"I dunno. Maybe five or six."

"Thank you, Mr. Hamm."

"Anytime I can help Detective. Goodbye."

"Mr. Hamm…"

"Yes."

"You're safe with Otto. This case will be over soon. Take care."

Hampton nods. The call ended. He laid Otto's phone on the table next to the chair. He sits back, closed his eyes, and starts to cry.

***

Freddy arrived at the golf club around 9:15 PM. It is about 9:30 PM before he found the driving range. The lights were so bright that the green of the driving range is lit like a football stadium. He glanced at the photo of Alvarez and compared it to the men on the driving range. There he is.

He walks up behind Alvarez as the man takes a swing. The ball went long into the distance.

"Nice shot," Freddy says.

Alvarez turned around. "Thank you. Detective Falcon?"

Freddy nods.

"Would you care for a cup of coffee?"

"A man after my own heart," Freddy says with a smile. "Always."

He motioned, and a well-dressed man in a waiter uniform steps over.

"Two coffees. One with cream and light sugar."

He looked over at Freddy.

"Just black."

The waiter nods and walks off.

"A waiter at a golf club?" Freddy asks.

"This is a high-end establishment. Think of it more as a resort."

"I see. There's a first time for everything, I guess."

"Do you play?" Alvarez asks.

"Only Mario Golf," he says with a smile.

"Mario Golf?" The man looked puzzled.

"It's a video game."

Alvarez smiles and continued. "It's an interesting sport. It requires strength, precision, and a cool head. Would you be interested in hitting a few balls with me? It's not a video game, but you will get the hang of it."

The man returned with the coffee. Both men take their cups and thanked the waiter. Freddy reached for his wallet to tip. Alvarez shakes his head.

"Not required."

"But," Freddy starts to say.

The waiter spoke, "Sir, my service does not require tipping. It is all part of the annual fees the members pay."

"Gratuities are built into the fees," Alvarez says.

Freddy put his wallet away and nods. The waiter left the two men alone.

"Would you care to hit a few, Detective?"

"Okay," Freddy replied.

Alvarez motioned toward the golf clubs. "Grab a club."

Freddy walks over, sits his coffee cup down, and grabbed a club. Freddy grabbed a ball and set it on the tee.

"The most important thing is to grip the club correctly," Alvarez says. Freddy watched how the man gripped his club. He watched and mimicked the way the man interlocked his fingers around the club. "When you feel ready, you swing."

He knows to keep his arm straight and not bend his elbow. He also knows not to take his eye off of the ball. His arm relaxed as he swung the golf club back and, in a rapid motion, directly toward the ball. The ball flew out onto the green.

"Impressive. You seem to have a knack for it."

"Just be the ball," he says with a smile.

Alvarez did not react.

The men swapped places. He takes a moment to take a sip of coffee. Resting his club on the ground, he places both hands over the top of the club. Alvarez swung.

"I'm assuming you didn't invite me here just to play golf, Mr. Alvarez."

The men swapped places.

"No. You're investigating Marcus's murder. You've been asking a lot of questions."

"That's right. I'm investigating a murder, Mr. Alvarez. I want to find out what everyone knows."

Freddy swung. The men swapped places.

"I'm an open book. Ask away."

Freddy sipped his coffee. Alvarez swung.

"Where were you that night?"

The men swapped places. Freddy places another ball and swung.

"I was with Juliana all night. I think you already know that, though."

The men swapped places. Freddy sipped his coffee. Alvarez swung.

"Did she lose her phone?"

"Her phone?"

Freddy nods. The men swapped again.

"We found a phone that belongs to Juliana Martinez."

Freddy swung. The men swapped.

The man nods. "Yes, Detective. She lost it after we left the set."

Freddy sipped his coffee. Alvarez swung.

"You didn't go back to retrieve it?"

The men swapped places.

"We did. By the time we realized it, we were almost home. When we returned, the place was locked up, and everyone had left."

Freddy places another ball and swung.

"You let her fly off to Germany without a cell phone?"

The men swapped places. Freddy sipped his coffee. Alvarez swung.

"Of course not. I gave her mine."

"And what are you using?"

The men swapped places again. Freddy places another ball and swung.

"I bought a burner phone."

The men swapped places. Freddy sipped his coffee. Alvarez swung.

"A burner phone? You mean prepaid?"

The man nods. The men swapped. Freddy swung again.

"You're asking a lot of questions about Juliana. She's in Germany and has nothing to do with this."

The men swapped places.

"Then there's nothing to fear from my investigation."

Freddy takes another sip of coffee. Alvarez swung again.

"You have no business investigating Juliana. She had nothing to do with it. I don't know why your officers keep showing up at her home."

The men swapped placcs. Freddy places another ball.

"With all due respect, it's up to me to decide who I want to investigate."

He swung.

"I'm an influential man in this town, Detective. I pay a lot to get what I want."

Freddy walks over and glared at the man. "Are you trying to bribe me?"

"Let's just say I'm trying to lead you on the correct path. How much do you want to stop investigating her?"

"I think you misunderstood me," Freddy says as he places the golf club back with the others. "I don't play that game."

"Don't investigate Juliana, Detective. You'll regret it if you do."

"Is that a threat to a police officer?"

"Not at all. She's a dead-end in your case. You will have waisted your time."

Freddy drank down the rest of his coffee and threw the cup away.

"Well, it's my time to waist. I am curious, though. How did you find out that Marcus Peterson was murdered?"

"Excuse me?"

"Several people informed me that you called them to tell them Marcus Peterson had been murdered. How did you know?"

"Adam called me."

"Adam Greenbriar?" Freddy says this with raised eyebrows.

Alvarez nods. "He said that Marcus had been found dead, and the filming had been postponed."

"That's interesting. He told me that you called him."

"I promise you, Detective, I did not."

"Well, someone is lying. Have a goodnight, Mr. Alvarez."

He turned and walks back to his car.

This has been an interesting evening, he thinks as he got in his car. He is glad the rain had slacked up enough he doesn't need his umbrella.

"Well, Mr. Alvarez, I wasn't investigating you or her. Not until our little chat," he says to no one. "Now, you have given me ample incentive to investigate you both."

He looked at the time. It is after ten. Too late to call Shawn. He knows that's all he would get for today. Tomorrow they watched the footage from the cameras. He is sure, after tomorrow, they would know precisely who they were after. Now, he is heading home for some much-needed rest.

Chapter Twenty-Five

What's in the Box?

"You've known Detective Falcon since childhood?"

"What?" Otto replied with a mouthful of potato chips.

"Detective Falcon. He says you two grew up together."

"Yeah. Now quiet. I'm watching TV."

His last conversation with the detective still bothers him. Why would the detective ask about Juliana? Why is he asking all of those questions about medical issues? Why is he so curious if Juliana had sent us wine? These questions keep confusing him. He has no idea how this relates to Marcus's murder. He concedes the fact that he may not know as much about Juliana as he thought before today. But he just knows that Juliana could not have done this. Besides the fact that she loves him and Marcus to death. She's in Germany making a movie.

He needs to understand how this man thinks. The only way to do this is to talk to the only person who knows him best. Unfortunately, that person is Otto.

The show ends. Otto mutes the television. He lays the remote on his belly, as if it were a shelf, and looks over at Hampton.

"Alright. What?"

"What?"

"What?"

Hampton isn't sure what the man is asking.

"You were chatty when my show was on. Now that it's off, you won't say a damn word. Now, what the hell did you want to talk about?"

The man put a cigar in his mouth, lit it, and leaned back in his chair.

"I'm all ears," he says as he spreads his arms out. "Talk."

"Well, how well do you know the detective?"

"Freddy? Hell, better than he knows himself."

Somehow, he doubts that. He decides to let it go.

"You guys grew up together?"

He nods. "Yeah." He lets out a sigh. "Look. Freddy ain't the same person he was growin' up. Hell, he ain't the same person he was before Harry's death."

"Harry? Your brother."

"My adopted brother. Freddy and Harry were in a relationship. They were pretty serious too."

"What happened?"

"Look. Let's just say that one event changed Freddy for the better. After that, he cleaned up his act. He joined the academy. Became a cop. Turned into the person you know today."

"What about you?"

"What? What about me?"

"Did it change you?"

"Freddy and I have the same goal. We just have different ways to go about it. Freddy became a cop and takes the legal route. I, on the other hand, decided to take other avenues to solve the mystery of my brother's death."

"Other avenues? Petty crime. Kidnapping. Harassing. Entrapment. Torture."

"Hey! Nobody's perfect. What about you? How'd you meet your dead husband?"

Hampton rolls his eyes. He wants to say something. Wants to let the man know how insensitive that is. He reframed. The man is legitimately asking. And he did care, in his own weird way.

"Marcus and I met in high school But it was not love at first sight."

"Nothing ever is."

He recants the entire story of how he and Marcus met, all of the times he was a jerk to Marcus, how they met again in college, and how they finally ended up together. He talks about how Marcus had always loved him, even when he was too stupid to realize he loved Marcus back. Hampton even explained the one time he almost lost Marcus. That one stupid mistake he almost didn't come back from. If it hadn't been for Juliana, then he wouldn't have. There is no way she could have murdered Marcus. She can't even be behind it. She loved them too much. He talked about all the drama they used to have on set. Then, he told the story behind the film that ruined Jacob's career and marriage.

"Okay. Sounds like this Jacob Wexler guy did it."

"Jacob. Never. I'd believe me before Jacob."

"Why?"

"What do you mean?" He is puzzled.

"Why do you place that jerk above yourself?"

"What?"

"Look. I ain't as smart as Freddy likes to make people think he is. Hell, I ain't even as smart as Freddy actually is. But this ain't my first rodeo either. Your buddy Jacob ain't completely honest with you."

"What do you mean?"

"I ain't saying he killed your husband. What I'm saying is, he still holds a grudge."

"How could you know that?"

"Because I'm human, and I have a brain."

Hampton is insulted. Is this man calling him an idiot? Otto must have picked up on his body language based on what he says next.

"I ain't saying your stupid. I'm not even calling you a dumb-ass. What I'm saying is, sometimes it takes an outsider to make sense of things. To see things you can't see because you are too close. This guy, Jacob, is still holding a grudge. From the way you explained it, I don't believe you destroyed his life. Most likely, he did it to himself. But he blames you. He blames you and your dead husband for ruining his career and his marriage. It took him years to build back up what he believes you destroyed in seconds. People don't just forget that."

He understands what the man is saying. Jacob did agree to the role far too quickly. Perhaps he had other plans. Maybe this is the opening he needs.

"Then there's your buddy, what's his name? The home wrecker."

"Adam."

He nods. "That's right. Adam. What's his deal?"

"What do you mean?"

"Well, from the way you explained it, he betrayed his best friend. He did the lowest of lows. How the hell can you call somebody a friend and turn around and sleep with his husband?"

"We weren't married then."

"That's not my point. I ain't perfect, but it takes a special kind of dick to do what he did."

"I was just as much at fault."

"Were you?"

"Yes. Absolutely. He didn't rape me."

"You gave into weakness. Yes, what you did was wrong. You betrayed him as well. But you guys worked through it. You still loved each other enough to work past it."

"Marcus never forgot."

"No shit. And neither did you. How the hell could you forget something like that. I'm sure a small part of him always wondered if you would do that again."

Hampton shakes his head. "I would never…"

"I'm sure you wouldn't. Remember, what you did was a betrayal of trust. You guys built a bridge over that rift, but the rift is still there."

He nods. He understands what the man is saying.

Otto continues, "Your buddy Adam never repented, did he? Never asked for forgiveness?"

"No, but Marcus forgave him."

"How the hell can anyone forgive someone that doesn't show remorse? Your dead husband may have been able to move past it. Hell, he may even be able to let it go. But there is no way anyone can forgive someone who isn't truly sorry for what they did. If there is no remorse, then there never is a lesson learned. No real change in behavior. Has his behavior changed? Is he still up to the same tricks?"

Hampton opens his mouth and closes it. He thinks for a moment. The man is right. He is a bit crass about it, but he is right. Adam still slept around. Adam still slept with all types of men: single, married, gay, straight. He doesn't care who it is.

"Yeah. Same tricks. He still sleeps with married men."

"See? No remorse. No guilt. In his mind, he did nothing wrong. You and your husband closed the book in his mind. You are the guilty ones. Not him."

Again, the man is right. Adam agreed a bit too fast, as well. That had causes an intense argument between him and Marcus. Marcus is too trusting. Adam still had a grudge.

"You see my point? There are at least three people who had motive to murder your husband. Freddy is only doing his job."

"I see."

He sits there in silence for what feels like an eternity. He is letting it all sink in. He is thinking about everything that had happened after his world changed. He is thinking about Marcus. He is thinking about his history with certain people on the movie set.

"I didn't mean to upset ya," Otto says. "You want to know about Freddy? That guy has his issues."

"Issues? What do you mean?" The man had his curiosity up now.

Otto let out a chuckle. "Don't get me wrong. He's a good guy. One of the best. But don't get him on one of his pop culture soapboxes."

"He's into pop culture?"

"Oh yeah," the man says as he lights another cigar. "You'd never know it, but Freddy's a geek."

"Oh really?"

Otto nods. "He's probably seen all of your stuff." He points the end of his cigar at Hampton as he says that.

"My stuff? The movies I've been in? He's a fan?"

He shakes his head. "Nah. Like I said, he's into pop culture. Movies, TV, books, comics, that sort of thing."

"Detective Falcon? He's into comic books?" he says with raised eyebrows.

Otto nods. "Just the other day, he and I had an argument over that cartoon Spider-Man movie everyone loved. Well, everyone except Freddy."

"That is a good movie."

"I know, right. Don't say that to Freddy, though. He has this long speech on why it would have been better without the multiple universe stuff."

"I see."

"And computers."

"What about them?"

"He and technology don't get along."

That explains why the man doesn't have a computer in his office, Hampton thinks. He remembers his first time in the detective's office.

"How did you two meet anyway? I know you grew up together...."

"That's it. See, Freddy was raised by his grandparents. His mom died when he was a kid."

"That's sad," he says with a frown.

"Yeah. Poor guy had it hard. His grandparents got custody of him and raised him as their son."

"What about his dad?"

"Dunno. Freddy never talks about him. I don't think Freddy really knows. See, his dad went to prison before he was born."

Hampton hangs his head. "And I treated Marcus like crap because of where he came from. At least he had a family."

"See. Goes to show. Ya never know people's situation. Never know where they come from."

He nods.

"So, yeah. We lived a few miles away from his grandparents, out in the country. His grandparents wanted him to have friends. They introduced us, and we instantly clicked. We were more like brothers."

"That's gross."

"What's gross?"

"He dated your brother."

The man laughed. "Me and Freddy were like brothers. See, Harry is a foster kid. We were teenagers when my parents decided to foster Harry. His parents died in a house fire. He'd been bounced around from place to place. My parents decided to foster him. They ended up adopting him."

"That's cool. So, all of you are the same age?"

"Me and Freddy are. Harry is...was two years younger."

"I get it. I still talk about Marcus in the present tense."

He nods. "See, we were all mischievous teens."

"Weren't we all?"

"Yeah, but that bled into adulthood. We turned into petty criminals. Small-time crooks. It lead to drugs and more dangerous situations. That's what happened to Harry. We think it was a drug deal gone bad."

"Gone bad?"

"Freddy found his head in a box."

Hampton squirms.

"Exactly." The man puts out his cigar and sits back in his chair. "See, all I know is Harry made me promise not to tell Freddy where he was going. Made me swear. That never works with Freddy. See, that interesting trait he has. That one that allows him to read people so well. That isn't learned."

"Oh?"

He nods. "Freddy has always had this ability to not just read people but to persuade them to tell him things. But in a way where they think it's their idea to open up."

He starts to think about those first couple of days after Marcus's death. All of that information he gave to Freddy. He gave it so freely. The man didn't ask. He just says that he's listening. He starts to smile.

"What?" Otto asks.

"He did it to me. I thought I was opening up to him. He's good."

"See? And that's what happened. He got me to spill the beans on the entire situation. He ran off. Freddy knew this guy Harry was meeting, and he was scared. Legitimately scared."

Hampton raises his eyebrows. "The detective doesn't appear to be the type that scares easily."

"Exactly. Nothing scares Freddy. Nothing. Except this particular person. I don't even remember his name now. I just remember Freddy coming back changed. He never talks much about it. Not even now. All I know is Freddy found a box with Harry's head in it. He buried the box somewhere. I dunno where. Freddy won't say."

"That's sad."

"Yup. So, he decided to join the police academy. I started my own quest. Freddy knows more than I do, but I can't get anything out of him. Freddy's promised to help me once he's found your husband's killer. I want more than anything to solve Harry's murder."

"And your brother's spirit can rest."

"What? What spirit? You watch too much TV."

He sets the remote on the table, stands up, and starts for the kitchen.

"You want something to drink?"

Hampton shakes his head. Otto enters the kitchen. Hampton watches the man grab a glass and the juice from the refrigerator.

"You drink a lot of juice."

"I have to. Can't have caffeine. Don't drink alcohol."

"You can't have caffeine?"

"Shhhh."

"I didn't mean any…"

"I said, can it! Listen."

Hampton listens. That's when he hears the sound. Someone is moving around upstairs.

"I thought Mario closed up already," Hampton says.

"He did." The man looks at Hampton. "Freddy is sure nobody knows you're here?"

Hampton shakes his head. He could feel his heart rate increase. He starts breathing rapidly. Panic is setting in. "No. nobody. He didn't even tell the other officers. Not even his captain."

"Well, somebody's up there."

Otto grabs his gun and starts for the stairs. He glances back at Hampton. "Stay there."

He didn't have to worry about that. Hampton has no intention of going anywhere. He watched Otto disappear up the stairs. A few moments later, he heard voices.

"What the hell are you doin'? You trying to rob Mario? What the…?"

He hears what sounds like a struggle, then a gunshot. He hears a tumble down the stairs. That's when he sees Otto. The man reaches the bottom and smashed his head on the bottom step.

Hampton ignores his fear and runs over to the man. He checks to ensure the man is still breathing. That's when he notices it. He sees the one thing that triggers a memory. Otto is holding his side. His hand is red from the blood. Otto turns into Marcus at that moment. It is happening all over again. Except now it isn't Marcus. It is this stranger who took him in. It is this stranger who risked his life to protect him.

This time he knows what to do. He knows he can't move the man. He knows he needs to find something to use as a compress on the wound. He knows he needs to call 911.

Hampton stands and starts for the bedroom. He wants to grab a clean shirt for the wound. At that moment, an arm goes around his neck. It is clad in black. His air supply is being cut off. He starts to struggle. He grabs the arm to try to pry it away. It is no use. The arm is too strong.

The grip loosens a little. The person grabs his arms. He screams out in pain. He can see the stranger now. This person is dressed all in black. This person's face is covered by a black ski mask. The more he struggles, the tighter the grip. As long as he doesn't struggle, the grip is loose.

He is being dragged upstairs. Whereto? Probably his death. He has no recourse. No way to call for help. Just a dying man lying at the bottom of the stairs.

The person drags him outside and into a car. He struggles the best he can. He places his hands on either side of the open car door. He tenses every muscle in his arms. He plants his feet. There is no way they would get him in this car.

He holds fast as well. This person struggles against his strength. Hampton is surprised at how much strength he has in his chubby arms. He is determined not to let go.

He finds his opening. There is a slight moment when the person releases to gain a better grip. He uses that moment to kick. He kicked hard. He heard a groan, and the person releases their grip. He turns around to see the person holding their shin.

Hampton starts back for the restaurant. He knows he has to call the cops. Hampton isn't sure what made him do it. He isn't sure what overpowered him at that moment. Something made him stop. He had to know who is under that mask. He walks over to the person on the ground, grabs the ski mask, and pulls.

He stumbles backward. The sight of the face startles him.

"You? You did this? You killed Marcus? You brought this pain on me? You? He trusted you! How? Why?"

He feels the rage build inside of him. It is overtaking him like water in a sinking ship. He is ready to beat this person to death. He wants to make them pay for what they did. And then…

A heavy hit to the back of his head. A searing pain spreads throughout his head. He collapses to the ground. He hears voices, but he cannot make out what is being said. Everything starts to fade into darkness. That is the last thing he remembers before everything goes black.

Chapter Twenty-Six

What Richard Did

"Is that it?" the officer asks.

"Yes," he replied.

"You sure?"

He leaned his head against the headboard and let out a sigh. "Yes."

"I could get you room service. I could order you a pizza. You need me to shine your shoes too?"

"Stop with the sarcasm. That's it."

The officer powered off the phone and placed it in his pocket. "Just relax, Mr. Olstroski. Let Falcon work his magic and figure this thing out. We'll find this guy, and you will be out of here in no time."

Now, why didn't he believe that? There was something about this guy he didn't like. Something he didn't trust. He decided to brush it off. He'd never been a good judge of character.

Just then, they heard a loud noise outside. The officer jumped up and looked out the window. What the hell has him so excited? he thought to himself.

"Shit," the officer says. He turned and pointed at Richard. "Stay."

Richard smiled, "Where am I going?"

The officer raced out the door like a bat out of hell. A few moments later, he heard a car engine, a siren, and the sound of a police car flying out of the parking lot.

"So, who's protecting me?" he says to no one.

He leaned back on the bed, resting his head against the headboard. He could not figure out how he got himself into this mess. He was offered a starring role in a Marcus Peterson film. A chance to play opposite Hampton Hamm himself. Hampton wasn't an A-list actor, but he was a star. Hampton was a big name in certain circles.

We're talking about the man that made you care about a mediocre sitcom set in a call center. The man that is the center of, what is obviously, a show that is a mix of The Office and Seinfeld. On all accounts, that show should not have succeeded. But it was the brilliant casting of Hampton Hamm that made that show's short two-season run a classic.

This is also the same man who made us believe he was a war veteran who lost his legs and suffered from PTSD. This man was brilliant in anything he did. He could make you believe anything. This was the man he had been offered to play opposite. This was the man he was honored to have a co-starring role with.

He felt terrible about that argument. What an asshole he was that night. He wishes he could apologize to Marcus. He still had a chance to apologize to Hampton. Hampton is correct. He had been a guest in their home. They deserved to have been treated better. He treated it more like his home than theirs. He took their hospitality for granted.

Well, there is always time to change that. He felt confident that, once all of this was over, he'd be able to make things right with Hampton. After all of the arguments the two men had, he still respected Hampton. Yup, he had all of the time in the world.

There is no way Hampton murdered Marcus. He can't understand how the cops could think that. He would believe he was the one who murdered Marcus before Hampton. Those men adored each other. Yes, they argued. Yes, they had their differences. But they were always honest with each other. There is a trust there, a bond that could not be broken. It's a bond he would never have, nor wanted, with Maggie.

"I just want to get out of here," he says.

There is no movie. He doesn't know why he lied to the cops. He panicked and just wanted to get away. Now he is stuck. He is committed to the lie now.

Where is this cop? What is taking him so long? He could easily run. He isn't tied up. He isn't cuffed. Hell, he isn't even under arrest.

They hadn't read him his rights yet. Nothing is holding him here. It wouldn't be hard for him to run.

But where would he go? Certainly not back to LA. What about trying to make a name for himself here? Hell, Cecil is going to cut him loose anyway. He could see that one coming a mile away. Certainly not back into Maggie's arms. Hell, she could barely stand to look at his face, much less wrap her arms around him and tell him everything is going to be okay. No. No more shit roles. No more bit parts. This is the new Richard Olstroski. He is ready for the next step. He is prepared to take his future into his own hands. He knows that this is the moment his life would change forever. This is the first day of the rest of his life.

It's time to work with the cops. No more being aloof. No more pretending to be someone he isn't. Marcus is dead. Hampton may get charged for it. He can't let that happen. Richard would work with the cops and answer any questions they had. He can't let Hampton go down for something he did not do.

Perhaps this is misguided guilt for not being there that night. Perhaps this is his conscious telling him to do the right thing. Hell, maybe this is him finally growing a pair of balls. Who the hell knows? All he knows is he needs to stop fighting the cops and start working with them.

That's when the phone rang. He looked over at the phone on the table. Should he answer it? Who would be calling? Cecil? It is too early for that callback. Cecil never came into the office until after ten. Besides, Cecil wouldn't care. He'd probably want to know what the hell this crazy shit is talking about. There's no movie. There's no role. Hell, he is so close to risking being dropped, as it is.

The phone kept ringing. What is it? Six rings now? Maybe seven? What the hell. He picked up the receiver and holds it up to his ear.

"Hello?"

***

Freddy had just finished drinking a cup of espresso. He is over at the sink cleaning up. The parts of the machine were spread out on the counter waiting to be washed: the portafilter, the portafilter basket, the steam wand tip, the drain grate, and the carafe. He had also removed the steam wand to clean it. His office door is open. It almost always is. He believed in an open-door policy with his fellow officers. They knew they were welcome to his coffee or anything in his fridge.

He had spent all morning contemplating everything he knows about this case. Reviewing all of the evidence and testimonies from everyone he had spoken with. He had five possible suspects. Miguel Alvarez inadvertently made sure that himself and Juliana Martinez were added to the suspect list. Richard Olstroski was, unfortunately, cleared the moment he was found dead. Hampton Hamm hadn't been completely cleared, solely because he was the husband, and he is still the only person that can be proven to have been at the crime scene at the time of the murder. Jacob Wexler has too sketchy of a story and has a motive based on his past dealings with the victim.

And then, there is Adam Greenbriar. Well, Freddy didn't need to use much deduction to determine why this man is a suspect. His past with both the victim and the victim's husband, combined with his inability to produce a believable alibi, places him on the list. Freddy had tried to find out the name of the person Mr. Greenbriar had over that night. He never could get a name, address, or phone number. None of the neighbors, including the kids with the lemonade stand, remembered anyone going in or out of his house during that time frame. There is too much that doesn't add up with this man to count him out.

The only thing he can say for sure is that Marcus Peterson did not kill himself. Unfortunately, the only reliable witness isn't talking. Mr. Hamm has no alibi either. A jury and prosecutor would find it hard to believe he slept through a violent attack and murder of his husband.

He turns as he hears a knock on the open door frame.

"Freddy? You okay?" Shawn asks.

"Yeah, what's up?"

He realizes how this looked. He had been standing there with the water running, holding the portafilter in his hand. It appeared he had lost himself in thought again.

"I've been calling you."

He smiles. "Sorry. I got distracted."

"I see. Thinking about the case?"

He nods.

"Make sure you don't do that while driving. I'd hate to get the call that our famous detective is found dead from a car crash due to him zoning out in thoughts while driving."

He glares at the man.

"I'm just kidding with you," he says with a smile. "We're all set up and ready to go. Interview room three when you are ready."

"I'll be right there. I don't want to keep the captain waiting."

Shawn shakes his head. "Captain's not part of it. He's meeting with the mayor today. It's just you, me, and Eddy."

"Oscar."

"Nope. Just us…"

"No. Bring Oscar. He's part of this too. I want to know everything that happened from his viewpoint. Every detail in that hotel room. Everything the owner says. Right down to the color of the shoes he was wearing."

Shawn nods. He turns to leave.

"Shawn."

"Yeah?"

"We're close. I can feel it. This is it. This will give us the identity of the killer."

"I hope you're right."

"I am."

"Hey, Freddy."

"Yes?"

"Who would have ever thought that Richard Olstroski, of all people, would be the key to solving this?"

Freddy laughs and shakes his head. "If you had told me that, the first day I met the man, I would have called you a dumbass."

Shawn leaves. Freddy continues washing up the parts of his espresso machine. He is excited and curious to see what this videotape reveals.

***

Richard ran out of the office of the motel. He had left the man's phone on his desk. He waited until the app placed the driver less than a mile from him. The driver should have been right around the corner. He started pacing. Every time he heard a vehicle approach or saw headlights, he readied himself to jump in. Where is this guy? The app says he is a couple of blocks away. There's not that much traffic. Another car was in the distance. It's slowing down. Finally! The car turns in and pulled up to Richard.

Richard opened the back door to get in.

"Richard Olgangly?"

"Olstroski."

"Sorry about that. I didn't mean to butcher your name."

Richard got in and closed the door.

"That's fine. Thanks for the pickup."

"No problem."

The car drove out of the parking lot and down the road.

***

He knows he is running late. Everyone is, most likely, waiting on him. He imagines them gossiping about how he can't go anywhere without coffee. They were probably talking about the fact he is waiting for coffee to brew before he appears. They would be correct.

It had taken him longer than expected to brew the coffee. The first time he brewed hot water. He had forgotten to put coffee in the basket. The second time, he had forgotten to put water in the reservoir. He had it all correct on the third try. Coffee is in the basket. Water is in the reservoir. Unfortunately, he forgets to place the carafe on the warmer before powering on the coffee maker.

After cleaning up the mess, he tries one last time. Finally getting it correct, he brews a full 14 cup pot of coffee. Now, he is rushing from his office to the interview room. He opens the door to interview room five.

"Sorry, I'm late, guys. You are…not here..."

Why are the lights off? Where is everyone?

"Shit!"

He is in the wrong room. Shawn said it is interview room three. He closes the door and walks down to the correct room.

"I knew it," Shawn says as Freddy enters the room. He is juggling his notepad and a large cup of coffee.

"Yeah, yeah, yeah," he says.

Shawn and Eddy smile. Oscar just sits there with a blank expression.

"I understand why they're here. But why am I here, Falcon?"

"Because you're the one who lost him," Shawn says.

"Shut the hell up, Braxton. I was asking Falcon."

"Guys!" Freddy exclaims. He is in the process of setting his coffee and notebook on the table. "Can we please be civil? Look," he directs this at Shawn, "who gives a damn how he got away? None of that matters. What matters is how he died and who killed him."

"But if it isn't for him," Shawn says as he motions to Oscar, "this guy would still be alive."

"Would he?" Freddy asks.

"Of course he would. He'd never have been at that place."

"Are you sure?"

"Of course I…" He stops talking. Perhaps he is catching on to what Freddy is alluding to.

Freddy focuses on Oscar. “And you. Stop being a dick. Stop blaming yourself for this man’s death.”

“But…,” the man starts to reply.

Freddy glares at him. The man closes his mouth.

“Okay, before we get started, I want you guys to know how I see things.”

Freddy sits down beside Oscar. Shawn and Eddy are on the opposite side. A laptop sits on the table. It is connected to a television that sits on a rolling stand at the end of the table.

Freddy folds his hands and rests them on the table. He made sure to focus his attention on all three men as he speaks.

“This man is not running. He isn’t trying to fly home. My guess is he had no intention of running. He had full intentions of obeying Oscar and staying put. He had nothing to hide. He took no part in the murder of Marcus Peterson.”

“Why did he run?” Oscar asks.

“Let me finish,” he says in a firm voice.

His voice changes to a more inquisitive one when he next addresses the man.

“You reported he made a few phone calls that morning. Who did he call?”

“What the hell, Falcon? We’ve been through all of this before. You damn well know the answers already.”

Freddy lets out a sigh. “Just humor me, Oscar.”

Oscar rolls his eyes. “Just his wife and his agent.”

“How did the conversation go with his agent?”

“He never spoke with the man. He left a message.”

“What about his wife?”

The man shrugs. “They need marriage counseling,” he says.

Shawn and Eddy chuckle. Freddy glares at them. The men quickly close their mouths.

“What do you mean?” Freddy asks.

"Well, just that there's no real communication. It was obvious she didn't trust him. She frustrated him. He had no agency in his home life. She seemed very controlling."

"No trust?"

Oscar nods.

"I got the same feeling when I spoke with her. She was headstrong, that's for sure. There was no communication with her. She likes to control all aspects of the conversation.

"Alright, here is what we know. At some point, after Oscar left, Richard Olstroski decided to run. He first went to visit Juliana Martinez's apartment. After being thrown out, he somehow traveled to this film set. There, he is murdered.

"So, let me fill in some of the gaps with my thoughts. Again, this is just conjecture. This videotape…"

"Video footage," Shawn interrupts. Freddy glares at him.

"I don't give a damn," he says. "This video," he emphasizes the word, "may prove my assumptions or disprove them. Either way, it holds the key to solving this."

"So, why don't we just watch it? Why all of the chatter beforehand?" Oscar asks in a grumpy tone.

"Because he wants to be proven right," Shawn says. "If he says all of this after we watch the video, then it's just his takeaway from the video. Saying it beforehand, and having the video back him up, makes him look as intelligent as he thinks he is. Am I right?" That last question, he addresses to Freddy.

Freddy didn't say a word. He just smiles. After a moment, he continues. "I think he received a phone call after Oscar left."

Oscar shakes his head. "Not possible. I still had his phone in my shirt pocket."

"Did he give the local number to anyone?"

"Yeah. In the message, he left his agent."

"I think he received a call on the phone in the room. The person on the phone said something that spooked him. The owner of the hotel reported that he appeared to be in a panic."

Shawn nods in agreement.

"We assumed it was because he needed to return to California for a movie. We later found out there is no movie. So, why was he in a panic?"

Freddy looks at all three men. None of them says a word. They were waiting for him to answer his own question.

"The phone call in the hotel. Perhaps this person threatened to murder someone else. Remember that witnesses claimed he insisted that Ms. Martinez's life is in danger?"

Eddy nods.

"I think he was picked up and driven to the film set. I believe he was lured to the far back of the set and murdered to keep him quiet."

"Quiet?" Oscar asks.

Freddy nods.

"And driven? By who?" Shawn asks.

"Whom?" Freddy corrects him.

"What?"

"It's 'whom' not 'who.'"

Shawn rolls his eyes. "Who the hell drove the damn car? Is that better?"

"Miguel Alvarez." Freddy ignores the tone and the last question.

"You think Miguel Alvarez murdered Richard Olstroski?"

Freddy shakes his head. "Juliana Martinez."

All three men are taken aback.

"Um, Freddy," Eddy starts in, "she's in Germany."

"Is she?"

The man nods. "Yes. Making a movie."

"Are we sure about that?"

"It was confirmed by several people at her apartment complex," Shawn replies.

Freddy nods. "They confirmed as much with me. But this could be something she, or Mr. Alvarez, informed them. Remember, he is staying there as well."

"So, you think Miguel Alvarez lured Richard Olstroski to this film set, and Juliana Martinez murdered him?" Shawn asks.

"Yes."

"Then who murdered Marcus Peterson?" Shawn asks.

"I don't know."

"What do you mean you don't know? What the hell are we doing here if you don't know who murdered the subject of your case?" Oscar asks.

"We're here to find out what happened to Richard Olstroski. I'm hoping this will give us clues to the murder of Marcus Peterson."

"Clues? What clues?" Oscar asks in frustration.

Freddy just sits back and smiles. "Let's watch the videotape. Shawn, would you do the honors of rolling the film?"

Shawn sighs. He starts to speak and then closes his mouth. He just nods.

***

The man was literally dragging Richard out of the building. His upper arm seared with pain from the man's grip.

"I swear to you I know her! Her life's in danger! You have to believe me!" Richard kept exclaiming to the man.

"Yeah. You and a hundred other people who find out where she lives. That damn Internet. People have no privacy anymore."

He realized he was wasting his breath. All of his pleadings lead nowhere. He decided to just let the man have his way. What is he going to do now? The call seemed urgent. The voice on the other end says Juliana is next.

The man slung him into the parking lot with so much fury he thoughts he was about to take flight. Richard hit the ground with a loud "thud." He sat up and just stared at the man.

"I better not catch you here again. Next time I do, the cops are getting called."

The man turned around and walked back inside. Richard stood up and brushed himself off. He took a step and felt pain in his right ankle. Another couple of steps, and he felt it again. He winced as the pain shot through his foot.

"Damn. Must have twisted it in the fall."

He started limping toward the street. Not sure what to do or where to go next, he stopped as he reached the sidewalk. He thought about going back to that motel where the cops had been watching him. The problem was, he wasn't sure exactly where that was. Perhaps he should start walking.

He started walking in the direction the driver had come from. Too bad he'd told the guy to drop him off before reaching this place. He hadn't been in there that long. Perhaps the driver is still there. Maybe he is waiting for the next ride. It isn't that far back. The walk hadn't been too bad. That's what he'd do. He'd find that driver and ask him to drive back. He could pay the guy in cash.

That's when a Tesla pulled up beside him. Richard, unkempt as ever, was limping down the sidewalk. The Tesla was driving slowly to keep up with him. The window lowered to reveal the driver.

"Mr. Olstroski, want a ride?"

He glanced over and just grunted. He couldn't tell who the driver was. It was too dark. The voice sounded familiar.

"Hop in. I'll give you a lift."

The car stopped. Richard stopped walking as well. The driver leaned over to open the door and leave it ajar. He approached the car and reluctantly got in.

"Sour Patch Kid?"

He looked over. The man held out a bag of Sour Patch Kids.

He takes the Sour Patch Kid from the man.

"Is that 'Oh yeah' by Yello that you're listening to?"

Richard is referring to the music playing in the car.

"Yeah. It's an 80's playlist."

The car drove off into the distant night.

***

Shawn starts the video on the computer. Freddy is amazed at how clear the image is on the television. He isn't that good with technology. He is aware that things like this are possible. Not sure how to do it, he'd never tried.

All they see is the view from the top of the building. Nothing much has happened yet.

"So, what are we waiting for?" Oscar asks.

"Can it," Shawn says. "It's coming soon."

"How soon? I have a cake in the oven."

Shawn looks at him in annoyance. "It's about fifteen minutes in. Quiet, you."

"Shawn, he's correct. Just fast forward it. There's no point in us watching fifteen minutes of nothing."

Shawn sighs. He forwards the video, and that's when Freddy sees it.

"There. Stop. Pause. Back it up."

Shawn backs up the video to the spot Freddy is referring to.

"There. Play," Freddy says.

They watched as a Tesla pulls into the drive. It stops in front of the building. After a moment, the passenger's side door opens. Out steps Richard Olstroski.

"Now, we have something," Oscar says.

"Shhh," Freddy says as he glares at the man. "Otto said there was a Tesla in the area that night."

"Otto?" Shawn asks.

Freddy shakes his head. “The guy Oscar stopped. We have a history.”

“Small world, eh Falcon,” Oscar says dryly.

The driver’s side door opens and out steps…

“Son of a bitch,” Freddy says.

***

“Why are we here?” Richard asked. “Isn’t this the film set for Marcus’s upcoming movie?”

“Yeah, it is.”

“So, why are we here?”

“I already told you.”

“Yeah, I know. I’m so sorry.”

“What for?” The man looked puzzled.

“I don’t remember your name. We worked on this movie, and I am embarrassed that I don’t remember your name.”

“No worries,” the man says with a smile.

“I’m just not good with names. Faces, yes. But never been good with names.”

“That’s fine. It’s Adam. Adam Greenbriar.”

“That’s right. I’m so sorry. You’re Marcus’s friend.

Adam nods.

“Come on,” he says. “He’s eager to talk to you.”

“I don’t understand why he would lie, though.”

“What do you mean?”

“I saw your phone display when he called. That is Marcus. Why would Hampton pull this charade? Why fake Marcus’s death?”

“The publicity. Marcus is a rising star. Hampton’s career has tanked. Hampton didn’t fake Marcus’s death. He tried to kill Marcus. Left him for dead. Right here.”

“Why didn’t he call the cops?”

"Too scared. Even though Hampton's career is on the downswing, he still knows people. Important people. He's connected."

Richard assumed the man was talking about the mafia. He had watched enough movies and television to understand what "connected" meant.

"I see," he says.

"Come on. Marcus is waiting."

***

"They're talking, but I don't hear anything," Oscar says in annoyance.

"It's a security camera. There's no microphone," Shawn replies.

"Look. We don't need to know what was said. The important thing is that Freddy is wrong," Eddy says with a smile.

The three men start to laugh. Freddy is calm and relaxed. He is wrong about the murderer but not about the rest.

"Alright guys, cool it. I want to see what happens."

It doesn't surprise him that Adam Greenbriar is involved. He'd love to know what the two men were talking about. Ah well, the only way to know is to press it from Mr. Greenbriar. There is about as much of a chance for that to happen as there is for a dead man to make a phone call.

The two men walk around the side of the building. Freddy is confused. Shawn isn't kidding. All windows. The view changed to the interior. But it is different somehow. The men were walking down the stairs.

"I'm confused," Freddy says. "How are they walking downstairs? Isn't he found on the first floor?"

Shawn nods and smiles. "It's a confusing layout. Remember the directions that I gave for the coroner to follow?"

"Oh, God. So, you had to go up two flights of stairs and back down again?"

"Yeah. Damn first floor is separated by a wall. The other side looks like a warehouse."

"So, when do we get to the murder?" Oscar asks.

"Just wait," Shawn replies.

"Well, we know who did it," Oscar says.

"We do?" Freddy asks.

"Yeah. That guy." Oscar points at Adam Greenbriar.

"Are you sure about that?" Freddy asks.

"Well, why the hell not? He's there, ain't he?"

They watch the two men enter a room.

"This is it," says Shawn. "This is where we found him."

The camera footage changed again. This time it displayed the inside of a room. The door opens and in walks Richard Olstroski and Adam Greenbriar. A new person walks into view. Freddy can only see the back of the head. He watches as the person starts to converse with Richard. The head turned slightly to reveal part of a face.

"Son of a bitch!"

Shawn pauses the video. "Deja Vu," he says.

Freddy rolls his eyes. He gets up and walks toward the television. "Zoom and enhance. Now."

"What?" Shawn asks.

"Zoom and enhance. I need to be sure."

"Freddy, you do realize that's not a thing, right?"

"Too much *CSI*, old man?" Eddy says with a grin.

"I don't watch *CSI*. Too fake. All of those shows are too fake."

"Well, however you saw it," says Shawn, "zoom and enhance is not a thing. The most we can do is magnify it."

"If that's who I think it is, then I know who murdered Marcus Peterson."

***

"Marcus is dead, Richard. I thought you knew," he says with a smile.

He saw the panic on the man's face, the fear in his eyes. Richard started to run. Adam blocked the exit so the man could not leave.

"Richard, you're too easy. When I called you and told you Juliana was in danger, you bought it just as I knew you would. And calling Adam from this phone." He holds up Marcus's phone in his right hand. "I knew you would look at the caller ID. I had to make it believable."

"Why did you do it? Why kill Marcus and frame Hampton?"

He could say anything right now. For a moment, he thinks about giving an elaborate story. He just smiled and decided to play along.

"Let's just say that he had it coming."

"Is that it?" Adam asks.

He looked up, and the smile faded. The anger showed on his face.

"You're leaving?"

"Look, I brought the man, as you asked. What happens next is between you both."

"I thought, you of all people, would want to watch the fun."

He shook his head. "No. Besides, my fun is yet to come."

He knew what the man was referring to. He knew he still had one last promise to keep. As per their agreement, Adam would deliver Richard to him, and he would deliver Hampton to Adam. He could give two shits about what Adam had in mind for Hampton. His primary focus was making sure this rat didn't squeal to the cops.

"Whatever," is all he said.

Adam left and closed the door behind him.

He acted fast and grabbed Richard by the neck. The man fought hard. He wrapped an arm around the man's neck and wrapped his other hand around the man's mouth.

"Shit!"

He felt teeth bite into his gloved finger. His arm pressed harder around the man's neck. He threw the man to the floor, face down. His hand still covered the man's mouth. The man was struggling less and less. He held tight until the struggling stoped.

***

They watch this poor man slowly suffocate to death. After a few minutes, Richard stops moving. The man is in full view as he stood up. Jacob Wexler left the room, leaving Richard Olstroski's corpse lying face down. The image vanished, leaving a dark black screen.

"Jacob Wexler murdered Richard Olstroski," says Freddy with glee.

"You know, the amount of joy in your voice scares the shit out of me," Oscar says, showing no emotion in that statement.

Shawn stops the video and turns off the television. All four men are seated again.

"That's a horrible way to die," Oscar says.

"I've seen a lot of painful and agonizing deaths, but suffocation. He had to know what was coming. He had to be scared out of his mind. I've woken up before, not being able to breathe. That's a scary feeling," Freddy says.

"I just imagine he was waiting for the inevitable," Eddy says.

"Anyway, so now we know what happened to Richard Olstroski. Now we need to find Jacob Wexler."

"Well, now we know who killed Marcus Peterson," Shawn says.

"How are you so sure Jacob Wexler is the one who killed Marcus Peterson?" Freddy asks.

"What other possibility is there?" he replies.

"What we know, for a fact, is that Jacob Wexler murdered Richard Olstroski. We know that a man, who could fit Wexler's description, broke into this building and tried to kidnap Hampton Hamm. We also know that Marcus Peterson is murdered, and no prints were left behind."

Shawn starts to argue his point. Freddy ignores him.

"What puzzles me is Adam Greenbriar. He was the messenger. If I were a betting man, I would bet money on the fact that he had no idea what was about to happen to Richard Olstroski."

"What now, Holmes?" Shawn asks.

"Well, my dear Watson, we bring him in."

"How?"

"We track him," he says with a smile.

"How?" he asks again.

"Marcus Peterson's phone."

All three men looked confused. Freddy has that smile on his face. The one that shows he is the most intelligent person in the room.

"Shawn, didn't you say you found Juliana Martinez's phone?"

He nods.

"And she received a call from Marcus Peterson after he died?"

He nods again.

Freddy sits there for a moment. He sees the expression change on the man's face. His face went from confusion to enlightenment.

"Son of a bitch," he says.

"Now you get it."

"What?" Eddy asks.

The look on Oscar's face changed as well. "I'll call the cell provider."

"What?" Eddy asks again.

"It's TL Link, I believe," Shawn replies.

"What?" Eddy asks a third time.

"It's simple," Freddy explains. "Juliana Martinez received a call from Marcus Peterson's phone. Probably the same way Richard Olstroski did. Whoever has that phone murdered Mr. Peterson."

A moment of realization appears on the man's face.

"Now you get it. Oscar, call the phone provider. You are our tracker. I'll be in constant communication with you. We've got this son of a bitch now."

The door opens. All four men look in that direction. Freddy sees a young officer, no older than twenty-five, standing there. He doesn't know the officer's name.

"Detective Falcon," the man says with a nervous voice.

"What is it?"

"A nine-one-one call just came in. It may interest you."

He pauses for a moment. Freddy sits there patiently waiting for the man to speak. Oscar finally breaks the silence.

"Well, what is it? We ain't got all damn day!"

"Y, yes sir., Detective, the call came from a restaurant."

Freddy's heart sinks. He displays no outward emotion. He waits for the next words to come, hoping they aren't what he thinks they will bc.

"It's the owner of *Hold the Anchovies*. He says somebody broke into his place last night. There appeared to be some type of struggle. The owner says that Detective Falcon would want to know immediately."

"Did he find anybody downstairs?"

"Sir?"

"Downstairs. It is set up as an apartment. Is anyone there?"

"Yes, sir. Well, he isn't sure if the guy is dead or alive. They called an ambulance to rush him to the hospital."

"The guy?"

"Yes, sir."

"He didn't say if there was a second person there?"

"No, sir. Just the one."

"Is he short and heavyset?"

"No, sir. This guy is tall. He is reported to be stocky, though. But not short."

"Thank you," Freddy replies.

The man nods and closes the door.

"Well, gentlemen, it looks like the stakes have been raised. We have a larger problem."

"Let me guess," Shawn says. "That's the place you were housing Mr. Hamm?"

Freddy nods.

"Now what?" he asks.

Freddy sits back in thought for a moment. He keeps running through all of the scenarios in his head. He keeps returning to the same conclusion.

"The plan doesn't change," he finally says. "Oscar, track down the phone. Shawn, you and Eddy will stay in contact with Oscar. Find Jacob Wexler and Adam Greenbriar."

"What are you going to do?" asks Shawn.

"I'm going to find Hampton Hamm." He pauses for a moment, not wanting to say what he is thinking. Saying the words out loud gave finality to it. After a moment, he speaks one final time. "Or his corpse."

Chapter Twenty-Seven

The Wooden Chair

He can't figure out why he is hanging his head. The last thing he remembers is struggling for his life. He had removed the ski mask from Jacob's head. That's when...when...when what? He can't remember.

He raises his head and slowly opens his eyes. Everything is still blurry. The light is a blinding white. It takes him a moment to adjust to the light. He is sitting down, though. That much he can tell. He could feel searing pain emanating from his wrists. It feels as if something was cutting into them. He can't move his arms. They appear to be pinned behind him somehow. He can't open his mouth either.

After a moment, he is able to open his eyes and look around. He is in a bedroom. The room looks familiar, though he knows he had never been in this room before. He is sitting in an old wooden chair with his arms behind him. He turns his head to see that they are not behind his back. They are wrapped around the back of the chair. His wrists are tied together with a rope. It appears to be a rope, at least. It isn't cutting into his wrists, as he initially thought. His wrists are wrapped so tight that it feel as if someone were cutting into them with a knife. Whoever tied him up, probably Jacob, tied his wrists too tight. He realizes that his mouth is covered by duct tape. He can't scream if he wanted to.

The bedroom isn't anything fancy. It is pretty average. It is a bit too tacky for his tastes, but who is he to judge? This is normal in his world. He and Marcus had been to many parties hosted by people whose homes were decorated in the gaudiest fashions. This is nothing compared to what he had seen.

His brain starts flashing on memories of Otto. The man was breathing, but he had lost a lot of blood. It would be hours before

Mario would return to open up. He hopes Otto would survive until then. He can't bear the thought of anyone else dying.

That's when his thoughts turned to Richard. He didn't know the man that well. The man always smelled as if he had been eating out of the garbage. He was a nice guy, though. True, they had had their arguments. Richard never respected the fact that he was a guest in their home. But the man doesn't deserve what happened to him. Found dead in an empty building. Nobody deserves that.

His only saving grace is Mario. Despite Otto's condition, Mario would open up and discover the break-in. He would find Otto, hopefully alive, and call nine-one-one. This would alert the police and...and Freddy. Yes, this would alert Freddy. Freddy would be looking for him. But would it be too late? He had no idea what Jacob had planned. If Richard and Marcus…

He starts to tear up as he thinks of his wonderful husband. The man would do anything for him. Marcus treated him like a king, even when he was acting like an idiot. He knows he would never "get over" Marcus's death. How could anyone ever "get over" the loss of their spouse? But he knows he has to heal once this is all over.

He shakes it off. It is time to focus. There would be time for grieving later. He is still here and alive. Freddy and the police are still out there. He would get out of this mess. Richard will be the last victim in this tragedy.

Freddy needs to hurry up, though. He's not much of a fighter. He doesn't know how well he would be able to fight back with his arms tied to a chair.

***

Freddy knows Hampton would be in one of two places. He would let Oscar and the guys work out where Marcus Peterson's phone is, and he would track down Hampton Hamm. He never intended on it going this far. How could he be so stupid? He had everything planned out perfectly. Nobody knew his relationship with Otto. Nobody knew where Otto lived. It was perfect. It was safe.

Obviously, it wasn't safe enough. The one thing he did not factor in is being followed. That's the only explanation that makes sense. Whoever broke into the Farmhouse knew it was a futile attempt. The goal wasn't to kidnap Hampton there. The goal was to scare us into moving Hampton. This was to ensure that we would move him to a less secure place. The kidnapper followed the Mustang that night. He was biding his time. Once the coast was clear, and he knows the path of least resistance was available, he took his shot. Now, Otto is fighting for his life, and Hampton is God knows where.

He shakes his head as the thoughts hit him. He doesn't want to believe it, but he has to acknowledge the possibility of two more deaths in this. The difference this time is these deaths would be on his head.

He is knocked out of this train of thought by an incoming call. He looks at the display to see that it is Shawn calling.

"You guys find anything yet?"

"Well, hello to you too."

"Cut the shit. One man is in the hospital fighting for his life. The other man is, hopefully, fighting for his as well."

"Well, we know where the phone is."

"Jacob Wexler?"

"Bingo. We're on our way to pay Mr. Wexler a visit now."

"Alright. My guess is that Mr. Hamm is in one of two places. I'm on my way to pay a visit to Mr. Greenbriar."

"Well, one of us will find the man."

"Agreed. And Shawn…"

"Yeah?"

"Be careful. This man has already murdered one person, possibly two, and attempted to murder a third. Not to mention the mysterious deaths of his previous wives. He's dangerous."

"Yes, Mama."

Freddy rolls his eyes. "Just be careful."

"Freddy…"

"Yeah?"

"It ain't your fault. Whatever happens, is all on this dirtbag. You did your job. It ain't on you."

With that, the call ends. Freddy brought his full attention back to the road ahead of him.

"Then why do I feel like it is?"

He shakes the thought off. Shawn is correct. Whatever happens, he did the best job he could have done. Everything was done by the book. Freddy Falcon always ties up every loose end and always solves his cases. And he would be damned if another person dies before this one is solved.

***

Shawn knocks a third time.

"Maybe they're not home."

"The car's in the drive. They're home."

"Maybe they're in the bathroom."

Shawn turns his head and gives Eddy a blank look.

"Maybe they're having sex," Eddy finally says.

Shawn just rolls his eyes. He raises his hand to knock one last time. His fist is a half-inch from the door when the door opens to reveal a little boy.

"Hello there. Is your daddy at home?" Shawn asks.

The little boy doesn't say a word. He just smiles, turns, and runs back inside. Shawn and Eddy look at each other as if to say, 'Now what?'. A moment later, Jacob Wexler appears at the door.

"How may I help you, Officers?"

"Jacob Wexler?"

Jacob nods.

"May we come in?"

"It's kind of a bad time."

"It will only take a moment."

The man hesitates for a moment. He nods and moves aside to allow them entrance.

"I apologize for the mess. We are getting ready for my son's birthday party."

The house had balloons hanging from the ceiling. There is a "Happy Birthday Matthew!" sign hanging above the dining room table. He could see a cake on the table that read "Happy Birthday Matthew" on it. The house doesn't look like a mess to him.

"Is there someplace private we can talk?" Shawn asks.

Wexler nods. He leads the men into the backyard. This is where they see more balloons and party fare. There is even one of those bounce houses that looks like a castle. Wexler leads them to the patio chairs sitting out by the swimming pool.

"How can I be of service? I assume this is about Marcus. I don't know what else I could tell you gentlemen that I haven't already told the detective."

"This isn't about Marcus Peterson."

"It isn't? Now I am confused."

"It's about Richard Olstroski."

He sees panic strike the man's face when he mentioned Olstroski's name. The panic changed back to a smile. Wexler let out a nervous laugh when he spoke next.

"Richard? I don't understand."

"Richard Olstroski was found dead in an abandoned building. This building served as a set for what would have been an upcoming Marcus Peterson film."

"Richard? Dead? I don't understand what this has to do with me."

"Mr. Wexler, you have the right to remain silent."

Wexler starts to panic. He can see the fear building in the man.

"What are you talking about?"

"Anything you say can and will be uses against you in a court of law."

"I don't understand. I didn't kill anyone."

"You have the right to an attorney."

"I don't need an attorney. I didn't do anything wrong."

"If you cannot afford an attorney, one will be provided for you."

"Daddy?"

Shawn turns to see little Matthew standing behind them. A look of confusion on his face.

"It's okay, Matthew. Daddy is just playing a game with the officers. Go back inside."

"We can't do this with the kid watching," Eddy says.

"Please. I beg you. I will go peacefully. Don't let my son watch this."

Shawn nods. He motions for Eddy to take the boy inside.

"Come on. Let's go find your mama." Eddy leads the kid back inside.

That's when Shawn feels a heavy force push him forward. The force is so swift it knocks him down. His face slams into the green grassy lawn with a "thud." He turns his head to see Wexler run out the back gate. He picks himself up and brushes himself off. He heard the sound of a car engine starting and the car driving off.

"Shit!"

Shawn runs out the back gate, just as Wexler had done. As he is running to the car, he calls Oscar on the radio.

"Oscar! Come in, Oscar!"

"What is it, Braxton?"

"Marcus Peterson's phone."

"What about it?"

"Please tell me you're tracking it."

"I am."

"Please tell me it's moving."

"Yeah. Why?"

Shawn lets out a sigh as he reaches the car. He opens the door and gets in.

"Jacob Wexler is on the run."

***

Eddy and Matthew enter the house and are oblivious to Jacob Wexler's escape.

"Where's your mama?"

"Sleeping."

"Well, we don't want to disturb her. Has she been sleeping long?"

The kid nods. "She sleeps a lot."

They were walking up the stairs when Eddy next spoke.

"Are you excited about your party?"

Matthew shrugs.

"I bet your mama's excited. You are going to get lots of gifts."

"Mama hasn't come out of the bedroom in days. She doesn't even know."

Eddy pauses at the top of the stairs. "Days?"

Matthew nods.

"Is she ill?"

Matthew looked confused. He realizes the kid may not understand the word.

"Sick. Is she sick?"

He shakes his head. "Daddy says she enjoys sleeping."

This statement set off an alarm in Eddy's head. He walks Matthew to his room.

"Stay here and play. I will check on your mama. Okay?"

Matthew nods. The kid starts to play with a couple of trucks on the floor as he turns to leave. He bolts to the master bedroom. The door is closed. He turns the knob and slowly opens the door. He can hear music playing inside. It is love ballads from the '80s. He never could understand people's fascination with that stuff. Give him hard rock or metal any day of the week.

He is taken aback at the sight as he enters. A woman is lying on the bed in a pure white dress. Well, it had been white at one time. Most of it had turned red. Her arms are above her head. Her wrists are tied to the headboard. Her legs and feet are tied together with rope. Duct tape covers her mouth. Her throat had been slit from ear to ear. That isn't the worst of it. This was not done in desperation. It was done in pleasure. Whoever did this atrocity, most likely Wexler, enjoyed every second of it. She had been gutted, and her heart was also removed.

He left the room and closed the door back.

"Oscar," he whispered into his radio. "Oscar, are you there? Come in, Oscar. This is Officer Hickly."

"Why the hell are you whispering?" The voice came across so loud it made the man jump.

"Oscar," he whispered.

"What?" He could hear the irritation in the man's voice.

"We have another murder."

"What? Who?"

"Wexler's wife."

"His wife?"

"Shhhhh. I don't want the kid to hear."

"Damn son of a bitch! It's bad enough he's screwed up his life! Now he's screwed up the life of an innocent!"

"We'll bring him in."

"We?"

"Yeah. Me and Shawn. When we bring in Wexler."

"Wexler's on the run. Braxton is after him now."

"What? When?"

"A few minutes ago. How the hell don't you know? Aren't you with him?"

"No. I mean, yes."

"Which is it?"

"Yeah. We were reading him his rights when the kid appeared. I took the kid inside so that he wouldn't witness it."

"That's when it happened then."

"Alright. Call a car to pick us up then. I don't want the kid to know what happened to his mom."

***

What the hell had he gotten himself into? He knew Jacob was crazy, but he had no idea the man was capable of murder. And he wants to murder Hampton too? Not Hampton. That is where he must put his foot down. He has to convince Jacob to let Hampton live. Convince Jacob to allow Hampton to be his. His plaything. His toy. But that is for later. Now is not the time to think of fun. Now is the time to get the hell out of Dodge before Sheriff Dillon figures out who murdered Festus. Wait. Isn't Festus a deputy? He shakes his head. It doesn't matter. The analogy is still apt. They are both scruffy and unkempt. The point is, he has to get the hell out before the redhead figures out who killed Richard. He doesn't know the law that well, but he knows it enough to know that he is an accessory to that murder.

Adam Greenbriar is in the middle of packing. He runs through the house, grabbing clothes, toiletries, food, and other things he thinks he needs. He is throwing what he can in suitcases. Truth is, he has no clue what he is doing. He'd never been on the run before. On the run? On the lamb? He isn't even sure what to refer to it as. All he knows is he has to get the hell out before the cops come knocking.

He can hear the noise from the guest bedroom. The chair is rocking. Hampton must be awake. Not now. That sedative is supposed to keep him knocked out long enough to ensure they are a safe distance away. He isn't supposed to wake now. Damn! Why did he have to wake up now!

A smile forms on his face as the thought occurs to him. He's mine to do with as I please. He's my plaything, my toy. Now that Marcus is out of the picture, Hampton is all mine. He thinks about everything he could do to the man tied up in the guest bedroom. He thinks about all of the fun they could have together now.

He shakes himself back to reality. There would be time to play with his toy later. Right now, he has more important things to do. His attention shifts to Richard's murder. Adam wanted no part of that mess. He knows he should come clean. But no. That means they would take his toy from him. That isn't going to happen. Hampton is his and would be his.

As for what happened to Richard, he had been a messenger. He was only supposed to deliver Richard. He had done that. It was done. Over. He will be leaving soon. He and his luggage and his toy would all be leaving this place. The cops would have no idea. He starts laughing as he pictures the redhead detective lost and unable to figure out what happened to poor Hampton Hamm. The entire time, Adam Greenbriar will have his toy hidden away in a secret place. A place only he knows about. A place only he will have access to.

He zips up the last piece of luggage and moves them all to the front door. He looks around to make sure he hasn't forgotten anything. The chair moves again. It is moving faster and making more noise. He is glad Hampton can't cry out. Thank God for duct tape. He grabs the handle of one of the pieces of luggage and opens the door.

"It's about time you open the door. I have a few questions for you, Mr. Greenbriar."

He freezes in stunned disbelief. Before him stands a tall, thin redhead with a knowing grin. What the hell is he doing back here? Just play it off. Be cool and stay calm.

"Detective! I am so sorry. I wasn't expecting anyone."

"No problem. May I come in?"

"Of course. Where are my manners? Please."

He moves aside to allow the detective entrance. He closes the door and sets the luggage back down. The detective glances at his suitcases.

"Are you going out of town? I hope I didn't catch you at a bad time."

He shakes his head. "No. Well, yes."

He can feel the sweat on his forehead. He wipes it away with his hand, hoping the detective wouldn't notice. He could feel his heart rate increase. His body is starting to shake.

"Are you okay, Mr. Greenbriar?"

"What? No. I mean, yes. Why do you ask?"

The detective shakes his head. "No reason," he says. "You are sweating profusely. I want to make sure you are okay."

"Oh. That. Just a little too much wine. Alcohol always makes me sweat."

"Wine? In the morning? Some might call that being a lush," he says with a smile.

Adam returns the smile. "Where are my manners? Please, sit down," he says.

The detective shakes his head. "I don't have long. I wanted to ask you a question related to the case."

"I already told you everything I know."

"I'm sure you have. I just have one important question. What room are you keeping Hampton Hamm in?"

He can feel the pounding throughout his body. Sweat is flowing down so much that he feels like he had just gotten out of a pool.

"H...Hampton? Wh...what do you mean?"

The smile fades from the detective's face. He speaks his next words in a stern, firm tone.

"No more games. We know you are working with Jacob Wexler. We know Wexler killed Richard Olstroski. We know Hampton Hamm is kidnapped. We know he's here. Now, one more time. Where is Hampton Hamm?"

"Jacob killed Richard?"

He tries his best to play it off. Just a little longer, and he would be free. He has to get this guy out of here. There is no proof of his involvement. All they have is Jacob tied to Richard. His part is circumstantial.

The detective nods. He opens his mouth to speak again. That's when they hear it. The chair rocking again. This time it is almost as if it were pounding on the floor.

"What is that?" the detective asks.

"What is what?" he asks stupidly.

Knocking could be heard again.

"That," the detective says.

The knocking continued. It is almost like a trail of breadcrumbs. Before he can make a move, the detective grabs his wrist and handcuff him to a nearby floor lamp.

"Stay," is all the detective says.

***

"Shit! Shit! Shit! Shit! Shit!"

He pounds his fist on the steering wheel with each word. How could he be so reckless? He had everything figured out. All of the calls were either made on a burner or on Marcus's phone. He uses Adam and Adam's Tesla to avoid anything being pinned on him. He wore gloves and a mask to keep his identity a secret. Everything was perfect. It was flawless. How the hell did those shitwads find out about Richard? Nothing ties him to that. Or is there? Had he made a mistake somewhere? Had he overlooked something? He ran everything through his head again. He wants to make sure he doesn't miss anything.

A car horn blasts. He swerves back into his lane. The man flipped him off. He returned the gesture.

"Same to you, asshole!" he yells out the window.

What the hell is wrong with people these days? Where is he? That's right. He shakes his head. No. It is too perfect. Not even that little pigmy knows I murdered his husband. Is it Greenbriar? Is he the rat? He shakes his head. He knows he should have killed Hampton instead of leaving him alive. He should have never let that shithead talk him into letting the fatass live. Now he's on the run.

And that detective. Redhead son of a bitch. How the hell could he be so damned smart? Damn! Good thing he took care of the woman, though. He'd be long gone before the cops found her.

He can't return home, that's for damn sure. Shit! Matthew! Those pricks caused him to lose Matthew. The kid is his reason for living. The kid is his most precious thing. And now he's lost that too! Damn pricks; took that from him too!

He laid down on the horn and screamed. The Prius flew down the highway.

***

He can't make out the voices, but he could tell two different people were talking. He starts rocking the chair harder now. He is forcing it to bang against the floor. Whoever it is needs to know he is here.

"What is that?" he heard a man say.

He keeps up the rocking. He wants to lead the person directly here.

"Stay," the voice says.

He keeps rocking. The footsteps are getting closer. His rocking continues. It wouldn't be much longer. He just hopes this is someone coming to rescue him and not to kill him. Closer now. Closer. The person is right on top of him. The door swings open. Standing at the entrance is a tall, thin redhead with a massive grin on his face. Hampton is bursting on the inside. He wants to cry out with joy. That's when he remembers his mouth is covered with duct tape.

Freddy just stands there in the open doorway. Is he not coming in? What is he waiting for? An invitation? He's not a vampire. He doesn't need to be invited in.

He starts to talk, but the only thing that would come out is "Mmm mmm mmm mmm."

"I'm sorry," Freddy says. "I must have the wrong room."

"Mmmm mmm mmm mmm."

"What is that? Well, I don't want to disturb you. You seem busy."

"Mmmmm mmmm mmm mmm!"

"Look, whatever is going on here, I'm not into it."

"Mmmmmmmmm!"

"I can't understand you with that duct tape over your mouth."

The chair starts rocking in anger and frustration.

"Mmmmm mmmmm mmmmm mmmmm!"

"Alright. Enough joking around."

Freddy walks over and places his hand on the corner of the duct tape.

"Like a band-aid. Right off!"

As he says the last two words, he jerks the duct tape off of Hampton's mouth. Pain radiated all around his mouth. He let out a scream.

"Aren't you a little short for a hostage?"

"What?"

"Just a joke."

"Very funny," he says as he glares at Freddy. The detective just grins. "Don't quit your day job."

"If I did, you would still be tied up."

He glares at Freddy. "I am tied up," he says as he emphasizes the second word. "Can you please get these ropes off of me?"

Freddy nods. He walks behind Hampton and glances at the rope binding his hands.

"Right off!"

He winced with pain and screamed out.

"You can't tell the difference between duct tape and rope?" he asks as he holds the duct tape in front of Hampton.

Freddy helps him move his arms from around the chair. He winces again with the pain. There is no telling how long his arms have been in that position. He can feel the stiffness in his legs as he tries to stand. Freddy grabs his arm to help him up.

"Don't rush. Give it a moment. You've been sitting like this all night."

He takes a step forward. Another. After a few steps, he finds it easier to walk.

"You good?"

He nods. "I assume you have Jacob." He winces in pain and grabs his shoulder.

Freddy shakes his head. "Give it time. Your arms will be sore for a while."

He nods, still holding his shoulder. "Then who is the other voice?"

"Oh, you don't know," Freddy says.

"Know what?"

Freddy just smiles. "Come on. Let's get you out of here."

He burst out laughing as he enters the living room. Sitting on the arm of the couch with one wrist handcuffed to a lamp is Adam Greenbriar.

"So, that's the other voice I heard. I could have sworn that it was Jacob under the mask."

"It was," Adam says. "He killed Richard. He kidnapped you."

Hampton looks around to carry on the facade. "Where? All I see is a short, chubby has been whose days of glory and fame are far behind him. You'll be doing your encore in federal prison."

"Marcus is better off dead! He is too good for the likes of you!"

Hampton feels the anger rise within him. He starts for the man. Ready to put his hands around the man's neck. He feels a jerk backward. He turns to see Freddy shaking his head. The detective had grabbed his arm to hold him back.

"Let it go. Let justice work."

Hampton nods.

"Now," Freddy addressed Adam, "Mr. Greenbriar, the three of us are going to go for a ride. And you are going to tell me everything you know about the murders of Marcus Peterson and Richard Olstroski."

***

"He's headed east."

Oscar's voice cracked up a little as it came through the radio.

"On what road?"

"Same as you."

"What?"

"You're on Lincoln, right?"

"West Lincoln. Yeah."

"So is he. Heading east."

"Shit!"

The tires squeal as he slams on the brakes. He makes sure no one is coming, and then he floors it. The police car made a u-turn and flew down the highway like a bat out of hell.

"Do we know what he's driving?"

"No."

"A Prius," came a familiar voice through the radio.

"Freddy!"

"The one and only."

"Where are you?" Shawn asks.

"Well, we just left Adam Greenbriar's. We are north of you."

"We?"

"I have Mr. Hamm sitting shotgun. Mr. Greenbriar is tied up at the moment."

He hears Hampton Hamm let out a chuckle.

"What do you want us to do?"

"Same as me. Follow Oscar's directions. Let's get this son of a bitch."

"10-4."

***

Freddy ends his part of the conversation. He glances into the back seat, where Mr. Greenbriar is sitting. The man's arms are duct-taped behind his back. He had let Hampton do the honors when they put the man in the car. Hampton had taken a little too much pleasure in the task. Greenbriar screamed out when Hampton pulled a little too hard on the man's arms.

"Mr. Greenbriar."

The man stays silent.

"Mr. Greenbriar."

Not a word.

"You can either talk to me or my captain. I can promise you he will not be as pleasant as I am."

He sees the man look up at him.

"There we go. Good. Now, who poisoned Marcus Peterson?"

Hampton turn his head and open his mouth to speak.

Freddy glances over to him as if to say, "Quiet." Hampton closes his mouth. He turns his head back to the road. The rearview mirror is slightly adjusted to see Mr. Greenbrier.

"Who poisoned him?"

"It was Jacob's idea."

"Thank you. So, how did you get the wine to Mr. Peterson?"

"I said that it was Jacob's idea."

"Yes. You did say that. But you were the one who did the act."

The man doesn't say a word. He doesn't even try to deny it.

"How did you get him to drink the wine?"

"It was a peace offering. A gift. I would leave a bottle a day on the hood of their car. It was a gift basket. There were cookies and candies. And there was always a bottle of wine."

"That was you?" Hampton asks. Freddy can hear the anger in his voice. He glances back over at the man. Hampton closes his mouth.

"Mr. Hamm. I understand your need to comment. Please let me do my job."

Hampton nods. Freddy looks back at the road.

"Were the other items in the 'gift basket' poisoned?"

Greenbriar shakes his head. "I didn't want to take the risk. I knew that Hampton doesn't like wine. The other items were for Hampton. The wine was solely for Marcus."

"Why?"

"Why what?"

"Why did you do it?"

"Jacob told me to."

Freddy let out a sigh. "Why did YOU do it?"

The man shakes his head and looks confused.

"Mr. Greenbriar, does Mr. Wexler tell you when to take a piss?"

"What?"

"You have agency. You have free will. Mr. Wexler doesn't control you. I ask you again. Why did YOU poison Mr. Peterson? What is in it for you?"

"Hampton."

"Excuse me!" Hampton exclaimed.

Freddy reacted quickly. The man has already unbuckled his seatbelt and is about to go over the seat. Freddy grabs his arm and jerks him back down.

"One more outburst, and you will be walking," he says in a firm voice.

The man starts to protest. Freddy glares at him. He sits back and closes his mouth.

"I get it. I would be just as frustrated and pissed off. Remember, he's trying to push your buttons."

"It's working," Hampton says.

"Don't let it. Let me do my job."

Hampton nods.

"Now buckle up. I'd hate to have to arrest you too," he says with a smile.

Hampton buckles up. Freddy continues his conversation with Mr. Greenbriar.

"I'm under arrest?"

"You tell me. Did you murder anyone?"

The man shakes his head.

"Let me ask this another way. Who killed Marcus Peterson?"

"Jacob."

"Why?"

"Freddy! Freddy! Come in!"

It is Oscar over the radio.

"What is it, Oscar?"

"Damn cell towers!"

"Please don't tell me you lost him."

"No. Well, sort of. The signal blipped out."

"What do you mean?"

"Well, I had him on Lincoln. The signal disappeared and reappeared there."

"Where?"

At that moment, a silver Prius cuts them off and pulls into traffic in front of them.

"Son of a bitch! I found him, Oscar!"

Freddy turns on the siren and flashes his lights. The Prius races around the cars in front and heads down the highway. Freddy pursues.

"I'm chasing him down North Carolina."

He sees the car turn onto East Madison. Pedestrians and cyclists have to jump out of the way. They turn and follow. They turn again and head north on North Indiana. Then turn on East Jackson. Another turn and then another.

"He's heading for the bridge."

"What?" he hears Oscar say.

"He's headed toward Maine."

"You don't think he's going to the airport?" Hampton asks.

"Possibly. But would he leave his family?"

"His wife is dead," Oscar says.

"What? When?"

"Eddy discovered the body a little while ago. Says it looked like Wexler took pleasure in the murder."

"He was tired of the old bag, anyway," Greenbriar says from the back.

"He has a son," Freddy says, ignoring Greenbriar's remark. "He wouldn't leave him."

Hampton shakes his head. "No. He wouldn't. He loves Matthew more than life itself."

Freddy swerves. He almost hit a pedestrian.

"That was close. Hey, this is like a movie. A real car chase," Greenbriar says with glee.

Freddy shakes his head. This is real life. People could die. They could die. This is serious shit, and he's acting like it's a damn video game.

"Forgive me, but I am about to do something stupid and reckless."

"What?" Hampton asks.

"Not with me in the car!"

He ignores Greenbriar. "Trust me," he says to Hampton. He grabs the radio. "Oscar. Call and have them raise the bridge."

"What?"

"Have them raise the bridge!"

"But…"

"Do it."

He pulls over.

"What are you doing? Aren't we going after him?" Hampton asks.

"We aren't. I am."

"What? I'm coming with you?"

"No, you aren't. I'm about to do something reckless, and I am not about to place your life in danger. Get out and keep watch over Mr. Greenbrier."

Hampton starts to argue. Freddy glares at the man. His mind is made up. Hampton nods. He unbuckles and gets out of the car. The chubby man pushes the passenger seat forward and pulls out Greenbriar. He let the seat back and closed the door.

"Good. Now, watch after Mr. Greenbrier until I get back."

"What are you going to do?"

"Something stupid and reckless."

With that, he drove off.

"Where is he?"

"Getting close to Maine."

"Do we have the bridge raised?"

"Working on it."

"Work harder."

"What are you planning?"

He cut the radio. He turns onto West Carter and then onto North Idaho. He is heading for Congress. He plans to hit South Maine and jump as the bridge is reaching its zenith. Well, as close to it as a drawbridge can get. The plan is to jump the bridge and stop Wexler in his tracks.

"Papa, I'm so sorry. If there was any other way."

Guilt starts to spread all over him. He suddenly thinks he is about to destroy the last remaining piece of his granddad. The guilt is almost too much. Then the fear creeps in. What if I don't make it?

What if I don't make the jump? Or worse. What if I did and hit Wexler head-on?

That's when another thought hit him. It is more of a memory than a thought. A memory of an earlier conversation. One he had had near the beginning of the case. The first time he met Mr. Hamm.

"Listen to me. I want to make this very clear. I know you did not murder your husband. Everything I have told you about myself is true. This case is personal for me because I know that loss. I know that pain. You are not just a number to me. I will do everything, including give my life if necessary, to prove that fact. We will bring this criminal to justice. As much as I don't want to, I have to take you in."

That's what he is doing now. Risking his life to bring this creep to justice. Let's just hope this works. He'd hate to end up in the bottom of the lake, and this asshole get away.

He shakes off these thoughts. All that mattered now is stopping Jacob Wexler. He turns off Congress onto South Maine. The bridge will be coming up soon.

"If I'm going to do this, I'm going to do this right."

He is glad he had decided to ride with the top down. He feels the sun on his face and the wind in his hair.

"Oscar. Where are we on the bridge?"

"Working on it."

"Work harder."

He can see Figaro Bridge in the distance. He is coming on it fast. Finally, it starts to rise. A smile creeps onto his face. He floors it straight for the bridge.

"Oscar. Where is he?"

"Close to Maine."

"Good. Tell them to lead him to Maine. Make the chase look real."

"What the hell, Falcon! It is real!"

"Just do it!"

"What are you planning? Where are you?"

"South Maine."

"South Maine? What are you…? Son of a bitch! Falcon! What the hell are you thinking!"

"Do it, Oscar!"

"Falcon!"

He ignores the man's protests. He didn't want to turn off the radio, though. He can hear Oscar continuing to monitor Wexler. Wexler is on Maine now. He would be on the bridge soon. The goal is to box the man in. Freddy has to be on the other side to ensure Wexler doesn't do the damn fool thing he is about to do. The bridge is rising higher now. He is getting close. Just a little more. The Mustang is going as fast as he can push it. If he plans it right, the bridge would be at the perfect angle as he hit the end of it.

He feels the car hit the bridge. Everything slows down. It feels as if he is on an incline for a rollercoaster, that rush and exhilaration. The fear of death a body subconsciously goes through. The rush of adrenaline. That excitement right before the plunge. He is approaching the top now. All he can see is the blue sky.

For a moment, it feels as if he was weightless. Flying through the sky. Nothing below him but water. He feels free. A calming sensation surrounds him. It is as if he had not a care in the world. He wonders if this is how the Duke boys felt when they were jumping some giant ravine while being pursued by Rosco P. Coltrane.

Then a sudden "thud" and jerk he feels as the tires hit the other side of the bridge. It causes his head to jerk back for a second. A Prius races toward him. He hits the flat part of the bridge and does not let up on the gas. The Prius is getting closer. All fear escapes him. Drive and determination are all he feels. This will end now.

He increases his speed. The Prius is staying its course. It is still heading right for him. He assumes that Wexler expects him to move. This is a game of chicken that Freddy has no intentions of losing.

Closer now. They will either hit, or Wexler will swerve. He is not stopping.

The Prius swerves at the last second. It swerves into the opposite lane. The car is unsteady. Freddy slams on the brakes and makes a u-turn. The car in front of him is out of control. It hits the corner of the incline of the drawbridge. The angle of its hit causes the vehicle to swerve off the side and into the lake.

Freddy slams on his brakes. He leaves his Mustang and dives into the water. The Prius is sinking like a rock. He attempts to kick in the window. It is no use. All he can do is watch Wexler panic as the car fills with water. The water rises, and the man panics more. Wexler is desperately trying to open the door. The flood of water makes it impossible. The man has a better chance of asking a brick wall to move. All he can do is watch as the water rises. The car sinks. The man starts to choke as the water goes into his lungs. He cannot watch anymore. He swims to the surface and heads for shore.

***

He laughs at the sight as he pulls up. Hampton had somehow managed to separate Greenbriar from his shirt. There they were on the side of the road, exactly where he had left them. A shirtless man standing there with his hands duct-taped behind his back. His shirt intertwined with the duct tape. At the other end, holding it like a leash, stood Hampton Hamm with a massive smile on his face.

"Good Lord, you two are kinky," he says with a smile. "First, I find you bound to a chair. Now I find you holding him like a damane."

"What happened to you?" Hampton asks as he slings Greenbriar into the back seat. "And where's Jacob?"

Hampton gets in the passenger's seat and closed the door.

"I went for a swim."

"And Jacob? Where is Jacob?"

"Jacob's dead, Hampton. Jacob's dead."

The Mustang pulls off into the distance.

Chapter Twenty-Eight

Four Cops and a Funeral

He is in the middle of pouring a large cup of black coffee when his phone starts to ring. It isn't his desk phone ringing. It is his cell phone. This is something he isn't expecting. He jumps, splashing coffee on the countertop.

"Shit."

He sets the carafe down and looks at the display. It is coming from a number he doesn't recognize. In the event this had to do with a possible case, he decided to answer it.

"This is Detective Falcon."

"Freddy!" comes the voice of a weakened, but still slightly energetic, Otto Von Snaut. For the first time in a long time, Freddy is pleased to hear that annoying tone in his voice. The fake innocence as if he were trying to hide something.

"Otto, I can honestly say that it is good to hear your voice. How are you?"

"I'm good. Hey, Freddy…"

"One second Otto. I'm gonna put you on speaker and sit you down on the counter for a second."

He places the phone on speaker and sets it down. He proceeds to clean up the mess as he talks to Otto.

"I don't recognize this number. Are you still in the hospital?"

"Yeah. I'm calling from the phone in the room. Damn Doc won't let me have my cell phone. Says it's too dangerous or something. I dunno. Old coot probably thinks it will cause cancer or something."

"Really, Otto? Do you have to insult everybody?"

"What? He is old. Has to be mid 50's."

"You're in your mid 40's," he says in an irritated tone.

"What's your point?"

Freddy shakes his head and decides to move on. “How are you?”

“I’m good. Doc says the bullet didn’t hit anything major. I should be outta here in a few days. How’s Hampton? Is he okay? Nothing happened to him?”

“He’s fine. No real harm came to him.”

“That’s good. You solve the case?”

“Yes. We released the body as well. The funeral is today.”

“You goin?”

Freddy shakes his head. “No.”

“Why not?”

“Shawn and Eddy are there. Anyway, glad you’re doing well. It’s open.”

“What’s open?”

Freddy is responding to the knock at his door. He can see Oscar through the glass. He motions for the man to come in and take a seat.

“My door. Another officer is coming in.”

“Freddy…”

“Yeah.”

“You ain’t gotta keep your promise.”

“What?”

“Helpin’ with Harry. Take some time off for a while. I know you’re good for it.”

“Understood. Well, let me let you go. I have another officer in my office who needs me.”

“Alright. Doc’s comin’ in anyway. What’s up, Doc.”

He hears the phone ”click,” and the call end. He places his phone back in his pocket, grabs his coffee, and walks back over to his desk.

“Hey, Oscar. What’s up?”

“Not much, Falcon.”

The two men sit in awkward silence for a minute. Freddy finally speaks.

"Did you...need...something?"

Oscar lets out a sigh. "Sorta."

Freddy rolls his eyes. "What is it, Oscar?"

"Falcon, I ain't good with my feelings."

"If you are going to tell me that you love me, this conversation is over."

"What the hell, Falcon? Stop being a smartass for a second and listen."

Freddy sits back and gives Oscar his full attention. The man across from him starts to squirm a little. He did have something personal to talk about. Freddy can tell how uncomfortable the man is. After a few minutes, Oscar speaks.

"Is it hard getting used to living with your grandparents?"

"What?"

"I mean, did you adjust well? Did they? The age difference, I mean. Them being up in years and all."

"Just spit it out, Oscar. You've never been one to beat around the bush."

"I want to adopt the kid."

"What kid."

"Wexler's kid."

Freddy sits forward with genuine shock on his face. "You want to what?"

"I can't let that kid go into foster care. He needs a good home. I just…"

"Oscar, that is the kindest thing anyone could do for this kid." He leans back again. This time he has a huge smile on his face. "Yes, I adjusted well. I never thought they were too old. You'll do fine."

"Thanks's Falcon. Eh, enough emotional shit. How's Mr. Hamm? The funeral's today, right?"

Freddy nods.

"You goin'?"

Freddy shakes his head.

"And why the hell not? You played a huge part in this."

Freddy lets out a sigh. "Shawn and Eddy are there."

"Eh. Whatever. I think you should talk to him, though. You ain't spoken to him since the day Wexler died."

"We're not dating…"

"What the hell? I never said you were. Look, Falcon, all I mean is that guy respects you and trusts you. You gotta give the case closure with him."

"I did. We released the body. He has his funeral. He's free. Wexler's dead. Greenbriar will stand trial. Case closed."

Oscar shakes his head. "Falcon, you have always done a debrief in the past. What makes this so different?"

Freddy just sits there in silence. Oscar is correct. He needs to speak with Mr. Hamm.

***

"Did the kid see the body?"

Eddy shakes his head. "The car picked us up and took us to the Farmhouse. I never let him go in that room."

"That's good."

Shawn and Eddy are waiting for Mr. Hamm. The funeral has been over for a little while. The man is still speaking with family. He finally makes his way to them.

"Officers," he says with a smile. "I am so glad you could make it."

"Thanks. It was a nice funeral," Shawn says.

"Yes, it was. He would have loved it. I wish he were here to appreciate what I am about to say. He would have gotten a great laugh out of this."

Shawn and Eddy looked on with curiosity.

"You two ever watch *Seinfeld*?"

"Yeah," they both say.

"Remember the episode where one of Elaine's co-workers thinks her name is Susie? They ended up "killing off" Susie and even had a funeral for her. Elaine had been asked to say a few words about Susie and can't think of anything. That popped in my head during the funeral. I started to chuckle. Anyway, that's the sort of thing Marcus would have loved. He would have died laughing at that."

"Perhaps he did. Perhaps that was his spirit or something."

"Perhaps so. Don't tell that to the detective, though. He'd have some logical explanation on how the soul doesn't exist or whatever."

Shawn smiles. "I have no idea if it does or not. I just know there has to be more to life than this. If not, what's the point?"

"Anyway, I want to thank you guys for coming."

"It was a nice funeral."

"Have you met my mom yet?"

Shawn nods. "She tried to convince us not to arrest you until after the funeral."

Hampton smiles. "Yeah. She told me she thinks you were here to arrest me for Marcus's murder. I tried explaining to her that you would not even allow the funeral if you were."

"She seems like a nice lady, though," Eddy says.

"She's wonderful. And she loved Marcus to death."

"Have you spoken with Freddy yet?" Shawn asks.

Hampton shakes his head. "Detective Falcon? No. Why?"

"Nothing really. He always likes to do a debrief after a case. You know, tie up loose ends and all."

"No. He didn't say anything. In fact, I haven't spoken with him since the day the case was solved."

"That's weird. Anyway, you should stop by sometime and speak with him."

"I will do just that."

"We do need to go," Shawn says.

Hampton nods. "Thank you again for coming."

***

The day after the funeral, there is a knock at Freddy's office door.

"It's open," he says without looking up.

The door opens and in walks Hampton Hamm. The man has a different air about him. He seems more confident and self-assured. He looks relaxed and chipper. He is wearing jean shorts and a tee shirt. This is the first time Freddy has seen the man in something outside of khaki pants and a short-sleeved collared shirt.

"Mr. Hamm," he says with a smile. "It's good to see you. Please sit. Would you care for something to drink?"

Hampton just smiles and shakes his head.

"I'm sorry that I missed the funeral. I didn't feel that it was appropriate."

Hampton shakes his head, "No. I understand. I honestly don't blame you. Shawn and Eddy looked out of place as it was. You know they came fully dressed in their uniforms?" He lets out a small laugh. "My mom thought I was being arrested after the funeral."

Freddy lets out a laugh at that.

"It was a good funeral. Marcus would…" He pauses for a moment and decides to rephrase the statement. "Marcus wouldn't have cared. He always said I could have whatever funeral I wanted for him. He always said that funerals are for the living and not the dead. 'What do the dead care?' he'd say. 'They're already gone.' And he's right."

"He sounds like a wise man."

"He is."

"Well, how can I help you? What brings you to my office?"

"I want to know something about the case, though. Something that's been bothering me."

"You want to know how Jacob did it."

He nods.

"It's quite simple. Wexler followed you home that night. He waited until you fell asleep outside. You already know how he got in."

Hampton nods. He draws the invisible line as he had done the night they figured that out. Freddy smiles.

"Wexler saw his opportunity from the moment your Husband approached him about the role. It was pure revenge. He never forgave either of you. The problem was coming up with the perfect plan and finding the perfect patsy. That opportunity came when Adam Greenbriar was brought on. He knew what happened between you and Mr. Greenbriar. He was aware that Mr. Greenbrier still wanted you."

"What do you mean, he 'wanted' me?"

"He called it 'love.' I would say lust. He claimed to love you. To me, it's more of an obsession or lust. Definitely not love."

"That man doesn't know what love is."

Freddy starts laughing as the *Foreigner* song "I Want to Know What Love Is" starts playing in his head.

"What?" Hampton asks.

Freddy began to sing the chorus of the song.

"Excuse me?"

He smiles. "The song."

Hampton looks puzzled.

"I Want to Know What Love Is."

Hampton still looked puzzled.

"Foreigner."

He still looked puzzled.

He shakes his head. "Never mind."

"Go on. I'm listening," Hampton says. The man chuckles. "Boy, if that's not a reversal."

Freddy laughs and nods.

"So, yeah, he thought that if your husband was murdered, then you would come running into his arms."

"Similar to John Hinckley," Hampton says.

Freddy pauses. “Mr. Hamm, I had not pondered that. What an interesting parallel.”

Hampton just smiles.

“Thus, a partnership is born. Greenbriar is the one who decided on the arsenic. See, wine already has arsenic in it….”

“I know. You’ve explained that to me several times. The poison didn’t kill him. It only weakened him. What about the wound? How was he murdered?”

“That’s the brilliance in it. At first, I thought it was a stiletto.”

“A stiletto? You thought my husband was murdered by a high-heeled shoe?”

“Not by. With. He was murdered by Jacob Wexler. You see, the proper use is ‘murdered with a high heeled shoe.’ Most people misuse it, but….”

He pauses as he sees the look on Hampton’s face. The man is rolling his eyes.

“But, you don’t want to hear that.”

Hampton nods.

“That’s when I noticed the smelly shoe.”

“The smelly shoe?”

He nods. “Richard Olstroski’s shoe that Shawn found. It had a broken heel.”

“A broken heel?”

He nods. “Mr. Olstroski wore specialty made shoes. It was a custom heel.”

“My husband was murdered with Richard Olstroski’s shoe?”

He nods.

“How did Jacob not leave any prints?”

“He was wearing gloves. The same gloves he wore when he broke into the Farmhouse and again when he kidnapped you.”

“Why was there no struggle? We weren’t expecting visitors.”

“He probably told your husband you invited him in. At some point, he probably asked to use the restroom or found some excuse to look in Mr. Olstroski's room. He knew about the shoes. Mr. Greenbriar says that he mentioned them to Wexler."

"So, he stabbed my husband and left?"

Freddy shakes his head. "Not exactly. Think back to that night. Did you hear a phone ring?"

He shakes his head.

"Think Mr. Hamm. Don't respond right away. Perhaps that morning?"

"Wait a minute! Yes. A phone did ring. I was out of it. It was before I called the police. I assumed it was Marcus's phone."

"It was. Wexler was hiding in your house. He was going to murder you next."

Hampton freezes.

He assumes the realization of those words was sinking in.

"That phone call stopped him. Greenbrier wanted you alive. Only you. Wexler hated both of you and wanted both dead. He sent a text to Greenbriar using your husband's phone. It said, 'Marcus is dead. Hampton is next'. Greenbriar called out of fear. Wexler panicked. He thought that phone call would startle you, and you would discover him. He ran. I guess you could say, ``You owe your life to Adam Greenbriar."

"I owe heartache and pain to Adam Greenbriar. Is that it? What about Richard?"

"He overheard Greenbriar and Wexler talking. He doesn't know the details. It isn't until your husband was murdered that he figured it out. Greenbriar had no idea Wexler was planning to murder him. He thought Wexler was going to keep him quiet."

"In a way, he did just that."

"That's disturbing."

"In what way?"

"The man was murdered, Mr. Hamm. Have a little sympathy."

"Perhaps you are right. One thing that puzzles me, though. How did Jacob know where I was being held?"

"You mean at Otto's?"

He nods.

"He followed us."

"What?"

"After his botched kidnapping, he waited outside. He followed us to *Hold the Anchovies*. That's how he knew."

"That man was determined to tie up all loose ends."

Freddy nods.

"Have you heard from Juliana Martinez?" he asks Hampton.

"Yeah. She flew in last night. Miguel told her everything that had happened. She called me immediately. Juliana could barely speak. She is devastated."

"You know, there was a moment when I believed she was the one who murdered your husband."

"Juliana? Never." He shakes his head.

"Never say never, again."

"What do you mean?"

"You've said that every time I mentioned a possible suspect. As I recall, you said that about Jacob Wexler and Adam Greenbriar."

"But Juliana…"

"Mr. Hamm, if there is one thing I have learned from my years doing this job, it's that everyone is capable of murder."

"What's going to happen to Adam?"

"That's for a jury to decide. I just enforce the law."

Hampton laughs.

"What is it?"

"I just had a thought that struck me funny."

"What caused it to make you laugh like that?"

"Who knows where it came from. It just appeared."

"I mean, what about? What was the thought?"

"Just about what we are doing."

"What do you mean?"

"This debriefing. It's not unlike the last chapter of a mystery novel."

"This is not a book, Mr. Hamm."

"I mean, you've read mystery novels and detective stories. We talked about it the night you drove me to Otto's."

"I remember."

"The last chapter has the main protagonist explaining all the loose ends from the story. To tie things up. Just reminds me of that."

"You read too much."

"What about the letters?"

"What letters?"

"Marcus's letters. The ones he would write to his mother. Did you find them?"

"Ah, yes." He had forgotten all about it. He had meant to return them to Hampton. He opens his desk drawer and reveals a stack of letters. He handed them to Hampton.

"Where were they?"

"Just as you suspected. Jacob Wexler had used them to write that note. To make it look like it came from your husband's hand. Adam Greenbriar had informed him that your husband wrote those letters to his mom."

Hampton nods. "Of course. The only other person who would have known. I have a question I'd like to ask about you, Detective Falcon."

"A question? What is it?"

"It's a sentence worded in a way as to elicit information, but that's not important right now."

He lets out a smile as he says that. Freddy just rolls his eyes.

"What is your question, Mr. Hamm?"

"So, what's next for the great Freddy Falcon?"

Freddy sighs and smiles. "A promise to keep."

"After that?"

"I have no idea. Haven't we had this discussion already?"

"Have we?"

"I think we have."

"Oh. Perhaps we have."

"What about you? What's next for the great ac-tor Hampton Hamm?"

"I don't know, actually. I thought about taking a break for a while. Figure things out."

"If you ever need anyone to talk to, my door is always open."

"As is mine."

"You know Hampton…"

"Hampton?"

"That is your name."

"Yes, but you refuse to call me Hampton throughout the case. You want to keep it professional."

"The case is over."

"It's killing you, isn't it?"

"What is?"

"You are dying to say 'Hampton, it looks like this is the beginning of a beautiful friendship.'"

"I was going to ask you if you wanted to join me for ice cream. There's this place a few blocks away on Garfield. They make the best ice cream you have ever tasted."

Hampton smiles. "I'd love to."

Acknowledgements

I still find it hard to believe this is real. My first novel. I hope you enjoyed reading this as much as I enjoyed writing it. There is no way I could have done this alone. There are so many people I would love to thank.

Unfortunately, I cannot thank them all. I apologize to anyone I miss here. It was not intentional.

First and foremost, I could not have done this without my loving husband. Jim, you have supported me throughout the entire journey. Thank you for reading the early drafts and giving me the constructive criticism that I desperately needed. Your suggestions helped to improve this story immensely. You are, and always will be, my rock.

Thank you to my parents. You were always there for us and did your best to ensure we were taken care of.

Aunt Millie, you introduced me to all the geeky things that helped shape who I am.

Thank you Kirsten for taking the time to edit this work.

Scott, you did a great job with the cover.

Thank you, God. You gave me the talent and inspiration to do this. You placed me in the right situations and surrounded me with the right people to help make this possible.

About the Author

RB Willis was born in a small town in Georgia. He graduated with a Computer Science degree and worked numerous jobs in the tech field. His legal blindness has never slowed him down. It has caused him to find new ways to adapt and push himself forward in most situations. He's a gamer, podcaster, tech enthusiast, and a fan of most things in geek culture.

www.ingramcontent.com/pod-product-compliance
Lightning Source LLC
Chambersburg PA
CBHW060633310726
48982CB00003B/761

9798218128630